The Briny Café

Also by Susan Duncan
Salvation Creek
The House at Salvation Creek
A Life on Pittwater

SUSAN DUNCAN

The Briny Café

BANTAM
SYDNEY AUCKLAND TORONTO NEW YORK LONDON

A Bantam book
Published by Random House Australia Pty Ltd
Level 3, 100 Pacific Highway, North Sydney NSW 2060
www.randomhouse.com.au

First published by Bantam in 2011

Addresses for companies within the Random House Group can be found at
www.randomhouse.com.au/offices

National Library of Australia
Cataloguing-in-Publication Entry

Duncan, Susan
The Briny Café / Susan Duncan

ISBN: 978 1 74166 820 9 (pbk)

A823.4

Cover and line illustrations by Nettie Lodge
Cover design by Christabella Designs
Internal design and typesetting by Xou, Australia
Printed in Australia by Griffin Press, an accredited ISO AS/NZS 14001:2004
Environmental Management System printer

10 9 8 7 6 5 4 3 2 1

FSC
www.fsc.org
MIX
Paper from
responsible sources
FSC® C009448

The paper this book is printed on is certified against the
Forest Stewardship Council® Standards. Griffin Press holds
FSC chain of custody certification SGS-COC-005088. FSC
promotes environmentally responsible, socially beneficial
and economically viable management of the world's forests.

For Bob

ACKNOWLEDGEMENTS

There are many people who have helped with this book. Some stand out. My husband, Bob, whose quiet wisdom and sound advice to wear it away kept me going. Caroline Adams, who came in at the last minute, dished up some much-needed faith and saved me from some awful clangers with her insight, skill and endless tact. Toby Jay and Dave Shirley, who let me ride the waterways on their beautiful lighter, *Laurel Mae*, while they pulled masts, serviced moorings, delivered building supplies and patiently explained the intricacies of swivel bolts and bow rollers. Thanks too to Barbara (Bell) Viljoen and Chris Bell, who really did live in a boatshed over the water long ago, and who kindly shared their memories. I must admit, though, that I have embroidered, exaggerated and extended their stories for my own purposes and to turn it into fiction.

I have also written about the preparation of food hoping to inspire anyone who has never found joy in the kitchen to have a go. To me, food is central to the pleasures of life. This might be a good spot to reveal that the cooking method for Peking duck came from world-renowned chef Heston Blumenthal and I have never tried to make it myself. Not yet, anyway. The other recipes mentioned are favourites. Especially the lemon delicious pudding which I love after a Sunday roast lamb. I must confess, too, that I have always yearned to run a seaside café. Now I've done it. Theoretically, at least.

Many thanks to Random House for its patience and to Beverley Cousins for her hard work in getting this book over the line. To Jo Jarrah, not just thanks, but gratitude.

To Heather and Cher. Two good women. Thanks for the laughs and for keeping the house on an even keel while I typed.

See you . . . on the water.

AUTHOR'S NOTE

Cook's Basin does not exist. Nor does The Briny Café. Nor do any of the characters or events that I've written about. This is a work of fiction but it is, of course, a homage to Pittwater and the fabulously quirky people who make it such a wondrous place to live.

CHAPTER ONE

Not long after schoolkids have rampaged through The Briny Café like a flock of hungry seagulls, Ettie Brookbank sits down, with a heavy sigh, at one of the scarred picnic tables in the Square outside. She's just returned from cleaning a house so filthy she'd seriously considered putting a match to it. She'd found used condoms at the bottom of a bed, a bathroom full of bloody tissues, and a kitchen strewn with dirty dishes and cooking pots burned beyond redemption. The house had always been a tip but this was a new low. To top it all off, the owner, a divorced mother of three, had forgotten to leave out her pay, which meant Ettie would have to waste time chasing up the money and put off grocery shopping for a couple of days.

For a while she'd put aside her anger, telling herself she was lightening the load for a woman raising her children alone. Then she'd stopped vacuuming mid-stream.

"Ah sod it," she'd thought. "I'm out of here."

The sun is now low in the sky as the steady pulse of Cook's Basin beats around her. In this sleepy offshore community there are no roads or bridges, no cars, trains, no buses or even bicycles. Just a cluster of dazzling blue bays with mouth-watering names: Oyster, Kingfish, Blue Swimmer.

For once, the beauty of her surroundings fails to soothe her and Ettie feels worn out and anxious. Every time she looks into the future, all she sees are her options fast running out. She flexes her arm muscles. She is strong. Her blood still runs hot. She considers her nest egg sitting tidily in the bank. The stash her mother left her wasn't much but she's never, ever touched it. The numbers, five of them now, are fat with comfort and mean she can make choices. She reckons that's about as close to freedom as most people ever get.

She could buy a ticket to Paris, find a tiny atelier to live in and get a job in a pâtisserie. Learn to bake meltingly light croissants. Stir crème anglaise dotted with vanilla seeds and rich with egg yolks that hint at decadence but feel light on the tongue. On her summer holidays, she could hitchhike from Paris to southwest France to make the 800-kilometre pilgrimage along the Compostelle de St Jacques. *First, all you can think about are the blisters on your feet. Next, you ditch everything from your backpack except a clean pair of knickers and your toothbrush. Finally, the rocks begin to sing to you.*

She wants to hear rocks singing, she wants to burn bridges, shout from mountain tops. She wants to lie on a remote, sunstruck island dotted with whitewashed houses in fields smelling sweetly of thyme, oregano and rosemary. She wants a man twenty years her junior to read to her from *The Iliad* in between afternoons of wild or – even better – languid sex. She yearns to drink absinthe and live every moment like it is her last. The years are being swallowed so fast, she thinks, how long before it is too late . . . ?

She tells herself there is no reason she can't do any of

this. Except that she is afraid. What would she become, she wonders, without her allegiances to friends, the Cook's Basin community and the landscape she loves so much? A drifter without purpose. Skimming, floating, flailing above the surface. Hardly even there. She is fifty-five years old. Her youth was so long ago she barely remembers it. Her future, if she is lucky enough to escape illness or accident, is old age. Nothing can change that simple fact. She is also painfully aware she doesn't have it in her to live dangerously.

Ettie resides in a rented timber cottage at the top of the gut-busting steep side of Cutter Island, which rears out of the sea at the mouth of the bays like an upended ice-cream cone. Every day, as she tackles the two hundred steps to her home, she tries not to resent the triple-decker waterfront houses with foldaway glass walls and private jetties. The ritzy boatsheds kitted out with soft white sofas, draped fishing nets and an extra fridge to take care of the booze in the summer holidays. The sleek commuter boats with powerful growling engines and taut biminies to keep the rain off. And truthfully, she doesn't begrudge anyone good fortune. It's just that sometimes she's completely frazzled and doesn't know where she's going to find the stamina to lug her shopping from way down at the silvery public wharf to way up to her sky-blue door. She sighs. Ah well. Clogs to clogs in three generations, isn't that the old saying? No one gets a free run from beginning to end. Not in her experience, anyway.

In the last light of day, she secures her dinghy and hoists her groceries over three equally tippy boats to reach the jetty. The light is on in the ritzy boatshed when she walks past. She sees a small group of kids standing in a circle, their backs to the outside world. Holiday-makers, she figures. She'd recognise the outline of most of the Island kids like the markings on a dog. There is no sign of the new owner, a sleazy bloke with rubbery lips and granite eyes. He must have handed over the house for a weekend party.

The rain that's been holding off all afternoon suddenly comes down like a grey wall. She squares her shoulders and takes off, the shopping whacking against her legs like a constant reminder that she's too old and it's all too hard. Halfway up, she's soaking wet and every breath feels like a hot blade. She doubles over with a stitch. How long does she think she can keep this up, for God's sake? She flexes her fingers to restore circulation as rain runs down her neck to the hollow of her back. Her clothes stick to her body like a second skin. Her shoes squelch. She has to remind herself once again that many women her age, without steps to keep them fit and healthy, wouldn't make it even halfway. She blames her breathlessness on the extra supplies she's carrying to whip up a "Welcome to the Foreshores" dinner for the skinny little woman who has just bought the rundown old house in Oyster Bay.

"Hey, Ettie, need a hand?" Without waiting for an answer, Jimmy, an Island kid who favours clothes as iridescent as his carrot-coloured hair, grabs her bags.

"How're you doing, Jimmy? You managing with your mum away?"

He cracks an ear-splitting grin and jiggles the shopping from one hand to the other, his wet synthetic singlet sticking to his boyish chest. His feet are never still – like a sprinter warming up before a race. "I'm nearly eighteen, Ettie. I'm grown, aren't I?"

"I'm always here if you need anything. Just until your mum comes home." But her words are lost. The kid, who lives in a harmless world that bamboozles strangers, is a disappearing streak of red and yellow already nearly at the top of the steps.

Oh for that energy, she thinks, bracing for the last dash.

She reaches her front door with a groan of relief. Her shopping is piled in a corner out of the rain and she shouts out a "Thank you", not sure if he will hear. She kicks off her wet shoes and dumps the dripping groceries on the kitchen bench, massaging the kinks in her neck. Not bothering to towel dry, she grabs a bottle of wine from the fridge and fills a glass to the brim, swallowing a good inch straight off. It slides down her throat like liquid gold. Better than sex, she'd joked out loud to friends the other day, feeling slightly winded when she'd realised she meant it. Relaxing now, she separates her mail from the groceries and drops it on the table. Probably all bills, anyway.

She steps into a pair of pyjamas and slips her arms into the sleeves of an old plaid dressing-gown that once belonged to her mother. Like an old spinster with no one to please, she thinks, looking around for her glass.

The wine spreads warmly, seductively, from her stomach to her limbs, smoothing, blurring the edges, sharpening her appetite. She decides on a slab of strong, crumbly Cheddar from the colder regions of Tasmania, a few slices of hot Spanish salami cut so finely they're transparent. A handful of salty black Ligurian olives which she arranges in a white bowl. She sets the food on a chopping board like the artist she is – although her name on the cover of three children's books and a few dozen canvases hanging on the walls of Cook's

Basin homes hardly adds up to a stellar career. Without the regular cleaning jobs that paid the rent, she'd be out on the street. A slight exaggeration, perhaps, but uncomfortably close enough to the truth.

She adds half a sourdough baguette and a bone-handled knife. At the last minute, she snips a small bunch of grapes and fills an empty spot on the board. It is a still life waiting to be painted.

Her wineglass topped up again – what the hell, she thinks, it's Friday – she flicks on the television and tunes in to a current affairs show where a whining bad luck story is being flogged into resembling serious news. So she takes her dinner onto the rain-sodden deck to watch the storm move out to sea instead. The air smells like gunpowder. *Alone again*, she thinks, the Willie Nelson tune looping in her head. She sculls the wine, overwhelmed by a dangerous yearning to feel the warm hand of a lover.

Sam Scully, a big man with hands like plates and shoulders so wide he has to twist slightly to get through doorways, slips his mooring in the dead of a night washed clean by the storm. He is amazed, as he always is, by the suddenness of the calm. In less than fifteen minutes, the lightning that turned the landscape a ghostly shade of blue has pranced off to sizzle and crack over the open sea.

Despite his steel-capped workboots, he makes his way almost soundlessly along the timber deck of his barge to the roomy cabin he uses as an office and, occasionally, a dosshouse. He hooks his index finger around the helm and spins it 360 degrees with a feather touch. He looks back to make sure he is clear of the buoy rope. Satisfied, he moves the throttle forward. Under his feet the engine thrums. The *Mary Kay*, his treasured canary-yellow barge, glides across water as smooth and dark as chocolate. Moonlight filters through the fleeing rainclouds, enough to find his way without the risk of ramming a million-dollar yacht or one of the many anonymous wrecks, engraved with the scars of their neglect, that litter the waterways.

He heads for Cargo Wharf to pick up a load of timber for delivery to the old house that Ettie tells him has been bought by some city mug for a knockdown price. Well, he thinks, the south-facing shore of Oyster Bay isn't called the dark side for nothing and a wood duck's born every minute.

At the peak of Cutter Island, he notices a couple of lights. He figures Ettie's awake and worrying as usual when there's no need. Community looks after its own if they earn it, and Ettie, who keeps an eye on every waif that comes or goes, has the runs on the board. A pot of soup or, if it's a fundraiser, one of her magical watercolours showing moody Cook's Basin moments. *Auction or price tag, whatever you think will bring the most*, she told him when old Pete the Dutchman died and there wasn't enough money in the family kitty to bury him. Sam was fully aware she'd have to cut back on the wine for a week or two to cover the cost of the frame. She was a giver who stood out in a community of givers.

A few minutes later he feels a shift in the damp night air as he sidles into the wharf, smelling more land than sea in it now. He's judged the tide perfectly. It's as high as it's going to get. If he wanted to, he could tap-dance from the barge to the dock without missing a beat. He's tickled by the idea. Humming tunelessly, his plain face split by a grin, he does a funny little soft-shoe shuffle in his clod-hopper boots to make the point, then gets down to the hard slog of barge work.

Onshore, he binds a pallet of timber in three strong canvas slings. Then back on the boat, he squats on an upturned milk crate to operate a crane that stretches skywards from the deck like a broken beak. Sliding the gearstick a millimetre at a time, he lowers the swaying hook until it is over the centre of the pallets. He jumps onshore again, clips the slings to the hook, tugs twice to make sure it holds, then returns to his milk crate to swing the timber aboard. He repeats the process with four pallets, spreading the weight evenly to keep the barge balanced. When it's all done, he tidies up and goes inside the cabin.

As he reaches for the nav light, he hears a low purr coming from the roadway. He can barely make out the shape of a car cruising in to park at Commuter Dock. He's immediately suspicious. No headlights. Dodgy as. He checks the time and decides to wait awhile. Just when he's convinced it's a drunk planning to sleep off the party before he faces his irate wife, he sees two blokes get out, closing the doors quietly behind them. A match flares and a flicker of light bounces off a shiny head. He hears another sound now. Oars scraping inside metal rowlocks. A rowboat drifts against the seawall next to the car. He catches the sound of murmuring that carries across the still water, but he can't make out the words.

Stupid bastards, he mutters. It's the stealth that gives them away. If they pitched up on a sunny day with an Esky, we'd all crack a smile and wave them off without a clue what was going on. He plays with the idea of sounding his horn for the simple pleasure of frightening the shit out of them but it makes more sense to see where the rowboat is headed.

He waits for the car to crawl away in darkness and gives the rower time to get well ahead. The tide is dropping. He reckons he has an hour before the water is too shallow for him to ease the barge close enough to the seawall in Oyster Bay to safely unload the city mug's cargo. Plenty of time to follow the rowboat.

Outside, in the cool night air, raindrops fringe the edges of her round table. Ettie picks up an olive, a little cheese, popping them into her mouth one after the other. Next, she breaks off a piece of chewy white bread, adds some salami and takes a bite. Back to the cheese again. Like a merry-go-round of taste and texture.

Even though she's old enough to know that playing *what ifs* is a loser's game, she wonders, for the millionth time, if things might have panned out differently had her mother lived a decently long life. Forty-odd years ago not many women were aware that a lump the size of a pea had the power to kill. Her mother just thought it would eventually disappear, like most bumps and lumps. By the time it was the size of an acorn it was too late for anything. Her mother retreated to her bedroom. Her father retreated into himself. Ettie retreated to the kitchen and taught herself to cook little dishes of nursery food she thought her mother might find tempting enough to at least try to eat.

She bites into a grape and struggles to remember the

features of her mother's face. She comes up blank. Instead, she finds herself thinking about the way her mother would half-fill a basin of water to wash Ettie's hands in soap that smelled of lavender. It was a ritual that even as a child she recognised as pure love. From her bed, her mother tried to pass on all the advice and wisdom she thought her daughter would need in the days, and years, ahead. But Ettie was a child and had no real understanding of death – how there was no going back from it – so she barely listened, figuring there'd be time when her mother was better. How she wishes she'd written down the words, if only to return to them for comfort every now and then.

It's not that Ettie hates her life nowadays. No, not her life. You have to be pretty damn dumb to hate life. Or crook in ways she doesn't want to think about. It's just that she can't work out why she finds herself with so very little to show for her fifty-five years.

There had been a husband once. Tick that box. One of those blue-eyed charmers with an easy way, who loved women. *All* women. "So why did you marry me?" Ettie had asked after she'd caught him in the pool house with a woman pressed up against the wall with her eyes closed and her skirt hoisted to her waist.

"I love flesh. I really do," he'd told her matter-of-factly. "If you're married, they don't see commitment as an option."

"So you can screw your brains out and still come home to a clean house and a hot dinner?"

"Yeah," he said, amazed she'd understood, as though there was nothing obscene about it.

A year after her divorce, when the marital assets had been

divided and Ettie was marking time in a city flat until she figured out what she wanted to do next, she'd stumbled upon a tiny advert in the back of her local paper: "For Rent: Cosy house in picturesque offshore location." She didn't fully understand the concept of offshore but it sounded exotic. When she called the agent and learned it meant living on an island, she packed her bags – and her paints – and rocked up at Cook's Basin, ready for a new start in life.

She'd been so young and full of dreams. First, she planned to ditch her old *good wife* persona and morph into a wild young hippie in streaming rainbow-coloured clothes, with hair down to her waist, who only wore shoes when she travelled to town. Second, she'd sit in her Island eyrie and paint inspired pictures that would be snapped up by art collectors around the world and eventually lead to wealth and fame. Or a decent living at least. Well, she got the hippie part down pat, anyway.

God, was it really *thirty* years ago now? She reaches for her glass. It's empty.

Damp creeps through her pyjamas, her backside begins to ache with cold. One more glass to warm up before going to bed, she thinks.

The moon breaks through the clouds at the same moment that she realises it is very late and she is seriously drunk. Old and drunk. Does it get much uglier? She leans on the rail and stares into darkness. Moonlight bounces off treetops. Way down in the bay, yachts hang still and silent on their moorings. The night air has turned sweet. Stars are out. It is utterly beautiful.

*

Sam follows the rowboat to a jetty next to Triangle Wharf on Cutter Island where it's been tied so close to shore it will be stranded at low tide. So it's a blow-in, he thinks, knowing that no self-respecting local would risk a rock through the hull of such a sweet little timber boat.

He swings away from shore. The clouds have scurried off. The sky is clear and laced with stars. Silver light plays on the water like tinsel. It feels as if the open waterway belongs to him alone and the corners of his mouth lift in a smile of contentment. Give him the sea every time, he thinks, where there are no boundaries to hold a man back.

The less he has to do with terra firma, the better. More like *terreur fermé* (according to the beautiful Frenchwoman with liquid brown eyes who'd worked on his accent for two years). The terror of being closed in, yeah. It said it all. When his feet hit the ground, he feels nailed in place, like some funny bugger has poured cement in his workboots.

Ten minutes later, he nuzzles the *Mary Kay* into the seawall in Oyster Bay with water under the hull to spare. Despite the time – just after 3 a.m. – the house is ablaze with lights. He toys with the idea of knocking on the door to introduce himself and maybe bot a cup of coffee. What's her name again? He fumbles on the dash, searching for the order form. *Kate Jackson*. He reconsiders. If she's heard the joint's rumoured to have a ghost, knocking on her door in the witching hour might scare her rigid.

Jeez. He'll never understand why anyone would want to buy a mouldy old pile of crumbling sandstone in the shadow of a dank escarpment. One season of monsoon rain like they had ten years ago and the whole shebang could quietly slip down the hill into the bay. If she'd bothered to ask around, any local would have explained the downside of *cheap* when it was applied to *waterfront*. Must be a dreamer, he decides, feeling a swell of pity for what lies ahead of her. More money than brains.

Cook's Basin News (CBN)

Newsletter for Offshore Residents of Cook's Basin, Australia

OCTOBER

SUMMER SHAPE-UP

Pilates classes will recommence in Angie's house on Saturday morning.

$15 per session or $120 for 10 sessions.

Concerned Resident's Letter (name supplied)

Recently, a lone mangrove, just 30 cm high, was removed from in front of our house.

We have nurtured that mangrove for twenty years in the hope it would multiply and provide fish nurseries to keep our waters teeming with life.

Also, we have lost our resident python, Siphon, who is harmless and keeps our rat population down. If he has wandered off, fine; if he has been removed out of ignorance, please learn an understanding of our wildlife or return to suburbia where the animals are mostly two-legged and often venomous.

Kingfish Bay Hazard Reduction Burn

The hazard reduction burn on the north side of Kingfish Bay is now complete. Residents (yes, that DOES mean you, Stinger) are asked to walk on the fire trail only for the next few days as the ground is hot and trees might suddenly drop their branches, with the potential to cause serious injury.

If you see serious flare-ups, please ring emergency services.

CUTTER ISLAND OFFSHORE WINE LOVER'S SOCIETY

Date: November 8

Time: 4 p.m.

Place: The Flahertys

The hard-working members of the Society – after much deep thought, serious consideration and tireless testing – have made their summer wine selection and will forward tasting notes, price lists and any other relevant information shortly.

CHAPTER TWO

The Briny Café hovers over the water at the end of a yellow streak of sand, a ramshackle building made from timber planks weathered to silver by the sun, sea and wind. It stands resolute – the beating heart of Cook's Basin – despite a long list of culinary inconsistencies and a slightly cartoonish lean towards the east, brought on by the annual hammering of the icy August westerlies.

On the deck, after a breakfast that is memorable for all the wrong reasons, Sam Scully pays for a newspaper at the cluttered front counter and strides into the Square looking for company. He has four hours to kill before the next high tide when he's due to transport six tonnes of soil to a garden project in Kingfish Bay. The new owner, a retired chef, has straightened and strengthened the old 1950s holiday house without losing its character (although if he wanted a posh garden, he's headed for heartbreak – the wallabies always win).

Sam sees the water taxi tied up at the end of the wharf and looks around for its driver Fast Freddy. Despite his racy moniker, Sam finds that spending time with Freddy is like relaxing in a pool of cool water on a sweltering day.

He spots him nursing a coffee at a picnic table under a couple of stringy shade trees and makes his way towards him through clutches of lily-white tourists, out frolicking on the first warm day of the season. Despite the sunshine, Freddy is still rugged up in his night-shift clobber – a warm red fleece, blue trackie daks and lambskin boots that come up to his knees.

"Business slow?" Sam asks, brushing a few crumbs off the bench and taking a pew beside him.

Fast Freddy shakes his head. "Just havin' a breather before going home for a zizz. I've got to square up for a twelve-hour shift later this afternoon."

"Weekend. Mugs everywhere."

"Yeah. Nothing changes . . ."

"My imagination, Freddy, or are there more about than usual?"

"A few ning-nongs showing off on the water. Not enough to spoil a beautiful day."

"Never seen you lose your temper. Not once."

Freddy shrugs. "No point. Shouting never achieves anything. Compassion takes you a lot further."

"You're a good man, Freddy."

Freddy swills the last of his coffee. "Filthy brew," he pronounces through puckered lips, squeezing the paper cup into a ball.

"That bloke who's moved next to Triangle, he's got some suss late-night habits. I reckon he's worth keeping an eye on when you're out and about."

Freddy nods and points towards Sam's newspaper. "Reckon I could read my stars before I take off?"

Sam looks confused at first. "Oh mate. Gotcha." He flicks

to the back pages, rips out the astrology column. "This stuff really tell you what's ahead?"

"Good a guess as any." And with a slightly bow-legged hobble, Freddy heads towards his apple-green water taxi with its powerful 150-horsepower engine, turquoise bimini, lime padded seats and bright pink carpet. Colour, Freddy explains to every astonished first-time passenger, lifts the spirits, you see.

Running thick fingers through his salt-stiff hair Sam looks around for someone else to entertain him. A group of dishevelled Islanders with south-facing houses sits in the sunniest corner of the Square, soaking in the warmth. They're in tight conversation, eating hot chips out of a bucket with a look of guilty pleasure on their pale, mildly hungover faces.

The *Seagull* – a scarred old timber ferry with a turned up snout – swings into the wharf, her shabby blue and red hull cutting through the green water. The magnificently raj rear deck is solidly packed with Saturday morning memsahibs, kids carrying cricket bats, and a few tail-wagging mutts travelling free as usual. The two Misses Skettle, twins who were born and bred offshore more than eighty-five years ago, alight last. Both have a single strand of pearls hanging to the exact level of their second buttons and, thrown over their narrow shoulders, sit purple cardigans that tone with their mauve hair. They pound down the gangway chirruping, and blow Sam a kiss like he's still five years old and hanging behind his mother's skirt. For old girls, he thinks fondly, they move like pink and purple rockets.

Sam checks his watch, pats his pocket, searching for his tobacco. Jeez. A month away from turning forty and his memory is on the blink already. Once and for all, mate, he tells himself emphatically, you have given up the freaking fags!

He feels a sudden pinch in his gut, then another that blossoms into a full-on cramp. He stomps inside the café, aiming to launch an enquiry into the freshness of the bacon. But pulls up short. A woman in blue jeans with straight black hair and a pancake-flat backside beats him to the counter. She puts her shoulder bag between sweets, peanuts, chocolates, cans of baked beans and some furry and green-tinted loaves of bread, all flung haphazardly like the flotsam and jetsam of a shipwreck. He watches her grab a newspaper and slip it under a paddle-pop arm, like she's in a city café where they're part of the furnishings. He winces and waits for Bertie, the cantankerous owner of The Briny Café, to erupt.

"Paper's not free, luv. Two-fifty on a Saturday unless you're planning to pinch it. Which I wouldn't advise," Bertie says in a killer voice. The old man stares at her boldly with dark brown eyes out of a bald, acorn head.

"Sorry," she says, without flinching. She orders a coffee and Bertie's famous egg and bacon roll. Sam toys with the idea of warning her off it but gets distracted when he notices the weird tinge on Bertie's usually tanned face. He's looking every one of his seventy-odd years today, he thinks. Haggard, yellower than the *Mary Kay*.

"Car smash or barbecue, luv?" Bertie asks.

The woman looks blank.

"*Sauce*, luv, what kind of *sauce* do you want?"

"Ah. Barbecue. Thanks." She turns away.

"Pay up front, luv. That's how we do it here. Like it or leave it."

"Oh right." There's a harder edge in her tone now.

Bertie takes her money, hands over the change then leans against the counter, bare arms crossed, smirking. The breastplate of his apron is flecked with small brown stains. His Beatles T-shirt and flared jeans are straight out of the seventies. He waits until she's almost through the door to the back deck: "We'll call your number, luv, when it's ready. Then you collect it at the counter."

Sam watches her search her receipt for a number, the expression on her face a mixture of embarrassment and anger.

"How about *one*, luv. You can remember that, can't you?"

"Yeah. Should be able to." Her tone is frigid. "Friendly place, this. Whatever happened to the good ol' days?" The flywire door slams behind her. It almost falls off its rusty hinges.

"Jeez, Bertie," Sam says when she's out of earshot. "Bit rough, weren't you?"

"My café, my rules. Best everyone knows upfront. What can I get you?"

"Nothing, mate. Just wanted to let you know I feel a bit off after me brekky. You might want to ram your nose up against the bacon."

"First sign of warm weather, everyone goes down with a tummy wog and blames me," Bertie says, unfussed.

"I'm not bein' critical, mate. Just wanted to let you know. And while I'm here, I'll have a bag of your hot chips. Best chips on the foreshore."

Bertie harrumphs. "Hold back the praise, Sam. Too much and I'm liable to keel over." His voice skids to a wheeze.

"Keep your shirt on. I'm not talkin' about your dodgy burgers, mate. Just the chips."

"Yeah. Go easy, why don't you? Wouldn't want to give a fella a swelled head after only forty years of flippin' the same old meat patties, day in, day out."

"You're a legend, Bertie. Everyone knows it."

"More faith in cash than compliments, Sam. Four bucks. On the nose. No mate's rates. Quickest way to go broke."

Sam scoffs his chips in the Square to avoid the extra twenty per cent loading Bertie adds for the privilege of dining amongst the shambles of broken tables and chairs on the back deck. In theory, the mark-up is to cover the cost of service, china and silverware but if those frills were ever there, they disappeared from the café long ago. Every order, no matter where it's consumed, comes wrapped in a white paper bag with grease leaking through the packaging like rising damp.

The Briny, an eccentric mishmash of decks, docks, jetties, storefront and attic and perched on pylons like an addled crab, has withstood fierce winter storms, raging summer bushfires and twice a modest tsunami. But Sam wasn't sure how much longer it could survive Bertie's increasingly risky food.

He sees Bertie's latest victim exit the fusty debris of The Briny Café with a muttered and insincere "Thanks" thrown over her shoulder. Bertie appears in the doorway, his glistening skull tilted in bored acknowledgement. She wanders to the end of the wharf where Chris, the ferry driver, a sun-raddled old fella with short legs and knuckles the size of doorknobs, is selling tickets. She buys one and steps aboard. A day-tripper, Sam thinks. Bertie probably hasn't done himself out of any long-term business then.

A seagull swoops on his bucket of chips and Sam bats it away with his newspaper. The bird flies off and lands neatly on a pylon where it chucks him a gimlet-eyed look. Always scavenging and searching for the easy way out, he thinks, like that clueless bastard in the rowboat last night. A small place like Cook's Basin, you try anything seriously shonky and pretty soon the wrath of the community comes crashing down on your head. He aims his parcel of rubbish at the bin. Curses when he misses by a mile.

On the other side of the bay, Ettie shuts her eyes against the daylight and gives sleep one more shot, counting an imaginary chorus-line of glittering fairies dancing in a garden of red-spotted mushrooms. Well, it worked when she was five years old. She gives up and stumbles into the bathroom. Under the fluorescent light, the face in the mirror looks hammered. As old as she feels. Two drinks max in future, she tells herself, knowing even as she says it that it's pointless. By the bottom of the second glass, all bets are off.

She crawls back into bed and hoists the sheet around her neck. The dull thud of a migraine takes hold of the back of her head and needles its way forward to a point behind each eyeball. A trickle of moisture leaks from under an eyelid that she hopes is the result of pain and not self-pity. She decides to delay visiting the new resident in Oyster Bay until tomorrow. It will give the rich spaghetti sauce she's planning to cook time for the flavours to develop. She allows herself to believe it's the truth.

By early afternoon, her hangover lifted, Ettie struggles out of bed to prepare the welcome feast, which is, in reality, an excuse to thoroughly check out the newcomer. Offshore life

life is a constant test of spirit and endurance, and locals are loath to waste time explaining tides, tinnies and tank water to residents who are likely to faint at a single tick bite or the sight of a python sleeping off a rat dinner on the verandah. One of her many (admittedly self-appointed) roles is to suss out whether newcomers are stayers or bolters, wusses or warriors.

As long as the woman doesn't turn out to be a nutter, she thinks, browning the mince in small batches over very high heat. Nutters suck you dry with no return. She tips a decent slug of a rough red into the pot and lets it reduce to a syrup before adding the homemade tomato pureé she bottles by the vat when tomatoes are at their peak. Leaning over the stove, her eyes closed, she sniffs the onions to be sure the bitterness has been cooked off and gets a strong whiff of the carrots and celery she's added to give the sauce complexity. All good. She brings the mixture to the boil, bangs on a lid and leaves it to murmur for at least three hours in her favourite old cast-iron pot that's as red as the sauce. She drinks three glasses of water, makes a pot of tea, takes two aspirin for her hangover. Then starts on the very rich and decidedly wicked chocolate cake, feeling much cheerier.

Outside the temperature is rising, the sun blazing, the sea glittering. The tangy smell of sausages cooking on barbecues drifts on the air. Thin spirals of smoke wind upwards. The good people of Cook's Basin are coming alive after their winter hibernation.

CHAPTER THREE

Sam Scully spreads his feet on the worn green paintwork in the wheelhouse, balancing his body with the instinct of a kid raised in a boatshed so low over the water his mum would roll up the floor rugs before every king tide.

Close to Cargo Wharf, he ditches a roll-your-own butt in a round boiled-lolly tin before he's tempted to light it. Two weeks since his last puff, he thinks, wondering briefly if there's any benefit in counting the days when the deal is open-ended. Oysters, mussels and other ugly sea creatures bulge off exposed piles in razor-sharp clumps of grit and shell. The muddy smell of low tide is rank. Ambrosia to him.

He spins the helm, sidles up to the wharf and tosses a for'ard portside line around a cleat. At the stern, he repeats a process he could carry out in his sleep.

With the barge secure, Sam hoists himself onto the wharf, feeling blindly for a foothold to give himself a final boost. Onshore, the truckie, ankles crossed, arms folded, watches from the rear of his semitrailer. There's no offer of a helping hand. Not that Sam needs one. It just rankles.

"Told you earlier, mate. It's low tide right now," Sam says, walking up to the truckie and brushing red dirt off his scabby hands. "Worst time on the water for taking a delivery."

"No choice, buddy. Got a full day booked and you were first cab off the rank."

The bloke has a *bugger you* air about him. Sam's eyes go hard. He chews his bottom lip. "Yeah. Well. Told you we could load at four a.m. or four p.m. You made a trip for nothing, mate. Crane won't hoist from eight feet below the wharf."

"Serious?"

"Serious as . . ."

The truckie swears. Sam feels a twinge of pity, but not enough to turn helpful. He walks away, tapping his boots to dislodge the dirt, unmoved by the screech of grinding gears against too many revs. Dust kicks up. A dirty brown cloud floats over the water. Consideration, mate, and a little humility, and it could have all unravelled so differently.

He sets off on the *Mary Kay* at an agreeably sedate pace, listening to the steady growl of a well-greased diesel engine, as soothing as a symphony to his bargeman's ears.

The barge suddenly lurches. "Jeez!" he explodes. A stink boat flies past kicking up a three-foot wake. Sam leans out of the cabin door. "Stupid bloody idiot," he shouts, knowing the lunatic driver is too far away now to hear. He shakes his head in disgust. First hint of summer and a fresh crowd of cowboys rolls in treating Cook's Basin like the last frontier, many of them pig-ignorant about boats and water. He's amazed more don't kill themselves, or worse some poor innocent boatie enjoying the waterways in the peaceful manner he's supposed to.

He follows the white froth of the disappearing wake, trying to place the boat. A runabout with dollar signs hanging off it stands out in a civilian navy of mutilated tinnies you'd be hard-pressed to sell for scrap metal. A new swanner then, he figures. He'll have a quiet word in his ear. The idiot needs to be set straight on a few basic local niceties. Even morons deserve one warning.

He tracks the runabout to a pen at the foot of a tall, glassy house with a boatshed featuring opaque sliding Japanese doors, wind chimes and decorative oriental ceramic pots filled with water lilies. Like a Japanese whorehouse, he thinks. He swings alongside, ties up, leaves the engine running and makes his way along the jetty.

"Yo!" he calls. He hears the whoosh of a sliding glass door, the clunk when it opens all the way. A red-faced bloke in a blinding white linen shirt sticks his head over the deck, close enough so Sam doesn't have to shout. Hallelujah.

"Lost something, mate?"

"You own that flashy little boat tied in the pen down here, next to that pretty timber rowboat?"

"Yeah?"

"Lovely things, timber boats. You got a name, mate? I'm Sam, by the way."

"Leo."

"Right. Now that we know each other, I won't say what I *was* gonna say. Which was that if you ever freaking roar through the moorings again, knocking toddlers off decks and tipping tinnies on their sides so people's hard-earned groceries roll overboard, I'll break your head."

"You threatening me, arsehole?"

Sam looks down at his scuffed leather boots. "Nah. Like I said, that's what I *would've* said if you'd been a weasel. But my father, you see, always reckoned good manners got you further in life than a fat wallet. So. Very nicely. And politely. There's a reason for an eight-knot speed limit when you're in a high traffic area. It's called *safety*. Do it again, mate, and I'm liable to forget I'm a good-natured sort of bloke. And the name's Sam. Not *Arsehole*."

He waits a minute for a response.

"Another quick word of advice, mate," Sam adds, "Around here it's best to keep any illicit habits inside the privacy of your four walls. Step outside with any even vaguely suspect behaviour and we'll come down on you like a ton of wet cement. And you might want to invest in a nav light for that rowboat if you're going to keep using it at night."

The door slides shut with a bang. Well, he thinks, he tried. He thumps down the jetty, jumps on board the *Mary Kay* and glides slowly away, hoping the weasel of a man picks up a few clues. Hoping there won't be trouble ahead.

With the noonday sun now high in the sky, Ettie packs her carefully prepared food in two waterproof carry bags and sets off down the two hundred steps to the wharf, on her way to visit the new woman in Oyster Bay. She's dressed in a profusion of colours and beads that she hopes doesn't make her look like mutton dressed as lamb, or worse, someone stuck in the 1970s.

The creep from the ritzy boatshed is standing on the deck, staring at her like she's naked. She feels a chill run down her spine and the hairs on her neck prickle. He inclines his head towards her. She ignores him.

"Picnic?" he asks, ambling towards her and pointing at the bags.

"Something like that," she replies. She bends to untie the bowline.

"Jump in your boat and I'll pass the bags to you," he says with a voice like thick black coffee. "Isn't that the way you do it around here? Everyone lends a hand?"

Ettie feels cornered. "Yeah," she says in the end. "Thanks."

She makes it into her boat and he holds a bag just out of reach, grinning, like it's a game. Ettie wonders if he was the kind of kid who set fire to cats' tails or pulled the wings off flies. She waits, refusing to play the game. The creep laughs and puts her bags even further away from her before walking off. Ettie lets go of her breath, and lingers a few moments to make sure he's gone before grabbing the bags and loading them into her boat.

She tucks her floating skirt under her bottom and pulls the starter cord four times until the engine revs with an unwilling splutter. Undeterred, she swings out of the melee of tinnies to navigate the sparkling blue waters on a brilliant spring day that's too good to be ruined by a deadset creep. She can't resist cranking to the max even though she knows the risk. The joy, she thinks, of the wind in your face. She feels reborn by the heat, the lustre of the landscape, the glory of Cook's Basin. Riding the waves like a rollercoaster. Scanning the water for the quicksilver flash of a single majestic kingfish. The blues of Friday night are all but gone.

Her strings of hippie beads are soon streaming out behind her, catching occasionally on the tiller. Quickly, she bunches them in a knot – she doesn't want to end up throttled like

Isadora Duncan. She checks the two carry bags containing an earthenware bowl of still steaming spaghetti bolognaise, a thermos of coffee, a green salad, a chocolate cake so moist it's almost a mousse and a bottle of a medium-quality red wine. Honest food, she thinks, made with the best ingredients she can afford. Still standing upright. All good.

Ettie hopes the latest arrival in Oyster Bay isn't vegetarian or gluten intolerant, and wonders if she should have called ahead. Perhaps even asked if it was convenient for her to visit. Sometimes she forgets that on the other side of the moat the rules are very different. Hardly anyone lives as casually as offshorers.

Too late now, she thinks, cutting the motor and drifting the last few feet. She steers her tinny alongside the pontoon with a light thunk. Way above, she makes out a woman with spindly limbs, tying empty cardboard boxes into bundles.

"Oy!" Ettie shouts, waving.

The woman looks up, uncertain, and calls out, "You okay?"

"You're the new owner, right?"

There's a nod.

"I'm Ettie Brookbank. The welcoming committee. Of one."

"Yes?"

"Come to explain a few, er, local customs." Why doesn't the bloody woman come down so she doesn't have to shout?

"Now?"

"No time like the present," she says, throwing a line around the cleat and tying on.

Reluctantly, it seems to Ettie, the woman makes her way from the gloomy shadows of the verandah to the foreshore, her hands balled in the pockets of her blue jeans. She takes careful steps, eyes fixed on the ground, her black hair falling forward and half-covering a face that has spent too much time indoors. Her T-shirt is blinding white, even though the bright noonday light is filtered by massive spotted gums. Ettie counts twenty steps from top to bottom and feels a twinge of envy. She'd trade her two hundred in a flash. Even for a house that's always given her the shivers.

"Here, take these, love, while I wring out the bottom of my skirt. Bilge pump's busted." Without standing up in the unstable aluminium boat, Ettie passes the orange bags across a six-inch gap of water. They're heavier than the woman anticipates and she stumbles forwards slightly.

"Don't drop them, okay?" Ettie fusses with armloads of sopping fabric, wringing little handfuls, one at a time, careful not to crush the tiny mirrored discs that wink along the hemline. She looks up, squinting into sunlight. "You got a name, love?"

"Oh. Of course. Kate. Kate Jackson." She puts down a bag and extends a hand.

Ettie folds it in her own calloused mitt and feels *white-collar* scrawled in the softness of the skin. She smothers a sigh and, not unkindly, mentally gives the scrappy woman about three months before she flees back to the reliable comforts of city living. Not that there's any shame in fleeing. Everyone's different, that's all. She bunches her skirt against her stomach and finds her barefooted way onto the rocking pontoon, admiring the toenails she's painted to match the bright orange of her embroidered Indian shirt. The platform sinks alarmingly under the weight of the two of them. Ettie ignores the water.

Kate hops backwards to keep her leather moccasins dry.

"Pontoon needs work," Ettie says matter-of-factly.

"Everything does. You call in on everyone who buys a house around here?" Kate asks, straight to the point.

"Only if they're alone and look incompetent," she grins.

"Ah. That bad, am I?" The first hint of a smile softens the sharp edges of a narrow face, makes its way up to eyes that are neither green nor blue but somewhere in between.

"Seen worse." Ettie reaches for the heavier bag, leaving the lighter one for Kate to carry, and leads the way along the jetty with swaying hips and tinkling anklets. She glances at the stacks of new timber on the seawall and shakes her head. She's seen offshore renovations rip the heart out of tough and experienced men who failed to factor in the high cost of barging materials and the expensive impact of fluky weather and unyielding tides. She wonders if this edgy woman has the faintest clue what she's taken on.

Halfway up a scraggy path overgrown with needle-sharp burrawangs and bitey prickly Moses, Ettie pauses. Under her bare feet, the sandstone steps are green and slimy. The stewy smell of rotting vegetation catches in her nostrils. She looks up at the gabled house with two chimneys and a red-tiled roof. Genteel once, maybe even cottage-style grand in its day, but right now "wreck" is the first word that springs to mind.

"You've heard the house is supposed to be haunted?" she says, turning to see how Kate reacts.

"Always had a soft spot for ghosts," the young woman replies evenly, coming up to stand beside her. "Even the unfriendly ones."

"There's an old codger, slightly mad. Lives in a log cabin

at the foot of the escarpment. Wouldn't be surprised if it was him scaring people off."

"What kind of mad?"

Not even a twitch, Ettie notes. "Harmless. Hiding his poverty behind crankiness."

"Ah. Sad then, not mad."

At the door, Ettie turns back and says seriously: "A lot of people come here to hide. Doesn't work. Not ever."

"Do I look like I'm hiding?"

"No one ever does, love."

A ruined wicker chair sags near the front door in slovenly welcome. Inside, it's no better. Mildew creeps up walls leaving a mark like a high tide. Ceilings are stained with water, soot and streaks from the mashed bodies of spiders. Ettie shivers. So cold, she thinks, on a day when it's hot enough to strip to your undies and dive in the water. "Which way's the kitchen?"

Kate points to a door at the end of a badly scuffed hallway: "Through there."

"Oh a wood-burning stove!" Ettie declares, unable to keep the nostalgia out of her voice. "We had one when I was a kid."

"The real estate agent suggested I fix the chimney before I try to boil a kettle. She gave me the impression the house might burn down if I didn't."

"Probably true."

"Nice of her to tell the truth. Lot of agents reckon that with a new carpet over the bloodstains and a fresh coat of paint, the past is consigned to the dump."

"Showing properties at high tide is about as shifty as we ever get around here." Ettie hoists her bag to the counter top. "Nice view," she adds, happy to find a positive.

"I like it."

"Right." Ettie claps her hands together lightly, feeling neither welcome nor unwelcome. "Let's have lunch, shall we? Spag bol washed down with an acceptable red."

Kate hesitates, confused.

"It's in the bags, love. I'm not expecting you to cook."

"Oh. I see."

"Furniture due to arrive soon?"

"Builders start tomorrow. I'll keep it basic until the work finishes."

"Good idea," Ettie says, thinking it might be a long time to go without a table or a comfortable chair.

Ettie sets out lunch on a packing box on the verandah where the atmosphere is less oppressive than in the house. She pulls up two smaller cartons labelled *BOOKS* for them to sit on and pours a decent slug of wine into a couple of water glasses scrounged from Kate's derelict kitchen. They clink. Ettie sips, swills and sighs with satisfaction. "Ah. A single drop. How it softens the edges."

She holds back from the food, letting Kate, who takes a polite amount, go first. Good manners or a sparrow appetite, Ettie's not sure which, although she'd put her money on the sparrow option. The woman's got about as much flesh on her as a cricket.

Ettie fills her own bowl generously and hoists a fat skein of heavily sauced pasta into her mouth. "Not enough salt," she pronounces. "Would have added chilli but I wasn't sure if you were the hot and spicy type." The joke falls flat.

"The sauce is perfect. This, um, is very kind of you."

"Saves everyone knocking on your door one at a time to

find out what you're up to. No prying of a personal nature, of course. None of us could survive too much scrutiny. More like getting and giving practical knowledge." Ettie hands over a list. "Stick this on your fridge door. It's the usual guff. Garbage pick-up days, fireshed fundraisers, twilight sails with the names of boats looking for crew."

"Ah. Thank you."

Kate – God, she looks so young, twenty-five maybe, thirty tops – sits with her knees clenched and her back straighter than a ruler. Ettie begins to wonder if dropping by uninvited was a mistake and decides to hold off the chocolate cake for another day. "So, how'd you find this place?"

"Short story. Got lost a few weeks ago when I was looking for a beach not far from here. Saw the ferry and took a ride on a whim. Bought the house the same day."

"That's it?" Ettie can't keep the incredulity out of her voice.

"Close enough." Kate forks some crisp salad and places it in the centre of her hot pasta.

Ettie tries not to wince and turns her head away from the sight of wilting lettuce. "Well, that's a first. Most people rent for a while to see whether a few rough commutes when the wind blows like stink knocks the romance out of offshore life. Look at many houses?"

"Just this one."

Ettie keeps her face blank. Wriggles to ease the pain at the base of her spine and wishes she'd arranged the boxes so her back was braced comfortably against the wall. "Any regrets?" she asks, thinking she'd be weeping into a case of wine if she owned this joint.

"None," Kate says, too quickly.

"None?"

"Truly. I've always loved wrecks. Not sure why. Maybe because no matter what you do to them, they improve. And this one looks worse than it is. The bones are solid. All it needs is a bit of love and care."

"Well. Early days. Plenty of time to find your feet." Ettie concentrates on her food. "How are you finding the isolation?"

Kate pauses, searching for the right words. "I feel like I've fallen down the rabbit hole, like the volume's been turned down, if that makes any sense." She flushes.

Something rare, like a feeling of kinship, flutters briefly against Ettie's ribcage. "Yeah, as a matter of fact it does. Perfect sense. Never heard it expressed better. You've got a way with words."

"I should have. I'm a journo. Financial. Nothing glamorous."

"Ah," Ettie says, beginning to think there might be a bit of distance in lunch after all. "S'pose you're used to hanging out with the rich and powerful, then?"

"They're only someone till you talk to them. You discover that quick smart."

Ettie nods. "Idols with clay feet."

"Something like that."

"Well then. Welcome to the rabbit hole, Alice."

The sound of a boat down below grows louder and Ettie stands up and walks to the edge of the verandah. She's expecting to see a few fishermen on their way to dredge for nippers in the sandbanks.

"You've got a visitor," she announces, when a water taxi swings into Kate's pontoon.

An elderly woman wearing stiletto heels, a city suit and a wide straw hat decorated with fake flowers topples headfirst out of the boat.

Kate gets to her feet, looking puzzled.

"Oh God, it's my mother. I'm so sorry. Can you just wait while I see what she wants?" She thrusts her bowl aside, then turns and sprints down to the foreshore.

"Invite her up. There's plenty of food!" Ettie calls after her.

The elderly woman picks her way up the steps like she's walking through a paddock of cow pats, waving a hand noisy with bracelets. She lets out small yelps at regular intervals, yanking her arms away from plants that scratch, nip, and rip at the silk of her immaculate turquoise suit. Ettie, who adores clothes, feels a pang of sympathy.

Kate leads her mother onto the verandah and, without any expression of warmth, introduces her as Emily Jackson. Red-faced from the steps, the woman looks as though she's dressed for the Melbourne Cup but has ended up lost in the jungle. She ignores Ettie's outstretched hand.

"Local, are you?" she asks, pinpricks of sweat pooling above lips thin with disapproval.

"Not born and bred but I've lived here long enough to qualify," Ettie says with the customary pride of all long-term off-shorers who feel they've earned a few points because they've been tough enough to go the distance. It takes a moment to realise the woman has no interest in her at all.

Emily Jackson turns to her daughter instead, and in a voice like splintered ice says: "So, you've found rock bottom at last. Feel comfortable, do you, hiding in this . . . this *hovel*?"

For the next half-hour Ettie listens with growing incredulity

– and indignation – as Emily runs her daughter down without mercy in front of a complete stranger. Every comment an arrow with a poisoned tip. *Have your pimples cleared up yet or is that one on your double chin? You're scrawny, dear, unattractive in a woman. What are you doing in this godforsaken hellhole? Are you completely insane? Or just plain stupid? I sometimes wonder if the hospital mixed up the babies when you were born and you're not related to me at all.*

That poor, poor girl, Ettie thinks. And it's at this moment that she irrationally, thoughtlessly, and without hesitation, decides to embrace Kate and help her find a place in the warm heart of the community that all those years ago had embraced her too. From the day she arrived in Cook's Basin and a bunch of local women turned up on her doorstep with a pot of boiling minestrone and a loaf of crusty bread, she'd felt wanted. And that was as good a definition of home as any.

Three hours later, Ettie climbs into her tinny feeling slightly tipsy. The sea breeze has died and the air is thick and warm. She motors home using the bottom half of an empty milk container to bail water. Travelling so slowly, the boat sends out ripples like radio beams.

She is horribly aware that she'd prattled on for too long at lunch, like one of those eccentric old women who unload their boring stories on anyone who's close enough to hear. A glimpse into her old age? She squeezes her eyes tightly shut against the image. If only her mouth had done the same, she thinks.

But she couldn't help herself. She'd waxed lyrical about the wild flowers in spring when the rain remembered to fall, the way wallabies held off giving birth, sometimes for years, until there was plenty of feed. She offered up advice too. Close your windows when you see whitecaps and batten down for a gale. Keep the gutters clear of leaf litter so the water drains into your tank instead of overflowing and running down the hill into the bay where it won't do you any good. And don't swim at sunrise or sunset, that's when sharks come in to feed. Don't eat the mushrooms that glow in the dark, either. Or any others unless you are sure they're the right kind. Check out the way spotted gums peel like sunburn in November until their trunks are smoother than a facelift. Wish it was that easy for us, eh? See leaves drop like torrential rain at the beginning of summer to hold moisture in the soil in the dry season. The clean, dusty smell of them. What a weird brown country we live in. On and on . . . Filling Kate's silence until she ran completely out of puff.

"You love this place, don't you?" Kate had said finally, with a wry grin.

"Shows, does it?" She'd managed a smile and held back, perhaps in shame, from telling Kate that in the beginning she'd seen Cook's Basin as an exotic playground. Sand, surf, boats and barbecues. A place where she could forget the pain of her marriage and divorce, live out her dream of becoming an artist. It took a couple of years before she experienced the emotional switch that had clicked for Kate in a second.

"I'm curious. What's Ettie short for?"

"Henrietta. Named after my granny. She made wonderful scones in a wood-fired oven."

"When the stove is fixed, if you have time, you might be kind enough to show me how?"

"Be a pleasure. An absolute pleasure."

By the time she's halfway home, Ettie has convinced herself that Kate is not so much a cold fish, but quietly tough. Which makes perfect sense having met her horror of a mother. If it had been up to her, Ettie would have grabbed the old woman's expensive suede handbag, hit her over the head with it and made her swim home. But Kate had dutifully summoned – and paid for – a water taxi to take her away. Good riddance to the old duffer.

God! Speaking of old duffers, when did she last check on Artie? With a sudden lurch of guilt, Ettie veers off course towards a yacht bleeding rust at the mouth of the bay. She eases her tinny alongside and whacks the hull so hard the boat rocks. Just when she's beginning to fear the worst, a thwack comes back.

"You sick, Artie? Or just taking your time so you can scare me to death?" she yells, cranky because she'd blame herself forever if he'd been lying there dead for days.

A stick makes its way out of the porthole towards her with a short shopping list and a twenty-dollar note pegged to the end. "Need a few supplies, luv. You up to it?" he calls.

"You should be in a nursing home, Artie, getting three meals a day and a regular hot bath."

"Me legs are buggered, girl, not me brains. I'd be done for in a week in one of them shitholes. Be like steppin' into a coffin while you're still breathin' and waitin' for the lid to crash down on ya. You gonna take the list or leave it hangin' there?"

She reaches for the note. "I'll drop by with the stuff tomorrow afternoon. You'd better answer quick smart when I knock or you'll be laying in that coffin sooner than you think."

"Still got a bit of distance in me. No need to panic."

"Good to know that, Artie, now that my heart's beating back in its proper place. How's your water?"

"You mean me storage tanks, right? Heh, heh. Got a tow for a fill-up this morning. All good. You and Sam. What would I do without youse?"

"Stop brownnosing, Artie. You're not up to it."

"Okay, luv. Off you go and sleep well tonight." He thumps the hull with a rat-a-tat-tat that sounds like a drum roll on opening night.

Ettie sighs. One day she'll find him rocking on the water without an ounce of life left in a body already one-third dead from a stroke. She checks the shopping list and consoles herself with the fact that at least the old bugger doesn't seem to be going through the rum at his usual terrifying rate.

CHAPTER FOUR

Not long after a pearly pink sunrise that fills him with joy, Fast Freddy heads for The Briny Café looking for his regular morning caffeine hit. The first cup may taste like filth but it fires up his tired old body after a night on the water dealing with babies in a rush to be born and kids puking their guts up after a party. He finds Ettie, who is dressed for hard yakka in a stretchy black top and khaki army fatigues, peering through the café's flimsy glass door.

"A fridge light in the corner but not a soul to be seen," she says, straightening with a loud sigh. She picks up her bucket of cleaning supplies, and a fake leopard-skin rubber glove with a hot-pink trim drops out. Fast Freddy bends to retrieve it.

"Very glamorous," he says, tucking it back in amongst a range of environmentally sound products. "Modern life, it's all about style."

"All gloss and no grunt, eh?" Ettie says, smiling a thank you.

Neither of them hears Big Julie sneak up behind them. "Bertie's not coming in today," she says, wrapping her arms around Freddy's waist and planting a loud kiss on his rough cheek.

"Easy on," he says, stepping back in a fluster. "Don't want to start a rumour."

"Why not? The grapevine needs livening up." Big Julie, a tiny woman with panda bear eyes and bleached blonde hair, winks at Ettie and flashes her cleavage at Freddy. All brass but plenty of class, too.

"Hit on some other poor sod, Jules, and leave a worn-out old boat navvy alone."

"Nah. You're too tempting, Freddy. Those scratchy whiskers, the delicate aroma of petrol . . ."

"Give it up, love, and fix a bloke a coffee, will you? I'm parched and about to topple off my feet with exhaustion. Ettie needs a kickstart, too."

"Another in a long line of knock-backs but I'll live," Big Julie sighs. She wrenches open the door, slides through a wall of plastic strips – Bertie's concept of a modern flyscreen. "Give me ten minutes."

"What's up with Bertie?" Ettie asks, while Freddy drags the pile of morning papers inside.

"Crook, love. That shyster lung of his is playing up again and the mean old bastard won't go to see a doctor. Told him the government's been picking up the tab for decades, but he still won't make the trip. Ask me he's scared. Got a head like an old turtle and acts like one." She lines up two paper mugs, presses a switch and gives the machine a hefty whack. A thin trickle the colour of weak tea dribbles from the spiggot.

"Want me to offer to take him?" Freddy asks.

"Nah. Just turn up at the funeral. Sorry. Bad joke. He'll be right. Old bugger's got nine lives and he's only used two." She hammers the machine a second and third time with the flat of her palm, then turns to face them with a shrug of frustration. "Busted, love," she says. "Just like its owner."

What would happen if Bertie retired, Ettie thinks on her way to work. Probably some cashed-up entrepreneur would swan in, knock the building down and put up a glass and chrome monstrosity. It would serve overpriced food and yes, she might as well admit it, drinkable coffee. But the spirit of past generations would be wiped out by a wrecking ball. The heart of The Briny lost forever. No amount of money could restore that. It was priceless. But, she reassures herself, The Briny, which has always been the central meeting point for the offshore community, is tougher than it appears. If anyone tried to pull it down there'd be an uproar.

She wonders how long Bertie had been hiding behind his sharp one-liners, grimly determined to ignore a new order of residents with their elegant laptops and rising expectations. Pretending the café was the last frontier so no one noticed the place and its proprietor were falling to bits.

For years now, she's had to suppress a strong desire to vault the dusty counter, grab a mixing bowl and whip up a fluffy sponge or fragrant orange cake. Instead, every morning, she smiles at the feisty old man and tells him his coffee has more character than any other brew in town. Well, at least it isn't an outright lie. She flexes her fingers like a pianist to stop the itch she feels every time she imagines how she could transform The Briny.

*

On the dark side of Oyster Bay, a small team of handymen begins work on Kate Jackson's house, ripping out rot, clearing debris, cracking awful ghost jokes. *What's a ghost boxer called? A phantomweight. Why did the barman refuse the ghost a brandy? He didn't serve spirits.*

She asks them if they know how and when the ghost stories began but they're not sure. Some kids, they reckon, probably after they'd been accused of camping illegally in the house and leaving a mess. Blame a ghost, right?

When the crashing and banging starts to sound more disturbing than constructive, Kate escapes. At the edge of the water, she flicks a few dead leaves out of the cockpit of her newly acquired secondhand kayak, crouches to check the murkiest recesses of the nose and stern for spiders. Satisfied, she pushes the boat into the water and wades in after it. The cold shock of the sea makes her flinch. Her skin goes bumpy. Sand, the colour of gold, squeezes between her toes. Further out but still in shallow waters, seagrass shivers in bright green pods.

Holding the kayak steady, she climbs into the cockpit and starts stroking away from shore, a red slash on tawny water. She is surprised by the power of the tide, the resistance of such a light breeze. Halfway across the bay, she comes across a sun-bleached plastic tank floating aimlessly. She hauls it into the cockpit, not sure if she's doing the right thing but then she spots the *Mary Kay* and paddles towards it. The barge is craning a sunken boat from the water, nose first. The canopy is ripped down the middle and seagrass hangs from the sides like wet hair.

"Hey," she calls, hanging onto the gunnel so the kayak doesn't drift off.

"Yo!" Sam makes his way along the edge of the barge and stands over her awkwardly. He recognises her immediately as the woman Bertie was winding up in the café the other day. So not a tourist after all . . .

"Bit of a mess," she says, looking at the wreck. "What happened?"

"Prop got caught on a rock and tipped the boat. Filled with water as the tide came in. Nobody noticed till this morning."

"Boats. There's a lot to learn."

"Yeah, well, you never know what'll nip a piece out of your backside if you're not concentrating. One good thing. That old turtle who lies around the bay with his belly up getting the sun will be happy. Won't be much racing back and forth to the Spit in this for a while." Sam crouches, almost eye level. "The seat's survived. Although the swivel might be a bit stiff for a while!" He smiles to show it's a joke, but he gets no response.

"Picked up a tank floating on the water. Thought you might know what to do with it."

"You're the sheila who bought that creepy house, aren't you?"

"Well, I bought the house over there, if that's what you mean," she says, pointing. "But the name's Kate, not Sheila. Do you reckon the tank belongs to this boat?"

Sam rests his elbow on his thigh, his chin on the knuckles of his hand. "Let me think . . ."

"Yeah, well. How about I leave it with you to sort out?" she snaps.

Jeez. No sense of humour. Uptight. Snippy. He lets his grin slip away and pushes himself upright. "I'll tell the owner," is all he says.

*

Over the next three weeks, Ettie and the Cook's Basin community watch the little slip of a woman in Oyster Bay charm or con (no one is sure which) the chippies into turning up five days a week. And on time, too – when everyone knows they juggle at least four jobs at once. The word is she can't cook, never offers them a cold beer when they knock off, and doesn't speak unless she has something worthwhile to contribute. They scratch their heads and mumble amongst themselves. None the wiser.

In a desperate effort to seduce the chippies away from the Oyster Bay renovation, one Islander promises slap-up hot breakfasts every day. To be followed, she adds seductively, by fresh banana muffins for morning tea and a warm, moist peach cake topped with caramel sauce with lunch. The offer fails dismally. The tiles for her new bathroom remain in boxes. She goes back to bathing out of a bucket.

A bloke with a leaking roof gets so fed up with tripping over saucepans every time it rains, he finally climbs a ladder and, to his absolute amazement, manages to fix the holes himself.

The pushy young couple waiting for new steps to access their house are told they're young and fit and they can manage with their goat track for a while longer. They're outraged, and also blissfully unaware that if an oldie rings in with a serious problem, they'll keep dropping to the bottom of the waiting list anyway.

When Kate travels on the old *Seagull*, loaded to the max with babies, kids, prams, empty outboard petrol tanks, shopping bags and floppy sunhats, women squeeze up to make room for her and their toddlers eyeball her with open curiosity.

But no one has the courage to nod more than a quick hello. Even the boat-mad mutts, who regularly hitch a ride knowing the ferry driver doesn't have the heart to toss them off, decide she's not the kind of person to leap enthusiastically upon with dirty paws.

Kate Jackson has everyone seriously flummoxed. Ettie is the only person who isn't surprised.

Cook's Basin News (CBN)

Newsletter for Offshore Residents of Cook's Basin, Australia

OCTOBER

The Fire Season is almost upon us once more – what can you do?

Maintain a fuel-free zone around your house. This means doing a clean-up! Get rid of cardboard boxes or other recyclable paper material from under the house, as well as any old timber you've been saving because it might come in useful one day. Stack your winter wood well away from buildings (and your neighbour's house!). Clear dead leaves and branches from gutters. Check that taps, hoses, pumps, etc., are ready for use and that your water tank is always full. Keep flammable liquids away from your house. Plug downpipes and fill gutters with water if fire threatens. Place buckets of water and wet towels around and outside the house to put out spot fires.

P.S. There will be a community pump check next Monday. Fire up your pump to make sure it's still working and celebrate afterwards by bringing a plate and a bottle of whatever you fancy to the beach near Triangle Wharf.

CANE TOAD ALERT

Residents have been asked by the Municipal Council to be on watch for cane toads in their gardens after a couple of recent sightings. According to a spokesperson, cane toads should be caught and restrained in a bucket (with a lid) and disposed of humanely. Cane toads compete with native animals for food and are toxic to larger reptiles such as goannas and snakes. Cane toads are easily recognisable by their large size and warty skin. Use rubber gloves when handling them.

ARTIE DUTY

Ettie has asked that the local community be reminded to make regular checks on Artie. When she last knocked on the hull, he was down to his last supplies and, as everyone knows, he's too proud to call up and say he needs help.

Car Stolen from Car Park

Mark's really dodgy, battered and banged up ute was stolen some time between Thursday and Monday by someone who was clearly extremely desperate. While we sympathise with battlers, we were not insured and we're not travelling all that smoothly ourselves. If anyone saw anything suspicious, please call Mark or me. Thanks. Even better, if you snitched it, put it back. No hard feelings. Well, maybe a few.

CHAPTER FIVE

In the middle of a chilly November, when spring's hot spell looks like all the warm weather they're going to get, Ettie's phone rings. She strips off her rubber gloves and wipes the sweat from her forehead, answering the call with a combative voice. "This better be good," she says straight off, "because it's taken me a year to get around to cleaning the windows and I've just hauled myself off a ladder to pick up the phone!"

"It's Kate. From Oyster Bay. Is this a bad time?"

"Thought you might be telemarketing, love. I try to shame them into hanging up first."

"Oh I see. Anyway . . . I now have a kitchen table, two chairs and a new hotplate. And I wondered, would you like to come to dinner this Friday?"

Ettie doesn't hesitate. "Sounds perfect. What are you cooking?" The moment she asks what is a ritual offshore question meant to indicate interest and appreciation, Ettie worries she's come across as impolite or, worse, critical. Kicking herself for being tactless, she rushes outside to shoo away a flock of white cockatoos that regularly swoops onto her deck, screaming abuse, tearing at the timber window frames and sidestepping along the rail like linedancers. The noise is so horrendous she almost misses Kate's reply.

"I hadn't thought that far ahead. Maybe a chop. A sausage as well."

Ettie's lusty foodie heart shrivels. She is certain she won't find echoes of garlic, lemon and rosemary on the chop and that the sausage will be a basic *butcher's special* pork banger presented with a bottle of tomato sauce on the side. Fair enough fodder if you're in a rush, but not the stuff of traditional Cook's Basin entertaining where home cooks do their utmost to dish up top nosh because no one wants to risk losing a car space by going to a restaurant. The genuinely hopeless cooks – and Ettie wonders if Kate might turn out to be one of them – get lumbered with the dishes.

"How will you cook the sausages?" Ettie says, once again without thinking before she opens her mouth. Since turning fifty, it's become a habit that she can't seem to break.

"Grilled, maybe, like the chop," Kate says, uncertainly.

"And then sliced into inch-long pieces and folded through a slow-cooked pot of spicy homemade baked beans with plenty of capsicum, carrots and onions?"

"Er . . ."

"I'm joking, love. But seriously, living offshore, you might want to learn a few basic recipes that work for two or fifty-two."

"I can assure you, Ettie, I will *never* invite fifty-two people to dinner."

"Ah but that was before you fell down the rabbit hole and your world turned upside down. Who knows what's ahead?" And then, because she can't help herself, Ettie plunges in again. "How about I work out a list of ingredients and come over late in the afternoon to give you your first cooking lesson? Got plenty of wood set aside? We could have a go at Granny's scones if you can get the oven hot enough to fire a brick kiln. I'm thinking . . . a lamb curry?"

With a massive effort of self-control, she closes her mouth and cuts off the nervous babble.

"Curry. My favourite. You're sure?" Kate says after a long pause.

"Got a pencil? I'll tell you what we need."

Two minutes later, with the phone back on its cradle, Ettie pulls on her rubber gloves to finish the windows, already planning a medium-hot lamb curry served amongst a gaudy array of tempting side dishes. It takes her mind off the grind.

She is certainly curious to see what Kate's done with the house. Curious to know how a city girl, living alone, is coping with the bloodcurdling night-sounds of the bush. Powerful owls on the hunt. Sneezing bandicoots, so human-like it's impossible not to imagine a stalker lurking in the darkness. The rhythmic thump of wallabies bashing through the bush. The isolation, too. So intense that it vibrates in the over-wrought pre-dawn hours when every tiny rustle feels full of deadly threat.

The dark side of Oyster Bay, where Kate lives without a soul in shouting distance, is no place for the faint-hearted.

Outside The Briny Café, which he feels has an even stronger than usual lean to the east, Sam Scully finds himself with time on his hands. He sweeps up leaves dropped by a straggly paper bark and a stringy casuarina, both of them struggling to survive against the constant battering of sand, salt and the icy westerlies that hung around until the end of September this year. A stray tan mutt, with a bowling ball torso, a flattened snout and an authoritative rear end, glares at the fuzz on the end of the broom, snuffles and pounces.

"You're not helpin', mate," Sam tells the dog, using the broom head to fend off the attack. The mutt responds with a tackle and locks on with a deep-throated rumble, savage now. Sam gives a hard yank.

"Give up, you mongrel," he orders. The dog instantly drops the broom head and slinks away.

"No hard feelings, but jeez, lighten up." He goes over to a tap and fills a dog bowl with fresh water. The mutt falls on it thirstily, drool flying in all directions.

Sam finishes his sweeping and the rest of the day stretches emptily in front of him. There's no cargo to pick up until the next high tide, which is late in the afternoon. No bugger has even rung up to have his mooring serviced to fill the gap. He's free as a bird.

He scans the Square. A pack of helmeted cyclists wearing tight black lycra and swigging water from designer bottles rest on the seawall like crows. There are a few tourists about but even though it's sunny, the weather is too cool for crowds. He's about to give up and head home when he spots Ettie struggling with a load of shopping bags. He sprints over and grabs them.

"Thanks, Sam," she says, flexing her fingers. "The trek from the car park seems to be getting longer every day."

"You're still a spring chicken and the answer to every man's dreams. Never forget it."

"In *my* dreams."

Sam leans Ettie's groceries against the leg of a picnic table that has the initials of three generations scratched into the wood and scatter-shot with birdshit. The mutt wanders up and stretches his back leg in a crooked arabesque.

Ettie yelps and snatches her shopping out of range. "Who owns this mangy mongrel?"

"Dunno. But he's definitely on borrowed time. How about a coffee? My shout."

"You going to send out a warning?"

"Eh?"

"Moth plague when you open your wallet."

"Easy on, Ettie, just tryin' to show a bit of dash around a lovely young woman. And that joke's older than time. Yes or no?"

"Why not? I'm game." She flicks a look at the bike riders. "Bet every single one of them would have bought a coffee if it was even halfway drinkable. Bertie's doing himself out of easy profit. Too pig-headed to admit his brew stinks."

"Bertie's never gonna change. Flat white, right? No sugar."

She nods. "It's such a waste, though."

Sam's eyes narrow as a boat flies through the moorings at high speed. "That freakin' weasel."

"The creep," Ettie adds, vehemently.

"Know him?"

"Arrived a few weeks ago. Bought the house next to Triangle Wharf. He hasn't quite cottoned on to the meaning of community spirit yet."

"Not sure he's the type that ever will. Any idea what he does?"

"Nope. Lot of kids hang out in that fancy boatshed, though, and the whole Island is keeping an eye on him. He's dead shonky, if you ask me. I'm just not sure exactly *how* shonky."

The wake from the boat pounds into the seawall like surf. The cyclists fly off their perch and rub their soaked backsides, looking over their shoulders to find out who's to blame. The boat is long gone. They drift back to their bikes, grumbling loudly.

"Well, he's a load short on manners," Sam says.

"He's a deadset slimeball." Ettie's face turns red.

"He make a pass or somethin', Ettie?" Sam teases.

"Don't be ridiculous. There's something missing in him. A link to the compassion part in his brain. He's cruel, maybe even sadistic."

"Has he hurt you in any way?"

She smiles. "Nah. He wouldn't be breathing. It's just a feeling, like looking into his eyes and finding no one at home."

"Well, you're better off keeping your distance. You want a burger? A sandwich? I'm feeling particularly generous today."

"No. Just the coffee. I'm on the way home. I've had a full week of scrubbing very dirty houses. I want to sit and watch the clean blue ocean from my deck and maybe rack up a few z's."

"Book publishing in a bit of a downturn?"

"Could call it that. If it ever had an upturn."

"You're the best there is, Ettie. Remember that. When you draw a seagull, it's a seagull. Plain as day. Even to a kid who's never seen one. You're an unsung genius, love."

Ettie smiles ruefully. "Yeah. That's the problem. Unsung."

Inside the café, Big Julie takes Sam's order. Infamous for low-cut blouses known to occasionally wreck a bloke's concentration, she leans forward on the counter provocatively and gives him a wink. "Nice work with the broom," she says. "Couple more years and you'll be an expert."

"I'm surrounded by critics. Where's Bertie?" Sam gives the café a quick squiz as though he might find the old bloke lurking in a dark corner. But there's only Fast Freddy skimming the headlines before he decides whether it's worth forking out for the newspaper.

"That lung of his is still playing games."

"Bad?" Sam asks.

"Well, bad enough for him to see a doctor for the first time in a hundred years."

Freddy looks up. "Aw, bugger. That's not good."

"Makes you wonder if he's at death's door," Sam quips.

Big Julie's face turns white. She hands Fast Freddy his coffee, thick and sweet the way he likes it. Freddy raises a thumb and leans across the counter to wipe a tear off her cheek.

"Steam," she says, dragging her wrist over her face. "From the stupid bloody espresso machine that's never really worked properly in its lousy bloody life."

Fast Freddy pats Big Julie's shoulder, his head bowed. Sam stares down at his scruffy boots.

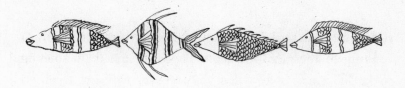

CHAPTER SIX

The next day, on an unseasonally cool Friday afternoon, Ettie packs her waterproof bags and sets off, leaving enough time to call in on Frankie at the Oyster Bay boatshed, a grizzly bear of a man, who has more luck with engines than women. She wants him to fix her navigation lights, and if he has time check out what's making her engine sound worse than a sick kookaburra. She scans the shoreline for any sign of the creep next door. All clear. She almost skips the last few yards.

She dumps her bags on the end of the ferry wharf and, feeling as lithe as a gazelle, makes her way across a row of rocking tinnies to reach her own. The engine starts on the first pull. She swoops in to scoop up her supplies without slowing in case the boat stalls. She feels like singing, like anything is possible if lady luck looks her way. The old black dog that visits if she lets down her guard for too long is back in his kennel. For the time being at least.

Ettie is puzzled by Kate's renovations. She'd expected to see walls knocked out, a state-of-the-art kitchen and one of those fabulous no-glass bathrooms with sloping floors so the water slides off into the drain without leaving stains. The kind that turn up in the glossy pages of home design magazines and make her spirit soar when she steps in to clean them. But while the house is undeniably transformed, it is essentially unchanged. It is still a dimly lit, turn-of-the-century cottage that's been shoved slightly off-kilter by the passage of time and the pummelling of storms straight off the Antarctic.

She wonders if Kate's insistence on keeping the past intact shows a lack of confidence, a lack of imagination or a lack of funds. Or maybe she just wants to preserve a slice of Cook's Basin history.

She murmurs quiet approval after a tour and pats the young woman on the back in congratulation. It is charming, after all. And she gets a full score card for bringing the project in on time and on budget – a rare offshore feat. Must have picked up a few clues from interviewing all those tycoons.

"So, you're a minimalist," she says, indicating the almost bare room.

"Not really. I don't want stuff to get ruined if the chippies have to come back with sanders and grinders or paint and varnish."

"Ah."

"Spills on sofas are expensive to remove," Kate adds, sounding slightly defensive.

"Pays to be careful, huh?"

"Watch the pennies and the pounds take care of themselves."

"So young and yet so wise. Have you met your neighbour up the hill yet?" Ettie asks, setting out her supplies on the newly sanded and varnished kitchen bench.

"I've caught a glimpse of him a couple of times. He has a

way of melting into the landscape. There one second, gone the next. He's definitely sad, not scary. Like he's been dealt some awful blow and never recovered." Kate shrugs. "I'm guessing, though. We've never exchanged a word. One day I'll get him to talk to me about surviving in a tough environment. Maybe I'll write a story about him."

Ettie can't think of a worse idea. She once tried to help the old codger haul his shopping all the way up to his shack on a day so hot even the cockatoos were slumped. He'd hissed at her so viciously she'd almost toppled backwards into the water in fright.

"Nobody knows much about him. Weird when you think about it, 'cause around here there are very few secrets."

"He's just an old man who prefers his own company. When I was a kid growing up in a small country town, we called loners like him hermits, not nutters. In India, people believe they're deeply spiritual and look after them. It all depends on your culture."

"Well, he's colourful, anyway." Ettie takes a deep breath and rubs her hands together. "Okay, the curry is done and only has to be warmed. We'll make the side dishes together and cook the rice when we're ready to eat. You want to fire up that gorgeous old stove to make some scones?"

Kate shakes her head. "Sorry. Still got problems with the chimney. Maybe next time."

They work side by side for the next hour. Ettie explains why a tomato is better diced instead of sliced for a relish. Why bananas should be cut as late as possible so they don't go brown – even when they're doused in lemon juice. She shows Kate how to pinch off parsley leaves. How to grind spices in a pestle and mortar to bring out their flavours. How to use a light hand when you stir so the food doesn't bruise or break. She finds a collection of colourful little dishes in a cupboard and raises her eyebrows in a question.

"Mementoes," Kate explains, "from assignments in different parts of the world."

"I've always wanted to travel," Ettie sighs, lining them up on the bench and asking for the origins of each one.

"Turkey," Kate says, pointing. "Morocco, Paris, Peru, Italy, Spain and good old Australia."

"The only travelling I've done was to Venice on my honeymoon," Ettie confesses. "It was so exotic to a plain suburbanite like me. Gondoliers singing, a string quartet in a tucked away church. Water and boats everywhere. I sometimes wonder if that's why Cook's Basin lured me in so easily. It reminded me of the most glorious two weeks of my life." Ettie's thoughts turn inward, stilling her hands as she remembers the glitter of the sun on the Grand Canal, the swoop of swifts chasing mosquitoes at sunset, the chiming of bells from churches all over the island. Mostly, though, she recalls the wild headiness, the sense of immortality and endless possibilities of being madly in love. The innocence of believing that vows were meant to last forever. She pulls herself back to the present abruptly, veering away from the memory of a miscarriage three months later that went so horribly wrong the possibility of children was wiped out forever. But she can't help wondering, as she has over and over, whether her marriage would have worked out differently if she'd been able to have a family. She shakes her head and picks up her knife again. "Tell me about your travels," she says, firmly closing the door on the past to tamp down self-pity.

Kate begins to open up a little then, talking about the giddy thrill of reinventing herself in cities that smelt of cumin; or spurted steam from sidewalks; or had stone angels toppling from rooftops. How she loved laying claim to a different personality to suit every new town.

Ettie understood that impulse. Hadn't she behaved the same way after her divorce? Playing the field, hunting for the excitement her husband said he couldn't live without. Only drawing the line when his friends turned up clutching bunches of service station flowers and bottles of cheap champagne like they were doing her a huge favour. *Thought you might be lonely*, they said, reading from the same script. It happened so often she stopped being polite.

Ettie grins. "So which Kate am I looking at now?"

Kate smiles shyly. "As close as it gets to the real one. As far as I know, anyway."

The kitchen is unheated and the night is cold. So they sit on plain white cushions on polished floorboards, in an essentially bare sitting room. One on each side of the large stone fireplace where a good blaze takes the chill off the room.

They tuck into a rogan josh that's more fiery than Ettie intended. "Chilli is hard to judge," she apologises. "The heat can sometimes depend on the time of year it is picked." Within reaching distance, side dishes in rainbow colours cover a glass-topped coffee table. Mango chutney. Tomato and red onion splashed with paprika and white vinegar. Banana and coconut drizzled with lemon juice. Yoghurt and cucumber spiked with mint. Eggplant and chilli fragrant with garlic. Peanuts stand alone. Pineapple teams with crystallised ginger.

"Traditional and untraditional accompaniments," Ettie explains, pointing out which is which. "Restraint has never been my strongest suit."

Over one of the smallest sound systems Ettie's ever seen, Chris Isaak sings smoothly about *tomorrow never coming*. Oldies' music, not the kind she expected to hear from a gung-ho reporter who must be at least twenty-five years her junior.

"Everyone wants to know how you managed to keep the chippies on site," Ettie says, spooning more rice into her bowl.

Kate looks up from her curry, surprised. "What do you mean?"

"Well, love, one day on, two days off, that's how most jobs are done around here."

"Really?"

"Word is you don't even feed and water them. There must be some secret."

Kate puts her bowl on a scrubbed stone hearth. She reaches into a basket filled with discarded builder's timber and throws a piece on the fire. Hot spots reflect off the bare boards, shadows dance on the freshly whitewashed walls. "If there is, it escapes me. All I do is clean up after they leave and get things set up so there's no mucking about the next day."

Ettie ladles curry sauce over her rice. "That must be it, then. They don't have to think hard first thing in the morning. Takes the sting out of their hangovers."

"Oh and I paid them at the end of every day's work. Cash in hand."

"Ah." Ettie nods. No waiting until the end of the job for their money. A brilliant strategy? Or dumb luck? She eventually decides Kate has the instincts of a born entrepreneur.

The music comes to a stop. Outside, a bullet of cold air whips down the gully. It tweaks the surface of the bay but can't find its way past the newly applied mortar and the tightly puttied windows. The room stays cosy and warm. Ettie goes over and crouches in front of a basket filled with CDs. She finds Frank Sinatra, another surprise. What strange forces, beyond a shocker mother, have shaped this young woman?

"You ever feel afraid here?" she asks, handing Kate the CD.

"Should I?" Kate gets up to replace Isaak with Sinatra. She presses the play button and Frank's voice spills over them warmly.

"No, of course not. The previous owner, the one before you, it was 'Old Timer's' that got him. His daughter went on with all that ghost mumbo jumbo to hide the fact that he was losing his mind."

"The ghost didn't send him mad then?" Kate says with a wry smile.

Ettie shakes her head, wishing she hadn't mentioned it. She collects their empty plates but Kate immediately takes them out of her hands and carries them into the kitchen. Ettie hears a tap run. She follows, unable to sit idly when someone is working. She grabs a spotless ironed tea towel when she notices there's no dishwasher.

"By the way, my holidays are over and I'll be gone for a few days from Monday," Kate says. "An assignment in New

York. I was hoping – if you're passing – that you could keep an eye on the house."

"New York!" Ettie almost drops the bowl she's drying.

"Trust me, it's not as exciting as it sounds."

"You mean nowhere near as exciting as a tinny ride to the Spit to clean a house trashed by three teenage boys who think shoving all their rotten food under the bed constitutes a tidy up? That's my day on Monday while you're sitting in business class sipping champagne." She hears the bitterness, tinged with despair, and goes quiet.

"You want to know how it really works?" Kate blurts, rushing on without waiting for an answer. "Right. For a start, scrap business class. It's cattle car all the way. It will take thirty-six hours to make it from my front door to my appointment. I will get forty-five minutes to do an *in-depth* interview that should take a week. I will return to my hotel room and spend the next twenty-four hours hunched over a computer positioning key points in a stranger's life until they make some sense. I will then order food from room service, grab whatever sleep I can and make my way back to the airport the next day. No time for museums, art galleries, a Broadway show, or even a quick look in the windows at Tiffany's. By the time I pitch up back at the office, the story will be laid out, subbed and hitting the presses. Already yesterday's news." Kate blushes and swallows whatever she is about to say with an apologetic smile. "Bit of a rant there. Sorry."

Ettie finishes drying the second bowl and stacks it neatly inside the other one. "If you want the truth, Kate, it sounds pretty amazing from my side of the fence. All jobs are hard yakka. That's why you get paid to do them."

"I'm not afraid of work. But I'm talking to a twenty-two-year-old brat who's just inherited a business empire without lifting a finger to earn it. He's famous for wild partying, fast cars and a very short attention span. I'm supposed to believe him when he tells me – as I know he will – that he's a changed man and looking forward to the hard work ahead of him to preserve the integrity of his father's legacy and the wellbeing of his employees. In fact, he and I both know he will sell to a corporate raider in the blink of an eye and float off to some hedonistic paradise without a second's thought for his father or the people who worked hard to help build the company."

"Ah," Ettie says, getting it at last. "It's the lies that are wearing you out."

"All I get is spin," Kate says, pulling the plug out of the sink. "One day, I'll hear the truth and I won't be able to recognise it and that's just plain scary." She uses the bottom of Ettie's cloth to dry her hands as water glugs down the drain hole. "You know, when I was a young cadet on a daily newspaper I used to pity the subs who'd been there for years. I was told they'd been legends in their day. To me they just seemed like cynical old men hanging out for their lunchtime beers. But now I worry there's a very real possibility that I could turn into them."

"So that's why you're in Cook's Basin. You're looking for a bit of sanity, which is a bit weird if you don't mind me saying so, 'cause most of the population thinks you've got to be nuts to live here."

Kate laughs. "Maybe my mother is right, then, and I have lost the plot."

"Or maybe you're just beginning to find it," Ettie says gently.

Kate's grin lights up her pale face. "Maybe I am."

Ettie tries not to think about her own scrambled existence. Was there a turn-off to fulfilment somewhere along the way that she missed? A fork in the road that failed to mention left was for battlers, right for swanners? She wonders if Kate is still young enough to believe that something wondrous will suddenly pop out of the ether to light up a new path. Ettie has been burned too often to trust in miracles herself. A failed marriage. An erratic career as an artist and illustrator. A few attempts at jobs such as corporate catering (the company went bust) and therapeutic massage (an ad in the paper prompted so many late-night calls for the wrong kind of massage she gave up).

There was also a brief, horrendously misjudged plunge into running a florist shop where she built the business but could never resist adding one or two extra blooms to a bunch, thus cancelling out the profit margin. Until then, she'd never realised generosity could send you broke. She also understood that it wasn't enough to be good at your job. If you wanted to run a successful business, you needed to understand the bottom line. And she just didn't get it, no matter how hard she tried. She quit at the end of her first year, wiser but with virtually nothing to show for twelve months of hard slog. Trusting in miracles, she believes, is borderline suicidal.

Kate crosses the kitchen to open the freezer. A puff of misty air spreads across the room. She removes the last of the chocolate cake and holds it aloft with her eyebrows raised in a query towards Ettie.

"Yeah. Why not? A little sweetness takes away the fullness."

"Chocolate does that?" Kate gives her a funny look.

"Works for me."

Sitting on his deck with his all-time favourite dinner of sausages, garlic mashed potatoes and peas, Sam automatically checks to see that his barge is still safe on her mooring. She's a miracle, he thinks, an indefatigable workhorse with shapely lines and a glorious rear end. He sips a frigidly cold beer and it hits him then that his fortieth birthday is a day away. He toys with the idea of throwing a last-minute bash but can't work up the enthusiasm. A sign, maybe, that his priorities are shifting? He is hit by a wave of nostalgia and half-closes his eyes. In his mind his mother wanders down the jetty to meet him off the school ferry. Ready with a story: a snake in the woodpile . . . a duck with ten ducklings paddling in her slipstream . . . a blank-eyed stingray cruising the shallows. She would always have a tea towel over her shoulder. A short-sleeved floral shirt. Plain cotton shorts. Her feet were bare and brown. Legs and arms, too.

"Good day?" she'd invariably ask. And he'd shrug by way of an answer.

"Daisy's boxer had her pups on the ferry this morning. Right at my feet. Just leaned sideways and out they popped, one by one. Like squeezing pips out of a cherry."

"Yeah right, Mum. Pull the other one."

"Honest as, love. Six pups. Did you know that Dottie *waxes* her legs? Never heard of it before. Must hurt like heck."

One summer day, she ran down the jetty to meet him, face

flushed with what he knew must be *big* news. He tried to guess. A shark in the bay? A giant fish on the line? Maybe a decent dinghy washed up at high tide that he might be able to keep if they couldn't find the owner?

"The bay ran dry today," she told him. Breathless. In the same incredulous tones you'd use if an alien had just dropped out of the sky.

"Yeah. Yeah." Sam was disappointed. Didn't his mother know he was too old to fall for dumb tricks?

"No, love, no joke. I was looking out the window while I did the breakfast dishes and the whole bay emptied. Like someone had pulled the plug. Got a bull's-eye view. Soldier crabs on the march, not sure which way to turn and crashing into each other. Water tanks. Rotting hulls. A cannon. A whole universe of sea creatures clinging to our rubbish and turning it into homes. Rent free!" She laughed, delighted with the thought. In the Scully family, the monthly rent payments regularly flattened the fizz in the household savings account. "A bold, new landscape. And a wee bit ghostly."

"Then what happened?" he asked, eyes narrowed.

"Well, I waited. Sort of paralysed with shock. I thought later that if I'd had my wits about me I would've run for the hills because it was crazy! Bays don't empty, not around here. Not unless some catastrophe is about to happen. I stuck my head out the window and watched, wondering if I was in a dream and didn't know it. Suddenly, the water came back in a mad, frothing rush. Fish were tossed high. Driftwood flew through the air. Water came up to my knees in the boatshed. The whole event took about ten minutes, and within fifteen it was as though it had never happened."

Sam grinned, sure now that it was a hoax. "You're havin' me on, Mum, aren't ya?"

She didn't reply. Instead she reached for his hand and walked him along the jetty to the beach. Then she pointed to a few dead tiddlers stranded way above the seawall.

"How do you think they got there?"

Sam was flummoxed. He trusted his mum, but she'd always told him to question what he hadn't seen with his own eyes. To seek the truth before making a judgement. And this was downright spooky. Fish didn't fall out of the sky. No way.

"Did Dad see it?" he asked, thinking witnesses were the only way to go.

"No. He was in the city. He doesn't do a ferry shift on Wednesdays, remember?"

"Anyone else see it?" No witnesses, no deal.

His mum smiled then, and pointed to a peeling old shack across the bay.

"The Heggartys were home. Want to row over in the boat and ask them?"

Sam dithered. The Heggartys were ancient and a bit potty. Once they got yacking, he'd be trapped for the rest of the afternoon. Still, old Mrs Heggarty cooked a decent shortbread biscuit and kept a good supply in a jar on the kitchen counter next to the tea. He had nothing to lose. He set off.

Two hours later he returned. "Tsunami," he said, looking at his feet, cranky he hadn't twigged earlier. "Mild. Caused by an earthquake a long way away. It's the second time the Heggartys have seen it happen here."

His mother looked vindicated but she wasn't the type to

gloat. "Mrs Heggarty have any biscuits?" she asked.

He shook his head. "She was about to make a batch when I turned up."

His mother ruffled his hair. "Come inside." She pulled a tray of scones out of the half kerosene tin perched on a gas ring that they called an oven, slathered on butter and honey. "You're a good boy. It never hurts to question even your old mother's words. Always remember that."

They had nothing in those early days, Sam thought. No phone, no electricity. No radio. The three of them ate, slept and played in a single room. A chip heater for hot water. The rise and fall of the sea cleaning away their sewage. He never once heard his mother complain, even when those huge king tides flooded her floors and wet her knitting if she'd forgotten to put the basket on a shelf. He remembered the awe of an early misty morning when he went off fishing with his dad and came home with a kingfish so big all the neighbours dropped by with their measuring tapes. He feels the old familiar ache of loss creep into his gut.

Sam sighs. Toys with the idea of another beer. He's watched the boat traffic all evening. Too many tinnies have come to a standstill at the Weasel's wharf and it's giving him a very bad feeling.

Kate lines up the chocolate cake on a plate.

"Cream's in the fridge, is it?" Ettie says, opening up to have a search. "Oh. This is the sort that needs to be whipped. Next time, buy double cream. Works better with cakes. Well, except for sponges. And it's less effort."

"Oh. Okay. I've always thought of cream as . . . just cream. Tea?" Kate asks.

"Coffee if you've got it."

"No coffee. Sorry."

"Tea's fine."

"Marco Polo, Earl Grey, Sencha or Russian Caravan? I don't have anything else that isn't medicinal, I'm afraid."

"Marco Polo," Ettie says, trying not to sound astonished.

She watches Kate, curious to see how a woman who is indifferent to food prepares a delicate brew of exotic tea. She crosses her fingers but expects the worst.

Kate warms and drains a fragile bone china teapot with a lissom spout and painted with tiny pink flowers. She adds two heaped teaspoons of tea and snatches the kettle off the heat a second after it bubbles. She waits half a minute before pouring water over the leaves. The mysterious scent of fruit, some floral hints and definitely vanilla, fills the kitchen. Flavours that would burn if the water was spitting hot. The lid goes on with a light clink. Ettie nods with approval.

Kate places two delicate cups and saucers, like props out of an Agatha Christie movie, on a tray with the pot. Ettie follows her back to the sitting room and watches her pour the copper-coloured tea with tight-lipped concentration. She passes Ettie a cup. Not a moment too long in the pot, Ettie thinks. Every flavour is distinct even if she can't quite pin them all down. The two women sit silently, each lost in thought until Ettie replaces her cup on the tray.

"Shall I make a fresh pot?" Kate asks.

"No. I'm feeling full and sleepy. It's time to go."

Ettie stands with a sigh of contentment and makes her way

to the front door. Kate holds her wet-weather jacket while she slips her arms through the sleeves.

"I'm thinking of buying a boat," Kate says. "Nothing flash. To go back and forth to the Spit. Who do you think I should talk to?"

"Sam Scully on the *Mary Kay*. You've met him, right? He delivered your building material. Get him to ask around. If I see him, I'll mention it. And don't worry about the house while you're away. Everyone will keep an eye on it. That's how Cook's Basin works. God, look at the moon. Magic, isn't it? Don't come down to the pontoon, it's too cold. I'll see myself off."

Carefully Ettie makes her way down the steps to the foreshore, grateful for the moonlight. Thirty years of offshore living, she thinks, and she still forgets to take her torch with her.

Frankie has left her boat tied to Kate's pontoon. She can see it's sitting higher out of the water and the greasy broth of oil, petrol and seawater that normally swashes in the bottom has disappeared. She finds a note wrapped around the tiller, held on with a rubber band. She fossicks under the dented bow for the torch and in the thin yellow light of a near-dead battery, she reads:

Dear Ettie.
Lights work. Bum scraped. Spark plugs cleaned.
One cake, a big one, in return.
Frankie.
Chocolate is best. The wicked one.

CHAPTER SEVEN

In the Square, Ettie fingers the latest rejection from a publisher, folded into a tiny solid block in her pocket. Not even a note, this time. Just an unsigned *With Compliments* slip. Was the irony deliberate, she wonders? She feels a whang-bang dose of the blues on the rise.

The stray mutt crawls towards her apologetically and flops at her feet. She rubs his ears. "Good doggie," she says. Inside the café, Sam is slouched over the counter, ordering their coffees from Big Julie.

How long before The Briny collapses? One day, she'll step inside for a flat white and put a foot through a rotten floorboard. Then she'll crash onto all those oyster-encrusted piles underneath, get slashed to thin little ribbons like calamari and end up crumbed, deep-fried and served in a paper bag for some passing tourist. Environmentally sound recycling. Images whizz through her head. She wonders if she can whip it into a cute little kids' story. Maybe not. It smacks ever so faintly of cannibalism. She sighs. Back to the drawing board.

Sam comes up to her and hands her a beer. She raises her eyebrows and points at her watch.

"Coffee machine died again. It was a beer or tea and, as we are all painfully aware, Bertie's tea is hard to pick from drain water."

Ettie sighs and takes the beer. "Tide's on the turn," she says.

"Yep. Comes in and goes out. As dependable as tomorrow's sunrise."

"You remember Kate? From Oyster Bay? She's after a commuter boat. I told her to call you for a few tips."

"Jeez, Ettie, what did you go and do that for? She's deadset scarier than my old schoolteacher who used to come after us with a rubber strap for no reason. You should have told her to ask at the boatshed. Frankie's the main man. Bloody hell."

Ettie looks at him in surprise. Why is he so worked up over nothing? she wonders. He likes Kate, *really* likes her. So much that he thinks staying clear of her will solve the problem. Well, well. After twenty years of sweet-talking the never-ending stream of starry-eyed young women who regularly drifted into Cook's Basin in search of romance and excitement, he might have met his match. She doubts Kate would fall for his usual moonlit picnic on a deserted beach and a casual fling. Well, well.

Sam glugs his beer and Ettie waits patiently, a smile lurking at the corners of her mouth.

"Listen," he says. "There's a sweet little tinny for sale on the Island. Solid as a rock and reasonably priced."

"You're a star, Sam."

Ettie finishes her beer and kisses his cheek like a sister. Still feeling down-hearted, she drags her feet along the stained seawall towards Commuter Dock where she's tied her tinny, dreading lugging her shopping up the steps to her Island home.

"Cool seawater on the way with the tide," she calls to the oysters, not caring if she sounds mad because everyone, even an oyster, needs a little encouragement from time to time.

As she reaches the dock, black globs are mustering behind the hills, blocking the sun. Spring is gathering for a final tantrum before bowing to summer. The light on the water is clean and smooth and battleship-grey. She searches for her boat in the mess of clanging tinnies tied three-deep off the pontoon. Only two boats to climb over and they're those lovely stable plastic ones. She sighs with relief.

On the way home, she veers off to check on Artie to remind herself that in the great scheme of things, she really hasn't got much to complain about.

Sam kicks himself for offering to help out the Oyster Bay woman. He hasn't got anything against her as such. She's polite, pays her bills on time and gives all the right specs when she books a job. Not like one or two penny-pinching bastards he could name, who consistently understate a load hoping to cut costs and then wonder why they find themselves on the bottom of his schedule. So he's got no argument with her. She just gives him the shivers. It's like she sees right through to his backbone and finds it hollow. Face it, mate, she makes you feel like an ignorant redneck and it sets your teeth on edge.

He considers wheedling out of the deal with any number of excuses that he knows won't stack up under close scrutiny. But then makes his way to the *Mary Kay* at the end of the ferry wharf. Once a commitment is given, it has to be honoured. He jumps on board. With a bit of luck, Kate won't be home.

She opens the front door on the first knock.

"Hi," she says, puzzled. "I'm not expecting a delivery." She leans against the doorjamb, her arms folded. Not an invitation inside for a cuppa or a chinwag. Not a hint of warmth.

Sam stands awkwardly. "Ettie says you're looking for a boat."

"Oh yeah." Kate's face clears.

"There's a bloke on the Island selling up and moving onshore. It's a strong boat with a reliable outboard. You could do worse but if you're feeling itchy after looking at it, you don't have to take my word, you can get a second opinion from Frankie. So there you go. For what it's worth. Ettie asked me to tell you." He turns and begins walking towards the waterfront.

"Hey, Sam," Kate says, hurrying after him. "I need a name and directions. Or a phone number. Something. I'll contact him now."

Sam pulls up, sighs. He looks at the water, the barge, the sky and the bush and comes up with ten good reasons not to offer to give her a ride to the Island to see the boat. The first and foremost of which is that if the engine ever blows up, she'll throw the blame straight at him.

"Hop on," he says, ungraciously, "I'll take you over."

The barge cuts a smooth passage through water as sleek as foil. Back in his comfort zone, Sam relaxes and steers one-handed. He figures they've got an hour before the storm hits. Plenty of time to check out the boat and deliver Kate back to

Oyster Bay safe and sound. Mission accomplished.

Like all first-timers on the barge, he can see she is unnerved by the lack of lifelines but makes a bet it will only take her five minutes to feel confident enough to let go of the doorframe. If she's got any brains at all, she'll stay within arm's reach of solid support. Only the genuine idiots go off on a wander around the deck.

"You know anything about boats?" he calls over the noise of the engine.

"Well, I can drive a car," she shouts snippily. Like *so what's the big deal?*

"Lady, the only thing a car and a boat have in common is fuel."

She is inside the cabin now, standing next to him so she doesn't have to scream. "Oh come on. I've seen four-year-old kids driving tinnies. It can't be that hard."

There it is, he thinks, feeling the hair rise on the back of his neck. That ice-cold snap in her voice. He considers spelling out the facts of boats. No brakes. No headlights. No stability. Then there's the power of wind, currents . . . ah jeez, why go on? She doesn't strike him as the type who listens anyway.

"Up to you, mate," is all he says.

She leaves him then, and wanders forward to stand at the tip of the bow where there's nothing to grab if the barge takes a hit from a wake. She hasn't got a bloody clue.

The commuter boat for sale is a rock-solid, former fishing boat with a strong fibreglass roof instead of a flimsy canopy, a key start, and an engine still under guarantee. Thoroughly reliable. Not pretty. Kate whispers to Sam that it is exactly what she's looking for.

She turns to old Des who's still got a gleam in his eye even though he's on the wrong side of eighty. "Tell me why this is better than any other tinny," she says, polite but no-nonsense.

"Low tide you can jump on the roof," he replies, pride in his voice. "Keeps you dry in the rain, too, or when a rogue wave comes crashing over the bow. Big enough to transport a wardrobe, sofa or a dozen cases of wine and it won't rock more than a baby's cradle in a swell straight from the ocean."

Under the stubble clinging to his deeply lined face, he chews his bottom lip and stares at water through slats in the jetty. He suddenly looks like a man at his best friend's funeral who knows he's seeing the end of an era.

"Where you headed next?" she asks, kindly.

"Off to put me head on a flowery pillow in the retirement village. Happy wife, happy life. Although I keep tellin' her it's livin' here that keeps us young. She won't have a bar of it, though, so we're on our way. No point in whingeing. What is, is."

"How much then, for the boat?"

The old-timer hoists his baggy pants, held up by a piece of string, and gets a squirrel look. He chucks a quick glance at Sam, who shrugs to show he's not going to get involved. Then he takes a seat on the starboard gunnel, fidgeting until he's comfortable. Points Kate towards the portside. She sits, leaning forward on her knees, her face intent.

Sam watches as they haggle like camel traders until it starts to rain so hard the old bloke sighs with disappointment and gives in. "Haven't had that much fun since a trip through the souk in Marrakech fifty years ago."

Kate shakes his hand, grinning. "Haven't enjoyed myself more since buying a rug in the Grand Bazaar in Istanbul. I'll look after her, you know. I'm careful about possessions. Does she have a name?"

The old bloke shakes his head. "A boat's a boat. You don't need frills just a lot of grunt."

"I'll call her *Ghost* then, if that's okay?"

Sam snorts. Kate and the old-timer beam at each other, water dripping down their faces, both flushed with the thrill of the deal.

Sam retires to the shelter of the *Mary Kay* as Kate signs a cheque and hands it over.

"Isn't gonna bounce, is it?" Des asks after a minute, forgetting the rain and holding the cheque up to daylight as though it might be counterfeit. He curses and shakes it dry.

"If it does, let me know."

"If it bounces I'll charge ya double next time."

"Deal!" They shake hands.

"Hey, Sam," he calls out. "This one's got a bit of spirit in her. Ya better watch out. She'll run rings around ya and she's too good for ya anyway."

Sam cups his ear to signal he can't hear.

With the rain coming down hard, Kate thanks Des then asks if there are any golden rules for boats.

"Check your petrol tank before every trip and assume every other bugger on the water is a mug."

"Oh sounds fair. And if I want to reverse, I move the throttle backwards, is that right?"

The old guy looks at her quizzically. "Yeah, well, that's how it mostly works."

She thanks him again and waves towards Sam to signal the deal is done. He gives her the thumbs-up.

"I owe you a beer, Sam," she says, sticking her head inside the wheelhouse. "Go home and get out of the wet. I'll find my own way back."

"You might consider a lesson or two before hitting the water solo with a storm on the rise," he says, trying not to sound like he's telling her what to do. Because he already senses that won't go down too well.

"I'll be right. Thanks again."

And just like that, he's dismissed. He feels his jaw go rigid, his teeth clamp down. He knows he should insist on seeing her safely to the pontoon but . . . He sniffs the air, checks the water for whitecaps to get a sense of how long till the storm hits hard. She's got time. Just. With the wind coming from the east, the worst that can happen is she'll get blown onto the rocks and, if she's really unlucky, end up with a hole in her hull. She won't drown, though. Unless she can't swim. Ah jeez.

"You know how to swim, don't you?" he yells from the doorway of the *Mary Kay* to save himself a soaking.

Kate nods, waves and steps into her boat. He hears the engine kick over with the first twist of the key. With a bit of luck, she'll make it. If not, well, she'll learn the hard way.

CHAPTER EIGHT

The two Misses Skettle, who live in a lopsided, rabbity anti-quarian boathouse tucked cosily inside the lip of Kingfish Bay, set a pot of red wine laced with brandy, sugar, orange and lemon slices, cinnamon, cloves and nutmeg, on top of the stove to mull gently. As they do at the first scent of every big storm. They wait patiently for the sugar to dissolve before reducing the heat to barely a frisson. Then they make their way along the hallway to the front parlour where they sink into their favourite armchairs. The ones with faded rosy-pink slip covers. With a small glass each – to test the balance of the spices – they begin their watch. Expertly trained as enemy spotters in 1942, after three Japanese midget submarines made a series of attacks on Sydney Harbour, they take turns with the binoculars to scan the water for boats in difficulty. In more than sixty years they have rescued too many vessels to count and, once or twice, the lives of their skippers. It is a mission they will never abandon.

Given their age they are no longer able to fly to the aid of anyone in distress as they did in the days of rowboats, putt-putts and skiffs. Instead, they call Sam Scully. Which is precisely what they do when they see a tinny die on the water just as the wind is starting to gust up to twenty-five knots and the waterway is beginning to seethe.

They recognise the boat instantly but not the driver, which leads them to believe, they tell Sam in a serious tone, that the boat could well be stolen.

Resigned to his fate, Sam closes his mobile and gives up the shelter of the Island to plough back to the open passageway. No good turn, he mumbles, goes unpunished. Never truer words spoken.

Five minutes later, the barge takes a knock from a gust and corkscrews on the rising swell. Thirty knots, he guesses, watching spume rise off the water. Thunder grumbles in the distance. A flash of lightning flares beyond the rugged escarpments. Through a blanket of rain, he makes out Kate's boat being buffeted towards Rocky Point. He drags out his wet-weather gear from under the banquette, pulls it on and heads towards her, swearing under his breath. If it had been anyone but Ettie asking for help, he'd have kept his big trap well and truly shut and, as a result, he'd be curled up nice and dry, watching the footy with a mug of Milo and a continental hot dog slathered with mustard and tomato sauce.

He gets a glimpse of a sodden Kate standing in the cockpit, gripping the roof against the bucking sea. Her skinny legs, like toothpicks, braced wide. She's looking straight at the rocks. He can't make out the expression on her face but she should be bloody-well terrified.

He eases the barge as close as he can without risking a collision. "What's up?" he yells through the roar of the storm.

She turns her head and ducks too late. A wave of deep

green water slams into her face. She slips and almost loses her balance. "Out of petrol," she calls.

"I'm going to throw you a rope. Tie it onto the bow, okay? Can you do that?"

She nods.

"Crawl through the front hatch to catch it. It's safer than trying to edge forward around the gunnel."

She nods again and ducks through the opening.

Sam dashes back to the wheelhouse, riding the movement of the barge like a showjumper. He pushes the throttle up a notch and eases ahead of the tinny then slides into neutral and rushes to the stern, trusting the *Mary Kay* to fend for herself like the noble warrior he knows her to be. He grabs a line, waits till a swell lifts the tinny, then tosses. Kate misses the first throw.

He reels in the rope, coiling it quickly. "If you miss this one you'll have to go it alone. In three minutes we're going to hit rock."

"Go for it," she yells.

The rope soars across the water, unravelling in the air like a snake. Kate reaches up with both hands. Grabs it and falls flat on her face. That must hurt like stink, Sam thinks. But she holds up the end in victory, kneels to wrap it around a cleat. Six loops, he notes with approval, but she hasn't tied off. It's full-on amateur hour.

"Get back in the cabin. Keep the end in your hand and do not, I repeat, *do not* let go," he calls out. Not hanging around to see if she understands, he races for the wheelhouse, slams the barge into reverse and hopes like hell there's enough length in the rope to stop the tinny rounding up and smashing into his hull. What a freaking disaster. He sees the tinny swing into the clear. Tension eases out of his shoulders at about the same rate as his anger fires up. He came so close to smashing his precious barge – his livelihood, for God's sake – on a pissy little outcrop of rocks. And all for what? A dead ugly boat worth a couple of grand and a woman that right now he could rip the head off. She launches herself in a storm without a clue how to even tie a knot! A bloody two-year-old can learn how to do a half-hitch in three seconds flat.

He lets go of the helm and rubs a hole in the mist on the back window. At least she hasn't dropped the rope. Her hands must be burning, he thinks, with something close to satisfaction.

He sees a light in the Oyster Bay boatshed. He presses his horn until Frankie emerges in his overalls and black cap. Sam waves and points at the tinny attached to the tow rope. Ignoring the driving rain, the boat mechanic strolls down the jetty like it's a sunny day. Sam swings wide, dashes to untie the stern line and throws it at Frankie. He catches it as casually as a set of keys tossed across a kitchen counter, ties it on and walks off without a word.

Instead of heading home like he intended, at the last minute Sam decides to dock the *Mary Kay* and have a firm word with Kate. He'll resist the urge to grab the dopey woman by the scruff of the neck and tell her ignorant fools on the water put other people and their precious vessels at risk. All he plans to do is suggest, nice and polite – as is his customary habit – that she take a few lessons from someone like Frankie, who is a lovely bloke once you understand him, and someone who knows more about boats than anyone else in Cook's Basin. A few easy pointers before she ventures further than her pontoon might be worth considering, he'll say. Sweet and accommodating. He runs through the spiel in his head once more to make sure he's got the tone just right. To him, it sounds quick and to the point. He marches off, blinded by the rain, hearing the squelch of water in his leather boots.

At the end of the jetty, he leans over the side of the tinny. Time to set her straight. He peers into the cabin.

"You can let go now," he says softly.

She drops the rope. She doesn't move.

"You did a good job. Honest. Most novices would have freaked."

She turns a face covered in blood towards him. She's crying. He steps on board and lifts her to her feet, pulling her against his chest. He feels her shaking – from the cold or from relief, he's not sure which. He wriggles out of his jacket and presses her head into the hollow of his shoulder while he drags the waterproof around her to keep the rain off. "It's okay. It's all good. You're fine."

"You'll get wet," she murmurs.

"No kidding," he says.

"Sorry . . ."

She looks up at him and fingers her bottom lip. "Lot of blood but it's only a small cut. I'm being pathetic. I'll be fine. Truly. I owe you." She steps away.

Sam feels the barrier go up between them. He covers what he realises with surprise is regret with a stab at humour. "Yeah, well. Around here you forget a debt and your name goes on a shame list." He forces a smile.

"Public or private?"

"Mate, nothing's private in Cook's Basin, you should know that by now. I'll see you home. Leave the boat where it is. Frankie'll take care of it in the morning."

"I'm good. Truly. Thanks for . . ."

"Nothing, mate. Nothing at all. Do the same for anyone."

He steps out of the tinny and turns to give her a hand. But she shoves the red bundle of his jacket at him and takes off at a run, her head down against the rain. His eyes follow her along the shoreline until she turns to race up the steps to her house. She doesn't look back.

He heads off to the boatshed to thank Frankie for his help and explain what old Des's boat is doing in a foreign port. Water runs down his neck. His shorts are soaked. No point in hurrying, he thinks, he can't get any wetter.

He ducks under the roller-door of the boatshed into a tangled mess of pipes, hoses, vacuums, grinders and clamps.

"You there, Frankie?" he calls, picking up a chisel, closing one eye and looking down the straight side, running a thumb across the blade. A loo flushes. A wire door squeals then slams. He hears the slap of bare feet on cold concrete.

"Yo," Frankie says, wiping his oil-stained hands on a rag.

"Your neighbour. She's bought Des's boat. Had a bit of difficulty getting it home so I helped her out."

"If it's no good, tell her to take it back," Frankie says flatly, returning to the spilled guts of an engine laid out on the chipped cement floor.

"No, mate, the engine's good. The old bloke forgot to mention the petrol tank was empty."

"Yar, well, he's always been a mean bastard, that one."

"Anyway, just wanted to say thanks for helpin' out."

Frankie shrugs.

"So, what do you think? She going to last the distance?" Sam nods towards Kate's house.

Frankie shoves back the brim of a battered black fisherman's cap that no one's ever seen parted from his head. He appears to be giving the question serious consideration. "You know what I think? I think nervy women with skinny bums don't last very long around here."

"Nervy, you reckon? Never picked that."

"She get a good deal on the boat?"

"Dunno. Stayed out of the way."

"Would've bought that house myself for the price she paid. The seller knocked fifty per cent off, I hear, just to get rid of it."

"Is that right? Nervy but smart, then."

That night, with the storm long gone, and when the evening star is a lone white light in a dusky sky, Ettie chugs across mirror-flat water to a low-lying house with huge windows on the sunny side of Oyster Bay. She hangs offshore with nine other members of the Blue Swimmer Bay book club, bobbing in their tinnies like ducks on a pond, waiting to tie up.

When the last boat is secured, Jenny, Jane and Judy – the Three Js, Island-born and bred – who are founding members of the book club, lead the way to Fannie's immaculate home. They gather round a candlelit table on the lawn, fill their wineglasses and spend the first half-hour gossiping. Midway, the talk turns to the man who's moved into the house near Triangle Wharf.

"He lurks in that boatshed of his like a feral cat waiting to pounce every time a kid walks past," Jenny says. "He's either a paedophile or a drug-pusher. Or both. I've told my two kids to stay away. But I'm not sure if that didn't make him sound more exciting than dangerous."

"He's bad news," Ettie agrees. "I'll keep an eye on what goes on in that boatshed . . ."

"We *all* will," shout the women in unison.

"If that slippery-eyed stranger thinks he can rattle the balance of offshore life, he's in for an almighty shock," Jenny says, vehemently. "It's been a while since we invoked some of those 'fine old traditions' Sam is always ranting about."

Ettie immediately leaps to the bargeman's defence. "His heart's in the right place."

"More like all over the place," Jane remarks, cynically.

"You know, I haven't seen him take off on the barge with a woman and a picnic rug for quite a while." Ettie is thoughtful as she sips her wine.

"He will. Leopards don't change their spots." Jane had taken a few barge rides before settling down and fails to keep the bitterness out of her voice.

The talk finally turns to the book of the month, a worthy biography of Marcel Proust.

"Right," Fannie says, topping up the wineglasses and calling the meeting to order. "Ettie, why don't you start? What did you think of this month's book choice?"

"Better than sleeping pills," Ettie replies without missing a beat.

*

By the next morning the Cook's Basin community is already buzzing with the news of Kate's reckless behaviour and Sam's heroic rescue. The general consensus is that she's either a complete floozy or an arrogant fool, and that Sam isn't far behind for risking his magnificent barge to save an ugly boat and its brainless owner. Jack the Bookie decides to offer appealing odds to anyone who reckons Kate will last longer than three months.

When the first ferry commuters see Fast Freddy drop her at the Spit with her laptop and an overnight bag, they rush him like he's a rock star to find out if he knows more than the sketchy grapevine has thus far provided.

While he waits for The Briny to open Freddy, who is firmly against gossip, nevertheless indulges his interrogators in an effort to set the record straight.

No, he says firmly, she has not been shamed into leaving. She is on her way to America – New York, if he remembers correctly – to interview somebody rich and famous. No, she didn't mention a name. Yes, she does have a split lip but no other injuries as far as he could see. What did they talk about? Well, he asked if she would mind if he detoured slightly so he could knock on Artie's hull and he was pleased when she agreed, even though she was rushing to catch an international flight. It showed good instincts. Although he adds, digressing in his usual way, he may have checked on Artie too early in the morning because he was greeted with an angry roar. He thought he'd be thrilled he was going to enjoy more of the day than usual since he'd roused him at the crack 'a, but well, everyone's built differently, he supposes. As long as there's kindness, compassion and patience in the world . . . He did, he admits, indulge in some similar philosophising to Kate about his long night shifts under a full winter moon, which she seemed to find interesting.

He continues. As everyone knows, he says, he mostly keeps his thoughts to himself. But during the taxi ride, without quite understanding the impulse, he'd found himself telling Kate about the magic of being awake while most folks were tucked in their cosy beds. About how the purity of the stars and the moon made him feel big and small at the same time. How when he was overcome by the vast clarity of the night sky, he sometimes forgot to breathe for a moment or two.

He recounts, then, that she asked him what were the most important skills to have on the water: *Good eyes, attention to detail – such as the weather and the level of your petrol tank (ha, ha) – patience and the ability to make quick decisions.* Same as life, when you think about it. She gave him a blaster of a smile that lit up eyes the colour of the deep blue-green ocean and as far as he's concerned, she's made a friend for life. She paid him with a decent tip that was neither too little nor too much, which means she understands the value of money but is not, as a fresh new wave of rumours suggest, a cheapskate. Then she shook his hand and thanked him sincerely for his advice.

If he is any judge of character – and anyone who spends as much time dealing with the general public as he does, knows a few things about human behaviour – Kate Jackson is a quick learner. He told her he'd be waiting for her return with open arms and he swears he saw a tear in her eye.

Cook's Basin News (CBN)

Newsletter for Offshore Residents of Cook's Basin, Australia

NOVEMBER

COME AND CELEBRATE SUMMER AT THE FIRESHED DINNER

When: The last Thursday of the month

Where: Oyster Bay Fireshed

Chef: Marcus Allender, the new resident in Kingfish Bay (he had a restaurant in the city before retiring here!)

Cost: $15.00 (adults) $5.00 (children)

Menu: To be announced

Remember: An extraordinary meeting (that doesn't mean it's replacing the AGM) has been called and will take place prior to the fireshed dinner at 6.30 p.m.

More Car Park Activity

Frankie from the Oyster Bay boatshed reports his car was broken into and vandalised two days ago. Thieves took his spare tyre, the tools to change a tyre and then busted the radio and CD player just for fun. If anyone has any information regarding these increasing attacks on private property please call the police. Illegal activities of any kind cannot and will not be tolerated. Some residents have suggested using CCTV cameras to catch the culprit. This must surely be a last resort. Keep your eyes and ears open and make our offshore community safe.

BREAKING NEWS!

Word sheets and music sheets for the Christmas Choir are now available on the Cutter Island Residents' Association website. They can be downloaded and printed so there is no excuse for anyone turning up without them. (Are you listening, Phil?)

The performance will be on Sam's beautiful barge, the *Mary Kay*, on December 21, barring bad weather. So dust off the Santa hats, oil the vocal cords according to personal taste, and get into musical training.

CHAPTER NINE

"Ettie!" Big Julie pokes her head out of the tangled plastic strips and waves a tea towel above her head like a lariat. "Bertie's been waiting for you. How about a coffee? On the house."

It must be something big, Ettie thinks. Bertie's never given away so much as a paper napkin without an argument.

"What's up?" she asks, a smile firmly in place.

Big Julie waves her inside the café. "Bertie wants to have a chat. He's on the deck. Says if you'd prefer a beer, he'll spring for that instead."

"Everything alright, Julie?"

"Up to a point. Yeah, that about says it. Just get out there, will you? It's almost closing time and he's a bit buggered after a long afternoon of appointments – of the kind none of us wishes to have."

Ettie pushes open the squealing wire door.

Bertie, haloed in the last gauzy light of day, is sitting at a table in the corner, looking out to sea. He wears a sports jacket with brass buttons over a checked shirt and his khaki trousers are sharply creased, his shoes well-polished leather lace-ups. If he'd had a hat covering his glistening head, she would never have recognised him. She's about to make a glib remark but he turns towards her and gives her a look that knocks the wind out of her.

He's dying, she realises in an instant. Nothing else would shift the cynical smirk that was as much a part of Bertie as his grubby apron, his Beatles T-shirts and his stained white sneakers.

She pulls out a chair and joins him at the wobbly table.

"How much money have you got in the bank, luv?" he asks.

The question is so out of the blue Ettie hesitates, trying to figure out where he's coming from. "I'm good for a loan, Bertie, if that's what you're after," she says eventually. Because when a man is dying he shouldn't have to worry about money. "Name the figure and if I've got it it's yours for as long as you need it."

To her horror, a tear trickles down the old man's yellow-stained cheek. He pulls a handkerchief out of his pocket and mops his face with feigned casualness, like he's dealing with a sudden sweat.

"You'd do that for a mean old bastard like me, would ya? No guarantees or nothin'?"

She nods, not entirely sure she hasn't lost her mind – and her nest egg – in one dangerously rash moment.

Bertie sighs. "No need for a loan, luv, but I'll take your money – in return for The Briny. It's yours, lock, stock and barrel if you want it. Just so you know, it's not a freehold. You'd been buying twelve years left on a twenty-five-year lease. What happens after that is up to you." He makes a job of folding his hanky and shoving it back in his pocket, struggling to get his breath. "You're sittin' there stiller than a stunned mullet. And I'm short of time in more ways than one. What's your answer, girl?"

He grins to soften the words and Ettie bursts into tears.

Big Julie races outside with a glass of wine. "Here, love, get this into you. I'm already three ahead and I don't drink." She bends to kiss Bertie's cheek in the first public show of affection Ettie has ever seen between them, pats his smooth head. Flies off again.

"I have some money, Bertie, but not nearly enough," Ettie manages at last. "So thank you, my friend, but you'll do better by selling the business on the open market." She swallows hard, pressing a wild surge of hopes and dreams back into a tight little box and slamming the lid.

"It's yours, luv. For whatever you can afford. And that's the end of it. Julie, darlin'," he calls on the back of a dry cough, "bring the paperwork. Then let's go home. Ettie, you start work tomorrow."

For a long time, Ettie sits in the growing dark, afraid that if she moves she'll wake up and find it was all a mad fantasy. Then she thinks of Bertie. How must it feel to look death in the face? To know that in a single, half-hour appointment with a specialist you've never met before, the door to the future has been slammed in your face? Forty years of The Briny relegated to history by a few horror-filled words.

She picks up the key sitting on top of the documents Bertie has left lying on the table and goes inside to turn off the lights. Her lights. She slides home the bolt on the door and snaps the padlock. Her padlock. Her café. Thank you, Bertie, she thinks, for trusting me with The Briny. I will make you proud. She listens to lazy waves splash against the seawall, the distant cries of gulls. For her, it's the equivalent of rocks singing.

Her mood suddenly swings from euphoria to terror. She looks back at her track record in business which, even with a positive spin, is pretty lousy. Realistically, The Briny Café is a rat-infested, leaning hole, with gaps in the floorboards so wide you can see diesel scum making rainbows on the water underneath. Get rid of the grease and dirt holding it together and the first big blow could send it off in a cloud stinking of deep-fried onions and burnt coffee. What was she thinking of, taking this on? She wants to cry. She wants the whole great burden of thirty years of fending for herself lifted off her shoulders. She wants . . .

She sniffs, using her sleeve as a hanky. This is her last shot at financial independence in her old age. She straightens her shoulders and throws caution to the wind. All or nothing, she thinks, but aware that no matter how hard she works, she won't be able to do it alone. She needs a partner who understands money and how to make a profit. Two key skills that for her, she is painfully aware, are as hard as learning Russian.

Out of the gloom, the long-lost mutt crawls towards her with a whimper and a beaten look in his sad brown eyes. "Still here? Where do you live, little doggie?" she asks, scratching the white blaze on his chest. His ratty tail wags, his face lights up. He leans his barrel body against her leg and plants his backside firmly on her foot so she can't get away. She sighs. He's been hanging out in the Square for too long to be a dog on the loose from a nearby backyard.

This is a dog that doesn't have a home. A café can't really keep a mutt but what's a barge without one? She dials Sam's mobile.

Ettie and Sam sit side by side on a bench in the darkness of the Square while Ettie explains that Bertie is dying and she is the new proprietor of The Briny Café.

"Poor bastard, but letting you take over is the right decision," he says.

She lays a hand on his knee and gently tells him that she's thrilled but she'd hand it back in a flash if it meant Bertie could see out the lease in robust health. The community, she adds, must be ready to help him whenever it can.

"It's a good buy, love, you've made a killing. It'll be a goldmine one day. Set you up for life."

"You really think so?" she asks.

"Yeah. No doubt. Might look like a dump, but it's *our* offshore dump. That shambolic little seaside shanty holds nearly two hundred years of the spirit of the Spit. You can't buy that in a hardware shop. You're starting from the bottom. There's only one way from there and it's up."

"You're a good friend, Sam." She pats his shoulder, rests her head against the warmth of his chest for a moment. "Yeah, it's all good, isn't it?"

He puts an arm around her, draws her closer, buries his face in her hair.

He's never been handsome, she thinks, not even when he had young skin and an athlete's body. His face is too flat and square. His jaw overbearing. The years have softened the jaw but he's broader now. Blocky. His skin roughened by salt, sun and the razor-sharp winter southerlies. Not everyone's idea of attractive, but being older and more worn-in actually suits him. He has an aura. Rock-solid. Ettie has always preferred that to conventional good looks.

In her experience, good-looking men were trouble, although she's always had a soft spot for the drifters who float in on the tide to scrape a living from cleaning the salt-crust off windows or cunjies from the bottoms of boats. Generous blokes, mostly, who'd pass you their last cold beer if you were hot and thirsty. Not like the penny-pinching tycoons you read about in the business pages that breezed in for a week or two and then skived off without paying their mooring fees or the price of their anti-fouls. She'd take a drifter over a tycoon any day.

They are both silent for a while. It's long past the last ferry run and the Square is almost deserted. One or two people go past without glancing their way. They jump into tinnies tied to the seawall and head off, filling the night air with noise and exhaust.

Ettie says: "I'm not going to be able to run the place on my own. I'll burn out within the year. I need a partner. Any ideas?"

Sam is silent for a very long time. "Are you asking if I'd like to come on board?" he says, eventually.

Ettie is so surprised by his response she laughs for the first time that day.

"Can't see you filling bite-size cupcakes with cream, love, if you don't mind me saying so." She holds up his huge hands, grazed on the knuckles, grease under the nails.

"There are people," he responds, haughtily, "no need to

name names, who think my sausage rolls and garlic mashed potatoes are world-class."

"One day shut inside the café and you'd be a basket case, but thanks for offering. I was wondering, though, about Kate . . ."

"Kate!"

"Yeah."

"Are you off your rocker, mate? I thought you said she's stretched to the limit to make toast. And she has a top job in town, doesn't she?" Sam gets to his feet and begins pacing up and down. The mutt follows in his wake with the same rolling gait. "She's not your problem, Ettie. She's a big girl who can take care of herself." He stops in front of her. The mutt headbutts into his heels. "Tell me you're joking, Ettie, 'cause taking on a novice when it's a question of do or die is like having a death wish."

"Maybe," she says, unable to meet his eyes. "But she understands the value of money. I watched her brew a cup of tea once, too. She did it beautifully, with respect and reverence, like it was a ceremony. There's a foodie spark in her. Deep, and lying in wait."

"Promise me, Ettie, no more bloody lame ducks."

She stands up, without answering. "One other thing . . ."

"I'm almost too frightened to ask."

"Every barge should have a dog and right now this one has nowhere else to call home." She gathers the mutt in her arms and holds him out. Sam does a quick spin.

"Jeez," is the best he can manage.

*

Sam guides Ettie safely along the seawall to the half-sunk pontoon at the back of the café. They step on together and it immediately groans and belches under their weight. One big wake or a cracker of a storm, he thinks, will send it straight to the bottom of the bay. He bends to untie the ropes of her tinny as she finds her place next to the tiller.

"If Frankie's working late at the boatshed, I'll ask him about that spare pontoon hanging off his jetty and doing nothing useful," Sam says. "He might want to store it here until he finds a buyer. I can see a few tables on it, or a couple of deck-chairs where customers can hang their toes in the water while they guzzle the crispest fish and chips on the coast."

She nods because she can't speak, squeezes and twists the throttle into neutral, pulls the engine cord.

Sam gives the boat a gentle shove with his foot and she guns off. The tinny rears, nose pointed to the sky, then settles on the plane. Very soon it's no bigger than a wash tub in the dark.

Later that night, Sam decides to do his own detailed research into the Weasel's highly suspect goings-on at the house near Triangle Wharf. The whole community is aware the bloke is dealing drugs and figures adults make their own choices. But according to the Three Js, an increasing number of kids are arriving home with sloppy grins and glassy eyes, lying about what they've been up to. Sam wants to see the evidence.

He sets off in the *Mary Kay* with a plan to doss down for the night in his wheelhouse. He intends to record the number of visitors, the time of the visits and the physical state in which those visitors depart. Cold hard facts are the first step in any battle plan. A good community weeds out its rotten wood quickly and cleanly. Calling the cops just means waiting for the slow wheels of justice to turn, which could be a costly mistake.

By ten o'clock, he is firmly anchored in place. It is a perfect night for a stake-out. Cool, calm, and bright with moonlight. He yanks off his workboots, leaving on his thick woollen socks, and puts his feet up to wait. He props a pillow behind his head. Comfy as. Removes a book from his neatly packed picnic basket, clips on a small reading torch and opens to page one of what he's been told is a gut-wrenching memoir about storms and shipwrecks at sea. The mutt lies on his blanket on the deck, quietly snoring.

After a short time, the smell of warm sausage rolls rising from the basket breaks Sam's concentration. They are underrated in the modern world, in his opinion. Made with fresh eggs, onions, parsley and a bit of pork mince mixed in with the sausage meat, they turn into a feast. It has to be puff pastry, too. The buttery sort that smells so good his dad used to reckon it enticed the fish when you were picnicking out in your boat with a rod over the side. They were fun days, he thinks, remembering kerosene lanterns, ice deliveries and wood-fired stoves. Back then, the ferry transported fresh bread, milk and newspapers to the strapped-for-cash adventurers living in roughly cobbled together houses or boatsheds perilously sited along the broken shores. For the women left home alone by their working husbands, the ferry's arrival was as giddily anticipated as a party, their way of touching base with the world beyond their wild bush backyards and the long, skinny arms of their listing jetties. A break from washing nappies in a banged up metal bucket of tea-coloured tank water heated on a single gas jet.

But the lack of electricity, sewerage and phones were regarded as small inconveniences when a round orange moon lit up the water like a carnival, or a silver bream bigger than a paddle finally took the bait from a line hung out of the kitchen window.

The odd property developer had turned up from time to time, with lawyers, cheque books and political influence, mistaking the casualness of the locals for ignorance. A few development proposals took years of relentless slog to beat. But the offshorers never tired of the fight to preserve a way of life everyone knew was rare and idyllic.

Thinking back, Sam can only remember one or two blokes with the same alley-cat morals of the Weasel moving in. Without too much discussion, they'd been quietly but firmly ousted by community pressure. When it came to defending their territory, Cook's Basin residents could be as tough and ruthless as the situation demanded.

Sam peels off the covering tea towel on the basket, for once mourning not so much the old days as the passage of time. He lines up a small blue bowl of tomato sauce, wondering why it is that the older you get, the more tempted you are to look back instead of forward. He mentally shrugs. No matter how you looked at it, thugs and bullies had to be stopped before they got the upper hand. He takes his first delicious bite of a sausage roll, deciding to limit himself to two. He'll save the rest for later in the night when he'll be cold, hungry and bored rigid unless the book is as good as Ettie says it is.

It was a Blue Swimmer Bay book club choice, and everyone gave it a top score. He was amazed to hear from Ettie that Kate was joining the book club next month. He'd never have picked her as a joiner. More like the type to run solo, as far as he could tell.

He gets up and puts the basket outside the cabin door where the delicious smell can't tempt him. He makes a mental note to remind her about those beers she owes him. In a small community, when you give your word, you deliver or someone might be left in the lurch. And if you welsh too often, people develop a case of sudden blindness when you need a hand. To be fair, though, it takes a while to take a whole new set of standards on board.

Keeping your word and looking out for your neighbours was bred in his bones. Even that old actor fella who towered over the lot of them babysat for his mum after Sam broke his arm when he fell out of a tree. He was about four years old and can't remember much about that day. Although he has a vague feeling he and the craggy-faced actor had shared an icy, long-nose bottle of beer while the old fella told lurid bedtime stories with even more lurid endings. He probably passed out, he thinks, reaching for a beer from his icebox and twisting off the top. Maybe that's where he first got the taste for the amber brew.

A tinny cruises close by. He kills the reading torch and fumbles for his notebook and pencil. The kid ties up and shuffles along the jetty, glancing over his shoulder with clumsy stealth. A touch of hubris, too, as though flirting with danger gives him kudos. Closer to the boatshed door, the kid pulls a hood over his head, knocks and waits. A light comes on. A blind drops with a clunk that carries across the water.

The mutt growls. Sam calls him inside the wheelhouse and gives him a sausage roll to keep him quiet.

Half an hour later, two more kids saunter down the Weasel's steps like they're headed for a bag of chips and a lemonade at a video night with their friends. Christ, he thinks, that's little Teddy. He can't be more than fourteen. Who's he with? Jenny's young girl? He feels a red-hot rage work its way up from his toes. He fetches the basket and fumbles for a sausage roll. The basket is empty.

"You're on borrowed time, mate," he hisses at the dog. The mutt pants happily and thumps his tail on the timber deck, a few flakes of pastry caught in the loose folds around his mouth.

At dawn the next morning, the apple-green water taxi swings by the *Mary Kay*. It's the end of Fast Freddy's shift and he's on his way to the Spit. His shout wakes Sam out of a dreamless sleep.

"Just checkin' you're all okay," he calls, with his head poking through the hole in the bimini. "Ya know yer on the wrong mooring, don't ya?"

Sam waves from the doorway, holding a doona around his waist like a skirt. Freddy grins and fingers his nose like he's in the know.

Probably thinks I'm dodging a woman, Sam says to himself, cranky for a reason he can't quite define. He's happy to know the nosy bugger keeps an eye out, though. Three petrol tanks were liberated from their tinnies last week. Piss-poor behaviour. No doubt kids selling it on to each other for a quick buck.

The penny drops.

He'll give the Weasel one warning. After that, all bets are off.

Up for'ard on the portside, the mutt lifts his leg and piddles against a crucifix bollard. It's been a long night.

CHAPTER TEN

Fast Freddy, resplendent in a sunflower-yellow jacket with red waterproof pants, sits in his usual spot waiting for the café to open, a green beanie pulled down to his woolly eyebrows.

"Combat gear for the fast runs, eh?" Sam says, taking a seat beside him. In the right light, Freddy could easily be mistaken for a lorikeet.

"As if anyone ever asks for a slow run," Freddy says, without rancour but with a hint of weariness. The sacks under his night-shift eyes are the colour of charcoal.

"Summer's taking its time." Sam rubs his hands together. "It's cold as."

"Soon as it arrives you'll be wishin' for a fresh southerly to take the heat out of the day," Freddy replies. "Human nature. Always lookin' over the fence when every day's a blessing, especially when you're on the water. Want my advice?"

"Is there a choice?"

"Try sleepin' in a warm bed like most sensible people."

"I was on a mission, mate, keeping an eye on the community."

"Ah. Gotcha. That questionable bloke next to Triangle, eh?"

"Got it in one."

They sit silently, both locked in the beauty of a day frocking up in massive strokes of light. On the water, on the escarpment and fingering its way into hidden green gullies.

"Bloody magic, isn't it?" Freddy says.

"Doesn't do it justice, mate." Sam looks over at the darkened café and checks the time, hoping Ettie hasn't woken up thinking yesterday's bonanza was a dream and rolled over to go back to sleep. "So have you heard, then?" Sam asks.

"Heard what?"

"About Ettie?"

Freddy looks so alarmed Sam rushes to fill him in. "Keep your shirt on. It's all good, mate. She's the new owner of The Briny."

Fast Freddy spins on his seat and stares across at the dishevelled café. "Eh?"

"Bertie's crook, and he's handed her the reins."

"Good news and bad news, then," Freddy says, after he's given himself time to think through the ramifications. "What's the drum on Bertie?"

"You don't want to know."

"Ah." They sit in silence once more.

After a while, Freddy says philosophically: "Well, everything that is born must die. That's the truth of it."

They both see her then, flying across the water in a tinny so frail the hull looks transparent. For the first time that either of them can remember, Ettie fails to throttle back in the go-slow zone.

"Jeez, she must be stressed," Sam says.

"It's a bloody big job," Freddy replies, shocked to hear himself swear.

Ettie, in plain black trousers and a white shirt, roars into the wobbly pontoon belonging to The Briny, ties up and hauls ten plastic containers out of the boat. They are filled with raspberry and coconut muffins, orange cakes, lemon cakes and freshly baked loaves of banana bread. She scoops the boxes into her arms and takes off along the jetty barely able to see over the top. She plonks them on a table at the back door to search for the key and a lid comes undone. The smell of fruit and spices drifts across to the Square riding the back of a light westerly. Chippies and early commuters sniff the wind like dogs on a scent and twist their heads in the direction of the café in astonishment. The world, as they know it, has just somersaulted, although they don't truly understand the magnitude of the change until later in the day when the news of Bertie's bad luck and Ettie's good fortune sweeps around the Island and the bays via the *Seagull*.

Fast Freddy and Sam rush to help her. She smiles to thank them and then indicates they should help themselves from the container that's lost its lid. They reach, with reverence, for a golden-topped muffin still warm from the oven and bite into moist, crusty sweetness. Both know in a single bite that they've found their mandatory morning comfort food for the years ahead.

"You must've been baking all night," Sam says, brushing crumbs off his grubby work clothes and licking sticky fingers.

"Most of it," Ettie admits. Her eyes shine and her skin has a youthful glow that's been missing for a long time.

"Well, love, these muffins are the answer to every man's dream."

"Like a coffee to go with them?"

"Oh Ettie, if you could manage one, Fast Freddy and me would fight to the death over your hand in marriage. Right, Freddy?"

"Yeah, yeah," Freddy says, embarrassed. "Any chance of a second muffin, Ettie? Full café rates this time?"

"Haven't worked out prices yet, my old friend." Her laughter is as rich and buttery as the muffins. "You're in the clear for today. Go for it."

Sam also reaches for another one. "You're a star," he says. Ettie slaps his hand away and he leaps like he's been scalded. "What's Freddy got that I haven't?" he whines.

"I wouldn't know where to begin." Still laughing, she pulls open the flywire door and marches into her new life as the proprietor of The Briny Café. Famous for dodgy egg and bacon rolls and heart-starter coffee. Taking a deep breath she clicks a switch on the espresso machine and hands Sam the key to the front door.

"Open up for me, would you? And take your scruffy mutt with you. No animals inside or the health department will close me down. I'll call out when your coffee is ready. You can have a slice of toasted banana bread to go with it. Let me know if you think there's too much cinnamon and make sure you give half to the dog."

Ettie grabs a cloth, smells it and tosses it in the bin. She scrabbles in gritty drawers until she finds a pencil and paper and begins a list. She plans to stay open all morning, every morning, to cash in on the early commuter trade and to advise customers of the changeover. She'll close every afternoon for one week to give everything – from floor to ceiling – a thorough scour. Plus she needs time to get her menus sorted.

Humming, she makes the coffees while Fast Freddy, in what will become his personal contribution to the running of the café, drags in the newspapers, cuts through the twine and stacks them on the counter with their edges neatly aligned.

"There you go, Ettie, now you're well and truly open for business," he says with a flourish.

"You're a good man, Freddy."

It takes her five minutes to set out the muffins and arrange the cakes on two chipped white rectangular platters she finds in a mouldy cupboard. She lines up her fresh, homemade goodies on the counter and steps back to judge the effect. She swoops on the fossilised Florentines in a single action and throws them in the bin. The waste hurts but she's been watching them for months and they've never moved. She dusts her hands. It's a beginning, at least. A taste of where she's headed. How the world spins, she thinks. Yesterday, she couldn't see a way out of endless drudgery. Today, she's overwhelmed by possibilities. Oh yeah, miracles happen. She's living proof. The trick is to recognise them when they come along, and to grab them unafraid.

At lunchtime, with his stomach rumbling and his tastebuds on overdrive at the thought of what Ettie might have cooked for lunch, Sam makes his way back to The Briny.

His hand is on the screen door when he hears a high-pitched yip that sounds more like surprise than fright. Two more follow in quick succession. He chucks a look at the ferry wharf where the two Misses Skettle, their iris-blue hair newly tinted and corrugated, stand side by side, the week's groceries piled at their feet. The old girls are resplendent in full skirts printed with pink cabbage roses, like belles from the 1950s. They are watching a tinny racing in circles.

"Jeez. That's Jimmy," Sam says when he reaches them. He shades his eyes and moves forward to make sure he's right.

"That boy's stark naked," announces one of the Misses Skettle calmly.

Her sister squints as the tinny completes another circle, its outboard motor dug so deep in the water the boat is almost vertical. "Maybe, I can't tell. There's a towel over his lap."

"Well, your eyes are better than mine. But I'm quite sure I saw a soft appendage."

"Better than a stiff appendage. At our age, anyway!"

Sam bites his bottom lip. "Well, we all know Jimmy's always been a bit impulsive. But he's coming good."

"Of course he is," the old women nod in agreement, their geranium-pink lips tightly puckered in confirmation. "Anyone can see that."

Inside the café, Ettie is firm. "The hamburger mince has a green frill and I'm frightened to even crack the eggs. It'll be a week at least before I'm running at full speed. Go home and make a sandwich, Sam."

"You'll have muffins again tomorrow, though, won't you? You can't get a bloke's hopes to such a high level and then let him down!"

"Get out of here. You're wasting my time." She flicks his backside with a damp cloth.

On the way out, he sees a bin overflowing with discarded food. He snaffles a handful of raw burgers and winks at the dog. "That's you done, at least."

Back on the barge, Sam checks behind for boat traffic and eases the throttle forward. He feels an instant, slight shudder in the *Mary Kay*'s response.

"Ah bugger," he groans, guessing there's a drag on the rudder. Boats are like people, bloody unpredictable, even when you nurse them like a newborn baby. He's aware there's no point in whingeing though. Whatever is wrong has to be found and fixed immediately. Law of the water. Maintain or sink. No half-measures. He swings back to The Briny, gentle on the helm to keep off the pressure. With the dog locked in the wheelhouse, he strips to his cherry-red jocks and jumps overboard, holding his nose. He's so quick, no one notices till they hear the splash.

"What ya got, Sam?" yells Jimmy when Sam comes up for air. The boy, who must have found a stash of clothes from somewhere, is hanging over the jetty rail, his orange hair gelled into a crocodile spine.

"Turtle with a fishing line down its gut and the line wrapped around the prop," Sam tells him, his voice full of disgust. Some lazy fisherman cutting the line instead of untangling it, he guesses. The hook lies hidden in the seagrass bed until some poor unsuspecting turtle nibbling its morning tea swallows it whole and the line wraps around its flipper and neck, strangling the poor thing.

Same bloke probably kept his rods in tip-top order, his house as neat as an operating theatre. Negligence isn't due to ignorance any more, Sam thinks. It's contempt for anything beyond your own needs.

Jimmy wobbles his head. "That's no good, Sam, no good. That poor turtle. We've got to save it."

Ah jeez, thinks Sam, squeezing water out of his nose. He'll jump in with me in a sec.

"Ask Ettie to come out," he calls, hoping to stall the kid. He looks up to see a spidery white body, in bright green boxer shorts patterned with yellow bananas, flying over the rail and heading for a sternum-splitting belly-whacker. The kid misses him by less than a foot.

And sinks like a bag of potatoes.

Sam dives, terrified he'll smash into the prop or go under the stern and lose his way. He grabs an arm, pulls the kid towards him and they surface together.

"'Preciate your concern, mate," Sam says, shaking his head to clear his ears, checking Jimmy for signs of blood. "Does you credit. But in future, hang on till we decide what to do."

"It's the turtle, Sam. It'll be drowning if we don't hurry," Jimmy splutters. Before Sam can calm him, the kid duck-dives. Sam curses. He checks out the growing crowd at the jetty rail for a local face but comes up empty. "Instead of watching the free entertainment, could one of you go into the café and ask Ettie to bring a sharp knife to the stern of the barge?" he yells. He sees a bloke break from the front row.

Christ! The kid is still under. Good lungs or half dead, he

thinks, hoping like hell it isn't the latter. He looks down to the sun-striped seabed and sees red hair waving like a flag. Heaves a deep breath and dives again. Thank God he's given up those shocking cigarettes.

Underwater, he taps the kid's shoulder and points at the surface. Jimmy shakes his head. No! His hands are full of fishing line, he is unravelling it from a flipper. Sam points at the surface again, his lungs busting. Then he yanks the kid and drags him up to open air.

"I nearly got him saved, Sam," the kid splutters, swallowing air in huge gulps. "I'm unwrapping the line. It's like a parcel, wound round and round. I'm nearly there, Sam. Can't you see?"

This time, Sam doesn't let him go. "Mate, we're getting a knife. We'll cut through the line, then you and I will lift the turtle onto the deck of the *Mary Kay* and we'll check it out. Okay?" He feels the kid pull away, trying to dive again and holds on tighter. "We're a team. We need to do this like a . . . navy exercise," he says, keeping eye contact and getting through to Jimmy at last. "We're a team, mate. You and me."

Jimmy nods. "Yeah, Sam. We're a team. Aren't we?"

Ettie rushes out of the café, leaps on the barge and runs to the stern. She kneels and sticks her head over the side, handing Sam a carving knife.

"Need an ambulance?" she asks, more calmly than she feels.

"No. A vet." Sam and Jimmy take deep breaths and dive together.

They rescue a sixty-pound, narrow-faced, long-necked turtle that bears a striking resemblance to Bertie, though no one dares mention it. Not with the old bloke in hospital and knocking at death's door. Still, Sam thinks, miracles do happen. You just have to be open to them. Look at Ettie.

He hoists himself onto the barge and drags the heavy reptile out of the water to the deck. Jimmy, his legs bent and straining forward, uses the fender to lift himself onto the boat in a single motion. He lands on all fours like a giant grasshopper. Clears his nose with a loud honk, then sticks his bony backside into the air to peer inside the shell. He looks up, puzzled.

"Where's the head gone, Sam? Did we leave it behind?"

"No, mate. The turtle's tired and gone inside to have a rest after all the excitement."

"What are these?" Jimmy fingers deep grooves in the turtle's shell.

"Prop scars," Sam says, thin-lipped. "Caused by boats that hoon through the waterways so fast little blokes like this don't have time to duck out of the way. Remember that, mate, the next time you're chuckin' wheelies in the middle of the bay."

"Did I do it, Sam? Did I hurt the turtle?" The teenager's eyes fill with tears.

"Not this time, Jimmy. But think before you take off next time, eh?"

In the cabin, Sam finds a stained old towel that stinks of diesel. He uses it to brush off most of the water before pulling on his shorts and T-shirt. He hands it to Jimmy.

"Dry off and make sure you get dressed, mate. None of this naked frolickin'. Okay?"

"Why not, Sam?" asks Jimmy, using the towel to dry the turtle's shell instead.

"Well, for a start, mate, the two Misses Skettle nearly fainted and they're too old for shocks."

"How old are they, Sam?"

"Just get dressed, mate, so we can get this turtle in the ute and I can take it to the vet."

"Can I come, too?"

"Need you here, mate." His face softens. "Your job while I'm gone is to look after the mutt. Let him out of the wheelhouse and take him back to the Island. No speedin', but. Remember the turtle. I'll track you down when I get back to give you a full report and that's a promise. Jeez. My head hurts. The water's still bloody cold, tell you that for nothing. Now get the dog and off you go."

"Why for nothin', Sam?"

"Never you mind."

"Is he a good dog, Sam?"

"The best, mate."

Inside the café, Ettie's dealing with a rush of tourists who've worked up an appetite after watching the turtle's rescue. They ignore the *Closed* sign and fall on what's left of her cakes like locusts. She cranks the coffee machine to full-bore and decides the cleaning can wait. The till is flush with notes. It gives her a thrill and, more importantly, courage and confidence in the future.

"Keep an eye on Jimmy, will you, till I get back?" Sam shouts over a few heads.

She's too busy to do anything but nod.

*

The local vet, a stringy woman with a horsy face, takes one look at the turtle and calls the zoo. She writes a name, address and phone number on a slip of paper and hands it to Sam. "Sorry. Wish I could do more. I'm okay with cats, dogs, rabbits, guinea pigs. Even birds, goats, horses and cows. But this is out of my league."

Sam tucks the turtle under one arm, resting the shell on his hipbone, and lumbers through a waiting room chockers with nervous dogs and yowling cats. The turtle remains hidden and silent in its shell. He wonders if it has the faintest idea what's going on, or if once it's pulled its head in, the outside world ceases to exist. Nice trick if you can manage it.

Sam returns to the café by mid-afternoon to find Ettie bent over a sheaf of papers.

"Is he going to be okay?" she asks, without looking up.

"It's a she," he says wearily. "About twenty-five years old and in her laying prime. Probably spends her time cruising the coast from northern Queensland to Cook's Basin. Maybe a little further south as well. The hook is stuck in her guts so she'll need surgery but they're certain she'll survive."

"You were gone for hours. I thought she might've died or something. Jimmy's been frantic. Looking for you every-where. He won't settle until he knows whether the turtle's going to live. Is it my imagination or is he getting even odder with his mother away?"

"Well, we're all a bit odd, but not everyone's good-hearted, so he's ahead. Just got a low attention span and a few behav-ioural quirks. A job'll set him straight."

"I'd take him on if I could, love, but it's a bit of a risk if he's going to turn up to work naked."

"Clothes or no clothes, he's got all the right instincts. Reckon you could manage a coffee? I'm beat."

"I can find a hamburger and chips, as well. That appeal?"

"No green frills?"

"Found a stash of patties and chips in the freezer. If you're game, so am I."

"Hamburger, love, with the blood running out of it. Go easy on the barbecue but load up on the onions. You're a star, Ettie."

As she goes to turn on the grill Sam wonders how long meat lasts before it goes off, frozen or not. He decides it's smarter not to count the days since Bertie took sick. "On second thoughts, burn it to a cinder, love."

The lip-smacking smell of frying onions and toasting buns follows him through the plastic curtains and out into the Square. "Where you hiding, Jimmy?" he yells. "And you'd better bloody be wearing your trousers."

Jimmy – clothed in baggy knee-length brown shorts covered in red hibiscus flowers and a grey windcheater that hangs off his shoulderblades like wings – pokes his face out of a crowd of after-school kids waiting for the ferry.

"How's the turtle, Sam?" He bounds over. "Is she okay? You sure? I could help look after her. She's a lovely turtle, Tilly. Where's she staying?"

Tilly?

"How'd ya know it was a girl?"

"No bollocks, Sam. Not anywhere."

"Er, good on you. Well *Tilly* is in the best possible hands. And when she's fit, she'll come back and you and I will take the *Mary Kay* out to sea and lower her overboard so she can find her way north to lay some eggs. Deal?" He holds up his hand, waits for a high five.

Jimmy ignores it. "Tilly needs a friend. She's been hurt bad."

"And you're a great friend, mate, the best. But she's too crook right now for company." Sam scrabbles for a way to lever Jimmy's mind off the turtle and into new territory. "Are you around on Thursday, mate? I'm gonna need some help on the barge. The pay's not great but it's fair. Hard work, though. Gotta tell you that upfront."

Jimmy hops from one foot to the other. "Yeah. I'll help. Count me in, Sam. Count me in. What's on?"

"Got a few planks left over from a building site. They're cluttering up my foreshore. We'll bring 'em over to the café to fix the deck where it's rotting."

"Cool, Sam. That's really cool. How much you gonna pay me? Is it gonna be enough to buy a car?"

"Well, not right away, mate. But all in good time." He wraps a beefy arm around the kid's pointy shoulders. "Not a word to anyone. Okay?"

"Not even to Ettie?"

"*Especially* not Ettie."

Back inside the café, Sam finds three hamburgers waiting on the counter.

"One for you, one for Jimmy and one for the mutt," Ettie explains.

On the other side of the world, in a city where sea turtles are found in zoos and cafés standing lopsided on a water's edge are a rare thing, Kate Jackson disembarks into dirty rain and gritty wind. She grabs a cab and directs the driver to take the Queensboro Bridge. When he wants to argue, she cuts him short. She lived in this city once, she tells him, and not so long ago so she'll know if he peels off to add another ten bucks to the fare. When he asks why she'd leave a paradise – ha, ha – like the Big Apple, she feigns sleep.

The speeding cab swerves, ducks and weaves along grimy streets of paint-peeled clapboard houses where youths lurk under hoodies and old women push shopping trolleys containing everything they own. When they reach the Queensboro Bridge, the night-time hookers, who tout deep in the shadows of massive stone pylons, are still at work.

She reaches the hotel a little before nine o'clock and joins the queue to check in, edgy from too little sleep and her customary pre-interview nerves. When she finally reaches the counter, the receptionist takes her name, punches a few keys and says, "You have a message." He prints it out and hands it to her.

Story's been canned. Make your way back to the office asap.

She takes her key, finds her room and strips off to stand under a scalding shower. By the time she turns off the taps, the fug that's been cluttering her mind for months is gone. She doesn't want to do this job any more. The fire in her belly is dead. It's as simple as that.

She switches off her mobile phone, hauls back the covers on the bed and lies down. She closes her eyes. In her sleep, she jumps icefloes that thaw under her feet, getting smaller and smaller until the last block dissolves into nothing and she begins to sink.

When she wakes, she types an email. Short, sharp and to the point.

I resign. Effective immediately.

Then she dials Ettie's number, appalled when she realises there is no one else she can think of who might genuinely care that she's just made one of the biggest decisions of her life. The call goes to message bank. "I did it, Ettie. I quit my job. I'm on my way home." Saying the words out loud, even to a machine, suddenly makes them a fact.

CHAPTER ELEVEN

From the very first day that Ettie takes control of The Briny Café, the locals are full of speculation. They are aware that in a very short time, a woman of Ettie's charm and talent will triple turnover and she'll be run off her feet quick smart. But if she tries to go it alone she'll burn out within the year. Or fail to maintain the new high standard they are already delighted to see emerging in the berry muffins and the lemon, orange and walnut cupcakes.

The question they are all asking is who she will approach to work alongside her. Jack the Bookie, never slow to see a business opportunity, has drawn up a list and is taking bets on what many people consider to be odds so short it's hardly worth having a flutter. The top three contenders, at even money, are the Three Js, with Jenny just a little in front of Judy and Jane but only because her kids are at the age when they can look after themselves after school. They're all first-rate cooks with a long history of dishing up spectacular fundraiser dinners, including two pigs cooked to golden perfection on a spit, a chicken cacciatore with a rich tomato sauce redolent of salty anchovies and olives, and a quite amazing jambalaya with perfectly balanced spices that people still talked about years after it was served. Their desserts, too, are spellbinding, but the standouts are the honey macadamia tart, tiramisu, baklava (which segued perfectly with the slow-roasted lamb shoulders fragrant with oregano, rosemary and garlic) and a mess of meringues, strawberries and cream swizzled with a raspberry coulis with exactly the right hint of tartness. The women are all good enough to knock the stuffing out of a three-star Paris restaurant according to the only local who'd ever been fortunate – or financially flush – enough to dine in such an establishment. And while it was generally acknowledged he was a bloke occasionally prone to exaggeration, no one doubted his noble intent to pay homage to Cook's Basin's cooks.

There was also talk of a newly arrived, professionally trained chef who might turn out to be a star attribute to the community. It was still early days but he was showing a bit of dash by preserving the quirky style of his 1950s waterside shack instead of ripping it down to put up a concrete bunker. With his renovations completed, he might be looking around for a new project. Jack put his name on the list in an effort to liven up the odds.

No one, in even a brief moment of madness, considered the runty little Oyster Bay woman with less heft on her than a plucked bantam as a contender. There was a tad too much *otherness* about her as well as a lack of the essential warmth and understanding required by a neighbourhood café that every local regarded as a second home.

With an impressive show of restraint, Sam resists the temptation to cream the pot with his inside knowledge. To him, it is the same as cheating and cheating, his father always told him, meant you never worked out if you had any real talent of your own. The end result, he said, was a person who had no idea who they were or what they stood for, which was a recipe for an unhappy life. He never doubted his dad then and he isn't about to start now. Anyway, if he throws Kate's name in the pot, Jack will smell a rat in three seconds flat.

Soon after sunrise on Wednesday morning, Sam ties up the barge at the Spit. The ferry wharf is jammed with chippies in ragged jeans, T-shirts and boots; painters wear speckled overalls and matching sandshoes; labourers stomp about in steel-capped boots, wearing ripped windcheaters, khaki shorts and navy singlets. A couple of tree loppers stand apart, chainsaws neatly clipped inside fluorescent orange canisters. Ropes are coiled thickly in a grey tub containing clips and hard hats. Tinnies cruise in from the bays and the Island under a new sky – each of them carrying potential customers for The Briny Café.

He sets off towards the open door, rubbing his hands in anticipation of a freshly baked muffin. Counting sixteen heads as he goes along and it's only a little past six o'clock, he makes a bet that within three months, barring some awful natural catastrophe like a tsunami or a cyclone, the place will be a great little earner. As long as Ettie comes to her senses and finds a suitable partner. Sometimes, Ettie's good instincts get the better of her commonsense. If she's not too busy, he plans to have a quiet word in her ear. He has a list of three names in his pocket that coincides with Jack's even money bets. Each one is a hard worker and a skilled cook with a firm understanding of the central role The Briny plays in community life. Kate, he suspects, doesn't have it in her.

Sam marches inside. There's already a disorderly queue at the counter and the muffins are almost sold out. He nods good morning to Ettie, orders a coffee and toasted banana bread and joins Fast Freddy at their customary table in the spindle shade of a casuarina. Engrossed in the newspaper which he reads over Fast Freddy's shoulder, he barely glances up when a cab arrives, figuring it's a weekender getting a head start.

A second or two later, he feels the hairs on the back of his neck begin to rise, followed by a strange sense of anxiety. He searches for the mutt, who's already sussed the softest touches and is happily bumming tidbits. He glances at the café. It hasn't caught fire. He hasn't heard the gut-churning crunch of boats colliding at full speed. There's nothing awry, as far as he can tell. But he's a man who always trusts his instincts, so he's alert now.

"Somethin' botherin' ya?" Fast Freddy asks, feeling the tension.

"Nothing I can pinpoint. Just a feeling of imminent disaster."

Kate walks towards him, like a hazy apparition, out of the misty morning light.

"Gidday," he says.

She nods and puts her bags on the ground.

"Been anywhere interesting?"

"Not really. Bit of a fizzer, in fact."

"Yeah. Know what you mean. Everywhere else always turns out a bit shabby."

"Something like that."

He marks his spot in the story he is reading with a finger. Fast Freddy bats it away like an annoyance.

"Easy on, Freddy! I'll lose my place," he exclaims.

"Buy your own paper, then," Freddy says calmly. "Welcome home, Kate. You look like you need a good feed, a cuppa and a long lie-down." He folds his paper and gives the mutt the last of his muffin, dusting the crumbs from his hands. "Right. I'm off for the day. Gotta catch up on my beauty sleep. See ya . . ."

"Thanks, Freddy. It's great to be back."

He walks off with a rolling gait, as if he's still riding the chop.

"Who owns the mongrel?" Kate asks, pointing under Sam's feet.

"No bloody idea. He's surviving on free bed and board on the *Mary Kay* till a better offer comes along. Hey! You wouldn't like to take him, would you? Go well over there on the dark side of the bay. Give you a bit of company."

Kate laughs. "Nice try." On a sudden impulse, she puts an arm around Sam's massive shoulders and leans in to kiss him on the cheek. Flabbergasted, he looks at her like she's gone mad.

She flushes. "So . . . Anything happen while I was gone?" she stammers.

Sam's face clears. "Mate, so much has happened it's impossible to know where to begin." He stands in his faded red shorts and sky-blue T-shirt, dragged down in the corners from clothes pegs. "Ettie's been waitin' for you to get home. She's in the café and got a heap to tell you." He gives her a little push in the direction of The Briny. "Off you go. And by the way, you still owe me a coupla beers."

"How about a slab? It's the least I can do after almost wrecking your barge."

His hackles rise. Jeez, he thinks, will she ever learn? It's not about the value. It's all in the gesture. "No need to go overboard, mate. Saving your backside wasn't worth that much."

"Your call," she shrugs, offended, and heads for the café.

The Briny is eerily different. And yet nothing has changed. Kate peers through the plastic ribbons. Same counter tops, shelving, fridges, ovens and gas tops. Same signs announcing Bertie's heart-starter coffee. But there is a sense of order instead of chaos, gleaming surfaces instead of grubby ones. The flotsam and jetsam of Bertie's latest food fads, for so long left mouldering on the counter in pyramids, have disappeared. The pervasive odour of bacon, stale fat, burnt toast and the tang of Bertie's toxic brew are still faintly there. But they've somehow been pushed aside by the mouth-watering scent of baking, fresh coffee, bananas, lemons and oranges, cinnamon and vanilla. Ettie is behind the counter, hands flying, working the coffee machine like a professional barista. There's a queue of uncombed chippies lined up in their scruffy work togs, their tongues hanging out.

Kate looks inside the display fridge to find that the gaudy chocolate Florentines, as traditional in The Briny as hot chips, are missing. She realises something truly momentous has occurred in her absence.

Ettie wraps an order and turns to the counter. "Kate, love, you're back! Here, whack this out to Sam, will you? He's waiting for it." She hands her a coffee and a warm white paper bag. "Give me ten minutes to clear the rush."

Outside Kate shoves Sam's breakfast rudely under his nose. "You want to tell me what's going on?" she says, her hands on her hips.

He opens the bag, sniffs and smiles, takes a slurp out of his cup. "Ettie is a fairdinkum genius," he sighs. He digs into his banana toast, chewing loudly. "Too good to share, mate. I recommend you order your own when you go back in there." He calls the dog, who runs up to him, eager to please, and leaves Kate standing on her own without another word.

"So much for the legendary Cook's Basin generosity you're always banging on about," she yells after him.

Ettie flicks the sign to *Closed*, pulls aside Bertie's red, white and blue plastic ribbons, and calls from the crooked doorway of the café. Kate scissors her way out of a seat at the picnic table, gathers her bags and walks slowly across the uneven paving stones of the Square. The *Seagull* eases into the wharf. Kids in school uniforms – shirts hanging out, shoelaces undone – spill out and roar up the ramp, still scoffing their breakfast out of cereal bowls.

"Coffee, love, you must be knackered? How did it go? All done and dusted? Wasn't expecting you home till tomorrow." She warms milk, wipes the nozzle on the machine, dusts benches, straightens platters and rearranges the few last cakes, whizzing tornado fashion, until a coffee, a muffin and a napkin are neatly lined up. "Right, let's go out and sit on the deck for some peace and quiet and I'll fill you in." She stands aside, insisting Kate goes ahead.

"Where's Big Julie? Bertie?" Kate asks, pulling out a chair that's essentially beyond repair.

Ettie sits down and reaches across the table to enfold Kate's hand in both of her own. She searches for the right words. "Bertie's crook. Seriously crook. Left it too late to see a doctor and now there's not much anyone can do. Lung cancer. Secondaries everywhere."

"Oh that's terrible. Poor man. And Julie? Those two have a thing going?"

Ettie looks surprised and releases Kate's hand. "As it turns out, they did. You're more perceptive than the rest of us. We never guessed. I suppose we couldn't believe anyone would want the grumpy old bugger. The thing is," she says, leaning back in her seat, "Bertie gave me first option on the café and I didn't hesitate. The Briny is now mine. Well, a twelve-year lease on it."

Kate smiles. "That's wonderful news, Ettie. You'll be brilliant. Everyone knows you're the best cook in Cook's Basin, and way beyond. So no more cleaning houses, hey?"

Ettie's face turns serious and she takes a deep breath before continuing. "The thing is, I'm looking for a partner. And I thought of you."

"Me!" Kate's coffee mug stops halfway to her mouth. "Why me? You can pick from any one of a dozen people better equipped than I am. God, Ettie, you know I find boiling an egg a challenge." She pushes back her chair, grabs her mug and flees to the edge of the deck.

Ettie leaves her be, giving her a while to absorb the idea. The sea is so blue, she thinks, and the sky is even bluer. Customers will see beyond the scruff and rot if they are the kind of people who appreciate food prepared with love and care.

When she judges enough time has passed, she joins Kate at the rail. "How's your coffee?" she teases, trying for lightness.

Kate looks at the empty mug in her hand like she's never seen it before. "The coffee? Excellent, really. You'll have to take down the sign describing it as a heart-starter." She faces her friend. "Ettie . . ."

"Yeah?"

"I appreciate what you're doing, truly, but I know zilch about food."

Ettie takes her time framing a reply, wanting to get the pitch exactly right. "I don't need another cook, Kate. That's my job. What I really need is a partner who's good with the big picture. You're a perfectionist. You never shortcut details. You know how to get things done quickly, efficiently and so instinctively you're not even aware you're doing it. But mostly, someone's got to watch the money, make sure there's more at the end of the week than we started with. Honest accounting all the way. No tax dodging, no raiding the till. I want to be able to sleep at night. Adding up figures isn't a strong point. I am also painfully aware that I'm lousy on bureaucratic detail and smart enough to know I'm never going to change. It's a glitch in the way I think. The artist part of my brain. That's my excuse, anyway. In essence, I'd need you to take care of the nuts and bolts."

Kate is silent for so long, Ettie plunges on. "The café is a gift you couldn't hope for in a million Sundays. I know the building is rough and there's plenty to do. But the bones are not just good, they're phenomenal." She closes her eyes and clenches her fists, feeling both passion and frustration. "Sometimes, I really believe the universe steps in to take care of you when you need it most. And sometimes, Kate, we've got to have the courage to take a risk. Or else how do we ever find out what we're capable of? I got your message. You need a job. I'm offering you one. The timing couldn't be more perfect."

Ettie stares at the water glittering through the gaps in the decking. Presses her lips together. No more babbling, not this time. The sun beats down on the back of her neck. The hot sweat of disappointment trickles down her spine. Without realising what she's doing, she holds her work-red hands out in front of her to count the oven burns down her arms, knowing they will soon turn into thin white scars. Like rites of passage.

Well, she thinks realistically, resigned to the fact that Kate is going to turn her down, the café probably isn't everyone's idea of the Holy Grail. She surveys the rotting deck, junky tables and chairs. Inside there's the mouldy, defeated kitchen. Singed. Chipped. Buckled. Shadowy with the erosion of time, wear and neglect. When she stacks it up against a top job and international travel, it probably looks like a third-world rat-hole. But it's *her* rat-hole, and therefore *her* Taj Mahal.

She is so lost in her dreams that she gives a start when she hears Kate's voice.

"It's a big project. Massive. Do you have any idea how much money it's going to take to bring the café up to scratch?

Right now, it would only take one wrong move with the health department and you'd be shut down overnight."

"I will not, I absolutely will not, let an opportunity like this pass by because I don't have the guts to have a go," Ettie says vehemently. "Go home and think about it. If you feel the same way tomorrow, I'll look around for someone else. I thought of you first because I felt this was the answer to your prayers." Her voice softens. "Your heart's here, Kate. I heard it in your voice the first time I met you. The volume's been turned down, you said. I've never forgotten it. It takes most people years to get what Cook's Basin is all about, and it hit you like an epiphany in ten seconds flat."

Kate's face reddens. "It's a wonderful offer. I mean it."

"The café's a way out, Kate. What's holding you back?"

"I understand words, facts. When people like me leap from mainstream journalism we go into public relations or some other media-related career. God, sometimes even politics."

"Public relations? Politics? I'm not an expert, but if *the* spin was wearing you out before, you'd be headed for an even bigger wipe-out."

"I suppose I think you'd do better with a gung-ho, cashed-up entrepreneur who understands the pitfalls of the restaurant business. I don't want to let you down, Ettie. I'm afraid that I will."

Ettie puts her strong arms around Kate's shoulders. "If I thought there was a chance of that, I wouldn't have asked you. I'm not a fool. Or a martyr. You're good at planning, Kate. You did a treat with your own house. Handled the council, worked out the tides, kept the blokes on site when they usually bugger off to other jobs. You came in under-budget when most offshore projects blow their budgets to smithereens. Don't look at me like that. You think we didn't talk about you when you first arrived? We didn't gossip about much else. Only eased up when Jack the Bookie creamed the pot. A month was the longest shot anyone gave you. We all thought you'd turn tail after the first bad storm."

"Who gave me a month?" Kate asks, curious.

"Freddy. He's always had more faith in you than the rest of us."

"God, I'm so sorry, Ettie. I'm really jet-lagged. Having trouble getting my head around so many changes so fast. It's all a bit much. Can you wait until tomorrow for an answer?"

"Sure," Ettie says, flatly. Wondering how an offer that was meant to be magnificent, magnanimous and utterly perfect suddenly has the stench of defeat about it.

Out in the Square, Sam sees the two women walk away from the deck and he dashes inside the café. He stops short when he sees Ettie's expressionless face. He shakes his head, sadly. "Decided to hang around for the celebration," he says. "Got that arse-up. See you, Ettie. I'll call you tonight. We can discuss a new plan of action." He stomps out the door giving it an almighty slam.

Kate flies after him. "You want to explain that look?" she asks, grabbing his shoulder.

He removes her hand. "Didn't figure you for a woman with the heart of a soft-boiled egg. What's your problem? Café not fancy enough for you?"

"*Failure*," she hisses. "That's the bloody problem. What if I fail Ettie and we lose our shirts and we're back to square one? We'd have nothing but the gutter to look forward to."

"Gutter! What d'ya mean gutter? No one's asking you to do it hard, mate. Bertie made a good living. With Ettie in control, it's a licence to print money. I thought you had a bit of guts the other day in the storm. Turns out you're custard through to the bone!"

Kate snatches hold of a corner of his shirt, then drops it, feeling foolish.

He stops and, unaware he's doing it, scratches under his shirt. "You know how I came to be on the barge? Took a risk, Kate. Took a risk because I was tired of some other bastard calling the shots when it was always my neck on the line."

He leaves her and stomps along the unevenly planked jetty, slapping a greasy hat on his head. The barrel-chested mongrel follows at a full trot, on a mission, and marches to the bow where he sits with his nose pointed into the wind.

"What if it doesn't work?" she calls out.

Sam bends to untie the ropes. A man born with salt in his lungs, the sea under his feet. In tune with his barge. He steps into the cabin, as though he hasn't heard her. Then he leans his close-cropped head out the door, a hand on the helm. "It'll work, Kate. One step at a time. It's like any problem. You wear it away."

She watches the beamy *Mary Kay* disappear into the distance, the crane cracked in the middle like an elbow.

"You got the account books here, Ettie?" she says furiously when she returns to the café. "I need to know exactly what this leaning pile of driftwood can do."

*

131

Sam and the mutt set a sedate course on the *Mary Kay* to service two moorings on the eastern side of Kingfish Bay. They cross water where the sun plays tunes and high on the hills the new growth on the eucalypts is the colour of limes. Sam rips off his windcheater. It's gearing up to be a spectacular day. He hopes it's a good omen for Ettie. If ever a woman has earned a bit of luck, she has, he thinks. Although Freddy would call it karma. Do good and good comes back to you.

He looks down at the dog, no definable breed, sitting to attention at his feet: "You're on trial, you miserable mutt. Behave yourself or I'll tip you overboard and not even Ettie will be able to save you." The dog's ratty tail thumps loudly on the timber deck. "And stop dribbling, it's indecent," he adds, scratching under the dog's chin where the fur feels softer than silk.

Sam finds the moorings easily enough in a pool of timber boats. Putt-putts graceful as swans, homey cabin cruisers, elegant gentlemen's launches. Every plank gently hand-bent and whittled to fit as snugly on the ribs as feathers on a bird. Each one a work of art that peeling paint and rust stains fail to disguise. His own barge, a concerto of spotted gum, huon, jarrah and cypress pine takes more looking after than a new relationship. She's a lifetime commitment. But of the kind that never falters.

He gets down to business on the first mooring, chipping away cunjevoi from the rope. The mutt suddenly finds the shovel offensive and crawls forward, growling.

"We've had this conversation before, mate. Same as the broom. Off you go."

The mutt locks jaws on the wood and shakes it like a dead rat.

"If that shovel goes overboard, you dumb mutt, so will you. Take my word for it." The dog slinks off to a shady spot under the curved eave of the cabin to keep a watchful eye. "Dumb mutt," Sam says out loud. Then figures it's time he has a name. Ponzer. Pouncer. Bowler. Bailer. Boag.

"Yeah," he decides. "Boag. After my favourite frigid ale." He scruffs the mutt. The dog snuffles his hand. "It doesn't mean you're on board for keeps, mate, so don't go getting any ideas like that. It's just until I find a proper home for you."

On the bow, the newly christened Boag sits solidly, starting to look more like a bo's'n than a deckhand. Maybe there's a bit of class in him after all, Sam decides.

Kate sits at a small round table tucked away in a dark corner of the café, checking Bertie's figures. The Briny perches on a financial razor-edge from year to year, decade to decade. Never quite toppling into bankruptcy but close enough to seriously test the faint-hearted. There's a clear pattern of summer profit and winter loss.

"This the real balance sheet, Ettie? Or the cooked books Bertie sent to the tax department?"

"Bertie didn't have a high opinion of paying tax. Loathed banks even more. He told me so with a wink and a nudge. I'm sure there's a fair bit of give, all his way."

"Phew. Because this wouldn't keep you and me in loo paper."

Ettie places a hand on Kate's shoulder. "You don't have to do this now. You're tired. Think about it overnight. Or just say no. Walk away."

Kate puts down her pencil and stacks the ledgers in a neat pile. "Hope I'm not being rude, Ettie, but where'd you get the money to buy The Briny? You've always lived so . . ."

"Hand to mouth?"

"Frugally."

"My mother died when I was twelve and she left me a small amount that stayed in the bank, quietly growing. It was my emergency money. I never risked a cent. It's the only security I've ever had."

"This is an all or nothing bet, Ettie. You must know that."

"Yep. And just so you understand, it's taken every penny I've got. I'm fifty-five years old. Almost too old for risks. But it's now or never. The best I can hope for is fair recompense for hard work. That's the goal."

"I'm curious . . . Why do you think Bertie let you have the place? The man seems to live for profit. He could have put it on the market and made a killing."

Ettie smiles, like it's a no-brainer. "He loves every warped board, cracked window and leaning pylon and he doesn't want anyone to pull it down while he isn't looking. He also knows this stack of rotting timber means as much to me as it does to him. That it's integral to the Cook's Basin community. He doesn't need money any more. He needs to feel good about himself."

Kate taps the end of a pencil against her mouth. "I might as well put every card on the table from the start. I have some money – I sold my city terrace for a good profit and bought cheap in Cook's Basin – but I don't have nearly enough to turn The Briny into a swish café."

Ettie laughs. "Swish? The Briny? The community would never let us strip away the character. There'd be a blockade before one plank was removed. Seriously, though, we'll go broke if we aim for swish. What I have in mind is a good clean-up, and a slow and gentle resurrection."

Kate turns back to the dusty account books with curling pages and the faint whiff of mould. She finds a blank piece of paper and draws a line down the middle. At the top of one column she writes *Urgent*; on the other she pencils *Essential*.

Late in the afternoon, Sam makes a cuppa and sips it on the deck of the barge. Boat traffic whizzes past and he wonders, not for the first time, what drives a woman like Kate. The café is the chance of a lifetime. If he weren't fully engaged with the lovely *Mary Kay*, he'd be beating down Ettie's door and begging to be involved.

Life is all about observation and then creating opportunities, he thinks. See a problem. Fix it. Hardly rocket science. The Misses Skettle, he reckons, have it sorted. Do your best, lend a hand, live and let live, they advised him when he was sixteen years old and faced with fending for himself. Simple as . . .

He straightens up, tosses the dregs over the side. Boag catches his uneasiness and jumps out of his basket. The Weasel roars past in his spiffy white boat, flat out, sunlight splintering off the chrome. He's dead meat, Sam thinks. Not literally, of course. There was a law against that, and rightly so. Otherwise there'd be bodies floating all over the bays. But where the hell has the bloke materialised from? It beggars belief that he thinks he can swan into Cook's Basin and ride roughshod over local life. He sighs. Which he's aware he's been doing quite a lot of lately. He heads for the Spit. See a problem. Wear it away. His list of possible partners for Ettie burns a hole in his pocket. He'll deal with the Weasel problem later.

The fly-specked *Closed* sign is still firmly in place when Sam rocks up at the café in the early evening. He peers through the newly cleaned glass and can just make out Ettie wiping down a soft-drink fridge in the far corner. A beam of daylight shoots through a small hole in the wall and lands on her head. He knocks lightly.

Kate jumps up and opens the door before she realises who it is. She goes beetroot-red and stands stiffly aside to let him in.

"Still here, are you?" he says.

"Yeah. Sorting the final details before making an appointment with the bank manager. I'm in." The words are out of her mouth before she knows it. She turns to Ettie: "What time do we start tomorrow?"

Ettie pulls her head out of the fridge, not sure she's heard correctly. "Eh? What did you say?"

"I'm in."

With a whoop, Ettie jumps up. She dumps her dishcloth, rips off her polka-dot headscarf and throws it in the air. Breathless, she triumphantly withdraws a bottle of champagne from the fridge. "Ta da!"

"Pretty sure of yourself, weren't you?" Kate smiles, but her voice is shaky and her heart beats faster.

Ettie turns serious. "You're not a fool, Kate."

"No doubts that we can do it?" Kate asks.

"None. Not about the business. Not about you as a partner. This is the opportunity of a lifetime for both of us. If we let it go, we'll spend our old age asking ourselves *what if*. Trust me, a cupboard full of *what ifs* is no comfort in the dead of night."

She pops the cork and pours the pale fizz into three chipped water glasses. They stand in a circle, sombre, marking the moment with a clink. Sam sculls. Ettie too. Kate takes a small sip. The two women grin and Sam forces a smile.

Outside, the water shines like a jewel in the rich afternoon light. Red. Yellow. Orange. Blue. Green. Two hoots blast in quick succession. Loiterers make a dash for the back deck of the *Seagull*. Dust motes play in a pool of sunshine pouring through the door. For a delirious moment, Ettie wonders if an angel is about to land in their midst.

The Briny Café seems to lift her worn and shabby shoulders, raise her head and shrug off decades of slough, while the two women whose hearts are reeling with hope, joy and plain old fear, try not to get teary.

When the champagne is finished and a jet-lagged Kate looks ready to wilt, Sam plonks his glass on the counter. He gives Ettie a scratchy kiss and turns to the weary traveller: "C'mon, I'll take you home in style on the beautiful *Mary Kay*. Kings used to travel by barge, y'know. It's God's own transport.

And I've gotta go that way anyway." He looks back at Ettie. "Will you make it to the fireshed for the residents' meeting tomorrow night?"

"God, is it the last Thursday of the month already? Yeah. I'll be there. Who's cooking?"

"That new chef in Kingfish Bay. Used to be someone big in town, so I hear. He's making slow-baked whole ocean trout with some kind of green sauce. Anchovies and a heap of herbs. The anchovies might be a bit of a worry."

"Classic salsa verde. Very trendy."

"Yeah. I was going to suggest him as a possible —" He stops.

"Possible what?"

"Ah, consultant. Just till you both find your feet. No need, probably. You girls'll cream it. Right, let's go." He reaches for Kate's bags, grabs her elbow and pushes her out the door in a rush.

"So what made you change your mind?" he asks bluntly when they're underway.

Kate gets up from the banquette where she was about to doze off. "Do you care?"

"I care about Ettie, so I want to know you're in for the long haul, not just fluffing around until something better comes along."

"Whoa! Don't hold back. Christ, I can't win with you, can I? One minute you're berating me for not taking Ettie up on her offer, and now that I've said yes you're still having a go."

He turns to face her. "I'm just saying that if you let Ettie down, the locals will all come after you with hatchets. When you walk through the Spit we'll turn our backs. When you

138

get stuck in a storm, not even the Misses Skettle, who have hearts of gold, will raise the alarm. Put one foot wrong, and I kid you not you'll be right back at the starting line that the confidence Ettie's placed in you has just pushed you over. Around here, you earn your place in the community. It isn't handed to you willy-nilly."

"Finished?"

"Just so you know. Wouldn't want you to be under any misapprehensions."

"It's clear as daylight. My turn now? You're like something out of the dark ages," she says, coldly. "A tragic figure clinging to an era that's been dead for nearly half a century. You want to get out a bit more and see what the real world's all about. Some of us from *the other side* actually have our own set of morals and ethics and try to live decent lives. We're not all numbskulls, either."

"If it's that good over there, mate, what are you doing here?"

"Cut the *mate* crap, okay? It's starting to wear thin."

They motor along the broken shoreline in a silent, angry fug. Before the barge has slowed to a standstill, Kate jumps off at her pontoon.

"You want these bags or aren't they any good to you any more?" Sam calls after her.

She stomps back and snatches them out of his hands.

The mutt leans against his leg and dribbles on his boot. The good thing about dogs, he thinks, heading for home, is they never turn on you and bite your backside like people.

Cook's Basin News (CBN)

Newsletter for Offshore Residents of Cook's Basin, Australia

NOVEMBER

Good News and Bad News

We're all sorry to hear that Bertie is too crook to continue in his role as the legendary proprietor of The Briny Café. We wish him well with what we know will be hard days ahead. He has sold the leasehold of the café to our own Island personality, Ettie Brookbank, who takes over the reins immediately. She has asked us to let everyone know it will be business as usual in the mornings but that the café will be closed every afternoon for a few minor repairs and restorations, including the dodgy eastern end of the deck where the Editor of this newsletter lost a shoe a couple of weeks ago when her foot went through the timber. We're all thrilled for Ettie, who, as we know, is a magnificent cook. Good luck with the new business, Ettie, and we're all here to give a hand when you need it.

FUEL TANK MISSING

I'm guessing someone ran out of petrol and needed to get home. Right? So when you've refilled the petrol tank you borrowed from my son's tinny, please put it back. If you can't remember the boat, leave it at Commuter Dock and we will look out for it.
Carol

Please Return

Our collection of *Doc Martin* DVDs. We loaned them out but can't remember to whom. If you – whoever you are – have watched them by now, we'd love them returned so we can settle in and run through them once again ourselves. Even if you haven't, can you let us know you've got them? Our senior moments are compressing, if you get our foggy drift.

Cheers, Myrna and Max

Car Park Vandals

This is getting to be a serious issue. Last night, five cars were broken into. Windows were smashed, tyres stolen and several caps on petrol tanks were busted and the tanks drained. Please, if anyone has any information or saw anything even a little bit suspicious, call the police. It's got to be stopped. Someone, somewhere, must have seen something!

CHAPTER
TWELVE

On Thursday morning, when the air is so still the kayakers are out on the water in colourful packs, Ettie hears a boat whack into the fragile café pontoon with a heart-stopping crunch. She rushes out, hair and apron flying, terrified someone's been hurt. At the top of the crooked timber ramp with too many missing planks to satisfy even the vaguest safety standards, she looks down at a tinny locked in a frantic struggle to dock. She lets out a belly laugh and wanders down to help, positioning herself on the end of the pontoon that hasn't yet sunk.

"Start again from out wide and take it really slowly," she calls out to her new partner.

Kate wrenches the steering wheel, throttles too far forward and the tinny roars straight at the shore. She jerks the lever backwards and the boat stalls to a sudden stop. She falls sideways, banging her head.

"Slowly," Ettie calls again, still laughing. "Gentle on the throttle."

Kate restarts the engine and does a snail-pace 360-degree circle that gives her a long, straight approach. But she mis-judges the width of the boat and is still too far out to reach the cleat to tie on.

"Throw me a rope," Ettie calls, "I'll drag you in."

"God, how hard is all that?" Kate moans when she's finally ashore.

"Wait until it blows like stink. Then you'll find out how good you are."

"We need to put up an off-limits sign on the pontoon," Kate says, thinking of lawsuits.

"No point. Boaties are notorious rule-flouters. Sam's work-ing on a plan, though."

They walk through the decrepit tables and chairs. Ettie, pink-faced and smiley, solid in her large white apron, rubber-soled shoes. Kate, slight and serious, neat in blue jeans, a navy T-shirt. A small, dark wraith.

"How about a coffee? On the house." Ettie slips an arm around Kate's waist and guides her inside the café. Her dawn baking is already on display. "Hope you had a good think last night. It's still not too late to back out."

"What about you? No second thoughts about taking on an ex-journo with a history of itchy feet and burnt toast?"

"No doubts here."

"Then I'm in. Full partner. If you're sure."

Ettie is serious. "Never been surer of anything."

There is a knock. Light. As if someone doesn't want to intrude on a private moment. The two women turn towards the doorway. Fast Freddy peers through the plastic ribbons, his blue eyes like glass balls in his face.

"You finished havin' a sob in there? Or whatever? Can a poor tired old fella get a heart-starter at the end of a long night?"

"Yeah, Freddy," Ettie says, laughing. "I'd give you a bacon and egg roll too, love, except we're not officially open yet, and Bertie's leftovers are definitely suss."

"Just the coffee, Ettie. That'd be good as gold. Prefer to leave pigs in the paddock where they're happiest anyway."

"Busy out on the water last night?" Ettie jams ground coffee beans into a dripper, fills a steel jug with milk and hooks a thermometer on the side. She turns a black knob fast and hard. The milk froths with a gentle roar.

"No more than usual. Got stiffed for the fare to the Island. Second time it's happened. Same dead-eyed kids with skin like strawberry jam." Freddy puts down the pile of newspapers he's carrying and twists to read the headlines upside down.

"Know who the kids belong to?" Ettie places his coffee on the counter with a smile. She's drawn a boat in the froth.

"Nope. Couldn't help wondering what they were doing arriving at that boatshed next to Triangle when it was long after visiting hours, though."

"Leave 'em behind next time, huh?"

"Not in me nature to leave a bloke stranded, Ettie. You know that. I'll take 'em, but they'll pay upfront."

"You're a good man, Freddy. I'd be spitting."

"Well, the way I see it, life's a pond. If you let a passing bow wave knock you over every time it comes along, you'll drown. Better to tread water, till the ripples fade away, or swim under them. You'll live longer. Betcha."

"You're starting to sound like a Buddhist, Freddy."

"Those Buddhists got a lot goin' for 'em," he says, looking at his feet, his neck stained red. He slams his coins on the counter, grabs his coffee and flees.

"Didn't get a chance to tell him it was on the house," Ettie murmurs. "Right. Ready for work? We start at the top and work down. Every pro cleaner knows it's the only way."

Twenty years of scum is caked into every corner of The Briny Café. A colony of black house spiders resides in the cracks in the ceiling, their webs spun as thickly as fabric. Shelves are covered in half an inch of filth. Nearly everything is outlined with a ribbon of mould.

"You'll find a ladder in the storeroom upstairs amongst a pile of broken tables and chairs," Ettie says. "Bertie couldn't bear to throw anything out. There's a cracker view from the top deck, though. It'll make you weep. You can see all the way to Cat Island."

"This is going to sound really dumb, but I didn't know there was more than an attic up there," Kate says.

"Bertie never used it. He didn't think it was structurally sound."

"It's not going to come down on our heads or anything, is it?" Kate asks, alarmed.

"No. Nothing like that. Sam says it's solid. Reckons Bertie couldn't be bothered with the stairs so he kept it closed off. Told everyone it was unsafe. He probably said it so often he believed it himself in the end."

Upstairs, Kate steps into a large room. She finds vintage soft-drink boxes, empty packing cases, cartons of cleaning supplies and enough cheap napkins and dangerously flimsy cardboard coffee cups to last for ten years. One of Bertie's "bargains", she thinks. They are now completely unusable. She picks her way through the mess, jiggles a stiff latch on the French doors and steps onto the spongy boards of a broad deck.

And catches her breath.

The sea is awash with diamonds, small clouds whisk across the sky, tinnies fly, gulls soar. Shags, with heads rising from the water like periscopes, dive deep. A fish jumps, then another and another. Underwater, a chase is on. Light flattens from yellow to white. Within the unflinching boundaries of the landscape, nothing is still. She is mesmerised. A plan begins to take shape in her head.

"You okay?" Ettie calls.

"Yeah, yeah, just getting the ladder." She finds it and bangs downstairs.

For the next few hours they toss away sundried tomatoes, capers, anchovies, olives and every other "fancy food" trend that Bertie had tried and failed to embrace. Discard chipped plates, rusted trays, cooking utensils with missing handles and plastic platters, yellow and brittle with age. Ancient cooking pots, still solid and useful, are put aside for scouring. All morning, garbage bags pile up outside the front door until the café is stripped almost bare.

When the shelves are empty, Kate gets a bucket of hot water and a bottle of sugar soap and starts scrubbing. A greasy, evil-smelling concoction of stale fat and dirt lifts in thick globs. The hulls of dead flies and shrivelled spiders float to the top and quickly the water turns black. But the acrid stink of Bertie's stale coffee fades slowly away.

"Sam give you a hard time when he took you home last night?" Ettie asks with a sidelong glance.

"More or less said I'd be garrotted publicly if I let you down."

"He's not known for his subtlety. It just takes a while to get to know that his one-liners are his own brand of humour and not to be taken literally."

"Humour? Is that what you call it? Anywhere else, we'd call it rudeness. Does he dislike all women or just me?"

"Sam? Sam loves women. He nearly married a gorgeous Frenchwoman about ten years ago. He was absolutely wild about her but she didn't want to live here for the rest of her life. When it came to the crunch, he chose the Cook's Basin over love. I've never been sure whether it's the biggest regret or the biggest relief of his life."

Kate looks at Ettie with a grin on her face. "Can't see Sam hoofing around Paris in his greasy hat and old workboots, can you?"

Ettie laughs. "No, you're right. It never would have worked and he was smart enough to realise it."

"I just can't work out why he dislikes me so much."

Ettie comes over and puts an arm around her shoulders. "Oh he likes you, Kate. You can be sure of that."

"Well, he's got a funny way of showing it."

Customers come and go buying coffees and cakes until they hang the *Closed* sign at noon. An antique till that rings up pounds, shillings and pence, pings regularly. Ettie spins a spiel about the new ownership while she warms the milk.

Come back next week, she invites, when the new menu will be up and running and the burgers will be made from fresh lamb mince, seared over high heat and dusted with allspice and cinnamon to give them a kick. She'll top them with yoghurt, mint and cucumber, a little tamarind chutney, and she'll lie them elegantly on crisp butter lettuce fanned on toasted Turkish bread because it has more oomph than traditional buns. There'll be a sign chalked on a blackboard in the Square, she adds, when they're fully up and running. Keep an eye out, okay?

Halfway through the afternoon grind the Three Js – Judy, Jane and Jenny – pitch up with buckets and rubber gloves. "Point and we'll scrub," says Judy. "We've got a few spare hours." The chat is nonstop. Ideas get tossed, discussed, discarded or written on Ettie's list.

"We could do with some of your special harissa and tamarind chutney," Ettie says to Jenny. "Be great on the burgers."

"Maybe, if stocks were guaranteed, we could set up an area to display and sell local produce," Kate suggests quietly. "Create our own label?"

Jenny looks at Kate thoughtfully. "Fannie has been bored rigid since she retired. She makes a silky smooth pâté from organic chicken livers, bacon and brandy that's wicked. Want me to ask her if she's interested as well?"

Ettie nods. The chat fires up again. No one hears the stealthy arrival of the *Mary Kay*.

Sam is dressed for hard labour in heavy khaki cotton shorts with a long-sleeve flannel shirt over his blue singlet. A worn leather tool bag is slung at his waist. He scans the deck, the water. There's no sign of Jimmy. He holds back a sigh and starts stacking tables and chairs in a corner near a couple of dead trees in large terracotta pots. Cigarette butts, some still wearing lipstick, are jammed in the soil. Filthy habit, smoking, he reminds himself, fighting the urge to roll his own.

He yanks down a piece of sagging trellis and chucks it on the growing pile of rubbish from the café. A couple of days ago, the neglect and decrepitude were so familiar he barely noticed it. Today, it's an eyesore. His face softens at the sight of his canary-yellow barge, glittering like a golden slipper at the end of the deck. One day, he thinks, The Briny will be restored to her former glory. He hopes Bertie lives to see it.

On the water, a tinny crashes and bangs, going too fast over a rising chop. He watches the hoon through narrowed eyes. The bow rises, points at a blue sky, then snaps flat on water as hard as glass. Thwack. Thwack.

"Dead meat within the year," Sam mutters, his brow knotted, then: "Ah bugger. It's Jimmy. That kid's got one speed and it's flat out." He shakes his head in despair.

Jimmy surfs to a standstill alongside Kate's boat and the huge surge of a following wake splashes alarmingly over the pot-holed pontoon. Sam waits for it to sink but it struggles and rights. The kid rafts up and roars along the ramp in flapping red board shorts covered with yellow lightning strikes that match his top. Arms wave. Legs fly. He's like a firecracker going off in all directions. His hair remains ramrod stiff.

"I'm here, Sam. Just like I said. How's Tilly? She back yet?" He screeches to a halt a handspan short of Sam's nose.

"What did I tell you about turtles and speed, mate? Have a

good think before you say anything because right now I'm so mad I could push you into the water, fancy clothes and all."

Jimmy's euphoria dissolves. He knuckles his forehead, trying to think where he's gone wrong. His feet tap-dance with worry.

"Ah mate," Sam says, ditching a long lecture because he's fully aware the kid just plain forgot, "Tilly's not back yet. She's got to have surgery and then . . . physio. Yeah. Physiotherapy, would you believe it? It'll be a while before she's fit enough to return."

Realising a tricky moment has passed, Jimmy brightens. "What's she gotta have physio for, Sam?"

"Because she does!" he says, almost losing patience. "Let's go, mate. We've got work to do."

"What work, Sam? Where do we start? I'm ready, aren't I? Didn't I say so?" Jimmy bounces off the deck rails like they're elastic bands. "What d'ya want me to do, Sam?"

Suppressing a sigh, Sam drapes an arm around Jimmy's gristly neck and scruffs his sticky hair. Then wipes his fingers on his backside, his nose wrinkled in disgust. "Right, mate. Follow me. Good to have you aboard. You got any work clothes with you, or you going to prance around like —" Sam breaks off.

"Like what, Sam?" Jimmy asks anxiously, eyes cast down, dragging his bare toes along the splintered timber of the deck. His cheeks are so red his freckles disappear altogether. He's been picked on, Sam thinks, for his highly individual, but nevertheless impressively *creative* choice of clothing.

"Like a, a . . . handsome stallion, mate. You look down-right sartorial." He grins widely to show approval. Jimmy beams right back. He has no idea what Sam has just said, but picks up it's a compliment.

"These *are* me work clothes, Sam. I'm ready, aren't I? Didn't I say so?"

They get down to business. Sam chalks some dodgy planks while Jimmy, his face serious, sticks so close Sam can smell the sickly scent of raspberry jelly frogs on his breath and catches glimpses of a red-stained tongue. He wonders if that's all the kid's had for breakfast and makes a mental note to ask the Three Js to keep a closer eye on him.

"Here," he says, passing Jimmy the chalk. "I'll point. You cross. Got that?"

"Point where, Sam?"

"Put a cross there, mate, right where my finger is." He thumps his index finger on a plank. "Ouch! Jeez." He tears what was left of a fingernail with his teeth and spits it into the water. "Now, a cross here. Press hard so we can see it plain as day."

"Am I doin' okay, Sam?" Jimmy tap-dances anxiously again.

Sam draws in a long breath and decides to go with the flow. Wear it away. One step at a time. "Yeah, Jimmy, you're doing a treat. Bloody impressive, mate. No question."

The kid makes a mark, breaks the chalk, but his face burns with pride. For a whole second, he manages to keep his bare feet still.

With the *Closed* sign firmly in sight to deter any hopefuls, Ettie and Kate are revved. Kate has a growing list of improvements, none of them urgent, except for replacing some rotting floorboards near the front counter and under one of the fridges. They agree they can reopen fully by the middle of the following week, then perhaps make the Saturday the official reopening day.

"That top deck," Kate says, wringing a cloth.

"Yeah?" Ettie rocks back on her heels, a strand of sweat-damp hair in her eyes, and closes the oven door with satisfaction.

"It would make a drop-dead gorgeous apartment. Not huge, mind you, and a bit basic until we can give it a proper renovation. The view would make up for a few rough edges for a while, though. What do you think?"

Ettie pushes herself to her feet, not quite sure where Kate is heading. "Hard to rent out. The only access is through the café."

"I meant for *you*, Ettie," Kate says softly, leading her to the table they've set under the stairs for an office. Pulling out a chair for her.

Ettie's heart flutters and a thousand emotions cross her face at once. The unfamiliar sensation of being cared for instead of caring for others makes her feel slightly dizzy. She falls heavily onto the seat, unable to speak.

Misreading the silence, Kate rushes on: "I know it looks like a dump right now, but a coat of paint would work wonders. There's a bathroom. Well, a loo and a shower, but they work. A storeroom where a small bed would fit. The main room would take a table, a sofa, a desk – whatever. There's already a kitchen area. A bit basic and shabby, but with everything you need downstairs, it would probably do. And no more steps,

Ettie. No more steps to climb at the end of a long day."

Ettie reaches towards Kate, lays a hand lightly on her arm. "I don't know what to say."

"Yeah, well, you made me the best offer I've ever had in my life. Good fortune goes round, Ettie. I never thought so before, but it's the truth. How about you put your feet up for a few minutes and I'll make a cuppa while you have a serious think?"

Suddenly the sound of hammering comes from the deck. Kate looks at Ettie, raises her eyebrows.

"No idea," Ettie shrugs and stands up, stretching her back.

They walk outside to see a bear of a man and a long, skinny kid on their knees, their backs bent, measuring, sawing, fitting and nailing while the sweat runs down their faces.

Without glancing up from his hammering, Sam asks for a couple of coffees. "Er, on second thoughts, make it one. Jimmy! What d'ya want to drink?"

"Coffee, Sam. Like you," he shouts, directly in Sam's ear.

Sam winces. "I'm not deaf, mate. Not yet, anyway."

"But I don't understand . . ." Ettie is pink with embarrassment. There's no money for renovations or even repairs until they are established and have a fairly accurate idea of what they can expect in profits or, God forbid, losses.

"Had some timber cluttering up my foreshore for too long. You've done me a favour by using it. I'm grateful to you." He slams in a nail with a single mighty strike. Jimmy passes him another nail from a leather bag that's in danger of sliding off his pencil-slim hips. "Jarrah, if given the chance," Sam adds, "will mature like wine and see out two centuries. So it should do you for a while." He straightens.

With the sun behind him, he's haloed like a saint in a medieval painting. Or maybe she's hallucinating, Ettie thinks. Too much, too fast. She's having trouble keeping up.

He puts his great battered paws on her shoulders and turns her gently towards the café. "Coffee, love. It's bloody thirsty work. And maybe water for Jimmy as well."

When Ettie is gone, Kate steps out of the shadows, hands in her pockets. "This can't be a one-way deal, Sam."

Sam sucks his teeth. His chin thrusts forward. "Coffee for life. How's that, then? Satisfy you?"

"Mmm. How many a day do you think that would be?"

He's about to explode when he sees the humour in her eyes. "Jeez. You nearly had me going!"

"How about a daily muffin – one only – as well. And only for a limited time. One month, okay?"

"There you go," he groans. "Overdoing it. I'll let you get away with it this time, long as you promise not to keep upping the ante when a bloke's only being a friend and neighbour."

"Deal," she says, holding out a slim hand to seal it.

Two hours later, Sam surveys a deck that suddenly looks firmer, straighter and safer. "Almost five-star," he crows. "A satisfactory day. Might have a go at those shocker chairs next. Jimmy, you think you could give me a hand tomorrow?"

"What are we gonna do, Sam?"

"Yes or no? Plain and simple."

"What'd I wanna say no for?"

"Aagh!" But Sam can't hide his smile. "Good on ya, mate. Now go and say goodbye to Ettie, and if you whomp that tinny home, I'll tan your backside. Don't think I won't know if you speed up round the other side of the Island, either. Eyes in the back of me head, the top of me head and the side of me head, so trust me, I'll know."

CHAPTER THIRTEEN

When word of Ettie's new partner spreads amongst the community, the only happy camper is Jack the Bookie, who hasn't had to pay out on a single bet. An historic result. Understandably, he is the only resident who approves of Ettie's choice, although no one's had a chance to ask Fast Freddy for his opinion because he's still sound asleep after his night shift. Freddy's judgement, anyway, is suspect. A growing body of people believe the shy man with a good heart and even better manners has a full-blown crush on the woman. No one can quite understand why he should feel this way. Although now that Ettie has shown such extraordinary faith in her – and Ettie's nobody's fool even though her emotions run away with her occasionally – they all intend to have a much closer look at what makes Kate tick. Maybe they'll drop in to help with the clean-up. Or drop off a spare chair or two to replace the shockers on the deck. Kill two birds with one stone, eh?

When the Kate debate eventually wanes, the conversations on the *Seagull* swing around to another favourite topic: food. With the fireshed dinner set for that night, there is widespread curiosity about how the once-famous, retired chef from Kingfish Bay with his fancy recipes will perform under the pressure of the community's scrutiny. The dinner, after all, is a fundraiser and cooks are judged as much on the quality of the food as the amount left in the kitty after all costs are deducted.

The general consensus is that the sweet, pearly pink flesh of the planned ocean trout is expensive, defeating half the purpose of the get-together. The chef will lose a heap of overall points if profits plummet. Even if the food is right up there with the flamboyant creations of those volatile French chefs who are said to live and die by the number of stars next to their name. Mind you, everyone agrees, the people of Cook's Basin are a forgiving lot and it's guaranteed the new chef will be given another go until he gets it right. Heh, heh.

No one is in the least concerned that the fireshed facilities, which consist of an oven rescued from the tip, a single sink, hot water boiled in a rusty urn, and discarded crockery and cutlery from the past century, might cause him grief. Rain, hail, sleet, snow or a blow that lifts the roof off the kitchen annex and the lids off the pots – in Cook's Basin you take what comes. It's how you separate the ninnies from the nongs.

Jack the Bookie considers running a book on the evening's performance but in the end he can't be bothered. Sometimes it's wiser to quit while you're ahead.

*

That evening, under a starry sky and on grass browning off with the lack of spring rain, the residents' meeting attracts the biggest crowd since the day a newly arrived fat-cat put forward a plan to open fire tracks through the National Park. A big man with a low-flying stomach, he was confident his offer to throw large amounts of his personal fortune into a legal battle for private vehicle access to offshore homes would be met with universal approval. And a suitable amount of gratitude for raising the value of their properties. His appearance at the fireshed was met with howls of fury as the local population bore down on him like rabid dogs and he took off never to be seen again. His house went on the market not long afterwards. Profit, everyone agreed, was pointless unless you wanted to sell. And who the hell would want to leave Cook's Basin?

Sam and the two Misses Skettle arrive on the *Mary Kay* a few minutes early, surprised by the numbers already gathered in colourful masses and taking up positions on white plastic chairs set out in wriggly lines on the hard ground. He gallantly hands the women off the barge, making sure their ankle-length, hot-pink taffeta skirts don't catch on the bollards.

"You're looking magnificent, ladies, if you'll permit me to say so," Sam says with a slight bow.

"Well, little Sammy, when we're on a date we try to look our best."

"You're not staying for the fireshed nosh-up, then?" He sounds shocked.

"Of course we are. *You're* our date." They giggle like teenagers and tiptoe along the uneven jetty in their matching pink slippers with kitten heels.

"Just checking you haven't dumped me for a younger bloke," he calls after them.

He adjusts the collar of his clean red polo shirt, brushes dust off his dark blue shorts and makes his way to the fireshed in a pair of light tan boat shoes. As sartorial as Jimmy, he tells himself. But perhaps lacking a little of the boy's instinctive pizzazz.

"Ah gidday, Kate," he says, spotting her hovering slightly apart from Ettie's group of women friends. She has a glass of, jeez, *water*, in her hand. "You owe me a coupla beers."

Under normal circumstances – when the meeting's agenda would include septic tanks, drainage problems, lack of tie-up facilities at public wharves, boat vandalism, the relocation of uninvited death adders or an announcement of auditions for the next Island musical – it would take at least half an hour for everyone to pour a drink, catch up and settle down. Tonight, however, the instant snap to attention is a sign of the significance of the problem facing the community.

The president, an endlessly patient and pragmatic man, who collects local art and spends most weekends polishing his treasured timber putt-putt, stands behind the wonky trestle table. He puts forward a motion to have the Weasel castrated, drizzled with honey and laid out on an ants' nest with a stake through his chest. It is meant as a joke. So he calls for restraint a little hysterically when the motion is seconded by a show of fifty hands all volunteering to do the deed. He thumps the table so hard it almost topples.

The meeting begins in earnest.

The Misses Skettle, in firm voices, read from a carefully prepared report that gives every last detail of activity at the Weasel's boatshed, including winds and tides – but refrains from naming names. It is so comprehensive, Sam decides there's no need to present the findings of his own night-long stake-out.

A retired cop is asked for his advice, but is quickly cut off when he suggests employing the services of a hit man who owes him a couple of favours. All the Island mothers offer to boil the Weasel alive in an old tank at the top of the Island. Everyone offers to help collect wood for the fire.

The audience is told that if it has anything to add that is based on fact, not fantasy nor a wishlist, each person has two minutes to speak. Even the usual troublemakers toe the line instead of ranting about noisy teenage parties, bad behaviour on the school ferry, dogs in feral packs or the rising problem of queue jumpers hitting the water main since the current dry spell kicked in.

The end result however is unanimous. The Weasel will be given one warning by the president. If it is ignored, the police will be informed that they believe he is selling and supplying prohibited substances to underage children and seriously undermining the delicate social structure of Cook's Basin family life. The aye-ayes ring out forcefully and everyone adjourns to the bar with relief just as the moon begins to rise, casting golden rungs across the bay, like a ladder to the black night sky.

At 7.45 p.m. when there's still no sign of Marcus Allender, the Kingfish Bay chef who is solely in charge of the evening's fare, there are a few nervous faces. He is still an enigma in the community – a man who is sometimes seen passing mysteriously through the Square in a fancy suit and smart shoes (crocodile, or a good imitation of it). But he certainly loves his fishing. Hot, cold, wet or windy, he's out there with his line, which counts for a lot in Cook's Basin.

Fifteen minutes after eight, his boat drifts alongside the seawall on a conveniently high tide. A brigade of men put down their beers to help carry to the kitchen twelve white Styrofoam boxes emitting a deliciously tantalising aroma.

Bob, the wiry, unflappable chief of the volunteer fire brigade, encourages the chef with a friendly pat on the back, then slopes off to run the bar, where the queue for a frigidly cold is already ten-deep.

No one is prepared for what happens next.

The chef, a tall man with shaggy silver hair, a lightly tanned face and soft brown eyes, emerges from the fireshed loo in blizzard-white trousers, a white double-breasted jacket with a black kerchief tied at his throat, and a soaring toque.

The crowd falls silent. Struck dumb. People watch, mesmerised, while he dusts off his hands and opens the fridge door with a theatrical flourish. Ready to go about his business. Then an agonised yowl carries clear across the bay. Every neighbourhood dog, locked at home so they don't snaffle the kids' sausage rolls out of their hands, joins in a chorus of frustration.

"There is no room for my berry jellies!" the chef yells in distress, a few silver hairs escaping from the clutch of his quivering hat. "The fridge is full of *beer*!"

Ettie, Judy, Jane and Jenny, who are sharing a Thermos of icy margaritas, roll their eyes and emerge from the crowd like sisters-in-arms. They politely offer assistance in a way that's meant to make the chef feel like he's back in his state-of-the-art, three-star kitchen with a bevy of anxious acolytes to boss around.

He responds immediately. "Remove the beer," he orders. "Bring me platters. Set the tables. Unwrap the ocean trout from the foil, with care, with care! Don't rip the flesh. We must hurry before the fish is cold and the jellies warm!"

When he shows no sign of calming down, they insist he takes a large gulp of Ettie's cocktail, purely as a restorative tonic. Ettie is then quietly assigned the task of whisking him out of the kitchen – no mean feat – and taking him on a leisurely walk. The women plan to have the dinner served well before his return for they instinctively know that the first person to ask the chef for a double helping, or sauce *on* instead of *beside*, will get his head bitten off.

Ettie obligingly takes the chef's surprisingly soft hand in hers and leads him to the water's edge. She instructs him to take off his rubber-soled shoes so they can go for a quiet paddle in the cool water of the bay. She removes his toque herself, with great tenderness and care. The jellies will be kept cool in an icebox, she assures him with such calm sincerity that he falls under her spell and trusts her completely. She stands his toque carefully on the seawall, like a marker to show the way back.

By the time they reach the far side of the bay, eighty people are seated at ten trestle tables covered in red gingham cloths. Candlelight dances over their faces. They murmur appreciatively about the moist fish, the heavenly balance of the herbs in the salsa verde and the aioli, so superbly light everyone knows the chef must have whipped it by hand.

When they return – the chef so tall he's forced to duck under the coloured carnival lights strung between casuarinas – the diners rise to their feet in thunderous applause.

"My name," bellows the chef, "is Marcus Allender. Once I had a restaurant called Stretton's. Now I am retired but I love to cook. Thank you for allowing me tonight." He beams at the diners, his eyes glistening. Then, to everyone's delight, he bends his long, solid but not overweight body in a formal bow. He straightens and applauds the diners with a slow clap that echoes in the still night. That's how it's done at the end of a gala dinner in Paris, someone whispers.

When the moment is over and conversations fire up once more, Marcus whips off his jacket, whisks out a chair for Ettie, and tells her to sit while he personally serves her dinner. She is a saint, he tells her passionately. She saved his life, his reputation, tonight. He had forgotten the pressure, the stress of cooking large quantities. And he wanted so much to show his appreciation for the people of Cook's Basin. How they preserve a way of life that is unique, hold strong to values and principles under the pressures of modern life. He firewalks across the stony ground towards the kitchen until someone is quickly dispatched to fetch his shoes from the seawall. And his toque.

Ettie's dinner – fleshy pink trout, new baby potatoes swizzled in a lemon, butter and parsley sauce, three spears of luminous asparagus, four thumb-sized, deep red, halved tomatoes, green sauce and creamy aioli – is a still life.

"The colours," she whispers in awe, "the arrangement, the balance. I would rather paint this than eat it."

The chef nods warmly and takes her hand. He smells, she thinks, of limes. Underneath that heady scent, she catches a whiff of strawberries that she supposes he's poached in sugar syrup and then drained through muslin to make the jelly. He watches as she chews and swallows every mouthful with appreciation. Then he wipes the dregs off her plate with his finger and licks it clean, his eyes locked on hers. She visibly swoons.

On the morning following the fireshed dinner, Ettie arrives at the café a little later than 6 a.m. for the first time since the day she became the proprietor. Nursing a slight headache, a rosy flush and a faraway look in her eyes, she potters around her workspace, enjoying the peace and pleasure of ownership. Once or twice she finds herself staring dreamily up at the cross-beamed timber ceiling as though she still can't believe how this shabby but amazing jewel has been delivered into her hands.

After a while, she checks the time and gets to work, hoping everyone's having a good sleep-in after a late night. She reaches for a mixing bowl from a high shelf, weighs and measures ingredients she knows by heart, tosses in two punnets of syrupy raspberries and folds the batter for her trademark muffins. At the last minute – and inspired, she admits, by the great chef – she grates a little lemon rind into the mixture before ladling it into four, six-hole trays. She opens the oven and stops, puzzled. She is certain she turned it on. It is the mandatory first step in her daily routine. How her working day begins. She panics, thinking the oven is broken and will have to be replaced at great expense. But she flicks the switch, a red light glows, the fan whirrs and heat rises. You're off in la-la land, Ettie, she says to herself. He is probably married. They always are.

There'd been a man who broke through all her defences. Not quite a drifter but near enough to one. He had golden skin, golden hair and lion eyes. He cooked splendid breakfasts on Sunday mornings and brought them to her while she lay in bed. They'd read the weekend papers side by side, swapping sections. She'd let him hang his polo shirts in her wardrobe and store his tennis racquets in the broom cupboard. One humid summer night, he threw back the sheet, pulled on his clothes, grabbed his racquets and without a word walked out the door.

After him, she'd let one or two into her bed when an occasional bout of skin hunger overrode her commonsense. A fool's game. By and large, she didn't much care for the way men shifted the goalposts every time the going got rough or tedious. It meant you never quite knew where you stood from one day to the next – and if there was one thing she valued, it was constancy. Sam, who is like a brother, she thinks, has been the most constant person in her life. If she'd been born twenty years earlier . . . She scraps the thought. Only fools indulge in *what if* games.

Then she firmly puts the chef out of her mind.

While she waits for the oven to heat she steps out on the deck to clear her head, woolly from too many cocktails and the almost forgotten thrill of flirting. She breathes in the cool morning air, ripe with the smell of oysters, brine and wet sand. In the distance, Kate's boat slices through the water in a way that looks almost competent. Ettie smiles. She knew she'd be a quick learner.

She goes back inside to make two coffees, one so strong it restores her commonsense. She slides the muffins into the hot oven with unnecessary force and cranks up the morning pace. By the time Kate walks in, looking as fresh as you'd expect from a woman who drank water instead of wine last night, she's washed up and made them both a bowl of fresh peaches and muesli. She dollops on a large spoonful of plain yoghurt spiked with honey perfumed by the masses of glorious white blossoms that cover Tasmanian leatherwoods in late spring.

"Yum," says Kate. "If I'd known breakfast could be this good, I would've started eating it years ago."

They dine on the sunny deck in the peace and quiet of the early morning, then Kate retreats to the attic to make it fit for Ettie's new home. She is methodical, logical, and carefully puts aside old pieces she thinks can be restored.

Quite quickly a huge pile of junk builds up outside the café door. Ettie tells Kate not to worry about disposal. It will be enthusiastically scrounged by offshore artists who are able to turn the most miserable rubbish into art. Chipped china, busted chairs, dead toasters and old signage. When Kate holds up a stinking piece of felt carpet she's ripped off the floor, with a question in her eyes, Ettie indicates it should also join the heap. "Fantastic for covering worm farms and compost bins," she explains.

Soon the attic is an empty, wide-open space. Kate scrubs the yellow bathroom tiles back to their original whiteness, takes the loo seat apart, plunging every screw, nut and bolt in a bucket of bleach. She scours a rust stain from a leaking cistern until it gleams. And then fixes the leak. She washes windows, wipes walls and skirting boards so forcefully paint flakes off like dandruff. Finally, she sweeps, mops and polishes. There are a few gaps in the walls between the planks, only one big enough to call a hole. Nothing that can't be fixed.

It is taking shape. It will be beautiful.

Ettie's penthouse.

Downstairs Ettie, who has been baking fiercely, carefully removes a tray of coin-sized golden biscuits from the oven, slides them onto a wire rack and leaves them to cool. She returns to the table under the stairs, now covered in recipe books, and goes back to her lists. To be absolutely accurate, she uses a calculator to increase portions to suit café requirements. By the end of the day, she will have sorted out the basic menu, the daily specials, the rotation of different cakes and the takeaway choices for anyone getting home too tired or too late to cook.

At the last minute, she decides to add a chicken bolognaise sauce, simmered with the rinds of parmesan to give it richness. Perfect for harried mums to throw over pasta when they're caught short by sick kids or a plain old dose of exhaustion.

Late in the afternoon, the two women sit, drinking their tea, the last niggling uncertainties vanishing with the completion of each new task. Every fresh idea.

The old café signs, liberated from where they'd been tossed in the attic, are wiped clean of cobwebs and grime and tell a story of the old days. *General Store, Takeaway Food, Souvenirs, Hireboats, Dockside Dining, Post Office. Est. January 1st. 1899, Coffee Lounge.*

The small grocery area, where the local cooks will sell their preserves, is taking shape. A jar will be placed on the counter for contributions to community projects. A blackboard will announce upcoming events.

Ettie believes there is a market for takeaway curries and celebration cakes made to order. Kate is certain weekenders could be encouraged to order pre-prepared party food: light lunches, picnics and three-course dinners. She will do the costing, set the prices and print menus on flyers they will display on the counter. Perhaps Jimmy might like to take on a job doing deliveries, if required. As long as he knows he's not allowed to speed. Or go naked.

"We're just about ready, although the place doesn't exactly sparkle," Ettie says.

"Old buildings like this are rare and full of character. They don't have to sparkle," Kate reassures her firmly. "You know what's really weird?" she says, leaning against the staircase, mug cupped in her hands, and not a speck of dirt on her anywhere.

"Mmm?" The throbbing pain in Ettie's feet is reducing to a dull ache. In half an hour she'll get a second wind but right now she could close her eyes and fall straight to sleep.

"My father was born and raised in a country town. His parents owned the corner store. Remove the sea and coast, and this could almost be a copy. He would have loved The Briny."

"When he died, is that when your mum got so . . . angry?"

"She's a disaster of her own making, Emily. Never been any different and nothing short of a hurricane could topple her. She's going to faint when she finds out about the café. It's everything she loathes. As a kid, I remember her standing behind the counter, not a hair out of place. With such a temporary, one-foot-out-the-door look about her, she set the locals on edge whenever they came in for a loaf of bread. Eventually, she talked Dad into moving to the city."

"Good or bad?"

"Neither. But nothing was ever the same. The awful irony is that if they'd kept the place, it would probably have morphed into one of those *character* country cafés you now find everywhere. Emily's not known for her patience, though. Nearly seventy and she still hurtles like she's constantly late for an appointment."

"Bring her in one day, and we'll see if we can soften a few edges," Ettie says, getting to her feet, ready to plod on. "Just give me a day's warning, okay? So I can brace myself."

Not long before locking up the café, all hell breaks loose in the Square.

The two women rush outside. "Oh God," Ettie moans. "It's Jimmy. He's off his face."

His face tomato-red the teenage boy ricochets off walls, slams into tables, kicks seats. His eyes are scared and violent at the same time.

A grey-haired tourist watches from the ferry wharf. A couple of young mothers grab the mail from their postboxes and shake their heads, shepherding their babies safely out of range. A group of joggers stop and watch. Like it's street theatre.

"He's out of control. Nothing anyone can do till he sleeps it off," one of them says matter-of-factly. He throws back his head and slugs water from a flask pulled from his belt. "You going to call the cops?" he asks Ettie.

"He's an offshore kid. We'll sort this out."

Jimmy seizes a table and tries to hurl it against the café wall. The bolts hold firm. Tears are streaming down his twisted face, snot runs into his mouth. He looks confused. Lost. Disoriented. He kicks garbage bins, whirls in circles, bangs his head against the café wall. Blood streams from his nose. It is pandemonium.

Ettie tiptoes towards him and puts out her hand. "Jimmy?" Without a word or a hint of recognition, he lets out a gut-wrenching sob and crumples into a pile of skin and bones on the ground.

"He needs an ambulance," Kate says, reaching for her mobile phone.

Ettie slips her palm beneath Jimmy's head and cradles it gently while she scuttles into a sitting position. "Call Sam," she says, "he'll manage." She bunches her skirt to make a cushion and settles the bloodied mess of his face into her lap. Stroking his head, she croons, "It's okay. You'll be okay." Skinny white legs stick out like dowelling from his hibiscus-printed board shorts. Ettie hums, waving away offers of help. Jimmy never stirs.

Minutes later Sam pounds up the jetty and kneels beside the kid, running his hands over his limbs like a doctor. He presses open the lid of one eye then the other. Jimmy groans, focuses for a second. A helpless look of trust in his eyes.

"Jeez, Jimmy. You're pushing all the wrong buttons, mate." His voice is gentle. Inside he's raging. He worms his arms under the kid's shoulders, about as solid as a chicken carcass. "Ready?" Ettie nods. They half-drag, half-carry Jimmy's deadweight towards the *Mary Kay*. A sneaker leaves a long white streak of rubber like a skid mark at the scene of an accident. One drops off. Kate picks it up and follows.

Jimmy makes a gurgling sound.

"You're okay, mate. No permanent damage. You're an idiot, know that? I'd be shoving a fist in your nose myself if I'd caught you with any of the shit that's done this to you." But he knows the kid's been tricked. He'd never waste his money on drugs. Every cent he earns, Jimmy tells him like a cracked record, is one cent closer to owning a car. They lower him tenderly to the deck of the *Mary Kay*.

Jimmy opens his eyes. The naked vulnerability rips something deep inside Sam. "Tilly comin' home soon?" the boy manages through a broken smile.

"How'd you get like this, Jimmy? Where have you been today?"

"Visitin', Sam. Near Triangle."

"That arsehole with the fancy boatshed," Sam hisses through clenched jaws. "He's dead meat."

He scrounges a blanket from the hold and tucks it under Jimmy's chin: "You've just signed on as chief mate on the *Mary Kay*. Which means bed and board for the foreseeable future. I'm not letting you outta my sight till your mum comes home. No buts. No bloody questions, either, for a change. And just so you know, I'm going to work your skinny arse off."

Boag crawls forward on his stomach, licks the blood on Jimmy's legs. Jimmy's hand reaches out from under the greasy blanket and rubs the dog's soft ear between two fingers. The mutt curls against the bony body with a satisfied harrumph.

"I'm running an orphanage. That's what. A freaking floating orphanage of waifs and strays," Sam mutters, looking at the two of them. He fetches his favourite red cushion from the banquette in the wheelhouse and tucks it under Jimmy's head.

CHAPTER FOURTEEN

Treetops are black lace against the silver sheen of a predawn sky. Sam rises from his tangled sheets and shuffles down the bare boards of the narrow hallway. He opens the door to the spare bedroom – yellow light streaks across the floor. Jimmy, his face black and blue, is cleaned up, sleeping peacefully. The mutt, ears pricked, is tucked tightly into the crook of the kid's bent legs.

Sam goes back to his bedroom to dress. By the time he steps outside into a morning smelling of dry eucalyptus and dust, the kookaburras are firing up and the white cockatoos are preparing for their ear-splitting turn. The noise, he thinks, should wake the dead but the Island sleeps on. He walks along the high track, avoiding the worst potholes.

A small, tangled rear garden of lantana backs onto the public track from the Weasel's house. The gate is securely bolted and padlocked. Sam vaults it easily. He walks without stealth to the closed door at the top of four pavilions connected by covered stairways and knocks loudly enough to be heard. When no one appears, he tries the door. Locked. He slips a credit card from his pocket and slides it between the lock and the doorjamb. The handle turns and he enters a kitchen. Clean. Tidy. No scent of cooking. Unused, probably. Sam moves on, quietly opening and closing doors.

He locates the Weasel in the third pavilion, sleeping in a tight ball on a bed the size of a football field. Fists clenched and naked except for a pair of black silk boxers. There's a rug on the floor striped black and white like the coat of a zebra, a chest of drawers, one half-opened with T-shirts spilling out. A pair of black flip-flops has been kicked off untidily by the side table. Floor-to-ceiling windows catch the view, straight up Blue Swimmer Bay, to a waterfall dry from the lack of serious rain. While Sam stands watching, the Weasel mumbles and turns over, suddenly restless. Without opening his eyes, he fumbles for the sheet, feeling a cool shift in the air, perhaps, from the open door.

"Hate to wake you with bad news," Sam says, like they've just run into each other at the mailboxes in the Square.

The Weasel shoots up, holding the sheet against his throat, one side of his hair flat against his skull. His chest and back are covered in a thick coat of curling black hair. He looks like a trapped animal.

"What the fuck —"

"Am I doing here?" Sam finishes.

"Get out, you mongrel. Or I'll call the cops."

Sam undoes the top pocket of his shirt and offers his mobile.

"Be my guest," he says, "although this won't take long."

The Weasel is fully awake now. He reaches for a T-shirt

under his pillow and slips it quickly over his head. Ruffles his hair into rough order. "Mate, mate. What's this about? I don't even know you. What's the problem?" His tone is conciliatory. Like they're old friends and it's all a misunderstanding.

He reminds Sam of a crocodile he once saw in the far north. A fat-bellied beast that lay submerged, except for empty eyes that followed every move. Sizing him up, patiently waiting for an opportunity. Lethal and sleazy at the same time.

The Weasel swings his legs onto the floor. "You wanna tell me what's going on?" he says, still placatory.

"Well, it's good that you asked," Sam says, his voice over-friendly. "Around here we see ourselves as a village. And in a close-knit village, we all look after each other. So we notice when the balance starts to look shaky. Mate, ever since you arrived, the balance has been very, very shaky. So pack your bags. Leave Cook's Basin. Crawl back into whatever sewer you came out of. End of story."

"You're nuts. A loony. Go home and sleep it off." The smarm has gone from his voice. He's dismissive. Unafraid now.

Sam shakes his head. "Blokes like you should never have been born. If you've got kids of your own stashed somewhere, I feel sorry for them." He walks across the polished floor, his heavy tread muted for a moment by the rug. "And stay away from Jimmy. Or I'll break your head."

The first thing Sam notices when he gets home is the dog sitting at the kitchen bench. On his own stool. Jimmy is next to him. On a different stool. The kid has a mountain of

Vegemite toast in front of him. So does the mutt. Jimmy has a mug of tea. The mutt has a saucer of tea. The Vegemite jar is scraped clean.

"That okay, Sam? No sugar for Boag?"

"Spot on, mate. How are you feeling?"

The kid's face is the colour of a gathering storm, but his clear eyes shine sweetly. He's showered and dressed in plain brown board shorts and an orange satin shirt that would radiate for miles across an open sea. He smiles at Sam to show he's good. Every so often, when the dog's furry backside slips on the stool, he shoots out a steadying hand and they resume chewing their breakfast.

"How's Tilly the turtle, Sam? When's she comin' home?"

"Soon, mate, soon." Sam grabs a mug out of a cupboard. The tea is still hot. The kid's remembered to use the tea-cosy. Sam places the last two slices of bread in the toaster and wonders if there's any jam in the fridge. He fixes his gaze on Jimmy. "When you're sorted, we've got a heap of work to do to help Ettie get ready for the opening of the café. You reckon you're up to it?"

Jimmy bends an arm at the elbow and flexes his biceps. A tiny lemon pops up under his blue-veined skin. With utter sincerity, he says: "I can do anything, Sam." The dog wags his tail and topples straight to the floor.

"Knew I could count on you, mate. On the deck in five minutes. Time to earn your keep. You know how to paint, don't you?"

"Yeah, Sam. I told ya, didn't I?"

"Nevertheless, it remains to be seen. Just remember. The paint goes on the walls. Nowhere else. Not the floor, the windows, the benches. Only the walls. And Jimmy, if it gets in your hair, you won't need to touch that poncy smelling gel for a month. Get my drift?"

"Be careful, is that it?"

"You got it. I'll get you started and then you're on your own."

"Ettie's gonna love it, isn't she, Sam?"

"No doubt about it. And jeez, clean your teeth, mate, before we go."

Outside in the fresh air, the sun glosses over night shadows and dusts the treetops with gold. A lyrebird runs through an impressive repertoire of imitation bird calls. Magpies. Parrots. Butcherbirds, and then a siren. It startles a few late sleepers out of their somnolence. The ferry master unhooks the *Seagull* from her mooring for the first morning run. A light goes on in the café. Sam breathes in the joyful, larrikin pulse of his chosen territory. You've got to look after your patch, he thinks. Or you lose it.

With very little direction or encouragement, Jimmy tackles the job of painting Ettie's new penthouse, as it is already known, with fierce concentration. To prepare, the serious-faced young man quickly whizzes sandpaper over surfaces in not quite logical order. But nevertheless meticulously. When everything is ready, he paints steadily and soundlessly except for the hiss and swish of the roller coating the walls in a soft off-white that Ettie chose from an old colour card she found in one of Bertie's drawers.

Jimmy is on the first adult mission of his life, trusted by

Sam – who regularly churns away from the café to pick up and deliver cargo – to do a thoroughly professional job without cutting any corners. The kid blossoms with a sense of purpose and the challenge of completing a task to the best of his ability.

"Where did you learn to paint?" Ettie asks when she calls the boy to morning tea.

"Me mum. She reckons changin' the colour of your house feels like a holiday but lasts longer and costs less."

"How's she doing, Jimmy? Home soon?"

"Christmas. How long is that, do ya know, Ettie?"

"Not long, love."

Ettie passes Jimmy a plate. He wolfs into a double-size slice of pale strawberry sponge, using the back of his paint-speckled hand to wipe the cream off his cheeks. The moment she turns away, he plucks a strawberry from the filling and wraps it in his hanky.

Kate, seated at the round table under the stairs where her laptop is now installed next to a printer, glances up. She catches what he's doing, shrugs, returns to trawling Bertie's list of suppliers, trying to figure out why quotes for virtually the same produce vary so widely. She decides it must come down to quality and begins ordering from the middle price range, figuring she can ramp up or scale down when they know more.

After lunch, Ettie announces she's off to a catering supply warehouse two suburbs away. She hopes to be back within three or four hours, with new cake stands, sandwich platters and oversize biscuit jars for the counter. She strips off her apron, powders her nose and waves goodbye, flicking over the *Closed* sign after her.

The moment she is out the door, Jimmy starts rootling through the large compost bin under the sink.

Kate goes over and touches his shoulder. "What are you doing, Jimmy?"

"Savin' it for Tilly the turtle," he explains. "For when she comes home."

"Ah. The strawberry, too, huh? What a kind thought. But how about we buy her fresh greens when we know she's on her way back here?" Kate suggests, easing the slimy hoard of food from his grip. "Only the best for Tilly, right?"

"Are ya sure, Kate?"

"Yes, Jimmy. It's a promise."

And off he scampers, spidery arms and legs flying, ascending the stairs three at a time, reaching the landing in four strides with barely a sound.

Not long after, the chef, Marcus Allender, stands to attention outside the café. He is casually but beautifully dressed in tan leather boat shoes, pressed fawn shorts that reach his knees and a navy polo shirt with a tiny green insignia embroidered over his left breast. In both hands, like a sacred offering, he holds a small box tied expertly with a red-and-brown ribbon. As though whatever it contains is so delicate, the smallest movement could break it. Kate opens the door.

He bows with a minuscule movement of his head but it is enough to send his lustrous silver hair flopping into his eyes.

"I am looking for Ettie. Yes? I was told I would find her here."

"I'm afraid you've just missed her. She's gone shopping," Kate says, unsure whether to invite him inside.

"Ah," says the chef, his face falling with disappointment.

"Is there anything I can do?" she asks. "My name is Kate, I'm Ettie's partner."

"Ah. Thank you." He looks at the box in his hands as if suddenly at a loss. "Does she understand chocolate?" he asks at last.

Kate smiles kindly and reaches for the gift. "Like a second language. I'll make sure she gets this. Do you have a phone number? I know she'll want to thank you. Come inside. I'll write it down."

The chef steps into the café, lifting his legs like a brolga, stepping over the threshold as though it is a gunnel. His nose twitches. "That terrible smell, the one of burnt coffee and grease, it is gone. Before, I could not come inside. Not even for a newspaper. My stomach, it pinched in despair."

"We've got a long way to go . . ." She breaks off.

He's wandering around, assessing the erratically shaped nooks and crannies, the old signage waiting to be hung, the timber floor worn smooth in places, the walls, the ill-fitting windows, even the ancient flywire door to the deck. A genuine plywood slammer from the kind of country town that boasted two pubs, one milkbar and a corner store.

"A gem," the chef announces, just when Kate is beginning to feel uncomfortable. "Do not change a thing. Not one thing." And without another word he turns on his heels, strides into the Square and disappears.

*

Late in the afternoon, Sam tidies and locks the cabin of the *Mary Kay*, and heads towards the Island. He's hoping that vagabond mutt, left at home for the day to stop him roaming the café, has kept his snout out of the Island chook pens and all the dog bowls left at back doors. Stomach like a bottomless pit. Eats every meal like it might be his last. Well, he *had* been dumped and forced to fend for himself . . .

Sam plans to call in on Lindy, the local real estate agent, to let her know that the Weasel will be leaving before too long. No need to go into details. Just a quiet word that the slimeball has found offshore life a little claustrophobic and he thinks he'll find more fulfilment somewhere else. She might want to knock on his door to suss out if there's a deal there for her.

He ties the barge at the end of his jetty and wanders a short distance along the honeycomb shoreline to Lindy's steps, pulling a few straggly bits of crofton weed before it spreads any further. He sees a thicket of Mother-of-Millions, ready to sprout on a brittle bank he'd cleared a year earlier. He curses and tells himself he's done his bit and can stride on with an easy conscience. Let some other lazy-arsed Islander have a turn.

Ah jeez, he thinks, it'll only take a second.

He spreads his feet, bends from the waist and begins easing the succulents out of the sandy soil.

"You giving up the barge to go into landscaping?" Lindy asks, coming down the steps. She is wearing gardening gloves and carrying a bag half-full of weeds. "Whack it in here," she says.

Sam stuffs the fleshy purple plants inside and takes it from her. "Just the person I want to see," he says, wiping his face with a bare arm. "Wanna tell me where to get rid of this?"

"Up the back. I'll put on the kettle."

"Prefer an icy cold beer. Only if you're askin' . . ."

"Might be able to find one," she says.

Lindy goes ahead and Sam takes a moment to enjoy the spectacle of the muscles in her smoothly tanned calves bunching as she climbs each step. She's a top sort. Unflappable. Cluey. Funny. Generous. Not a snotty bone in her body when anyone can see she and her husband are riding high on the sudden boom in offshore properties.

At the rear of the house, he lifts the lid off a compost bin, empties the bag. He feels a slight sting. Another. His legs begin to burn and itch. He strips off his shorts. Red lumps. Black dots. *Bloody ticks*. He dumps the bag and races into Lindy's kitchen in his jocks. "Covered in ticks, love. Hold the beer. Gotta go home."

"Have a bath filled with bicarb," Lindy advises without a twitch.

"Mate, I don't *have* a bath. You should know that, you sold me the bloody house."

"Oh. Yeah. That's right. Well, strip off and get into ours. I'll bring in some bicarb."

"You're a saint, Lindy. Always knew it. And if you've got that beer . . ." Sam scuttles towards the bathroom, ripping off his shirt. "Ah bugger, they're all over my chest. Better make it two beers, Lindy. One at a time, though, if you don't mind. Like 'em to stay cold. Then I'll tell you about a bloke who's planning to move on."

"Sure, Sam," she replies, thinking she'd make her husband fetch his own drinks no matter how many ticks he had.

Sam turns on the water full-bore, his old mantra – *No good turn goes unpunished* – playing in his head. Still, he's in a nice hot bath and about to enjoy a teeth-rattling cold ale. There is always an upside if you take the time to search for it.

Lindy knocks on the door. "You decent?"

"Nope."

She walks in and hands Sam a beer through the steam, ignoring his naked body.

"Here's a clean towel," she says, hanging it on a rail. "And the bicarb." She sprinkles it into the tub.

Sam, striped white where his socks, shorts and sleeves end, churns the water with hands like fins. The bicarb fizzes. The water turns satin smooth and thickens like a sauce. "Suffocate, you suckers," he orders, hooking the tiny seed ticks out of their burrows one by one with a ragged little fingernail, until his chest looks like a bout of teenage acne. "Thanks, love," he adds, suddenly bashful and holding off having a go at the ones in his groin. "If you weren't married to Jason, I'd be proposing marriage myself. He's a lucky man."

"Yeah. Tell him that every day," Lindy says, closing the door and thinking he looked like a stranded, red-spotted beetle. A rare breed. Like him. And the day he proposed any-thing beyond a moonlight barge ride to a sandy beach to any woman, she'd shout the whole volunteer fire brigade a round of drinks.

She hears a rush from an opened tap. "Easy on the water, Sam," she yells. "No telling when it's going to rain next." She wonders why anyone would want to sell on the brink of a languid, steamy, blue-bathed Cook's Basin summer.

*

Sam sips his icy beer. Condensation plops from the bottom of the bottle into the tub. He feels the hot water ease his muscles, take the sting out of the bites. Kings didn't live better than this, he thinks, giving in to the warmth and drifting into a beery doze.

The door swings open, whacking the side of the bath.

"Jason! Mate. Gidday." He lifts his beer in a friendly toast.

"Ah?"

"Just havin' a hot bath."

"Yeah. Well. Right." Jason hesitates.

"Want me to leave the water in for you?"

"No, mate. Er. Another beer?" he asks.

"Thanks, mate. Love one."

Jason finds his wife in the kitchen stirring a pot of chicken stew.

"Sam's in the bath," he says, trying not to make it sound like an accusation.

"Yeah. Probably ready for another beer. Take it in to him, love, would you?"

"No worries. Er. He staying long?"

"No. Just until he gets rid of the ticks."

"Ah." His face relaxes into boyishness. "Want me to find some of my clean clothes for him too?" Jason suggests, not meaning it and remembering too late that sarcasm is wasted on his wife.

"Good idea, love. Thanks."

Jason sighs, beaten. He kisses Lindy's cheek and inhales the rich scent of garlic and onions rising in a hot cloud from a bubbling mass. He squeezes her backside in appreciation. She puts down her wooden spoon, a smile playing at the corners of her mouth, and turns off the simmering pot.

"See yourself out, Sam," Jason yells, grabbing his wife's hand and leading her downstairs at a gallop.

"You had a visitor," Kate says, when Ettie returns at the end of the day.

Ettie lowers her shopping bags to the floor, a flush creeping up her neck. She pulls her hair into a ponytail and wraps it into a bun that quickly falls apart.

"He left something for you," Kate adds, pointing to the box. "I told him you were fluent in the language of chocolate."

"Marcus?" Ettie whispers, even pinker. She raises the box to her nose and inhales. "Ah, smell the bitterness? And Cointreau, maybe cassis or framboise as well."

"Open it!" Kate says, laughing.

Ettie lifts off the lid. There are six almost black handmade balls, silkily smooth and swirled to a breaking wave at the top. "Oh my God. This is *serious* chocolate. If I had to guess, I'd say he started by roasting his own beans. It would have taken at least two days to complete the process."

Kate peers inside. "He's keen. Definitely."

Ettie looks affronted. "Let me explain. First the beans have to be roasted, then cracked and winnowed. The cocoa is then cooked slowly with butter and sugar, never so hot it burns. Burnt chocolate seizes—"

"Okay, okay!" Kate holds up her hands in mock surrender.

"You're in the food business," Ettie says tersely. "Even in a café like ours, you need to know more than an egg comes from a chicken." She snatches a hefty volume from a shelf above her work table, bound in crimson cloth, faded to pink. "This is my bible, the accumulated knowledge of centuries of cooking. I suggest you start at the beginning. And no, I'm not sharing the chocolates. Not until you understand the effort, skill and, dare I say it, *affection* that went into making them. Now, did he leave a phone number?"

Speechless with the shock of feeling Ettie's disapproval for the first time, Kate points sheepishly at a yellow Post-it note stuck on the computer. "He declared the café a gem," she says, finding her voice.

"He did!" Ettie spins with excitement. "He really said that?"

"Yep. Don't change a thing. Those were his exact words."

Ettie sighs. The erratic hormones of middle-age notch up a couple of gears. It is the intimacy, she thinks, that she yearns for. The feel of another body alongside, skin on skin, loneliness swept away for a while at least.

Cook's Basin News (CBN)

Newsletter for Offshore Residents of Cook's Basin, Australia

DECEMBER

Offshore general clean-up

The next offshore general clean-up will take place on the week commencing December 15. Council is recycling electronic waste wherever possible. Electronic waste means TVs, computers, printers, scanners, DVD and VCR players, modems and gaming machines. An external waste contractor has been requested to carry out the following procedures: Collect any electronic wastes that are presented at the roadside or at offshore public/private wharves. The electronic wastes will then be transported to a nearby recycling and waste facility. All further enquiries are to be made to the Municipal Council Environmental Health Officer.

Volunteers Required

Now that Christmas (don't wince) is getting closer and closer, we are in need of cooking, craft and woodwork teachers to help our kids to make gifts to put under the tree. Anyone adept at making fishing flies is guaranteed a full class.

Materials supplied.

Call Lou.

Grand Reopening of The Briny Café

Ettie says there's not long to go before the official reopening of the café. She'd also like to advise that they are up and running, business mostly as usual from the middle of the week, so they can iron out any problems before opening day. Everyone is invited to call in and have a good squiz. One free coffee per person on opening day only. Accounted for by an honour system. (Take note, Seaweed.)

NAVY DIVERS

We have been advised by the navy that from this afternoon, there will be unmarked Navy divers in the vicinity between Knock's Point and Bearded Point for seven days, both day and night, excluding the weekend. The divers will be supported by three boats, a white Steber and two small black Zodiacs forming a triangle. It is requested that should you encounter these boats, you don't pass between them but pass astern of the last Zodiac. Should you require any further information, please contact Lieutenant James McFarlane through the Navy.

CHAPTER
FIFTEEN

With an overcast sky and the tinny smell of rain on the wind, the *Mary Kay* noses into the back deck of The Briny. Jimmy leaps out of the wheelhouse and scampers forward with the mutt nipping at his heels. He ties on and dashes back to the wheelhouse, raising his hand in a salute that almost pokes his eye out.

"You and the mutt. In the cabin. And don't move," Sam says. "You're on duty, mate, and we're a team, right?"

"Right," Jimmy says, dragging his banana-boat feet to attention.

Kate is on the deck of the café filling the terracotta tubs and a few old buckets with fresh soil and healthy plants. Snow White, Sam thinks, checking out her spotless trousers, shirt, apron, sandshoes. Bet she's still as pristine at the end of the day. In his experience, over-fastidious women rarely kept you toasty at night.

He rubs his hair with both hands in a dry wash, spits on his finger and smooths his eyebrows. He dusts off his singlet with greasy palms, brushes his shorts, bangs his boots on the gunnel to dislodge any mud and hops onto the back deck.

"This place is getting so toffy I'll have to dig out my funeral tie before long," he says to her.

"Ah. And there I was wondering if you were sprucing up for a hot date."

"Word is Ettie's a genius, which we all knew, and you're getting the knack, which we were all a bit doubtful of. Thought you'd like to know the lie of the land."

His mobile phone suddenly goes off like a drill in his pocket and without a word he heads back to the barge, pointing his finger at both bow and stern to let Jimmy know to untie.

Ettie waits a whole day to call Marcus to thank him for his gift. She tells herself anticipation is a large part of the thrill of romance and he will understand that fact. She tells herself that to rush forward without considering either of their pasts is foolish. She also tells herself that she is on the brink of a distraction that could demand more time than she can afford to give right now.

But the truth is, she is afraid. Afraid that when she lifts the phone and he answers, she will find the gift was to say thank you. Nothing else. That any other hopes or dreams are a figment of her imagination. And oh the horror, she thinks, of a word out of place that kills all possibility of more.

Eventually she dials his number, intending to say nothing beyond polite acknowledgement and thanks. He picks up on the first ring. "I have been waiting by the phone," he announces. And she knows all reason is gone and she is tumbling into whatever lies ahead. Without a thought for where it might lead.

Late in the afternoon, Marcus Allender strides into the café for the second time in his life. Hair uncombed, his khaki shirtfront smeared with blood and guts and his old boat shoes sodden. He holds a glistening silver kingfish high in the air like a trophy. "A noble fish deserves a noble end," he announces. "If you would do me the honour of dining with me tonight, Ettie, I will prepare this giant warrior in the way he deserves."

"You're turning into a flaming orator, mate," Sam says, wandering in behind him.

Marcus is euphoric, a man who's fought a great battle with a fish and emerged victorious. "And you, my friend, are also invited. We will make it a small party, yes? Kate, you must grace the table, too. I am a man on a winning streak. Impossible, therefore, to refuse."

Sam runs his tongue along a sun-split bottom lip. "Well, mate, reckon I'm up to it. If Kate's game. How about it?"

She nods. "Yeah. I'm game."

Marcus beams. "I have been out hunting and gathering to prepare a feast for you, Ettie."

The object of his affection stands mute behind the counter, unable to think of a single word to say to this wildly passion-ate man who is wooing her in such heroic ways. She smiles and nods.

Marcus does a funny little jig and disappears – only to return moments later with a gesture of apology. "Seven o'clock, please don't be late. Food spoils easily and can never be repaired."

"Rock up to the back door," Sam advises the two women when the chef is gone again. "I called on him to offer the services of the *Mary Kay* a few months ago and he told me that front doors were for bailiffs . . . Anyway, I came in to tell you Jimmy's done upstairs. You can move whenever you're packed and ready."

Ettie, who once again feels like her world is speeding beyond her control, collapses in the office chair so heavily the wheels take off. She rolls across the café until she hits a ridge in the floorboards and nearly tips over. "I am a lucky woman," she sings, softly. "Lucky, lucky me."

The evening sun whacks out a little warmth. Ettie, Sam and Kate gather at Marcus's pontoon, where every rope is coiled into placemat perfection. Shards of light bounce off the cleats. A varnished timber boat, which looks suspiciously like a genuine Monte Carlo runabout from the Grace Kelly era, is tied to one side to make room for their battered tinnies. His house – a recently renovated and extended cottage that sits on the seawall like a stranded boat – blazes with light.

Ettie is suddenly overwhelmed by so much perfection. Her dress is old and out of date – mumsy even – when she'd meant it to be casual, hippy retro. Her sandals are scruffy. She hasn't had time to polish her toenails. Her thighs are dimpled, her stomach soft, and her breasts are pendulous. His standards are way beyond her. She has to fight an impulse to leap straight back into her calamitous tinny with its mess of buckets, rags, paddles and ropes.

"Off you go, Ettie. You first," Sam says, pushing her forward. She wonders if he's read her mind and shut off a quick exit on purpose.

She hauls in a breath that hits the far corners of her lungs, takes a leap of faith. Lifts her flouncy, tie-dyed blue peasant skirt, and makes a charge along the jetty that leaves the others way behind. By the time they catch up, she is standing uncertainly at a half-open door. What the hell? she thinks. She sticks her head inside to shout hello. Gets hit with a whiff of wood polish and eucalyptus oil when she'd expected garlic and thyme.

"Come in!" calls the chef. "Kitchen is straight ahead. I am at a critical point with the grilling."

Ettie turns to the others: "Should we take off our shoes? This basket says 'Shoes' in French."

"Nah." Sam is firm.

They pick through a small anteroom of mops and buckets, brooms and fishing rods, and a large round copper tub of logs. Marcus is standing by a wall of ovens, elegant in biscuit cotton chinos and a white cotton Indian shirt. The kitchen is sleek, functional and as spare as a doctor's surgery. He looks immaculate. It all does. Ettie's heart sinks once more.

He waves a wooden spoon in welcome, then pulls a tray from the oven and slides it carefully onto a marble bench. He switches off the grill, discards the gloves, dusts his hands and turns to them with open arms. He kisses everyone on both cheeks. Even a stupefied Sam.

"Champagne. I hope it suits." Without waiting for a reply,

he fills four long-stemmed cut-crystal flutes with wine the colour of ripe wheat and hands them around. Sam quietly shoves his six-pack in a dark corner. "To The Briny Café," the chef says, raising his delicate glass and leaning forward to touch Ettie's with a gentle clink. "Now, go inside and I will bring dinner in a few minutes. When you start work early, you must eat early and go to bed early. I was a chef. I know these things."

"Can I help?" Ettie puts down her drink, waiting to be told what to do.

"It is your night off. I am here to spoil you."

More accustomed to being asked to peel lychees, chop garlic, cream the butter and sugar, she almost purrs.

To everyone's astonishment, the sitting room, though as orderly as the rest of the house, is shabby and faded. Cracked and worn dark leather armchairs reside on either side of the stone fireplace. Barley-coloured linen sofas with blood-red piping sit against the walls. Gold-framed paintings, small and quietly evocative of the dusty Australian landscape, hang in careful groups. There's an antique pine sideboard covered with blue and white china. It looks European in origin. Odd chairs are scattered around, like a catalogue of changing trends. It is a room of old family treasures, Marcus's history neatly exposed. In a way, it is how The Briny would look if it were a home instead of a café. Relieved, Ettie relaxes.

With the instinctive nosiness of a journalist, Kate wanders around. She reads the spines of books. Hemingway. Steinbeck. Irving. Karen von Blixen. Xavier Herbert. Eclectic, she thinks. Lots of travel books. Both kinds: ones with big and beautiful pictures and captions, others all text. No cookbooks.

She picks up bleached photographs in battered silver frames. Silent, motionless people, looking serious and awkward in front of the camera, stare back at her.

"Looking for an old wedding picture, are you?" Sam asks, peering over her shoulder. In his huge hand, the fragile wineglass is like a Christmas bauble.

"Curiosity and an open mind, Sam. It's how you learn. You might want to think about that." Kate replaces a photo of a leathery man, a frail woman and a blurry-faced baby trailing a christening gown. They stand in front of an old Valiant with mud stuck to dark duco above the wheels.

Sam flops into a chair that gives a blurting noise. He grins. Ettie gives him a look that makes his toes curl.

With a clap of his hands, the chef calls them to dinner in a small formal dining room. It is bare, not even a watercolour hangs on the wall, so there is nothing to focus on but the food. Sam stands aside for the women to enter but turns the polite gesture into mockery when he pulls a handkerchief from his pocket and flags them ahead like an Edwardian fop. He knows he is being boorish. He cannot stop himself.

The room flickers and glitters in light thrown by two tall candles. An oval table is draped in a stark white linen cloth.

"Take your seat, please," Marcus says, pointing at their places.

Sam glances at the table setting and battles to mask the fact that up against a toff like Marcus, with his silver and fancy linen, he feels more than a bit unpolished. But he knows at the precise moment that Marcus pours him a glass of dry white wine – *to bring out the delicate flavour of the fish* – that he is not just unpolished but from a completely different league. There weren't any crystal glasses or bone-handled knives in the roughly cobbled boatshed where he was raised. His mum, a demon for *value for money*, bought up big when peanut butter and Vegemite was sold in drinking glasses instead of screw-top jars until she amassed a solid collection. She scavenged the family cutlery from Vinnies. Once or twice, Sam remembers, the knives and forks matched. Their plates were odds and ends, every colour under the sun. Back then, he thought it looked festive. Clothes were secondhand, too. What was the point, his mum said, of running wild in new shorts when they'd get ripped by the bush? Nearly all the neighbours were doing it just as hard, so none of the kids had any idea they were poor until they went to the city for a doctor's appointment. Even then, the lush extravagance on display was so irrelevant to Cook's Basin life that they couldn't see the point of it all.

Marcus lifts a heavy china dome from a gilt-edged serving plate and draws his catch of the day towards him. He runs a sharp knife down the fish's spine, carefully peels away a crisped skin and expertly eases hunks of snow-white flesh from the bone. He serves it slightly off-centre on almost transparent white plates, tumbling roasted red and green capsicum and quartered potatoes alongside. A salad of mixed baby lettuce leaves, highlighted with saffron-yellow mustard flowers, waits on an austere sideboard.

"You're a real showman, mate. One trick a minute." Sam holds out his plate, indicating with a jiggle and a nod towards the fish that a larger portion would be appreciated.

The chef obliges. "A man with a healthy appetite. Good."

But Kate kicks him under the table and he nearly drops the plate. He recovers and slurps a large slug of wine, leaning back in his chair until he balances on two fragile, antique legs. He opens his mouth to speak. Kate cuts him off.

"Sit up, Sam!" she snaps. "You'll break the chair and your neck."

He is so shocked he does as he's told. He withdraws his linen napkin from a silver ring engraved with initials. "A family heirloom, is it?" he asks, laying it in his lap with a triangular fold that he hopes finds favour with the assembled gathering.

"Yes. My parents brought it with them from Germany. It has been in a tea-chest for many years." Marcus swirls his wine, sniffs and sips. Satisfied, he tucks his own napkin into his shirt collar and nods that they should all begin eating.

"Too good to use, huh?" Sam says.

"My father did not have the heart to use it after my mother died. And on the farm, well, it was rough, you know. I was too young to appreciate finer things."

Sam's face is hot with embarrassment. "Sorry to hear that, mate. Must've been hard."

Kate decides to come to his rescue. "What kind of a farmer?"

"The struggling kind. But of course, that is all there is in Australia. My father, accustomed to rich German land, saw only the size of the farm when he bought it. I remember only the cold. Windows white with frost. My mother coughing."

Sam shakes his head with sympathy, trying to make amends.

"Every winter," Marcus continues, "I helped my mother stuff old towels under the doors to stop the wind. Made her cups of hot tea. She always sat so close to the fire in the kitchen stove. But she was never warm. Not even in summer. The cold, it was in her bones, you see."

The room is silent except for the occasional clink of cutlery on china. Ettie gazes at the chef.

Encouraged, he continues. "My father, he told me that she started to catch her breath. It was a year after I was born. Eventually, the effort to breathe wore her out."

Ettie reaches out to take his hand. "How old were you?" she asks.

"I was nine."

"Oh you poor, poor boy," she says, as though he's now standing before her in his school shorts, rat-tailed shirt and scuffed leather lace-ups.

Sam is the first to break a long, charged silence. "Best fish I've ever tasted, mate. Cooked to perfection. You're nearly up there with Ettie."

"How's Jimmy doing?" Kate asks Sam, to give the chef time to pull himself together.

"Good as gold. And mate, you wouldn't believe it, but his room's as clean and tidy as an operating theatre."

"Doesn't his mother feel kind of weird, knowing her son's living with you?"

"Nah. She's thrilled to think someone's keeping an eye on him."

Kate looks at him in amazement. "That's *her* job, surely?"

"Bit hard to manage when you're in the clink."

"She's in jail? His mother's a criminal?" Kate puts down

her knife and fork, turns her shocked gaze on Sam.

"Wouldn't put it quite like that. A case of mistaken identities. All of them registered for the dole."

"Ah. Fraud." She returns to her plate. Spears a piece of potato.

"You journos have a nasty habit of leaping to conclusions before all the facts are assembled. She did it to find the money to send Jimmy to a special school."

Kate snaps back: "Doesn't make it right."

"No. Just desperate, I s'pose." He nods towards the wine, asking Kate to pass the bottle. Knows he's hit a nerve when she ignores him.

After a dessert that Marcus describes as an old-fashioned lemon pudding to which he's added fresh blueberries and lemon butter, Sam apologises for having to skip coffee and make an early dash from a *splendid evening*, but he has a dawn cargo pick-up. Kate says she is exhausted and, if Marcus doesn't mind, she too will take her leave.

Ettie, relaxed and sleepy, volunteers to help clean up. Marcus suggests she slips off her shoes, gets comfortable on the sofa and he'll bring her a very decent cognac instead.

"Lovely," she murmurs.

"Jeez," Sam blurts when he and Kate are out of earshot. "What a night. Next time I'll dig out me Sunday best."

"Stop it. It was wonderful. Beautiful food. Excellent wine."

"I reckon he's got the hots for Ettie. What d'you think?"

Kate looks at him like he needs a lobotomy. "Very observant of you, Sam." They reach the end of the jetty. "Haven't you always said that Ettie is the answer to every man's dreams?" She smacks her forehead with the palm of her hand. "Oh God, Sam. You sound like you're jealous. Well, what did you expect? That she would wait until you were ready to throw down your anchor?"

"Throw-down-my-an-chor?" He repeats the words, syllable by syllable, like he can't believe what he's heard. "Even for a journo that's a shocker line." He swallows a belly laugh so he doesn't wake the good Kingfish Bay residents out of their peaceful sleep, shakes his head one last time and leaps into his dinghy. Chugs off without saying goodnight.

His piddly fifteen-horsepower motor sounds tinnier than a spoon banging inside an empty can. Kate, he thinks, has the insight of a mosquito. *Throw down his anchor?* Jeez. If there's a wrong way to read a situation she goes for it like a cat after a rat. And for a second there, he'd thought she was showing signs of settling into Cook's Basin like a native. He'd even been tempted, on a mysterious impulse he couldn't quite pin down, to invite her on a stroll to a lush green wonderland of rainforest lying under a lazy little waterfall hidden high on the escarpment. He'd found the tiny slice of paradise as a kid and knew, even then, to keep it a secret for its own sake. Magic, it was. Moss three inches thick on boulders tumbling like an emerald ocean swell. A canopy of rippling cabbage palms singing a whispery chorus. Thick, damp air ballooning with fecundity, while shafts of lemon light landed softly on chocolate earth. And the mist. Wisps of it rising like the spirits of ancient generations. Damned poetic, the land and water.

But *throw-down-his-anchor*? Nah, he decides. He'll give showing her that beauty spot a miss. She'll see the details plain enough, but with the cold, disengaged and judgemental eye she gets when she thinks you're trying to put one over on her. Maybe suspicion is all part of a journo's job. If it is, it sure as hell must take the spontaneity out of life.

He gazes up at the star-splattered sky – the Pointers, the Southern Cross, the Saucepan, the Milky Way. The certainties of his physical world. So what if he doesn't rate a rave review in a restaurant guide, or an interview in a newspaper? He's a bloke who never shirks the hard yards. And that has to stand for something.

He thinks of Marcus. Dig deep enough and you'll find everyone has a cross to bear. He's a good man. Perfect for Ettie. A stayer, if he's read all the signs right. With a bit of luck, they'll make a go of it.

On the spur of the moment, he makes up his mind he'll return the chef's hospitality with a Cook's Basin-style get-together. Prawns on ice in tin buckets on the pontoon, their shells thrown straight back to the sea. Freshly caught fish, pan-fried in butter over a fire in a washing machine drum at the water's edge. Served on enamel plates with a waxy spud cooked in hot coals. Some quartered lemons for zing and not a single fancy sauce in sight. Bread maybe, to mop up the juices in the frying pan. A few frigidly cold ales to wash it all down. Kings used to live like that.

Jimmy better be asleep in bed, he thinks as he heads home. Kids should come with a warning attached. *Proceed at your own risk.* Who knew one boy could manage twenty Weet-Bix at a go?

Halfway there, Sam nears the Weasel's pontoon. Feeling reckless and more than slightly drunk, he decides to stop off and perform a little maritime surgery. Despite the warnings, the Weasel is showing no signs of curbing his activities.

No time like the present to crank up the pressure, Sam thinks. While he searches in the bottom of his tinny for tools, a boat surfs in on a massive bow wave and almost crumples his boat.

"Need a hand, mate?" asks a knockabout Islander with a legendary thirst. He holds a stubby like he was born with one attached to his hand. Even in the dark, his face glows ruddily.

"Got a shifter on you, mate?"

Not caring that it's too early in the night for criminal deeds, they brazenly loosen a heap of new nuts and bolts. The Islander pockets them, knowing they'll come in handy one day. There is no sign of life from the house. They give the pontoon a shove then the Islander raises his beer in a toast and roars off, leaving Sam to tow it to a bank of mangroves. He ties it securely so there's no possibility a boat will bang into it in the dark. He heads home, giving the night sky a last look of appreciation.

A moment before the Weasel's house disappears from sight, he checks if any lights have come on. It's blacker than tar. All good.

Ettie reclines in softness with a blood temperature cognac held in the bowl of her hand. Fumes rise in dizzying spirals, tickling her nose, heightening her senses. She hears Marcus's footfalls as he approaches and swings her feet to the floor. He lowers himself beside her, placing his liqueur on a small side table.

"No, no," she says, resisting his attempt to lift her feet back to the sofa, afraid that he will find them unattractive.

"Chefs' hoofs wear scars like a map of their career," he says. And he begins to rub her battle-worn toes. Ettie smiles inwardly. If anyone had told her that she'd be seduced by a simple foot massage, she would have laughed out loud. If only all men realised how utterly erotic kindness could be. If he asks her to sleep with him, she thinks she will say yes. At fifty-five, there's no point in wasting time. Coyness, anyway, can be mistaken for lack of interest. She'd hate to risk him thinking that.

In a while, he leads her by the hand to a bedroom that is mostly white. There are books stacked in mountains and, to Ettie's immense relief, no sign of a woman anywhere. Only feathery pillows and cool linen sheets that snap under the weight of their naked bodies.

"Your skin is like butter," he says, his hand stroking her thighs.

She turns towards him, and without any rush they find ways to move together that allow each their small vanities and the frailties of their years.

Ettie is woken by the smell of baking when the sun is high enough for her to realise morning is well underway. She wraps herself in a sheet and stumbles into the kitchen, rubbing sleep from her eyes. Marcus greets her with a strong coffee, a plate of warm, sweet pastries and a kiss that makes her knees buckle.

"Kate has already opened the café," he tells her. "I baked and delivered enough pastries for the breakfast rush. I have never needed much sleep. I hope that is acceptable to you."

"I am never, *ever*, going to let you out of my sight," she says. To her horror, she bursts into tears and blubs into his wide chest like a baby. He licks the tears off her face, takes her hand and leads her back to bed.

Two hours later, Ettie wanders along the ramp from the café pontoon wearing last night's dress, trailing a long red scarf, her face flushed and dreamy. Instead of the dull ache of aging (which she is so accustomed to she barely notices any more), she feels lush, ripe. Immortal. Everything around her suddenly looks deeply erotic, when yesterday it was just seagrass, oysters, the lapping sea.

"Slept in," she says sheepishly. She looks down at her bare feet. "Sorry."

Kate smiles. "Let's have a cuppa."

CHAPTER SIXTEEN

The Weasel flies into a spitting rage when he finds his pontoon missing. He paces up and down his jetty, ranting, screaming, cursing. He is heard so clearly at the top of the Island that mums slam shut their windows to prevent their young children picking up any new and inappropriate words.

Passing by on the barge, Sam casually drops in to inform him that he's seen a pontoon washed up on a beach in a forest of mangroves east of Wineglass Bay.

"Stuck good and proper," he says, shaking his head, like it is a fairdinkum tragedy. "Must've rammed in there on a high tide. You might want me to get rid of it for you before you cop a littering fine. Prefer payment in cash, if you don't mind."

The Weasel throws a punch.

"Mate," Sam says, blocking the move and twisting the Weasel's arm behind his back, "if you wanted someone else to tow it away, all you had to do was say so." He lets go, turns on his heels, strides along the jetty and leaps onto the *Mary*

Kay which he'd left idling. "Full throttle. We're outta here."
The barge powers away. He orders the mutt to the bow, tells
Jimmy to stay in the cabin.

The Weasel takes a minute to react, then he roars down the
jetty like a feral pig.

Sam checks the distance between them. Eight feet and
growing. Unless he's an Olympic long jumper (doubtful
given his stumpy legs and egg-shaped gut) the Weasel is all
bluff.

Sam relishes the feel of the smooth timber under his hands
as he swings the helm and points the duckbill nose of the
Mary Kay into the glittering open sea. A top day and it's only
just begun.

Fast Freddy skips along the jetty, dodging through the early
morning white-collar crowd and a few rheumy-eyed, Coke-
clutching chippies still waiting to be ferried to their offshore
jobs. Ettie sees him and waves from the door of The Briny,
miming drinking a cup of coffee. He nods.

With summer hanging back like it is waiting for a deckle-
edged invitation, Ettie reckons Freddy has a couple of merci-
ful weeks left before the full-on party palaver begins. There
are seasonal signs on the way, though. Pollen on the wind.
Bleached skies. The racket of magpies with squawking babies.
It won't be long, she thinks, before Freddy's chirp gets worn
out by recalcitrant drunks on nights when the heat refuses
to fade and the bays are furnace-hot along with everyone's
tempers. On an impulse, she yanks down the plastic ribbons
hanging from the doorway.

Fast Freddy pops up like an apparition on the other side. "Glad to see the last of them. Risked permanent blindness every time I walked in."

"Useless things," she says, crumpling them up and tossing them in the bin. "Meant to keep out the flies – except nobody told the bloody flies that. Coming off work, then?"

"One more pick-up and then I'm heading home. Just had a call – it's a doozy. A bloke spewing his guts on a yacht on the western shore of Cat Island needs rescuing. He's offered two hundred bucks if I deliver him from purgatory. A gift. And a good deed if I can find the boat. All I need is a double-shot espresso to carry me over the finish line."

"Coming right up."

"You're looking good, Ettie," Freddy says, sensing a difference but unwilling to speculate what's caused it. Although like everyone else he's heard the rumour of a new romance in Ettie's life.

"We're nearly there with the café, Freddy. Kate and I have got the scars to prove it." She holds up red and chapped hands, the fingernails ripped and ragged. Kate stands next to her, hands also raised for inspection.

"Honest work never hurt a soul, ladies. Some say it nourishes it."

Five minutes after Freddy departs, the two Misses Skettle descend on the café in a head-spinning wave of Yardley's April Violets talcum powder. Their summer dresses are held tightly at the waist by wide red patent-leather belts. They step through the doorway and automatically reach up sparrow hands to tweak their lilac hair into place. They pause, mid-stream, puzzled.

"Ah," one says, approvingly, when they note the missing strips over the doorway. "Another of Bertie's health hazards hits the dust."

"Aside from his coffee, of course," says the other. "Good work!"

They place three antique biscuit tins in pristine condition on the counter. "We thought these might look pretty in the café." Then they take off again like two pink flamingos on a mission, slap-banging into a portly Kingfish Bay sailor. His Coke-bottle glasses fly off his sunburned nose. His mate, a tow-haired Island photographer, is flung sideways into the wall.

"Step aside, young men," says one Miss Skettle.

"Where are your manners?" admonishes the other.

And off they tootle, their rosy skirts afroth. Straight to the supermarket for the best-value red wine sturdy enough to hold up their much-loved, life-affirming spices, and stay fragrant during the application of a moderate amount of heat.

While his mate fossicks on the ground for his specs, the photographer sticks his head inside the café. "Any chance of strong, hot coffee? Feeling a bit dusty this morning."

"Good sail last night?" Ettie asks, reaching for a large container of milk and filling a jug. It is the morning after the Stony Point twilight sail.

"No wind. Boring as batshit. Missed the start by three and a half minutes. My comrade," he nods towards his mate outside, "was bent over the stern trying to count the legs on a jellyfish. He insists ten. It's definitely eight. Although technically a jellyfish can have up to two hundred legs. Which are, technically again, tentacles not legs."

"Hard one to check out," Ettie says.

"Nah. It's all on the net. The real issue is how many *our* jellyfish has." He waves Ettie forward. "Follow me."

Without pausing to help the sailor still fumbling on the ground for his glasses, they pick their way through a few late commuters and early shoppers to a plain white car. The photographer pings open the boot, revealing a large, bulbous orange jellyfish floating in a tub of water.

"I'm taking it to my studio to photograph so that even he" – with a flick of his head towards his friend who is wiping clean his glasses on the bottom of his shirt – "will be satisfied."

"What about an impartial opinion? I'd be happy to have a close look."

"Won't do. I need irrefutable evidence or that stubborn, myopic layabout will never admit he's wrong."

"Ah, cold hard facts," Ettie says, realising it's a bet and money is at stake. She peers intently into the tub. "Do jellyfish have eyes? It's so weird, looking at a creature without being able to find its eyes."

The photographer sighs. "How come everyone around here is a budding naturalist?"

"Have you got a lid for the tub? One sharp turn and your boot's going to flood."

"Nothing important is ever gained without great sacrifice," he says, with mock pomposity. "Don't mention it to my wife, though. It's her car."

*

By late morning, while Ettie is off doing some personal shopping, the muffins are sold out and the number of notes in the till is increasingly heartening.

Kate mulls over whether it would be appropriate to ask Marcus if he would like a permanent space to sell his luscious pastries. Suitably signed, of course, and in a prominent position. She was a journalist and understands that linking his famous name to the café will bring in business. In the end, she decides it is a call that only Ettie can make.

A shadow falls across the scratched timber floorboards and she looks up.

"Freddy!" she says, pushing back her chair. "Didn't hear you come in. Those plastic strips were good for something, eh? Ettie's not here right now."

Freddy, white-faced, trembling violently, stares silently at her.

"What's wrong?" Kate asks, gently taking his arm and leading him to her chair. "Are you sick? Or hurt?"

He waggles his head and opens his mouth. But whatever he is trying to say stays strangled in his throat.

"I'll call Sam, okay? Whatever it is, it will all be fine, Freddy. Give me a minute to call him. Hang in there."

His shaggy head falls on his chest and stays there. Tears spill from his eyes and roll down his cheeks, catching on the grey stubble like pearls. He sucks in a breath and drags a hanky out of his pocket. He holds it under his nose, more to hide his face than to mop up.

Kate dials Sam, bringing Freddy a glass of water with the phone glued to her ear. Outside, the hum of traffic carries on the wind, waves smack against the pylons under the floorboards. A car door slams. There's laughter. A shout. A baby bawls.

Freddy lifts his sad, crumpled face and blows his nose with a sound like a foghorn, just as Sam answers the phone.

Ettie returns on a wave of floating fabric, wearing a new flowery fuschia dress the Misses Skettle would definitely approve. She pirouettes in front of Kate, showing off, laughing. Feeling gorgeous.

She stops mid-circle, her skirts catching up a second later.

"Freddy?" she says, then looks towards Kate for a hint.

"I've called Sam," she explains.

Freddy looks towards Ettie pathetically. She swiftly crosses to him. Wrapping her arms around his narrow shoulders, she leans her cheek against his, engulfing him in her softness, hoping the strong and steady beat of her heart will reassure him.

"What's happened, love? What's the matter?"

He swallows a gulp of air like it is solid. "Boag's dead," he whispers, trembling hands clenched in his lap. "Nailed to that lone mangrove in Kingfish Bay. Like a . . . sacrifice." The words come out in sharp little jerks and end with a whimper.

"Are you sure, Freddy? No mistake?" Kate asks.

He shakes his head.

"Oh Freddy," Ettie says softly, rocking him like a child.

They hear the thrum of the *Mary Kay* then and feel the building shudder as the barge nudges against the deck. Kate pulls open the screen door and steps out as Sam walks towards her. "Where's Freddy? Any idea what's up?"

"It's not good, Sam. Where's Jimmy?"

"Gone off to find Boag. He disappeared after breakfast."

"Oh my God."

Inside the café Sam listens, his face expressionless. He leaves without a word, fists at his sides, his jaw bunched hard. Kate offers to go with him but he shakes his head and she backs away.

Meanwhile Ettie puts a mug of hot chocolate in front of Freddy. "Drink up, love. It'll do you good." She takes his hand and wraps it around the handle.

"What if it's one of us that's done it?" he asks.

"Not a chance. We both know that for sure, my friend. Now drink, Freddy," she says again and helps him to raise the steaming brew to his lips.

"Can't, Ettie. Sorry. It'll make me sick."

"Sure, love." She passes Kate the mug. "I'll take you home to tuck you in. You need to rest, and tonight I'll come back with some of my famous chicken soup that works better than penicillin. We'll all take care of you. You're a good man, Freddy."

"Wish you'd all stop saying that," he mumbles. "Once and for all, I wish you'd all stop saying that."

"Okay, my friend. Sorry."

"Gives me the shivers. Like I'm tempting fate."

"Sure, Freddy."

On the barge, Sam makes his way across a mirror-flat sea, hoping he'll find Freddy was suffering from an hallucination brought on by overtiredness at the end of a long nightshift.

Maybe he saw a branch snapped halfway and hanging like a dead thing. Or a shirt blown into the branches by the wind. It's easy to read things wrong if you're knackered.

When the single mangrove at the mouth of Kingfish Bay is close on portside, he sees a swarm of flies. A dirty black cloud of them. And another flying in. The frenzied whine is the kind that sends people mad. He wipes his face with the back of his hand, pretending the dampness is sweat. He slips into neutral and walks to the bow to drop the anchor. Then searches the deck for the shovel. Finds it buried in the dog's old blankets, like a kid's favourite toy. He yanks off his boots and socks and slides over the gunnel to wade ashore.

He'd expected retribution. He'd looked forward to it, if he was honest. But his big mistake – his freakin' *gargantuan* mistake – was to give the creepy little shit more credit than he deserved. He should have known the slimeball wouldn't have the decency or courage to go after someone his own size. But what kind of spineless low-life picks on a harmless mutt without a mean bone in his body?

He keeps his eyes focused on the clean, clear shallows all the way to the outer spread of the branches. The excited hum of feeding flies grows louder. He bends over and dry-retches. When he feels he can, he raises his eyes.

Before him, the dog is impaled with a plain old garden stake. Blunt-tipped and clumsy. It must have been an excruci-ating death. He charges forward with a roar, grabs the stake and hurls it aside to catch the stiff little body before it falls to the ground. He gently wraps Boag in his blankets and sits on the beach cradling the bundle in his lap. My fault, he thinks. My fault.

Eventually he buries the mutt on the point of a woody finger of land that juts out to sea like the bow of a boat. He places the spade alongside. A grave marker. Then he phones Jimmy and tells him he's confined to barracks for a few hours. He disconnects before the kid has time for a single question.

Jimmy manages to hold firm for two lonely hours, then cracks under the pressure. He roars up to the café in his tinny and flies inside. His face bleak with worry, hippity-hopping from one foot to the other at full speed, looking for his captain and the faithful mutt.

"Where is he, Ettie? He said he'd be home by now. Boag needs his dinner, doesn't he? Where's Boag? Why'd he confine me to barracks? What's barracks, Ettie? I'm followin' orders, just like I said I would. Now he's gone. What'd I do?"

It's as if the safety rug provided by Sam's stability has been pulled from under him, and Jimmy is falling back into old ways.

"He'll be back soon, love. It wasn't anything you did. Truly. You eaten?"

The kid's face clears. "He's gettin' Tilly the turtle, isn't he? It's a surprise, isn't it? Tilly and me and Boag and Sam. All together."

"How about some cake? A lovely rich cake with plenty of fruit in it. Would you like that?"

"Does it have custard, Ettie?"

"Not today, love. Next time." She cuts a thick slice and gives it to him on a plate.

"Where's Sam, Ettie? Where'd he go?"

"We'll all wait here together for him, love. He'll be back soon. Don't you like the cake?"

"I'm savin' some for Sam. And Boag."

"No need for that, love, there's plenty for everyone."

Sam enters the café with an overbright face and red-rimmed eyes. He spots Jimmy immediately. "What are you doing here, mate? You were confined to barracks." But his voice is kind. It is a question, not an accusation.

"He's been looking for you. Worried sick," Ettie says. "And you might want to tell him what a barracks is next time . . . You okay, Sam? You managing?" she adds softly, coming up to him. She lays her hands on his chest, slides them down and circles his waist with her arms. She feels a shudder, like a sudden chill. The tension drains out of his body and he touches her head lightly.

"Been trying to find ways to plug the holes, Ettie. Took me a while."

"What holes, Sam?" Jimmy asks.

"Nothing big, mate. And it's good you're here. I need a hand."

"We're a team, Sam, aren't we?" Jimmy says, feeling the equilibrium coming back into his life.

"Always, Jimmy."

Sam and Jimmy carry Tilly the turtle from the car park to the edge of the seawall, holding her between them like two ends of a sack. They load her into Sam's tinny and lay her on a bed of scrappy old towels to cushion the ride to the Island. Tilly, with a slow blink and a nod, withdraws into her shell.

"Is she home, Sam? Or gone out?" Jimmy asks, searching both ends.

"Home, mate. Guaranteed. And that's where we're going. Tomorrow we're gonna take the *Mary Kay* all the way to Cat Island and we're gonna lower Tilly over the side so she can go off to find a quiet spot on a deserted beach to lay her eggs."

Jimmy holds a paddle and pushes them out into the deep. Sam drops the outboard down and pulls the starter cord, twists the throttle into gear. They set off slowly homewards across still water and under a fleecy white sky, rocked every now and then by the wake of a passing tinny.

"Where's Boag, Sam?" Jimmy's eyes dart around the boat as if the dog is hiding like the turtle.

"His owner came for him, mate."

"That's you, isn't it, Sam?"

"No, Jimmy. I was just looking after him for a while."

"That's sad, Sam. You loved Boag. Boag was a good dog."

"Yeah, mate. The best."

"You cryin', Sam?"

"Don't be bloody stupid."

After locking up the café, Ettie and Kate visit Fast Freddy with a basket of life-affirming treats. They find him in bed, unshaved, wearing yellow-striped pyjamas, looking a pale wreck in the glow from a bedside lamp. A moth pounds against the light bulb. Freddy flinches with every collision. Ettie is reminded of a song about a moth that couldn't resist the flame but died happy thinking it had reached the moon.

"What makes a moth crave the light when it must know it will kill it?" Freddy says, solemnly. "What is the point of life if the pursuit of it ends in death?"

"What do you think, Freddy?" Ettie asks without a hint of sympathy in her tone, trying to force him to reengage in the everyday. He looks startled by the question.

"Well . . ." he begins, drawn in despite himself. "There are many schools of thought. Some think procreation. Others seek enlightenment . . ."

"*You*, Freddy. What do *you* think?"

"Being useful is a good place to start," he ventures after a moment or two.

She reaches out and turns off the light. The battered moth rests on the shade, deprived of death. "Every day is a gift. You told me that, Freddy. A long time ago when I was so broken-hearted after that tennis player dumped me and I thought I might never get out of bed again."

A small smile reaches the corners of Freddy's mouth and struggles all the way to his round blue eyes. "Saved ya, did I?" he whispers.

"Yes, Freddy. Now it's my turn to save you. With chicken soup, lasagna, salad and a slice of buttery lemon cake. You're going to have to get out of bed by tomorrow, too. I'm moving from the Island to my beautiful new penthouse on the top floor of The Briny Café. I need your help, my friend. Once again, I need your help. Are you up to it? Can you see to the packing and give Glenn a hand?"

"I'm up to it, Ettie. No worries."

"Bless you, Freddy."

"Thank goodness you didn't call me *a good man*," he says, coming out of his shell a little more.

"But you are, Freddy. Or we wouldn't say it," Kate says.

"How's Kate doing with the coffee making?" he asks, as if she isn't in the room.

"She's ace, Freddy. A natural."

"Knew she had it in her."

"Me too."

Kate steps over and plants a kiss on his hoary cheek. He blushes furiously, bright enough to stir the moth from its somnolence. It swoops and dives and follows the two women out the door, determined to die somewhere under the full glare of a spotlight it believes to be the moon.

CHAPTER SEVENTEEN

After leaving Freddy, Ettie and Kate stand on the dirt track that circles the Island separating foreshore properties from the higher blocks of land. Kate says she plans to visit Sam on her way home. Ettie offers to come, but Kate shakes her head. "You're only thirty steps from your front door. Go home, have an early night."

"Give Sam my love. Tell him I'll be there in a flash if he needs me," she says.

"You and Sam. You ever have a fling? Or, you know, something?" Kate asks, in a voice that's disinterested enough to put Ettie on full alert.

She looks for somewhere to sit. Tramps over to the nearest set of steps, bunches her skirt around her thighs and sinks down with a sigh. The burn in her feet starts to cool. "Maybe he had a crush, years ago, when he was barely old enough to drive a car and I was almost, but not quite, old enough to be his mother. He was a lost, sad young man, Kate. Like everyone else I helped to look after him. There was never anything more."

"Where were his parents?"

"Car accident. It was early summer. A gorgeous day. Two policemen came looking for him. That's how we found out they'd been killed. After that, we gathered in the Square. People from the bays, the Island. Full-timers, weekenders. None of us knowing who should be the one to tell him. There were so many people. And the Square never so quiet. We couldn't find him. Not for ages. Turned out, he was off fishing. He'd decided at the last minute to skip the trip into town because the kingfish were running hot."

"Who told him?"

"Well, I did. My mother died, you see, when I was even younger than he was. We all thought that might help Sam to understand. Tragedy just lands on you sometimes, for no reason at all. In the end, I hardly said a word. He looked at our faces and he knew. He got back in his rowboat and just kept rowing and rowing and rowing. The Misses Skettle and I, we followed at a distance. They had a small cabin cruiser in those days, a river boat, but they took it out to sea without flinching. Never lost sight of him. Even out beyond the heads where the swells swallowed and spat him up over and over. There was a full moon that night, otherwise he'd have been dead alongside his parents. He was never alone after that. Not until we knew he was through the worst."

Kate walks a little away, facing the sea, hands in her pockets, shoulders hunched. Lights dot the hillsides, the only clue to the separation of land and sea.

"God, no wonder he's so stuck in the past. Must have been awful."

"They'd saved and saved for a new car. Bought a lovely little red bubble. They were so proud of it. It was brand-new, you see, not secondhand. They were nearly home when a truck roared around a bend, crossed into their lane and wiped them out. And not a thing any of us could do to set things back the way they were."

"How old was he?"

"Sixteen."

"So that's why he collects orphans. And watches over the community."

"Kids, dogs, turtles. Anything that's lost."

"He really loves you, though. You can see it in the way he's always looking out for you. It goes way beyond helping out a friend. He's . . . sort of protective."

"And I love him. God, we go back thirty years. In a typical Cook's Basin way, we're as close as family."

"Someone has to tell him to back off the Weasel problem, Ettie. The guy's a thug. He knows no boundaries. The stakes will skyrocket in ways Sam couldn't even imagine."

Ettie stands, brushing the dirt off her skirt. "Sam can take care of himself. And he'll never be alone, not in Cook's Basin. Now I'm off. I'm completely exhausted and you should go home to bed, too. Leave Sam. He's had a shocker day. He needs time to sort himself out."

"Yeah, I guess so. Goodnight, Ettie."

On the foreshore, in the dark shadows of tall trees, Sam sits on the seawall, a stubby in his hand, drinking a beer in quick, angry sips. Cook's Basin has always had its share of miscreants, bludgers and even a few light-fingered layabouts, but executing a dog is an all-time low. A desecration of every code the community holds to its collective heart. He is cold with rage.

He hears an outboard engine and sees the blurry outline of a boat swinging close to the spot where the *Mary Kay* is moored. He puts down his beer and rises to his feet, bracing mentally and physically for a fight. The sky, the water, the night is the colour of pitch. The moon is an hour away. He walks silently to the jetty, flexing his fingers. The hairs on the back of his neck stand up. He inches further forward. The boat aims for the barge.

Slows. Idles.

Ah jeez. He returns for his beer, then makes his way back to the end of the jetty, rolls up his jeans and sinks his feet in the water.

"Lost, are you?"

Kate spins towards his voice and sees him. A dark shape less than twenty feet from her.

"As it happens, I'm not. I came to make sure you and Jimmy are okay," she says across the water.

He stands and points at his jetty. She slips into gear and eases alongside the pontoon with half an inch to spare, a perfect manoeuvre. They both know it is pure luck.

He extends his hand to help her out but she ignores it and stays in the boat, leaving him feeling wrong-footed, as usual. He says nothing. He tells himself she's going to make a fine partner for Ettie. She works like a demon. And her idea to turn over the attic was a stunner. She's even managed to make a coffee for him that was almost up there with the best. She's okay. More than okay. She'll do for Ettie and the café, even the community. It's the chemistry between them that's off. They speak a different language.

"Thanks for checking but we're all good here," he says.

"It's a no-win battle, Sam. Give it up." Her tinny rocks on the water.

A voice calls out in one of the houses strung along the foreshore, televisions flicker in blue pods, the sound carrying across the bay.

Sam sits on the jetty and hoists his legs over the gunnel, holding her boat steady. "I'm going to keep repeating myself till it sinks in, Kate. If there's a problem, you wear it away."

"The Weasel is the kind of problem that wears *you* away. Permanently, Sam. Stay out of it. Or you'll end up with concrete instead of leather boots."

In the green and red glow of Kate's nav lights, his face shuts down. He stares along the shoreline, raises his beer to his lips. Empty. "You can't let scum rise. Soon as you do, it takes over like algae, suffocating everything underneath."

"Vigilantes are no better than thugs."

"What's the alternative?"

"Call the police. Let them handle it."

"Kids at risk, Kate."

"Kids make their own choices."

"Kids don't even know there *are* choices," he says.

She is silent for a while. "You spend your whole life in Cook's Basin?"

"Born and bred. Wear my boots to hide webbed feet," he says, trying to ease the tension.

"Onshore the Weasel is about as dirty as it gets. Cook's Basin isn't the real world, Sam. Not even close."

"That's why we've gotta look after it. You've gotta stand up for what you believe in, Kate, or you lose it."

"Yeah, well, in my experience, idealists are the first casualties."

"Thanks for dropping by." He gives her boat a shove with his foot and stands. A hulking dark figure. Arms crossed. Legs apart. Like he's riding choppy seas.

"It's only going to get worse."

He waves, undefeated, and walks back down the wharf.

The Cook's Basin grapevine buzzes and the community seethes. Phones run hot with the combined forces of outrage and horror at Boag's terrible fate. It is universally decided this is not the moment to sit back and wait for the police and what will almost certainly be an unsatisfactory end. No more verbal warnings. No more detached pontoons. This time, the damage planned will be expensive, extremely inconvenient and even permanent. Sam is informed of the chosen strategies but asked to stay away from the action. If confronted by the Weasel, no one is sure what he might now be capable of.

With the full support of the community, three men steal into the Weasel's boat pen. With a sense that the ides are in their favour by providing a heavy fog that rolls in thickly from the ocean, they unscrew the cap of two petrol tanks. Add a dose of sugar to the fuel. They replace the caps, lift the containers to shake them vigorously, and depart into the mist. As silently as they came.

At the rear of the house, three women, all of them mothers of teenage children, gather in silence, carrying hessian chaff bags and an aluminium ladder. They place the ladder against the Weasel's water tank. While one holds it firm, another climbs to the top and empties the contents of a bag into the water. Two more sacks are passed up. The remains of a long-dead possum and three dead rats are left to quietly decompose in the water supply. The women slip away, sure-footed on paths they have walked since they were children.

High in the trees, an owl hoots. Somewhere, a dog barks. Nothing in the Weasel's house stirs.

The Weasel, they mutter amongst themselves, has absolutely no inkling of exactly how ruthless a tight-knit, united and outraged group of people can be when Cook's Basin's rules are casually snapped in two.

Cook's Basin News (CBN)

Newsletter for Offshore Residents of Cook's Basin, Australia

NOVEMBER

LOST

Dave's brand-new iPhone at Bomber Cove yesterday. Proud owner for ONE day. If anyone has found it, please call him.

Island Brunch

Brunch in the Park is on again.

10 a.m. to noon.

Free-range eggs, bacon from happy, free-range pigs, great coffee and tea.

It's a fundraiser so try to wake up in time!

COMMUNITY CELEBRATION

Cutter Island will celebrate 200 years of Island history next year. Get ready to be cajoled and threatened into digging out old photographs, postcards – anything relating to the early days – from under beds, in lofts or boatsheds, and put pen to paper to give accounts of earlier offshore life. Let's create an exhibition that will make the residents of 200 years in the future know whether they've stuffed it up, or got it bang on the money.

Thank You!

A big thank you from our young daughter who slipped on the ferry wharf steps. We are newcomers to the Island and were overwhelmed by the help, love and support from the community. Many thanks to the red boat that ferried us ashore. I was too flustered to get your name. I am happy to report our daughter is fine, with just a few stitches in her arm. Her parents are recovering and her mother is finally reducing her dependency on herbal relaxing tonics. We are still so glad we moved here. Truly!

Felicity

Note from the Editor

For all those caught up in the jellyfish legs controversy, the number for *our* jellyfish is ten. The photographs prove it. All bets are off from now on.

CHAPTER

EIGHTEEN

Fast Freddy wakes disoriented at a time when it is normal for him to go to sleep. He dashes onto his deck to see if it is the world that has slipped into reverse, or just him. He remains befuddled until he realises fog has wiped out the spot where he usually finds the horizon. Then he remembers. He bows his head, brings his hands together in the shape of a steeple. His prayer asks that when Boag returns to begin a new life, in whatever form he takes, he will find love, peace and tranquillity. And tidbits in abundance.

After an appropriate time of respectful silence, he showers, shaves and dresses to make his way to Ettie's house. He finds Judy, Jane and Jenny already hard at work and the small house almost packed up. The Three Js, who have taken time out from cooking a large pot of spiced pear and saffron chutney destined for The Briny, leave him to finish. He is given three departing cuddles in a row, followed by three smacking kisses on the top of his greying head.

Freddy carefully wraps the remainder of Ettie's belongings

– lamps, a few large serving bowls, a wall clock, some books – and places them in boxes, sealing them tightly with tape. With the weather bureau predicting choppy seas, a simple crisscrossing of flaps will invite disaster if Glenn's flimsy old punt rocks and rolls excessively.

The fog lifts by mid-morning. Sam calls Jimmy out of his bedroom where he's been glued to Tilly's side. Between them, they carry the turtle to the waterfront.

Smelling the brine, the sand, her familiar territory, she emerges from her shell, fixing her eyes on Jimmy and then Sam in what they choose to believe is affection. They hoist her onto the deck of the *Mary Kay* and set off for Cat Island, a wildlife sanctuary where Tilly can spend a few days adjusting to freedom if the big swim feels a bit beyond her for a while. When she is fit enough, it is only a short paddle to the open sea where she can turn north or south, depending on her mood.

They reach the corkscrew bay where rivers, oceans and closed waters meet. Sam stands aside while Jimmy squats beside Tilly, his long legs folded like a picnic table, patting her shell.

"Goodbye, Tilly. Come back and see us," he whispers. The turtle looks at him through obelisk eyes, dips her head and drags her flippers across the deck in a lumbering walk. With a gentle nudge from Sam, she flops over the side and sinks into the water without looking back. They watch until her black shape disappears into the deep.

"D'ya think she'll remember us, Sam?"

Sam takes a while to search his memory for one of his mother's timeless affirmations.

"You love Tilly, Jimmy?" he asks.

"Yeah, Sam."

"Well, mate, sometimes the hardest part of love is letting go."

"Oh it's hard alright," says the kid, sniffing. "Ya got that right."

The community truck – an aging ute with a rusting tray and gears that have never moved higher than second – bounces along the rutted Island tracks towards the water. Ettie's belongings sway and jiggle, but nothing breaks loose, tied down by Fast Freddy who's a stickler for doing things right so there's never any cause for regret later. Pleased the fog has lifted to coincide with the high tide, Glenn and Freddy, two men who have known each other since childhood, pull into the delivery wharf. They shuffle from ute to barge, thankful for once for the lack of rain.

"A good omen," Freddy says about the weather. He's struggling with his end of Ettie's heavy sofa, which he remembers helping to install at the top of the Island a couple of years ago.

"Nature," mutters Glenn, who flatly refuses to let Freddy get away with a single hokey-pokey ounce of superstition.

Soon cartons, a bed, a table and four chairs, odds and ends such as mops and brooms are loaded, all without a single rope to hold them steady. Glenn jumps in his leaky old tinny. Freddy takes up duty aboard the punt. Glenn fires up a fifteen-horsepower engine and nudges it away from the wharf.

Freddy, eyeing a necklace of rusty holes the size of cannon balls, says a quick mantra.

"Prettier than a party boat," Glenn shouts gleefully, referring to festoons of chewed tyres for fenders. They make their snail-pace way towards The Briny on a rising chop. The air crackles and snaps around them. A storm is on the way.

"I lived in that house for thirty years and that's all there is to show for it," Ettie says, watching the punt approach. "Doesn't say a lot, does it?"

"Maybe you had a sixth sense that one day you'd leave," Kate says.

"Nothing so esoteric. Too many steps to lug too much, that's all."

Fast Freddy and Glenn wave and the two women walk along the jetty to meet them.

When everything is delivered upstairs to the attic, Kate pushes a dithering Ettie out of the way. "Let me get to work up here while you keep cooking. I've moved so often I'm borderline genius at it."

With relief Ettie withdraws and returns downstairs to her baking.

Kate tells the two men where to put the furniture and then says they're free to go, she will do the rest. They take off like a pair of rabbits, terrified she might change her mind and ask them to spin the room one more time. That sofa, they agree, is too damn heavy to pick up more than twice in one day.

Kate unpacks boxes, makes the bed, fluffs the pillows, places frangipani soap in the bathroom along with shampoo and towels. She wires the sound system and programs "Blue Skies", Ettie's favourite, to come up first. She resists the impulse to hang a huge canvas of wind-ruffled seagulls on a wall that catches the morning sun. Art is personal.

Last of all, she puts a bottle of vintage French champagne into the fridge. It was given to her by a tycoon who appreciated what she'd written about him. She's been waiting for a suitable moment to open it and right now is as good as any. Only the paint-splattered floor is bothering her. She forbids Ettie to peek upstairs, races to Oyster Bay in her tinny and returns with a jewel-coloured Turkish rug.

"It's on loan," Kate tells Ettie when she finally allows her upstairs. "But if it grows on you, keep it."

Ettie stands still. Struck dumb. She wanders around touching familiar objects like she's never seen them before. Throws wide the doors to the deck, as if the view is an unexpected surprise. She opens and closes drawers in the bedroom. Checks under the pillow where she finds a pair of pyjamas neatly folded.

In the bathroom, she holds the bar of soap to her nose and runs the hot water tap until it steams. At the back wall of the apartment, where a rudimentary kitchen is set into a long bench, she picks up the kettle and fills it with water for no reason at all. A subconscious ritual. Settling in. Settling down. Claiming the space. She opens the fridge and sees the champagne.

"For you and the chef to celebrate. You can shift stuff around to suit yourself later. But you can sleep here tonight in comfort."

She gives Kate a hug of thanks. Unable to trust herself to

speak, she walks back to the deck, stares out across a sea of whitecaps. "It feels like a dream," she says at last. "And I am so afraid I might wake and find it all gone."

"This is only the beginning, Ettie."

Downstairs in the café, the blokes hang around having a beer and a coffee, a juicy hamburger, a cheese omelette. Without a twinge of personal guilt Ettie listens as they argue the pros and cons of alcohol. Since taking over the café, she's resisted the night-time vinos. Too busy, anyway, plotting how to turn a rundown eatery into the best food and coffee shop on the coast.

"A grog brings out your groovy wild side," Glenn insists. He blows across the top of the bottle, making a sound like a foghorn in the rhythm of reggae. Guzzles.

"Only side I ever see on the water taxi is dangerous, reckless and self-destructive."

"Only when you push drinking too far, Freddy. That's a different issue. Right, Ettie?"

She shrugs, knowing she's not on solid ground, refusing to be drawn into the debate.

Freddy wags his head in despair. "Everyone pushes it too far, 'cause all it takes is two drinks and you forget when to stop."

"You're bein' a bit tough, Freddy. Man likes a glass or two with his dinner. Lifts the flavour of the food. Helps with digestion."

"First, the man he takes the wine. Then, without even noticing the switchover, the wine it takes the man."

"Old Buddha say that?"

"Nah. Tom Russell."

"Philosopher or somethin', is he?"

"Singer. Country."

Glenn frowns and looks twitchy. "Not gonna make me listen to it, are ya? Country music, mate. Just can't go there."

"Your loss, Glenn. Your loss."

Glenn turns to Ettie, who's leaning on the rail of the deck and staring across the water. "C'mon, Ettie. Help us out. What d'ya reckon?" His tone is whining.

"About alcohol or country music?" She is dreamy, only half-listening, wondering how it will feel to live on the edge of the Square without two hundred steps that, while keeping her fit and strong, she is not sorry to escape forever.

"Both!" they reply, in unison.

She kisses their cheeks, thanks them for their help, their kindness, and avoids the question.

"See you," she says, laughing.

"Aw, c'mon, Ettie, give us an opinion," Glenn implores.

So she takes a moment of serious thought. "Each unto his own," she declares, eventually. Because everyone has to learn the truth for himself.

"I win!" they shout, once more in unison.

By late afternoon, the sky is the colour of charcoal. The smell of rain is in the air. Gusts flirt with the water, then race off, leaving long grey shadows in their wake. Bertie and Big Julie appear at the café door, arm in arm. The old man, bent almost double, shuffles his feet forward a few inches at a time until he's inside. Looking ninety instead of seventy.

"Bertie! You look great," Kate lies, blinking to hide her dismay.

"I look like I'm at death's door, Kate. You journos never could tell the truth." He coughs, dry and hard. Every breath sounds as rough as sandpaper. He is wasting away in front of their eyes. Big Julie holds him firmly under his elbow, a sack of bones in the palm of her hand, to stop him toppling.

"Bertie!" Ettie flies around the counter to grab his other arm and steer him to the table under the stairs. "You look like you need a decent burger and a bag of hot chips. Sit down. I'll bring you a selection from The Briny's new menu. We're still testing before opening day, and it might be a bit flashy for your taste, but we'll do our best." She kisses his shiny head and pats a scrawny shoulder. "Coffee, love? Or a glass of red wine?"

"Coffee'd be great, Ettie. Ta. I'll give you a hand," Big Julie replies, stepping behind the counter like old times. "He's not allowed to drink alcohol," she whispers. "Drugs have buggered his liver."

"God, Julie. You managing? Can we help?"

"Nah. Nothing to do. He's got a few months, tops. He knows it although no one's said a word. Life's a cack, isn't it?" Her mouth is turned down at the corners and she speaks softly. "I've loved the silly bugger for more than twenty years. Hell, we could've had some fun together. Why'd we wait? I keep wondering why we busted our butts at the café when the heart for it had died in both of us."

"One day at a time, love," Ettie says. "Take what comes, as it comes."

Big Julie grabs saucers and slides them under the cups. "How you finding it, Ettie? It's bloody hard, bloody non-stop, bloody backbreaking, bloody work. You've got to be mad to run a café."

"I love it, Julie. I like the process so it doesn't feel like work. Not yet, anyway. And we're only doing half-days until the reopening."

Big Julie looks around. Bertie's chaotic displays of batteries, lures, key rings, torches, matches, every blokey thing, hung strategically to hide cracks in the walls, have been ripped down. Counter tops are uncluttered. Polished glass jars spruik homemade biscuits. Lemon thins. Madeleines. Jam drops. Sold by the kilo or the piece. The blackboard menu is freshly drawn and lettered in brightly coloured chalk. Beautiful, like all Ettie's work.

"Seen the local produce corner?" Kate says, pointing. Big Julie wanders over, picks up a jar.

"Ettie's drawing of The Briny on the label?"

Kate nods. "Perfect, don't you think?"

Big Julie does a full turn in the soft glow that comes as much from scrubbing as from the patina of age. "You've tarted it up a treat, I'll say that," she says. "Still feels like the old Briny but it's . . . cleaner and tidier!" She glances guiltily over her shoulder to make sure Bertie hasn't heard. Then giggles.

"You girls up to no good?" he wheezes.

"Here's your coffee, love. Not as good as your old brew but it'll still put a bit of backbone into you for the rest of the day."

Bertie reaches for Julie, grabs her hand tightly in his yellowed paw.

"Reckon you could manage a wedding reception one day?"

he asks Ettie in a scratchy voice. But he's looking straight at Julie.

"No need for that, love," Julie says, recovering quickly. "You'd hate to tie yourself down. And I've never been an honest woman anyway."

"No time for jokes. I owe you. Twenty years of cheer. Debts don't get much bigger than that."

Big Julie leans over Bertie's hunched back and lays her cheek alongside his. "A wedding certificate isn't going to change anything. Why don't we think about it when you're feeling better?"

"You and I both know there isn't going to be any better. Like to make it legal, luv. Leave you set. Peace of mind for an old fella."

"Christ, Bertie, now I'm *really* worried. You've never done anything legal in your life. You trying to curry a few gold points before you pitch up at the Pearly Gates?"

"Might have left me run too late for the Pearly Gates."

"Never, Bertie."

"So what do you say? Are we on?"

"Suits me, love," she says, with a small hiccup.

Content, Bertie sips his coffee. Then looks down at his cup and grimaces. "Girly stuff."

Ettie pulls up a chair next to the old man and lays her hand on a thigh as thin as a wooden spoon. "Better pass on the secret recipe, then," she teases.

"I mean it, Ettie. About the wedding. Can I leave it to you? A dying man's wishes."

Ettie nods.

"I'd expect a good discount. Seein' as how I gave you the

place for a song." The old glint is back in his eye. He sits up a little straighter.

Kate jumps in. "For you, Bertie? Double the normal rate, okay?" she says with a smile.

"Hard to get good help, isn't it, Ettie? Always has been." He sounds breathless. He takes a moment to steady himself, his hand on his chest like he's holding his heart in place. "Business all done for the day?" His eyes seek out Big Julie, who appears from behind the counter, her cheeks wet.

"Sure, Bertie. All done. Let's go home, shall we?"

"Yeah. Got a few weddin' invitations to send out."

"Leave it to us, Bertie," Ettie says, her arm through his to stop him tipping off his chair. "We'll get Julie in for a meeting. Sort the lot."

The old man shuffles outside, a woman holding each arm. In the sunlight he looks transparent. Light enough to be carried off in a single puff of wind.

When Ettie comes back, she gives Kate a strange look. "Why'd you make a joke of the price? I would have done the wedding for nothing."

"He was testing you, Ettie. Making sure you kept your heart out of the business."

"Not sure about that, Kate."

"Trust me on this. Okay?"

Half an hour later, the storm hits. The bay is churning, yachts strain on their moorings, and halyards clang like church bells. The roar of the wind in the trees is like a stampede. Sporadic rain clatters on the tin roof of the café like stilettos on a tile floor. The first flash of lightning is a long, serrated wire that explodes like a cracker. The sky goes black. A couple of tinnies, outboards whining, their drivers hunkered low, are lifted high on the waves and crash down hard on a volatile sea. The women rush to secure the café.

Out of the gloom the *Mary Kay* appears. Sam nurses the barge alongside. Jimmy, in faithful attendance, expertly ties up.

The four of them dash to stack tables, chairs and umbrellas out of the way of a wind that Sam says is tipped to gust up to forty knots. He tells Kate he's going to swing her tinny around, nose to the wind.

"Why?"

"So the waves crash over the bow and not the engine. Try trusting me for a moment, why don't you? You might learn a trick or two."

"I'll do it. You stay here."

He strides across the deck and yanks her arm, pulling her back from the ramp. "I am not going to risk the *Mary Kay* to rescue you this time. Either let me do it, or kiss goodbye to your boat. Your freaking call."

"Fine. You do it then. I'd hate to get in your way."

Jeez. He unlashes the ropes, reverses at speed, keeping away from the rocks. One day, he'll learn to keep his trap shut and let her see how she manages with less know-how on the water than Jimmy's got in his little finger. He swings the boat in a wide circle, surfs a wave to the dock, ties up and kills the engine. He marches up the ramp as a gust knocks him sideways.

Kate waits for him at the top. "Thanks," she says, ungraciously.

"You're welcome," he responds, not meaning it.

When the furniture is tied down, they take shelter inside the café. Lightning strobes. Thunder rumbles, full of promise. They wait for a deluge that will soak the ground and raise the drooping heads of trees that have struggled through an almost bone-dry spring. The drops are big but they fall from the sky like a handful of marbles, not enough to wet the ground. They check the horizon for the orange glow of bushfires. One lightning strike and the tinder-dry National Park will explode.

"This'll get everyone off their backsides to check their water pumps and fire hoses instead of waiting till the flames are close enough to barbecue their sausages," Sam says.

"That's a bit unkind," Kate snaps, still angry.

"I've lived through four big blazes, mate, and there's nothing uglier if you're unprepared."

"Oh of course. I forgot. You're a man of vast experience. Always the expert."

He bites his tongue as they troop upstairs single-file to watch the progress of the storm from Ettie's apartment. Sam, who hasn't seen it since the furniture arrived, glances around and whistles. "Nice work. You've made it look great, Ettie. And Jimmy, you did a good paint job. Proud of you."

"Kate unpacked and arranged the furniture," Ettie says. "It's all her doing."

"So, you finally found something she's good at, eh?" Sam marches past Kate to the deck and checks the horizon.

Kate glares after him. He doesn't flinch.

"I'll make a cuppa while the storm wears itself out," Ettie says, hurrying off. Ego and pride, she thinks. Thrilled that she and Marcus are beyond caring about either.

Friday – the day before the official reopening of The Briny Café – is bedlam. The rush is on to finesse every last detail. Sam makes good an early promise and turns up not long after dawn with a new pontoon on permanent loan from Frankie. For a rental fee of one (large) chocolate cake a week.

Kate arrives with a tub of beeswax to polish shelves that are filling with preserves, jams and fiery curry pastes made by the best local cooks. Ettie has five pots on the go, as well as three mixing bowls, and the oven is chockers with the sweet little pick-me-ups she is so fond of. The café fridges fill with deliveries of fresh ingredients for Ettie to conjure her culinary magic.

Out of the blue, Ettie announces she's terrified that if a customer's first experience is ordinary, it will hurtle them towards bankruptcy. There are no second chances in the hospitality industry where word-of-mouth makes or breaks, she says. They must get it right first time or they will go under. Kate has never seen her so flustered.

Around nine o'clock, Jimmy arrives at the café at a pace so sedate Sam is prompted to slap him on the back in praise. The kid blushes and his skin clashes violently with his carrot hair.

Ettie wanders onto the deck to tell them that while her cakes are baking, she'll cook a good healthy breakfast that will keep them going all day.

"A few mushies on toast'll do, love. That'd be tops," Sam insists.

Ten minutes later two plates, piled high with eggs, bacon, sausages, tomatoes, mushrooms topped with spinach and drizzled with a homemade tomato sauce spiked with the flavour of grilled capsicum, are ready. Kate grabs them and pushes open the flywire door with her foot. "Come and get it," she calls.

Sam's eyes light up. "A couple of slices of toast would have done. Ettie can't help herself," he says, rubbing his hands together in anticipation. Eggs just how he likes them, firm at the edges, runny yolks. The tomato is cooked through and looks sweet as a watermelon. The bacon is crisp but not burnt. And the mushrooms? Pan-fried so hot they didn't get a chance to turn soft and wet.

"You complaining?" Kate asks.

"She's the only woman in the world who could get me to eat spinach." He pats Kate's backside absently and pulls a list of jobs for the day from his pocket.

Kate pauses at the door, which no longer squeaks. "Sam," she says sweetly. "If you ever pat my backside again without a personal invitation, I'll knock your head off. Do I make myself clear?"

"Eh?"

The door slams behind her.

Mid-morning, the chef arrives with a massive bouquet of pink Oriental lilies, trimmed of their lower leaves and messy gold stamens, and arranged in exactly the right size vase to fit at the far end of the cake display fridge. He puts them in place without consulting Ettie and she feels a niggle of uncertainty. Perhaps she's not the main attraction after all. Maybe he harbours desires to muscle in on her territory.

"I was unable to personally deliver them to your home, Ettie, because I have no idea where you live," Marcus explains. "Please forgive."

"Ah," she says with relief. "I'm about to have a coffee. Like one? I've made a little biscuity ginger cake. Almonds on top. We can take it upstairs. That's where I live. Just moved in."

His face lights up. Ettie goes ahead, her hips swaying in a way she hopes lifts his spirits. In the privacy of her apartment, he reaches for her with a hunger that a small piece of ginger cake could never appease. She falls into his arms with a sigh.

Later, she asks if he would like her to set aside a space in the café where he could sell his chocolates, or pastries, or whatever. She would have to discuss it with Kate, of course.

The chef takes a long time to answer. "Why are you inviting me?" he says, his velvety voice unusually tight.

"Well, we are asking the best local cooks and it would be rude not to include you."

"Ah. So you are being diplomatic, only. You do not want my name?"

Ettie is appalled. "Good God, no! This is *our* café, *our* triumph or disaster, whatever it turns out to be."

The chef's brow clears. "I was so afraid. The fame. If that was all that attracted you."

"And I wondered, I must admit, if it was the café that really tempted you."

"So we are both uncertain, then, in our different ways."

"It's just . . . I am hardly a trophy," Ettie says, softly.

"No," he replies.

Ettie's heart almost stops.

"You are a gift," he says, finding the right word at last. Unaware she has just died a small death at his hands.

"Oh! Your coffee, the ginger cake," she says, making a slight move to go and get them.

"I am finished with being a professional chef, Ettie," Marcus says. "Cooking for a fundraiser, yes. Creating small delicacies for us to share in bed, yes. Running a café, no. My ambitions now are selfish. I must tell you all this because it is the truth." He speaks the words gently but passionately. "I wish to read books that take me on journeys of the mind and spirit. To go fishing in the light of dawn. To wake in the morning and make buttery pastries for a beautiful woman. To seize not just each day but each moment, because I have reached the age when there is far more time behind than ahead. But I must tell you this, too, because it is true and I am a man of my word. If you ever need my help, you have only to ask and I will don my toque and stand beside you. For you, I will go into battle once more. But Ettie, most of all, I wish to love and to be loved in return." There are two deep furrows between his brows. A query in his soft brown eyes. "Is this acceptable to you?" he asks, deeply serious.

"Oh my dear," she whispers.

"I was prepared to find my way alone. But you were a strike from lightning. With you, I am more alive."

"Chemistry," she murmurs, her mouth close to his. "It's all about chemistry."

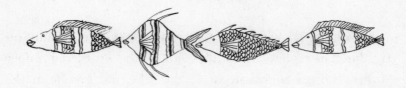

CHAPTER NINETEEN

The grand reopening to celebrate the fact that The Briny is back in full business takes place on a balmy, cloudless day with a lightly perfumed breeze wafting south from the tropics.

Ettie is calm and splendid in full chef regalia: checked trousers, white double-breasted jacket, black apron to her knees, a cloth over one shoulder. Her hair is tied back and tucked under a flaming orange bandana with tiny round mirrors sewn on. She pipes passionfruit cream into the scooped out hollows of lemon cupcakes. When she replaces their lids they look like wedding-day millinery.

Kate, with a navy-and-white butcher's apron over her blue jeans, goes outside with a cloth to wipe the night dew from deck rails, seats and tables. She straightens furniture, fills salt and pepper shakers, sweeps the deck and checks the opening balance on the till for the third time.

"Ready, set, go," says Ettie, without looking up from her cakes.

Kate flicks the sign from *Closed* to *Open* at 6.30 a.m. on the dot. The repaired door folds against the weathered timber wall, although flecks of paint still flake and puddle at the base. She hooks it in place with a shiny new latch and drags a blackboard outside that announces the café is open for business. *Free coffee, today only*, she adds in red chalk, to lure customers and give the day a sense of festivity.

They have agreed that Kate makes a fine pot of tea and Ettie is the queen of coffee. Kate will serve pre-prepared food. Ettie will do the cooking. Kate is the toast chef – Turkish, raisin, sourdough or ciabatta. Banana bread also falls into the toast category but involves a different process. It must be seared on a flat hotplate until it forms a crisp skin and is warm, but not red-hot, all the way through. Banana bread, Kate learns, is harder to get right than it appears.

Ettie has repeatedly told Kate that there is no time for mistakes, which, in any case, are expensive and wasteful. If she is unsure, she must ask questions. There can be no winging it with fingers crossed. Consumers are quick to judge and slow to forgive.

"Tourists, I mean. Offshorers will let us know if we've stuffed up and order us to have another go." Ettie wipes down her workplace and checks the clock on the wall. "Time to make the sandwiches, Kate."

At 6.45, their first (official) customer, a middle-aged bloke on his morning walk, strolls through the door. Kate steps up to the counter and takes his order for poached eggs, bacon (soft not crisp), sourdough toast, butter on the side. Coffee with a double shot. She clips the list to a rack above the grill. Ettie is already cracking two eggs into ramekins with a small amount of water in the bottom, ready for the microwave. She watches the seconds ticking down, no longer equating them – as she once did – with her future drizzling away in tiny electronic increments. He selects a newspaper.

"Twelve dollars and fifty cents," Kate says at the till. "The coffee is free. Today only, our opening special." She hands back his fifty-cents change and he drops it in a jar for community good works. She smiles a thank you, passes him a knife and fork wrapped in a napkin and tells him she will bring his food to him when it is ready.

He takes his newspaper outside on the deck where terracotta plant pots are lush with healthy young lemon trees. Old tin buckets, set out on a bench in a sunny, sheltered corner, are planted with fresh herbs: parsley, basil, thyme, oregano, chives, coriander. The fringes of strawberry-red umbrellas, donated by a coffee supplier hoping his beans will win favour, ripple like fingers over a keyboard.

Fifteen minutes later, the crowd from the *Seagull*'s first morning run swarms inside. "Like the banner outside, lovelies. Very creative!"

Ettie and Kate look at each other blankly. What banner? Ettie flicks her head towards the door and Kate dashes outside. And there it is, strung between two casuarinas, big, red and bold, written in a spidery hand:

Opin! Fri cofee. 2day

Sam and Jimmy sit at a picnic table under the sign.

"You, Jimmy?" Kate asks, pointing upwards.

"Yep!" Jimmy's head wobbles like a jack-in-the-box. "I did it all, didn't I, Sam?"

"You're a genius, mate."

Kate laughs. The Square is a parade of offshorers off to do the grocery shopping and take the kids to cricket practice. Early joggers. Mums wearing leotards and loose T-shirts, pushing prams. No chippies – not on a weekend. Plenty of dog walkers. All shapes and sizes – owners as well as dogs. Kate fills the water bowl under the outside tap, pushing aside the image of a snouty tan mutt with a white blaze who never harmed a flea.

A chunky, dark-headed figure lurks at the end of the wharf. Pacing impatiently, a mobile to his ear, his bark carries towards them.

"Is that the Weasel?" Kate asks in disbelief. As though she's conjured him by thinking about Boag.

Sam squints. "Yeah. Skin of a freaking rhinoceros."

The Weasel saunters towards them, his hands deep in the pockets of loose linen pants. His aftershave arrives ahead of him. He indicates the café with a casual roll of a shoulder. "Tell Ettie that timber like that wouldn't even need a match on the right day," he says in an oily voice.

"Insured to the hilt. You'd be doing us a favour," Kate shoots back.

"Should we tell him about the bad lemonade he gave me, Sam?" Jimmy is anxious.

"He knows, mate. He knows."

The Weasel makes his way back to the end of the wharf. Locals wrinkle their noses and step around him like he's rotten meat.

Fast Freddy cruises in on his last run after a nightshift made even longer because his newly married offsider overslept.

The Weasel jumps aboard the water taxi, giving the finger to everyone in general.

"Wondered why we hadn't heard a squeal from his jetty before now. Looks like he's been gone a couple days. Reckon he'll go for a spin in his boat first off," Sam says. "Roar past the Spit, trying for the biggest wake he can manage, just to make a point. There's time to pick up a couple of coffees and then watch the show." He slaps Jimmy on the back.

"Can I drink coffee too, Sam?"

"How about a fruit juice?"

"What show?" Kate asks.

Sam grins.

The pace is steady all morning. Kate and Ettie establish a rhythm to avoid crashing behind the counter or double-filling orders. When the breakfast rush ends, Ettie's cakes sell well but the sandwiches remain untouched.

"Do they look weird or something?" Kate asks, worried she's made a mess of them.

"Of course not. Wait till lunchtime. Then they'll move."

The two women finally manage to take a break on the deck in a short lull between morning tea and lunch. They see a boat – it looks like the Weasel's – stalled on the water, drifting east towards the ocean. They sip their coffees while a tide that's fat and full sings loudly under their feet.

A tinny glides alongside the seawall and a couple of Island musos disembark. "Think that boat out there needs a hand," Ettie says, pointing.

Phil, six and a half feet tall, says with a knowing smile:

"Not that boat." He has a red polka-dot bandana tied on his shaved head. His offsider, Rex, bare-chested under greasy overalls and wearing fancy cowboy boots with red leather flames, follows him with a guitar in his hand.

"Thought a little concert might help to kick off the opening," Phil explains.

Rex squints through the smoke of the cigarette hanging from his bottom lip. "Cost you a coupla burgers. Full works. Even the blinkin' beetroot, if you must. Suit you both?"

The two women nod, lost for words.

Phil rocks back on his heels and scans the crowd, like a cormorant looking for fish. "Good opportunity to show the mob on this side of the water how life should be lived. Poor pissants think a garage is the meaning of life."

"Not all of them, surely," Kate says, defensive. It wasn't so long ago that she hungered for a garage. And to be truthful, would still like one if it meant bypassing the frequently vandalised car park.

"Yeah. But it makes us feel good to think we're ahead occasionally." Phil grins.

Soon, there's a riffle of chords, a half-tune from a keyboard and they kick off with a full-bodied roar that stalls the joggers and sends the dogs cowering under the picnic tables, where they lie with their paws over their ears, emitting low, pathetic whines.

All afternoon, the music rocks on, bringing business from the bays, the Island and mainland. At one point, Kate goes onto the deck to clear the tables.

She stops dead when she sees her mother wandering the Square. Dressed in a flouncy red-and-green summer dress, set off with chunky costume jewellery that catches the light as she moves. Her face is painted into a ruddy clownishness – green eyelids, pink cheeks, red lips. Tiny black holes for eyes.

Kate takes a deep breath, slings a tea towel over her shoulder and marches up to her.

"Emily. You should have rung to let me know you were coming. I would have saved you a prime table."

"Is it true?" Emily asks. "You've bought into this . . . this . . . revolting disaster!"

"Around here we call it character. How'd you find out?"

"How do you think? I rang the magazine asking for you and some total stranger said you were in the café business. I laughed and she hung up on me. Me! I'm your mother, Kate, and you couldn't even be bothered giving me a call. I felt like a fool."

"Yeah. Well. Never mind. Listen, we're flat out. Opening day. If you want to eat, have a coffee, fine. Otherwise, I'll call you next week."

"Eat?" Emily shouts red-faced, waving her arm to take in the wharf, the café, the Square. "Here? Are you completely mad? I'm not sure why you've done this, Kate. All that time, money and effort spent educating you for something better and here you are, a waitress in a stinking rat-hole. Now call me a taxi. I can't bear to watch this . . . this horror show any more."

"There's a pay phone on the main road. You can't miss it." Kate's voice is hard, her blue-green eyes granite.

Emily's voice goes soft, which makes it all the more lethal. "You'll ruin this like you ruin everything, Kate. You're a loser. Have been from the start. If this is meant to hurt me, well, congratulations, it's worked. I'm appalled. Disgusted if you want the truth. Did you never consider for a moment how I might feel about this . . . this step into the gutter? Of course not. You've never shown the slightest interest in my wellbeing."

Kate looks at her mother, standing there like an over-decorated Christmas tree. "Don't come back, Emily," she says, softly. She reaches out a hand, almost touches her mother's shoulder, lets it drop. Emily's arms are folded tightly across her chest in the constant barricade of Kate's childhood.

As her mother backs off her heel catches in the sand and she almost falls. Before Kate can reach out, Sam appears out of nowhere and rescues the old girl. Emily is instantly flirtatious.

"There you go," he says, dropping her arm like it's on fire. "If you don't mind me saying so, mate, you're a bit on the wrong side of seventy for heels like that."

Her face hardens. Lips are pulled into a tight thin line. "Seventy!" she hisses, already on her way. "Seventy!"

Sam slings an arm around Kate's shoulder. "What was that?"

"My mother."

"You sure?"

"Yep."

"Jeez." He kisses the side of her head. "You know the saying *Like mother, like daughter*? Well, I can guarantee, Kate, you need never worry you're going to turn into a woman like that." He stares at the receding figure of Emily Jackson with a mixture of pity and disbelief. "Has it always been about her?"

"Yep."

"Well then, that makes you another in a long line of Cook's Basin miracles. You got out while there was still hope and we're all here to save you." He wraps his beefy arms around her and pulls her against his chest in a hug that knocks the wind out of her.

Kate looks into his eyes and gives him a smile that for some unfathomable reason shoots him straight to the moon.

On the deck, in the Square, it is a kaleidoscopic muddle – shorts and singlets, swirling skirts and sarongs, tail-wagging dogs dropping balls at bare feet, hats swatting sticky flies. The breeze is no more than a warm tickle. Phil's molten voice floats above Rex's tapping Cuban heels.

Ettie and Kate lose control of the kitchen. Jimmy leaps to the rescue.

"I'm gonna help, Kate, is that okay? I'll be great. You'll see." He hip-hops from one foot to the other and plunges his hands into boiling water without a yelp. Suds skyrocket and dishes fly. Fast Freddy grabs a tea towel while he waits for his cheese, tomato and herb omelette.

"You're a genius, Jimmy. No scungy bits at all." Fast Freddy, accustomed to fireshed clean-ups when the helpers' attention to detail fails dismally after a few glasses of red, is full of praise.

With the sink clear Kate sends Jimmy on a round-up of empty plates. Then has second thoughts. She watches and listens for crashes. One. A fork. Through the deck slats and into the water with a splash. No problems. She keeps him away from full plates of food, there is no point in pushing your luck.

The dishes pile up again. Jenny and the other two Js waltz in with smiley faces, rocking to the beat. They bump Kate out of the way. "This is a day for pros," they say with big smiles. "Watch and learn!" They help Ettie regain control of the orders, the kitchen, the cleaning up, before wafting off back into the sunshine. When the pressure builds again, Marcus quietly slips behind the counter. "Today, I am your sous chef," he announces to Ettie with a happy grin. "It is good to feel humbleness. But of course, only occasionally."

They battle on till the sun dips below the hills in an explosion of red, gold, orange and purple. As a final gesture, Ettie asks the chef to deep-fry three huge baskets of salt and pepper squid. She drops the crispy white slivers into little paper bags, stacks them on trays, then wanders through the crowd. Every dog in the square follows in a conga line, noses raised to the scent, hoping for some charity on a day that feels historic.

"On the house – thanks for being part of the celebration," Ettie says, handing out the food. "See you again. The Briny Café is back open for business."

CHAPTER
TWENTY

On Monday morning, after the early morning rush of chippies and commuters, Ettie offers to do the banking. "I need to do a bit of extra shopping," she explains. "The weekend almost cleaned us out."

Kate says she'll get on with restocking the fridges. She passes Ettie a pillowslip heavy with cash. "Don't get mugged or leave it at the checkout," she says, not joking.

In town, Ettie heaves the pillowslip onto the bank counter where it lands with a thunk. "Won the lottery or something?" asks the bank teller, a surfie-looking woman with sun-bleached hair, a deep tan and a body hard with muscle. She eyes it nervously, peeks inside. Finally reassured, she tips it upside down. "Had a bloke bring in a red-bellied black snake in a bag once," she explains. "He had a few banking issues at the time. Frightened the shit out of me."

"What did you do?"

"Took off, with all the other tellers, locked the bank and

called WIRES. Then we cancelled the bloke's accounts and suggested the bank next door."

The counter is awash with cash. Ettie feels ridiculously proud. "It's our first weekend in a new business. Not quite organised yet, the money's all in $100 bundles. The coins are sorted though."

She waits for twenty minutes while the teller weighs and counts so fast there is no hope of keeping up. The final balance is forty cents under. Kate is a natural with money, she thinks, trying not to feel smug that her partner is proving all the doubters wrong.

The teller indicates Ettie should wait a minute and slides off her stool to go through a heavy metal door, her backside as tight as a drum under grey trousers. A couple of minutes later she returns with a leather satchel and cotton bag.

"One for notes. One for coins. Bit classier than a pillow-slip," she explains with a smile. "Good luck."

After the first rounds in the battle to remove the Weasel are fired without any instant results, the Misses Skettle ask Lindy, the real estate agent, to do a property search to find out whether he owns the house or is a tenant. If the latter, could she locate the owners and advise them of the problems he is causing? Perhaps an eviction might be in order?

Lindy tracks down the background of the property that, unusually, she knows very little about. After some digging, she discovers the owners are living overseas. She taps out an email containing what she hopes are tactful but relevant questions.

The owners, it turns out, have never set eyes on their tenant – the deal was done over the web. Lindy discusses the issues and advises they use a respected agent in all future dealings. She is immediately hired to manage the property from now on. She begins by evicting the Weasel, then phones the Misses Skettle and fills them in.

The Weasel – real name Leo Merrizzi according to Lindy – accepts his fate. His tank water is putrid, his pontoon is a wreck and his commuter boat is still being repaired by Frankie who has been quietly advised by one and all to do his best but not his utmost. And if Frankie finds – after a suitable amount of time has passed – that the engine is beyond help, then the general consensus would be that that is a perfect result. It is, of course, his call.

Frankie, a loner who stays out of local feuds, politics and issues, and who lives by his own moral code, gives no verbal undertaking one way or the other. No one is fussed. Not many engines survive a serious dose of sugar that caramelises with heat and seizes most of the engine parts. The Weasel, to put it mildly, is stuffed.

Meanwhile, a troop of Islanders is assigned to drain the polluted water tank the moment the Weasel departs. It must be cleaned out, and anyone queuing for a top up from the mains water supply is advised he will have to wait a little longer for service while the tank is refilled. The new tenants, a family with three young children, plan to live on the Island full-time and are due to move in shortly. For once, no one gets narky about water rights.

Finally, the Weasel packs his clothes and few belongings and calls Fast Freddy to pick him up. In the midst of universal celebrations for a plan well executed, however, everything goes pear-shaped.

"I never asked where the Weasel wanted to go," Fast Freddy reports to Sam when he catches up with him in the Square. "I was on the way to drop him at the ferry wharf when he tapped my shoulder. Jumped like a startled ant, I did."

"And?" Sam asks, trying not to sound impatient.

"Well, we're not rid of him yet. I delivered him to a yacht anchored deadset centre of Oyster Bay. An old boat, *Ciao Bella*, almost alongside Artie. It hasn't shifted off the mooring for as long as I've been drivin' water taxis."

Sam is silent while he thinks through the ramifications. "Wise up Artie, did you?" he asks, hoping that having a vital role to play in the welfare of the community might put a bit of spark into the old fella, who's been showing signs of going downhill lately.

"Second call off the rank," Freddy says, with a hint of smugness. "He's on full alert. He's offered to set off his emergency siren, which he reckons will have the double benefit of alerting us to the arrival of any customers and scaring them off. He says he paid a fortune for the siren and he's never used it. He'd be pleased to get his money's worth."

"Civilised hours only, mate, or there'll be an uproar. What's it like below at Artie's?"

"Stinkin' mess."

"Life-threatening?"

"Just a crippled old man with dirty dishes piled up, lying in a fug of overripe sheets. Nothing too desperate."

"I'll see if I can round up some volunteers."

"Startin' next week. I've taken care of it for now."

"You're —"

Fast Freddy holds his palm outwards like a cop stopping the traffic. "Don't say it, Sam. Or I'll have to hit you, which would go against all me instincts."

"Star, mate, that's all I was going to articulate."

A few leaves skitter in front of them. The two men look towards a blow that's building in the west. The single-note yammering of cicadas carries across the water. A gust hits the umbrellas on the deck of The Briny. They crack like whips. The cicadas suddenly go quiet.

"Gotta fly while I still can," Fast Freddy says. "Shapin' up to be another doozy. Might get some real rain this time."

Sam dashes for the shelter of the café and bangs on the door. After a minute Ettie peers through the glass before opening up.

"Thought you might be a hopeful punter begging for an after-hours burger," she says, waving him inside and locking up after him.

"Get many of those?"

"Never ceases to amaze me."

The storm rockets through Cook's Basin not long after midnight. The drumming sound of rain on tin roofs is like music to the Islanders' ears. They turn over in their beds with sighs of relief, and fall straight back to sleep. But the rain, in what seems to be a recurring pattern, is blown out to sea before it does much more than dampen the ground. The wind keeps up until the first light of dawn, when flocks of birds come down from the trees to flutter about in a few shallow puddles. By noon, the ground is dry and hard once more.

Sam Scully wanders around his property checking for damage. The towering eucalypts look wind-whipped but they're holding on. They're like old Artie, he thinks, who fights like hell to stay alive but one day he'll stub his toe and keel over. Worn out fending off too many assaults for too long.

Back inside, he checks on Jimmy who's splayed on his bed like a starfish, sleeping soundly. He decides to leave him be. The kid runs at a thousand miles an hour most days and needs his rest. He'll pick him up on his way back from delivering a load of sandstone to Marcus.

Sam stops off at The Briny Café on his way to Cargo Wharf. As soon as the doors open, he'll grab a coffee. Ettie's foamy extravaganzas have become one of life's essentials.

The Square is a mess. Rubbish, dumped by a wind that racked up to thirty-five knots, is jammed into nooks and crannies, almost waist-high. The casuarinas look flayed and ready to collapse. Sam grabs the broom off the barge and begins sweeping up.

Twenty minutes later, the Square is tidied and the café is open. He goes inside looking for a garbage bag and a dustpan.

"Ask Kate," Ettie says, removing the first trays of raspberry muffins from the oven. "She knows where they are. I'll get your coffee on the go."

"You're the answer to every man's —"

"Dreams," finishes Kate. "Time for a new line, Sam. Ettie's dumped you for an older, handsomer and infinitely greater cook."

"You're laying it on a bit thick for this hour of the morning, aren't you?"

"Nah. You can take it. No brain, no pain." Kate swishes past him with the bag. "You've done a treat. Thanks. I'll finish up."

He chases her outside. "You got a minute, Kate?"

She turns to him, puzzled.

"You're a journo. Well, you were before you saw the light. How do you reckon I'd go about finding out about the Weasel?"

"What's it matter? The bloke's gone, isn't he?" She opens a bag and passes it for Sam to hold while she scoops up the rubbish.

"Yeah, well, that's the point. He's gone. But not quite."

"What the hell does that mean?"

"Mr Merrizzi has formally taken up residence on a wrecked yacht in Oyster Bay. Bloody peculiar if you ask me. You'd reckon he'd race back to town and his fancy ways, wouldn't you? He doesn't look like a bloke who's used to slumming."

Kate straightens up. "So let me get this straight. Instead of calling it quits and leaving, the Weasel chooses to live in squalor . . ."

"Because he's planning to keep dealing from the boat, don't you think?" Sam shakes the bag and Kate goes back to scooping.

"Yeah. Probably. But there's got to be more to it. He's a man who likes luxury. Nice linen. Soft shoes. And hot water, definitely hot water. You want to know what I think?"

"Why do you think I'm asking for your opinion, for Chrissake?"

"He's got nowhere else to go."

"Nah. He's rolling in it."

She shrugs. "It's the best I can do. Here, your turn to scoop. I'll hold."

Sam ignores her. He ties up the garbage bag and slings it over his shoulder.

"Hey, we're not finished. It's your turn."

He kisses her cheek and takes off. He's got five minutes flat before he's due at Cargo, and if he's late, he'll lose the upper hand.

Big Julie appears as a gang of commuters exits the café, each clutching a coffee and a muffin to sustain them on the slog through heavy traffic to the city.

"Sorry about the short notice, love, but can we hold the wedding this Sunday?" she asks Ettie, trying to say it lightly but her face is serious.

"How's Bertie?" Ettie lays an arm around her friend's shoulders. "Is he up to it?"

"Are *you* up to it? It's a hell of an ask. He wants the full catastrophe. Money no object for once in his life, the silly bugger."

"He's a romantic under that cranky veneer. Always known it." Ettie smiles. "Soft as a marshmallow." She puts a cup of coffee in front of Big Julie who is eyeing the cakes. "Want a rundown on the flavours?"

"No. I was remembering the Florentines. How the counter was always chockers with them. Bertie was a big fan. Not that he ate them. He reckoned the profit margin was a boomer and they kept for months."

"Jury's still out on that one," Ettie says, only half-joking. "Anyway . . . we've got orange, lemon, almond and coconut cakes and a strawberry sponge. Last but not least, a pear and almond flan. A sliver of one or all of them?"

Big Julie points at the flan. "Only a sliver. I'm really not hungry."

Ettie cuts a thin slice and ladles on the cream. "Honest opinion, okay?"

Julie takes a bite and nods. "Really delicious." She swallows another mouthful with difficulty and nudges the plate away from her, looking up apologetically. "Sorry, it's superb but if I eat any more I'm going to choke." She takes her plate to the sink.

"What do the doctors say?" Ettie asks.

"Not much. There's nothing to say. And neither of us believes in miracles, not any more." She looks ready to cry, her characteristic brassiness dulled by grief. "No point in wasting time denying the facts. Not when there's not much left."

"How's Bertie managing?"

"He's so brave, Ettie," she says. "I sit beside him and there's not a damn thing I can do except ask if he'd like another hit of morphine, which I know he hates because it gives him nightmares. Meanwhile, the bloody experts talk about pain relief, comfort and palliative care like it's a list of extras at a top hotel. No one ever mentions the horrors.

The whittling away of a life and spirit until there's nothing left. Not even dignity."

She turns her face aside. "You want to know what's truly terrible? Sometimes I want him to die. I want it to be over. For him. For me. There's nothing noble about death. And if one more person tells me that life goes on, I'm going to club them. Only death goes on. Then all that's left is a bloody great hole that can never be filled." Her voice catches on a sob.

"You're tired, love. Worn out."

"No, you don't understand. Every morning I wake up and want to run away."

"But every morning you get up and do everything that has to be done just the same. In my view, Julie, that makes you a hero."

"I want the past back, Ettie, because I'll know how to make the most of life this time."

"There's no going back. There never is."

Big Julie sighs, pulls a tissue from her pocket and blows her nose noisily.

"Come upstairs. Let's go over the wedding plans. You found a dress? I've got mine from a hundred years ago if you'd like to borrow it? Bit retro but I hear that's all the go."

"He'll think it's new, Ettie. He's been stuck in the seventies for most of his life."

Kate gets a ladder and writes the wedding details on their menu board to alert the locals. Ettie makes herself a double-shot espresso and takes it over to the table under the stairs where she slumps in a chair with a sigh.

"You okay, Ettie?"

"I swore I'd never do weddings. The bride always has a meltdown. The groom gets smashed. The parents on both sides argue. And the caterer gets the blame for the seating arrangements."

"But this is Bertie and Julie. Family."

"Yeah, I know. It's just that it's all so sad. Poor Julie. Poor Bertie. He doesn't look strong enough to get dressed let alone get married. God, sorry, love, I'm tired that's all. We really should do the wedding for free, you know. We owe him." Ettie doodles on a brown paper bag.

"No!" Kate is firm.

"He gave us a deal on the café, Kate. This is payback time."

"Definitely not. Let me handle this. If he wants to keep costs down, we'll make sure the food is inexpensive. I'll ask Julie how much he wants to spend and calculate backwards."

Ettie scrunches the paper into a ball, shoves her pencil into an old mug. "He's dying, Kate. It's our only opportunity to thank him in a way he understands."

"You have to trust me on this, Ettie. From what I've heard and know about Bertie, charging him the full rate will vindicate his faith in us and in the future of the café. He'd be appalled by a freebie. Asking for a discount was a test. If we'd said yes, I'm quite sure he would have reamed us out."

Ettie still looks doubtful.

"I'm not being hard, Ettie. I'm trying to let Bertie know that he's left the café in good hands. The Briny is his memorial. He wants to be sure it's going to live on long after him."

*

The locals greet the news of Bertie and Big Julie's wedding date with a mixture of joy and sadness. Everyone agrees that on the big day they will dig out their best clothes, their most festive hats and even a decent pair of shoes. They will raid the Island, the bays and any municipal garden for enough flowers to cast on the water in a thick carpet, wishing them health and happiness. But mostly health because if they get the chance they can manage the happiness themselves. They will smile like angels and toast the bride and groom until they go hoarse.

They will never, ever ask Bertie how he's feeling. And if either of the two notorious Island pessimists utters a single word that's even slightly questionable, they will be thrown like javelins over the rail of the deck of the new, very acceptable version of The Briny Café. It's going to be the cracker of all cracker weddings. A blaster to keep Bertie and Julie alight through the dark days ahead. And no one, absolutely no one, has permission to shed a single tear, let alone break out in a full-bore sob – or they too will find themselves kissing sharks in their best duds!

Late in the afternoon, when Ettie feels like her feet are on fire and her legs are filled with concrete, the chef wanders into the café with a basket over his arm. Kate takes one look at his lovesick face and disappears into the Square, where the sky is black with the promise of real rain, the kind that falls steadily and heavily.

Ettie goes over to Marcus and kisses him passionately.

"I have prepared a salmon tartare with capers, mint, lemon juice, olive oil and vodka. Cooked a goat's cheese, caramelised onion and sage tart with a flaky pastry. For dessert, a white chocolate mousse with Frangelico. I also tracked down six perfect, honey-sweet figs. Did you know it is lucky to make a wish on the first bite of new season fruit?"

"Oh Marcus, it sounds wonderful . . ."

"I had hoped a picnic on a small beach somewhere, with a blanket, some good wine and a full moon. But the weather is not obliging."

"Bertie and Julie are getting married in the café this weekend. I need to plan the menu tonight. I must work, please understand."

"Ah yes, but you must also eat to keep up your strength. Perhaps, instead of the beach, we could share our picnic upstairs on your deck, while you tell me your ideas for the wedding feast? We can watch the storm together?"

"What a wonderful idea," says Ettie, seeing the sense of it. "I'd like to take a shower after we close. So if you returned around seven-thirty . . ."

"May I wash your back? You have a glorious back."

"Lovely," she sighs, feeling her stress drain away.

He drops the basket, takes her in his arms and swings her around the café in a tiny waltz.

She kisses him once more and tells him to take the basket upstairs, she will join him shortly. And if he has any tips on easy fingerfood, she'd love to hear them.

Snug in the penthouse, the Cook and the Chef read to each other from recipe books that lie piled at their feet on the jewel-coloured Turkish rug. On the wall, Ettie's painting of seagulls looks down on them. They graze on picnic food in small, delicious bites, weighing the merits of one dish or another for Bertie's last hurrah.

"All day, you spoil your customers. Now it is my turn to spoil you," Marcus says, fetching the mousse from the fridge. He places it in front of her with reverence. Hands her a small teaspoon so that she will savour the smooth richness in tiny mouthfuls.

"Where have you been all my life?" she says.

"It is the timing that brings about opportunity. But we must always be ready for it," he replies, seriously. "Would you like a cup of coffee or green tea – with fresh mint?"

"You decide," she sighs, retiring to the sofa and dragging a knitted patchwork blanket over her feet before lying back amongst the cushions. She holds up a list and reads out loud:

Fresh oysters.
Fresh prawns.
Pork and fennel sausage rolls (for Sam).
Lamb cutlets (especially for Bertie).
Salt and pepper squid (by popular demand).
Antipasto platters and a selection of wonderful
Australian cheeses.

"What do you think?"

"Perfect. And the cake?"

"Oh God, I forgot about a cake."

"If you agree, I will make it. Three tiers. Fruit, of course, Bertie is a traditional man, I believe. I will make the marzipan and cover over it with white icing. But I can do no more. Decoration is not my forte."

"As it happens, decorating *is* my strong point. If you would like to make extra marzipan, I could create a replica of the café with figures of Bertie and Julie."

"So. We complement each other then," Marcus beams, handing Ettie her tea. "May I spend the night?"

Ettie indicates her extremely narrow bed with a rueful look. The chef is thoughtful.

"Perhaps," Ettie suggests, blushing, "if I lie on top of you?"

His face clears instantly. "I adore a practical woman."

A little before eleven o'clock, Ettie and Marcus hear a low growl, like a plane high above and a long way off. There's a massive crack. Ettie jumps in fright: "Whoa!" The bay strobes ghostly grey for a split second. The wind hits like a slap, riffling the pages of her cookbooks. The chef drags shut the door to the deck and turns the key.

Outside, sheet lightning pulses like a rock concert and rain hits the tin roof with the sound of an army on the march.

"God, what if it pours on Sunday? It'll be a catastrophe." Her voice barely carries above the din.

"We adapt," he says, unflustered.

"Well, if there is a higher authority, I reckon Bertie might be close enough to exert a bit of influence."

In the small hours of the morning, Ettie and Marcus are spooned together in a way that suggests they have slept like this for years. When the phone rings, neither of them stirs. The noise of the wind, the sea and boats creaking on their moorings screens the sound. But the ring goes on and on until it finally wakes Ettie. She is instantly fearful. No good call comes in the dead of night.

She reaches for the phone. "Hello?" she whispers.

"Ettie, thank God you're there. It's Julie. Can you get over here? Fast."

"Is it Bertie?" Ettie asks, thinking the worst.

"No. No. He's fine. But I need help."

"I'll be there in ten minutes. I'll run."

"Not a word about this."

"Right."

Marcus rouses a little as she's pulling on some clothes. "Go back to sleep," she whispers. "Everything's fine." She races down the stairs, grabs her wet-weather gear from a hook under the stairs.

The Spit glistens in the dark. Out to sea, the moon breaks through cauliflower clouds for a second and frosts the water. She runs along the flooded road until the moonlight disappears and the night is black again. Stormwater streams down the hill and large lakes pool where drains have blocked. The streetlights, knocked out by vandals, are useless. She stumbles in a deep pothole and curses, the pain shooting along her spine. The rain starts up again, pounding down in a thick wall of water.

Bertie's shabby weatherboard cottage is one street back from the waterfront and two hundred metres south of the café. A winding brick pathway sprouting weeds a foot tall leads to the front door. On either side, roses are copping a hammering.

Ettie pushes open the gate and runs for the shelter of the

verandah. She sluices water off her jacket. Knocks lightly. Within seconds a porch light comes on and Julie yanks her inside, quickly switching off the light.

"What the hell is going on?" Whispering although she's not sure why.

Julie is dressed in gumboots and a short floral nightie, which just manages to contain her voluptuous figure. She puts her finger to her lips and waves at Ettie to follow. They tiptoe down a cluttered hallway and through a kitchen straight out of the 1950s.

Without a word, Julie leans her shoulder hard against a broken back door and pushes. The bottom scrapes over a few loose bricks and finally opens wide. They dash to a corner of the house where Julie lifts a hatch to reveal rough brick steps leading into a basement.

"I'll go first. Take off your shoes and roll up your trousers, it's like a swimming pool down there."

"You need a plumber, Julie. Not me," Ettie whispers back.

"That's the last thing I need."

The basement is dark and smelly. Viscous muddy water comes up to their knees. Ettie has to grab hold of Julie to keep her balance. Something bumps her leg and she kicks sideways, hoping it isn't a dead rat. Julie switches on her torch and flashes it across the basement.

"Holy kazoo!" Ettie gasps.

Thousands of banknotes, in every denomination, float on top of the water. Pink, red, blue, green, even grey. A paper flotilla swirls, bobs, drifts but never sinks.

Ettie scoops up a few notes, shining the torch on them. "This real? Or did Bertie have a printing press somewhere?"

"It's real, alright," Julie says. "Bertie's private bank. Thank God Australian notes are waterproof."

"Holy kazoo!" Ettie says again. Lost for words.

"When I realised the basement was flooding, I went to call Emergency Services and Bertie was so distraught he nearly choked. He kept pointing at the back door. I thought he might be spinning out on his drugs but he dragged himself outside and showed me the trapdoor. He didn't calm down till I said I'd take a look. The silly old bugger stashed all his money in drainage pipes stuffed with dirt at each end."

Ettie – cold, in shock and knee-deep in water – begins to laugh. Silently at first, then in muffled shrieks. "Gives a whole new meaning to the term *money laundering*. Sorry. Not funny. God, what kind of a bloke lives like a miser and keeps his money under the bed? Or, more precisely, in a drainpipe?"

"An anarchist," Julie says, seriously. "A bloke who'd rather live off the radar than on it."

"Well, we'd better collect it and hang it up to dry," Ettie says, because she is, as Marcus pointed out, a practical woman.

The hilarity of the women carries through the floorboards to where Bertie lies in bed, his heart banging against his ribcage in a race to the finish. Slowly, his pulse returns to normal. He closes his eyes and sleeps.

It takes two hours to clear the basement. Ettie estimates there is more than half a million dollars hidden there. Bertie, no doubt, has money stashed all over the house and buried in the backyard as well. A tidy little retirement fund.

"Get him to draw a treasure map," she says, "or whatever he's hidden will be dug up and enjoyed by the next generation when it knocks down the house to renovate."

Finally, at the first hint of dawn, Ettie walks home. The rain has cleared and it's eerily quiet after the racket of the storm. She wades through even the deepest puddles, so wet already it makes no difference. She turns into the Square and sees the café is blazing with light. Marcus paces like a lion. He breaks into a run the moment he sees her.

"I was so worried." He wraps his arms around her. "An accident, I thought. Perhaps in the water."

"I'm fine," she says, smiling.

"Please, next time, wake me."

"Too many years of fending for myself."

"Tell me what is happening. If I know, I can prepare."

"Julie called to say the storm had upset Bertie. She needed help. He's fine now, completely settled down." Well it was the truth, just not quite all of it.

Cook's Basin News (CBN)

Newsletter for Offshore Residents of Cook's Basin, Australia

DECEMBER

GRAND REOPENING OF THE BRINY CAFÉ

What a party it was! Ettie and Kate would like to thank Phil and Rex for their wonderful music, Jimmy for his banner, and everyone who turned up throughout the day to make it such a special event. Especially the Three Js and Chef Allender, who made a one-time-only guest appearance and announced Ettie's lamb burgers would rival the Rainbow Room's. No kidding!

They would also like to announce a new takeaway menu (ask for a brochure) and to say that opening hours will be from 6.30 a.m. until 6.30 p.m.

Comedy Acts Wanted

Do YOU always see the funny side of life? Are YOU a natural comedian? If you are and would like to spread your humour to a wider audience, why don't you create a 5- to 10-minute performance to present to our panel of judges (sorry, we've got to have judges to ensure the content is not too outrageous!). It's for our show, which is tentatively listed for February 10 at the Cutter Island Community Hall. Have a go. Make us laugh!

Enquiries: Lazlo Timberland.

COMMUNITY VEHICLE

The Community Vehicle will be moved off the Island for repairs and maintenance for one week. We apologise for the inconvenience.

Wharf Repairs

Apologies for the short notice but we have just been informed that repairs will be carried out to the ferry wharf on the south side of the Island today. There will be no services until after lunch. Anyone wishing to use public transport will have to hoof it to one of the other wharves.

SHARK ALERT

An alarming number of large sharks (possibly bull sharks) have been sighted cruising around the shores of Cutter Island. One three-metre monster was sighted off a jetty in Oyster Bay and several have been seen feeding off Triangle Wharf. If anyone has any more up-to-date information, please contact the Editor.

CHAPTER TWENTY-ONE

It rains all the next day. The water in the bays is cloudy brown with run-off from the land. Spume, like dishwater, is lacy along the shore. Commuters rush past in gumboots, their laptops and briefcases wrapped in garbage bags to keep them dry. Everyone scratches leech bites on feet, legs, ankles. Slimy, fat and full, they drop off on the jetty or inside the café, oozing blood in slippery red puddles. But the trees lift their heads and their withered leaves begin to fluff. The big fish – kingfish, flathead, bonito – return and jump high out of the water, the sheen on their silver bodies like mirrors. King parrots appear, deep red and green, along with shy black cockatoos and whole families of tawny frogmouths that line up on branches looking inscrutable. Skinks come out to rustle amongst the wet leaves. Frogs sing torturously loud night-time arias. The humidity is thick enough to slice with a knife. Summer at last!

There are reports of long dark shadows that could be sharks cruising the bays. Mothers forbid their children to swim at dawn or sunset when they traditionally feed. Fast Freddy promises to keep an eye out, even though – as he patiently explains – the chances of spotting much at night are pretty slim. Still, anyone tempted by a risky midnight skinny-dip might want to think twice before stripping off and plunging blindly into the deep.

The two Misses Skettle tell anyone who cares to listen that it wasn't so long ago that the bays were so thick with sharks you could walk across their backs from one side to the other, without getting your feet wet. The kids go goggle-eyed. A few sceptics grimace. The old girls shake their heads, as they often do, at how quickly history is forgotten. They ramp up to full alert, and work out a system of shifts for the next few days so one of them will always have her eyes glued to the binoculars. Searching not for sailors in distress, this time, but for the sight of a deadly fin cutting through the water like a silver sail.

In the café, where it's been a slow morning and looks like being a slower afternoon, Kate sits at the office table drawing up plans for the wedding. It will be a tight squeeze on the deck. They need a table for the beer keg, another for the wine and glasses, another for food. Leaving no space for the bride and groom to take their wedding vows.

"Maybe the top deck?" Kate suggests. "We can dress it up like a stage."

Ettie nixes the idea. "Too many steps for Bertie."

"Good point." Kate chews the end of her pencil. Fundamentally the café must be at the heart of all that takes place.

Ettie goes back to making sausage rolls to freeze for the big day as Kate calls a supplier to check on the price of prawns and oysters. Both women look up when the screen door slams.

"Ladies," Sam says like a toff, touching a finger to his brow in a salute.

Jimmy beams at them. "No sharks. Not one."

They both make wet puddles on the floor.

Ettie looks from Sam to Kate. "Are you thinking what I'm thinking?" she says, raising her eyebrows. Kate nods and turns to Sam with a radiant smile.

"Eh?" Sam asks, nervously.

"Boys, let me fix you a couple of my already famous burgers. Kate's got something very important to discuss with you."

"It's about Bertie's wedding," Kate says, her tone wheedling. "You may have a bigger role than you thought."

"You're not saying I'll have to stand in as proxy or anything, are you? I know Bertie's crook but he'll turn up on the day, won't he?" Sam's a man who likes to help if he can but a bloke has his limits.

Kate laughs. "Relax. Nothing like that."

Sam frowns, still suspicious. Women on a mission, he thinks. Nothing more bloody terrifying, especially when there's a wedding involved. There's no sense to be had until it's all over and the last drunks cleared away. He chews a hangnail, thinking hard and fast. He decides he'll agree to move the furniture, he'll happily do keg duty, he'll even wash up. But he'll say a firm no to all other requests.

"We'd like to include your magnificent barge in the celebration. She's such an integral part of Cook's Basin. As iconic as The Briny. Would it be okay to tie it at the end of the deck for a little while on the big day?" Kate smiles at him in a way that fuddles his head for a moment. He registers *barge*, when he'd expected *furniture . . . keg . . . bar*. Easy as . . .

"No worries," he says, happy to be helpful, falling for the spin.

Ettie brings over his hamburger, arranged like a work of art. She calls Jimmy to the counter and gives him a large bowl of hot chips with plenty of tomato sauce as well. Keeping him out of the way of what she suspects might be delicate negotiations.

Sam tucks into his burger as Kate hands him a paper napkin with a smile, and from the look on her face he knows in a flash he's about to be hung out to dry.

"The rest is really easy," she says, leaning forward. She lays out the plan using a fork to make invisible lines on the tabletop. Sam swivels and twists, leans backwards and forwards, narrows and widens his eyes, trying to make sense of it. He picks up on a few keywords that make his heart sink. Flowers. Bowers. Froth and bubble. Jeez, he thinks. No good turn goes unpunished. He feels a twinge of remorse for his noble barge and in his head apologises to the old girl. He silently promises to make it up to her with a grease and oil change. And a thorough anti-foul.

He bolts the rest of his burger, grabs hold of Jimmy and skedaddles before Kate has time to think of anything else.

That night, when the shore is swathed in the clammy mist of high humidity and not even a zephyr stirs the deep black water or the leaves on the trees, the Weasel's yacht mysteriously comes adrift from its mooring. He wakes at sunrise to find himself beached amongst a thicket of gnarly mangroves.

"You're dicing with death," he hisses when Sam answers his call. "It's only a matter of time."

Sam holds the phone in front of him and looks at the screen, puzzled. "Not sure who you're calling, mate, but you've got the wrong number and, if I may say so, a dodgy sense of humour." He clicks off. Sighs when it rings again.

"Listen, you moron, I want my boat back on its mooring in an hour."

"No idea what you're talking about," Sam replies, recognising the Weasel's voice now. He struggles into a sitting position in bed just as the line beeps and cuts out. Far as he knows, the Weasel has gone off the local radar. Everyone figures Mr Suave will give up the wreck, which is a prison when you think about it, and return to civilisation within two weeks. No further action required. Boats sound romantic but the reality is cramped bunks, the stench of mounting garbage, bunged-up dunnies and airless cabins where the mossies are slow torture from dusk till dawn. Jack the Bookie is giving odds-on at the ten-day mark.

Scratching his chin, Sam throws back the sheet, in need of a piss. He shuffles quietly past Jimmy's room, struggling to make sense of the call.

"Hiya, Sam."

Sam jumps. "Jeez, Jimmy! You're gonna give me a heart attack one day. No creeping around. Thought we'd settled that."

"Everything okay, Sam? You got an early load? Am I on deck?"

"No mate. Back to bed. Nothing till later. Off you go."

But the kid sets off for the kitchen instead. Sam sighs and follows. "Right, mate. On your toes. Breakfast first. Then we're gonna find a missing yacht. You want bacon and eggs after your Weet-Bix?"

The *Mary Kay* cruises the bays on a summer morning that gets hotter and hotter. The waterways are busy with early holiday-makers, one or two wakeboarders, plenty of noisy stink boats with twin engines heading off to lunch somewhere where they'll catch any breeze that's going. Blokes out fishing stand holding rods lightly, alert for a twitch, tug or a full-on grab. Maybe he'll buy the kid a fishing line for Christmas, Sam thinks, then scraps the idea. Jimmy couldn't kill a fly.

He watches the kid coiling ropes in tight circles and feels a pang. He imagines fathers must feel like this when they see their sons growing into decent young men. Jimmy might not be the full quid in some people's eyes but if Sam could choose a boy of his own, he'd pick Jimmy without hesitation. All courage and heart. And not a lazy or nasty bone in his long, skinny body. Lot more going for him than some of those hard-eyed kids in tight school uniforms that hang around the mall with their foul mouths and fast-food jelly-bellies.

"Over there, Sam. Do ya see it?" Jimmy stands and points.

The Weasel's yacht is skewered in the mangroves, heeling in the mud.

"You've got the eyes of an eagle, Jimmy my boy. Good on ya." Sam spins the helm 360 degrees and points the *Mary Kay* back the way they've come. Three weeks to Christmas. He needs to think of something to put under the tree for Jimmy.

Maybe a surfboard. Dumb idea. There's no surf in enclosed waters such as Cook's Basin.

"Jimmy," he yells out the cabin door.

The kid pounds along the deck. "Yeah, Sam, everything's alright, isn't it?"

"Good as gold, mate. Just wondering what to get you for Christmas."

"A dog, Sam."

Ah jeez. "Fenders over on the portside, mate. Quick as a flash."

"Aye, aye, captain." He gives a salute that somehow tangles in his gelled hair. He licks his fingers clean and gallops to carry out his orders.

Sam eases the *Mary Kay* alongside Artie's yacht and knocks on the hull, waking the poor sod out of a dreamless sleep.

"Gimme five, till I pull on me strides," Artie wheezes.

"Take your time, mate. There's no hurry."

Artie coughs, triggering a fit of ragged spasms. Sam holds Jimmy back from flying to his aid.

"Leave a man his dignity, mate. He'll call if he's desperate."

Ten minutes later, Sam sits opposite Artie in the close air of the cabin while a kettle whistles on the stove. "I'm outta milk if you're passin' by soon," Artie says, nudging a mug of pitch-black brew towards him with a set of arthritic knuckles.

"No worries. You on your regular watch last night?" Sam asks, trying to sound casual.

Artie nods his sparrow head up and down. Fluffs of grey hair rise like horns from behind his ears.

"Many visitors?"

Artie makes a throat-cutting motion with his index finger.

"None?"

Artie nods again and slurps his tea with noisy pleasure. "If no one heard me siren go off then that's 'cause there was no one around."

"Well, somehow the Weasel's boat slipped its mooring and ran aground in the mangroves north of Kingfish Bay. Any ideas?"

"Busted rope. Been waitin' for it to happen. Wore out years ago. Miracle it's lasted this long."

"Ah," Sam says, agreeing. He swills his tea and stands, bending his head under the low roof of the saloon. "Ask Artie what needs doing, Jimmy. Be back for you in a few hours." He whacks his mug in the sink along with a dozen others.

"Don't forget me, Sam?" Jimmy says.

"Not in this lifetime, mate."

Out on the water, boats whizz past and people turn to look at the stranded yacht, not sure if some mug has run aground after too many gin and tonics or if it is a botched insurance scuttle. No one stops to help. The boat is cast until the tide floods back. There's nothing to do but wait.

On the other side of the bay, Sam fixes the mooring rope and returns on the barge to hang off the mangroves, waiting for the stranded yacht to right.

The day gets hotter and hotter. It must be hell below, Sam thinks, hearing *Ciao Bella* creak and groan with every shift in the level of the water. As soon as she's floating, he nudges the barge up close enough to attach a towline. He sets off back to the mooring, slowing when he's close enough to let *Ciao*

Bella drift alongside. He reaches for a boat hook and drags up a buoy attached to a new, bright white rope. He tosses it to the Weasel who's only just appeared on deck, looking so strung out Sam almost feels sorry for him.

"Fixed it for you," he says. "Big storms predicted next week. If you're planning to hang around, you might want to get your mooring serviced. Not that I'm worried about you, mate, but I wouldn't want to see Artie's boat rammed and sunk when the poor bloke's legs are buggered."

Sam waits for a response. None comes. Sam lifts his hat, scratches his head. "You seem to be having trouble catching up."

"You wanna do the mooring?" The Weasel's words slide out in a slur. He is in dire need of a shower, shave, a haircut and a set of clean clothes. "Cash upfront."

"Cash."

"When?"

"How about Monday?"

The Weasel nods and disappears back into the dark hole of his current existence.

If it weren't for Artie, would he have left the Weasel to drown? Sam hopes not. But he isn't sure.

Two days before the wedding is due to take place, Big Julie pokes her face through the café door. She is on the verge of tears. "The wedding's off. Sorry to mess you around but Bertie's cancelled." She points at the blackboard. "You better rub that out soon as you can."

"Oh love, too crook, is he?" Ettie says, quickly putting a

couple of cakes on a plate. She lines up three cups and hits the espresso button. "What a shame."

"Nothing to do with his health. He's been nervy since he discovered he had to produce a birth certificate and fill in a few forms. He was still prepared to go ahead until the, er, *accident* put the wind up him."

"What accident?" asks Kate.

Julie throws a quick glance at Ettie. "Um, he lost his tax records when the basement flooded in the big wet."

Ettie tsks.

"Poor bastard," Julie adds. "He's at death's door and still haunted by the thought that he might have to hand over money to the government." She breaks off when a customer wanders in looking for bait and ice-cream. Kate takes care of him, trying to figure out whether it is too late to cancel orders with the providores and, if not, how much of a financial hit they'll take.

Big Julie says, "He knows it's a late call and there'll be expenses. He'd be grateful if you'd give him a bill for what he owes."

Kate feels a twinge of remorse. Bertie might have made a religion out of stiffing bureaucracies but she should have known he'd never cheat his friends.

"I have an idea," Ettie says, softly and slowly, as if it is still taking shape in her head. "This is how I see it." She sits down and leans forward, elbows resting on the tabletop. "We've already done a lot of preparation and we know Bertie hates waste, right? So why don't we have a naming ceremony instead of a wedding? No forms, no certificates, nothing official. Just two people who love each other making their vows amongst a community that loves them." She sits back, slapping her palms lightly on the table.

Big Julie frowns and says nothing, spooning the froth at the bottom of her cup into her mouth.

Ettie continues, earnest: "Don't you see? Sam can conduct the service, make the speeches and take you sailing off into the sunset when it's all over. Like a ship's captain. It'll be glorious. Totally romantic."

Big Julie is still unconvinced. "I'll talk to Bertie. He's pretty adamant, though."

"Turn him around, Julie. This isn't just about him. Oh I know he's crook but this is for you. His grand gesture. He needs to make it for his own peace of mind."

Two hours later, Big Julie rings the café. She sounds like a different woman. "It's on!" she says, excited. "Bertie's even going to wear a black tie with his T-shirt!"

"Good on him, love," Ettie says. "Tell him he's showing his true romantic spirit at last!"

CHAPTER TWENTY-TWO

On the Sunday of Bertie and Julie's naming ceremony, the sky is overcast, the grey water as smooth as sharkskin. Sam sits at a table on the deck with a pencil and paper, watching Kate setting up. She has the knack now, he thinks. Stack, wipe, straighten chairs, cluster the sugar and salt and pepper in a neat circle. Quick as a flash, she lines up her world. Who'd have thought a five-star journo could turn her life upside down and make a go of it? Or maybe chaos scares the hell out of her? That mother of hers, she'd scare the bojangles off anyone.

Kate catches him staring. He grins, happy to see it tips her off balance.

"Reckon it might rain?" she asks, looking up at the sky, worried they don't have a perfect back-up plan, although the chef has kindly offered his home if the heavens open.

"Could build to a storm or fade out to sea," Sam says, without checking for signs. His face is creased with concentration. Christ, the longest note he's ever written is an invoice, and they're challenging enough. What the hell is he supposed to say at a naming ceremony, whatever that is? A feeling of dread builds inside him like the bloody storm.

He licks the tip of his pencil, writes a word, crosses it out.

"Want me to write it for you?" Kate asks, looking over his shoulder at his pathetic efforts.

"Would you, mate? I'm stuck." His face glistens with relief. He thrusts the paper towards her in a flash, throws the pencil after it and pushes back his chair.

"No way! That was a joke, Sam. You've known Bertie all your life, and Julie for twenty years. You can do it, just take your time and think about it."

Sam looks so miserable, she takes pity and picks up the pencil. He leaps to his feet like a kid who's been let off the hook and plants a kiss on the top of her head.

"Owe you one," he chirps, taking off before she changes her mind.

Kate writes:

1. Describe how they met.
2. How they fell in love.
3. How they are loved by the offshorers.
4. Any funny stories (the coffee jokes are old hat so don't go there).
5. You might want to ask other people for stories as well.
6. Explain what a naming ceremony means.
7. Pronounce them partners for life (do not cry or even sniffle here or everyone will howl).
8. Anything else you think appropriate.

She finds Sam in the Square. "There you go. Nothing to it."

He snatches the paper eagerly, but his face falls. "Mate," he says, "where's the good stuff for me to read out?"

"It's all in your head, Sam. I've given you the pointers. Now talk from your heart."

He looks doubtful. "Okay. Yeah. I'll wing it. Only way." He folds the list and stuffs it into the back pocket of his shorts.

"You got all those flowers attached yet, Jimmy?" he calls, heading for the barge.

Jimmy looks up from where he sits cross-legged amidst a sea of white gauze. He's holding a basket of cut roses and a roll of thin wire. The long crab claw of the crane hovers over his head. "It's gonna look magic, isn't it, Sam? How many of these flowers you want?"

"All of them, mate. That's what they're for. And make sure you can't see any bits of wire poking through the edges. Ruins the effect."

"Nice and romantic, is that it, Sam?"

"You got it."

Jimmy reaches into a huge basket of roses. "You think anyone will marry me?"

Sam catches a tone in Jimmy's voice, holds back a flippant remark. He walks over to the boy and squats alongside him, picking a red rose out of the basket and winding wire around the stem.

"Well, mate, that's a big question, 'cause there's plenty of ways of looking at the institution of marriage. Me? Now, remember, I've never been married, right?" Sam holds up a hand to block the question forming in Jimmy's head. "Never felt right. Don't know why, but it didn't. And that's the thing about marriage, it's gotta feel so damn right that to keep loving someone without it feels all wrong. You get my drift?"

Jimmy's hand shoots up.

"No questions. Not yet. Now there's another complication I've got to mention if I'm going to do this right. Just 'cause you think marriage is a great idea doesn't necessarily mean the woman you want to marry feels the same way. It might hurt to know she doesn't love you as much as you love her but it's got to be a two-way street or it'll never work. You getting this, Jimmy?"

Jimmy is bursting. "How do you find a girlfriend, Sam?"

Sam grins and pushes himself to his feet, handing Jimmy his wired rose. "Mate, they find you," he says. "Trust me. They find you. But only when the time is right. You've got to be patient. Sometimes it takes longer than you'd like."

Sam checks his watch. Noon. Three hours to go. He glances towards the south. The light is eerie, bruised and bright at the same time. Touch and go whether the whole shebang will be washed out. He picks up another rose and wires it to his T-shirt. "All my life I've been saying good morning to Bertie and I never knew he was a mad rose grower. Everyone's a mystery, mate. Deep down, we've all got hidden passions."

A large sign announces the café is closed for a private function, but no one takes any notice. Locals and tourists wander in and out and Kate makes coffees and toast so no customer is turned away or offended. She feels a quiet thrill every time the till pings. She is turning into a rabid capitalist, not unlike the people she used to write about, she admits. Even more alarming, she really, really likes the feeling.

Ettie and Marcus arrange platters of salami, cheese, olives, grilled vegetables and dips. Singing, bumping hips and shoulder-swaying in time to a tune about life being a cabaret. The oven is filled with bite-sized fish pies, salmon quiches and mixed mushroom tartlets, the chef's last-minute contributions because he is, after all, a man who is passionate about food, and even more passionate about a woman who understands that passion.

Ettie has prepared a mountain of lamb cutlets marinated in garlic, rosemary and grated lemon rind. Pounded calamari, dunked in heavily salted and peppered flour, is ready for the deep-fryer. The chef's boozy celebration cake, a towering edifice decorated with marzipan sculptures of café tables and chairs, and astoundingly accurate figures of Bertie and Julie, stands in a safe corner. Ettie worked late for three nights until she was happy with the result. She took a vote on whether to add a cup of coffee. Everyone said yes, so she decided it was a bad idea.

By three o'clock, with the storm holding off, the barge looks like a florist shop and the back deck of the café is crammed with guests clutching bunches of flowers to throw in celebration. Phil croons songs from the fifties. Bertie told him rock music sung flat out would be the death of him and he was near enough to last rites as it was. He'd like a lovely rendition of "Ave Maria", though, if they could manage it. Phil generously offered to go solo when Rex visibly buckled at the prospect.

Jimmy, resplendent in electric-blue satin shorts and a red

satin singlet, is on sentry duty in the Square, under orders to alert Ettie as soon as the happy couple rolls up in the hire car.

"Not yet!" he calls, sticking his spiky head through the door every five minutes until Sam feels compelled to tell him they don't need a *no-show* report. Only a *they're here* announcement.

Sam has changed into dress-up blue jeans, a crisp white shirt and wears a double-breasted navy jacket with one of Bertie's yellow roses pinned to his lapel. His steel-capped boots have been replaced by soft boat shoes, he's cleanly shaven, his hair damped into order with a squeeze of Jimmy's much-maligned gel. His hands are so well scrubbed, the freckles stand out like dollar coins. He paces up and down, rehearsing his speech.

"You're going to wear a hole in the floor," Kate says, laughing.

"This is real pressure, mate," he admits, shaking his head. "You have no idea."

Kate puts a hand on his arm. "You've got it back to front, Sam. Forget about yourself. This is about Bertie and Julie. Think of them and you'll be fine."

He takes a second to absorb what she's saying, then picks her up, swings her around like a rag doll and gives her a smacking kiss on the mouth. "Mate, sometimes you show so much dash I'm floored. Might as well have a beer then, since the pressure's off."

"Once and for all, I'm not your bloody mate," Kate says, crankily.

By four o'clock the sky is threatening. The excited chat has quieted to an uneasy murmur.

"Is this fashionably late?" Kate asks Ettie.

"Bertie's never done anything fashionable in his life."

"Didn't think so. Should we call? Or shall I run over and see what's happening?"

Just then, Jimmy pokes his head through the café door. "They're here!" he yells triumphantly. He races off and comes back in a second. "Nope. Only Julie. No Bertie."

"Oh God." Ettie rips off her apron and flies into the Square.

"He died," Julie tells Ettie in a broken voice. "The silly old bugger went and died on me an hour ago." She stands beside the hire car, glorious in Ettie's ivory wedding dress, her face wet with tears.

"Oh love." Ettie puts her arms around her.

"His heart gave up. I don't know what to do," Julie says, not moving. "I keep wanting to rush somewhere but I have no idea where to or what for. It all feels weird without Bertie."

Ettie takes her hand. "Do you want me to tell everyone to go home? We can go back to the house and I'll spend the night with you. We'll toast the old bloke and tell stories until we drop. What do you think?"

She shakes her head. "Don't think I could manage an empty house right now."

"Then how about we go on with the show and turn it into a celebration of Bertie's life? He'd like that. Value for money, even if it's not quite what he planned."

Julie cracks a tiny smile. "A wake before the funeral, is that it?"

"He'd love it. A wedding and a funeral for the one price."

"Bit unconventional."

"So was Bertie."

Ettie takes her hand. On the other side, Jimmy sticks out his scrawny arm like a wing for Julie to hold onto. Together they lead the widowed bride towards the barge. "Baby steps, love, and let's remember the good times," Ettie says.

Julie walks towards the crowd. Dramatically blonde and beautiful in a silken bridal gown that shimmers creamily against the greyness of the day. A cheer goes up. Applause breaks out. There are a few wolf-whistles. Julie's courage falters, and Ettie holds on more tightly, afraid that if she lets go, Julie will run away. They reach the barge and Jimmy helps her to step aboard the *Mary Kay*. There, under a mossie net bower wired with cascades of Bertie's prized roses, Julie brushes tears from her eyes.

"Bertie," Julie says in a broken voice, "is here in spirit."

The crowd rocks backwards with a groan. Without any prompting, Jimmy passes Julie a crumpled handkerchief out of his pocket. "It's clean. Promise."

Kate, who's found Sam next to the keg, pulls him through the crowd by the hand, instructing him to tell every Bertie story he can think of – the happy ones if he can.

Sam looks nervous and hesitates.

"Just do it!" she hisses.

He clears his throat, straightens his cuffs and steps for-ward, giving Big Julie a comforting hug before turning to the crowd.

"Bertie," he begins. "Well, as we all know, Bertie was a good man. Er." He scrabbles for Kate's list, pulling it out of his pocket. Reads for a second and looks back up at the crowd. Beside him, Julie is still, her head bowed. He sees a tear trickle down her cheek. Nearly weeps himself. He coughs. "Under his sharp one-liners – which were, I admit, a bit off-putting until you got to know him better – Bertie was a man who cared. About community, family, friends and the environment. Because he understood they were the real driving forces of everyday life. Now to be honest – sorry, Julie love, but I'm sure you understand what I mean – he, er, often hid these sentiments well."

There is a faint ripple of cautious laughter. "But we all know that in a real crisis he was the first to shove a hand in his pocket. Even though they were deeper than most."

Genuine laughter now. "He saw a lot during his forty or so years as proprietor of The Briny Café. But he knew how to keep a secret. And he never told a story that might do harm. Bertie stood up for his beliefs. Understood the true meaning of loyalty, even if it cost him. Long as it didn't cost him too much."

He turns to Julie. "It's a joke, love. So we're still good, right?" She lifts her head and smiles then, standing up straighter.

Seeing she's okay, Sam continues: "Bertie loved Cook's Basin 'cause he understood it was one of the last pure places and its ways needed to be preserved for future generations. And anyway, we're the only ones who would have put up with him for so long. Julie love, I'm on a roll." The crowd gees him on with a few whistles. "Seriously, Bertie was, in every way, a gentle man and a gentleman."

"You're repeatin' yourself, Sam," Jimmy cuts in, trying to be helpful.

"Thanks, mate. Good to know you're listening."

"He made the best chips in the world," Jimmy offers, determined to say his piece.

"And the worst coffee!" A shout from the back.

Sam holds up a hand. "Any comments regarding his coffee should be held for a later date out of respect." He sees Kate standing at the rear of the deck, slightly apart from the crowd as usual. She gives him a nod. A thumbs-up. He smiles with relief.

Beside him, Julie takes a deep breath and finds her voice. "Let me tell you about my Bertie," she says and the guests, trussed up in their wedding finery but finding themselves at a wake, are still and silent. "He could be a cranky, stubborn and miserly old bugger. But he never let anyone down in his life. And when he loved, he loved completely."

"Hear, hear."

"Jimmy?" she calls.

"Yeah, Julie?"

"Fetch me a glass of champagne so we can all toast the finest man I ever knew."

"Hear, hear."

Jimmy returns with a glass and a bottle in a flash.

"To Bertie," Julie says, raising her glass. Slabs of golden light break through the sullen mass of clouds. In a blink, the threatening storm is shunted over the horizon and a stampede of wispy pink clouds race across a blazing blue sky. The bay sizzles red and silver. Sunlight strikes the deck, setting hair aglow.

"It's Bertie," a voice shouts out. "Callin' in to The Briny Café one last time. Here's to Bertie!"

*

The celebration of Bertie's life ends with draining the last drops out of the keg. The water police, having heard the news of his death, call in to pay their respects and end up ferrying the worst drunks home. Fast Freddy babies the last crying partygoers into his green water taxi and hands out clean tissues from the box he keeps on his dashboard. He does at least ten runs back and forth until the café is an empty shell. It is his best turnover since Christmas Eve almost a year ago. He takes the trouble to say a private thank you to the former, much-loved proprietor of The Briny Café, whom he is sure is already returning to life in a new guise.

"Bertie's on his way back already. Reincarnation," he tells Sam, driving him home on the last taxi run.

"Turtle, prob'ly," Sam suggests, seriously smashed.

Freddy gives him a hard look to see if he's sending a fella up for his beliefs. Then he thinks back . . . Old Bertie did have a sort of turtle look about him. He is consoled by the thought.

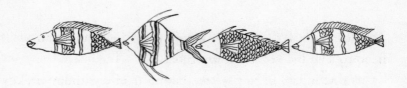

CHAPTER TWENTY-THREE

On Monday morning, Sam opens his eyes and finds they won't stretch wider than a couple of slits. Due, he is sure, to the bastard drilling from one side of his skull to the other.

"Ya look half dead, Sam," Jimmy says, standing anxiously at the end of the bed. He is dressed in his favourite outfit – blinding red trousers with mint-green stripes and a mint-green shirt with strobing red lines.

Sam feels the room tilt and a queasy tide of bile rise from his stomach. "That for me?" he croaks, reaching for the tea.

Jimmy passes him a star-spangled mug. Sam shuts his eyes against the glare.

"Ya look awful, Sam."

"Yeah. Thanks, mate. No need to go on. I get the picture." He sips the tea. Scalding hot, smoky and sweet with sugar. "Do us a favour, Jimmy, will ya? Those khakis I bought you. Reckon you could wear those today?"

"Ya sick, Sam? Want me to call Ettie?"

"No, mate. It's all good. Give me half an hour and we'll head to The Briny for a slap-up brekky."

"On Monday, Sam? Are we gonna have a Sunday brekky on Monday?"

"Does you good not to get set in your ways, mate. First sign of old age."

The kid bounces out of the room. His bony ankles poke below his trousers and his feet slap the floorboards. He sticks his head back inside. Serious. "Bertie won't be back, will he, Sam? He's gone for good."

"Yeah, mate, for good. Life is terminal. Helps to remember that when you're feeling a bit bogged down. Now go and change your gladrags, Jimmy. I'll stick my head under a cold shower and we'll be on our way."

By the time Sam is ready to leave, rain is falling with a steady intensity that puts the kibosh on work for the day. He wonders whether Bertie is doing him a favour in the afterlife. He hasn't felt this banged up since he hit the turps with a vengeance at his twenty-first birthday party. It's another sign, he mutters out loud. He's starting the uphill climb. Or is it the downhill slide? He plugs a shaving nick with a torn tissue and yells for Jimmy.

"How much money you got saved?"

"Not enough for a car yet, Sam."

"Guess I'm paying for brekky then. It'd be nice to think I can look forward to you taking care of me in my old age, mate. What do you reckon?"

"You and the dog, Sam. No worries."

Ah jeez, Sam thinks, the sugar wearing off and his head-ache squeezing like a vice. "We'll discuss the mutt issue later, mate. I'll be watching to see you eat your spinach. Don't think I won't. No spinach. No muscles. Remember that and you'll have no regrets." Right now, he is full of freaking regrets. Next party with a keg, he's giving himself a curfew.

The rain, delivered by a low-pressure system that plods in from the west, dumps forty millimetres in less than two hours. Chippies, fairweather workers by the nature of their tasks, have a Monday sleep-in. Instead of the usual morning bedlam, Kate and Ettie have time to restore order at a manageable pace.

Mid-morning and the café is still empty, the humidity rank. Outside, low cloud covers the hills and raindrops bounce off the water like sprites. The gloom is all-pervasive. Kate shudders for no reason and orders Ettie, who looks exhausted, to put her feet up. There is nothing to do except the cleaning.

"You'll get in my way," Kate insists, pushing her upstairs. "I'll call you if a busload of pensioners drops in looking for scones, jam and cream." She picks up a dishcloth and attacks the creeping mould in the rubber seals of the fridges. Next she'll obliterate all those arachnid tenants who have returned to camp in the far corners of the café.

Half an hour later, Ettie appears. "Can't switch off the monkey in my head. Poor Julie, nothing will ever be the same for her. And here we are cleaning, cooking. Getting on with the daily routine and everything is all so . . . normal . . ."

"Yeah. I know what you mean."

A voice calls from the front counter.

"Anyone home? Kate? Ettie?"

"Gidday, Rita." Ettie goes behind the counter, wiping her hands on her apron. "Didn't think you'd be out on a day like today. What can I do for you?"

Rita, an Islander with hair the colour of strawberries, silver earrings the size of pomegranates, is spitting mad.

"Bloody car won't go," she says. "New car with less than ten thousand kilometres on the clock. I jump in, turn the key, slip into gear. Nothing! Abso-bloody-lutely nothing!" Her eyes dart all over the café, like she's looking for the culprit. Kate offers her a coffee, which she declines. "I'm waiting for Brian. Got him out of bed, the lazy bugger. Knew he'd sneak back the second I walked out the door." She points to an orange and almond cupcake. "I'll have one of those. To calm me down."

"Cream?"

"God, no. I'm on a diet."

Ettie covers her snort with a cough and Rita rips into the cake.

Twenty minutes later, soaked and furious, her husband pokes his head inside the café. "No wheels, Rita. Didn't you notice some bastard has snitched your wheels?"

Without missing a beat, Rita strides up to him. "Wheels are wheels, Brian. They're one of the few certainties about a car. Why would I think to even look at the bloody wheels?"

They leave, still arguing. The soaked and muddy legs of Brian's blue-and-white-striped pyjamas hang below his wet-weather gear like dirty dishrags.

If Sam had been feeling a bit grubby when he surfaced that morning, he is absolutely ragged by the end of the afternoon.

The rain has moved on and steam is rising off the hills in thin spirals from a late burst of sunshine. He is contemplating an early night, maybe a quick game of Scrabble with Jimmy, a couple of fat sausages each for dinner, with a hefty serving of his special garlic mashed potatoes. He'll add some peas. According to the irrefutable wisdom of his mother, a kid needs greens at least twice a day to grow strong bones. He'd never questioned her then and he doesn't intend to start now.

He is fishing out the sausages from the freezer while Jimmy is on spud duty, when the phone rings. He is tempted to let it go but weakens.

"Yo!" he says, gruffly. It better not be some bloody nincompoop calling about his bilge pump not working. Live on the water, learn the basics. Or suffer the consequences. Amazing the number of people who don't get it.

"You coming to fix my mooring or not?"

Christ. He'd forgotten all about it under the weight of a chronic hangover. And frankly, if the Weasel was blown out to sea and never heard of again, it would be doing the world a favour. "Had to wait for the rain to stop."

"So you coming?"

Sam hesitates. He remembers Artie. How the poor bugger will keep wondering whether tonight's the night he'll cop a ram through the hull. One that'll sink him before he has time to sound his siren.

"Yeah. Cash up —" The call suddenly cuts out.

Sam closes his phone. "Jimmy! You're in charge of catering, mate. Whack on the spuds in an hour. Low heat. Shove on the sausos soon as you see the lovely *Mary Kay* making her way to bed down in home port. I'll deal with the peas out of the freezer myself."

He finds *Ciao Bella* looking forlorn on her mooring, her nose pointing into a soft breeze from the west.

"Oy! Merrizzi. You there?" He waits a whole minute, nursing the barge alongside. Nothing. He bangs the hull with his fist. "Merrizzi! Where you hiding?"

There's no sign of life. He throws out some fenders and ties up to the yacht. He swings his legs over the lifelines and drops onto a deck smeared with mould, decay and birdshit. A few tough weeds sprout like topknots along the gunnel. How the mighty have fallen, he thinks, taking less pleasure from the knowledge than he expected. He heads for the open hatch, his unease growing.

Downstairs in the seedy cabin, foetid with the stink of sweat, seawater and damp, Sam finds a dirty sheet, a stained pillow and two dozen warm stubbies. Catches the faintest whiff of the Weasel's expensive aftershave. He searches further. A bag of toiletries. Looks inside: toothbrush and toothpaste, a box of aspirin, the foil sleeves punched empty. The cupboards are empty too. No food. No mugs. No plates. Not even a water glass. Sam tries the tap – a syrupy brown trickle of evil-smelling fluid. He stands there. Sweat drips down his face and spine. He sees a couple of dead flies on a counter near the stubbies and begins to think the Weasel is playing games. Curses himself for a fool.

He calls out once more, then climbs the ladder to the fresh air on deck. The boat's a health hazard. For the life of him, he cannot understand why the Weasel is staying here. Unless he's hiding from someone. Or, as Kate suggested, has nowhere else to go. The light is fading fast. Standing in the cockpit, he looks up forward, searching. Something suss flickers at the edge of his mind. He can't pin it down.

He decides to swing past Artie on the way home to find out if the old fella knows anything, then he'll call it quits. A man like the Weasel is owed nothing and the weather is due to stay calm for a day or two before a new round of summer storms. He closes the hatch and takes another large bite out of the fresh air, feeling his sweat dry in the cool of the evening.

That's when he sees her, on the far side of the barge, holding onto the gunnel to stop her tinny from banging against the hull of the *Mary Kay*.

"Out of petrol again, are you?" he says, jumping off *Ciao Bella* and back onto his own vessel.

"I try not to make the same mistakes twice," she says, with a wry smile. "Saw the barge. Wondered what you were up to."

"The Weasel's hellhole," he says, pointing at the yacht. "He called about the mooring."

"Didn't think I'd live to see the day you'd do him a favour."

"I'm not, but if there's a blow he might come adrift and crash through Artie's floating palace."

"Ah."

Neither of them moves. Neither says a word. The sun drops out of sight behind the hills and the bay turns silver in the light of dusk.

"You want to come over for a beer?" Kate asks.

He plays it cool. "Never said no to a beer in my life. Give me five. I'll call Jimmy and tell him to start dinner without me."

"I could find some spaghetti, if you like."

"My favourite."

"I'm short on salad."

"Rabbit food."

"Right then. See you in a few minutes."

"Look forward to it."

He forgets about Artie. His hangover vanishes.

In the kitchen, Kate hands Sam a beer and goes back to stirring a pot of sauce. The rich scent of garlic, tomatoes and onions rises up in a hot cloud. She swirls the pasta to stop it sticking, the way Ettie's shown her.

"You ever been married, Kate?" Sam asks.

"No. You?"

"Nope."

Silence. Maybe he should change the subject. "Smells delicious. Didn't know you could cook."

"I can't. I keep a supply of Ettie's sauces in the freezer."

He picks up a spoon and tastes it. "You've added something," he says.

Kate looks at him, eyes wide with surprise. "As a matter of fact you're right. I chopped up a bunch of basil and threw it in."

"Ettie better watch out. You're showing signs of genuine talent." He takes another taste, puts the dirty spoon in the sink. "Ettie and the chef, what do you reckon? Think it will last?"

"None of our business, but for what it's worth, yes. They know what they want and recognise that they've found it."

"What about you? Do you know what you want?" He

props his backside against the bench, crosses his ankles. His arms are folded.

Kate hauls the pasta pot off the stove and drains the boiling water. Steam clouds her face so Sam can't read her expression. She bangs the colander against the side of the sink and tips the spaghetti back into the saucepan. "I've never been good at long-term relationships, if that's what you're asking. I have a habit of moving on when things get serious."

"Maybe you haven't met the right bloke." He waits a while. She says nothing.

"Ever thought about kids?"

Kate laughs unpleasantly. "I was a late-life baby and a big mistake. My mother tells me often that I ruined her life by being born. It's not much of an incentive to have my own family."

"Wouldn't set much store by your mother. She's . . ." He stops. "We're all responsible for our own decisions."

Kate serves the food in large white bowls, pouring them both a glass of red wine without asking Sam whether he wants it. They sit at an old timber table in the middle of the kitchen floor. She passes him a grater and a piece of parmesan, but he fumbles with it and she goes round the table to grate it for him.

"Like this," she says, standing next to his chair.

He slips an arm around her waist and rests his head lightly against her body. "You want to go on a real date sometime?" he murmurs, heartened when she doesn't immediately step back.

"What's this then?" she says, like it's a joke. When she goes back to her seat, he feels like he's let a golden opportunity slip away.

He likes her. It bothers him but it's a fact. He'd tried to write her off as a city mug but she'd proved that in her own quiet way she was smart, tough and loyal. He twirls a strand of spaghetti onto his fork and hopes like hell he can eat it without flicking sauce in her face.

"Should have cooked penne, it's not so messy," she says, reading his mind.

"I know everyone reckons a leopard's spots never change. Never believed the saying myself. Look at you. Less than three months in Cook's Basin and you're almost unrecognisable from the nervy —"

"Nervy!"

"You took a risk, Kate, and I'm not talking about the café. A house with a dodgy reputation, boats, chucking in your job because you knew it would kill you in the end. Takes guts, all that."

"Maybe I was desperate," she says, so quietly he almost misses it.

"Maybe. Only you would know. But what I'm getting at is that risks are at the heart of life. You and me, we're like chalk and cheese, but sometimes you find that opposites soften the hard edges in each other . . ."

"Are you making a pass?"

"I'm taking a risk 'cause I'm hoping that every time you bit my head off it was because you were worried you were getting to like me. And yeah, I'm making a pass."

Kate looks directly at him. "I'm a bad bet, Sam."

"It's a risk I'm willing to take."

"I've got to ask . . . why?"

He reaches across the table and grabs her hand. "I can't

explain it. Not in a way that's all flowery and romantic. Christ, I'm not even sure why, if you want the truth. Maybe I just feel better when you're around."

"Definitely not romantic . . ."

"Yeah, well . . ." Sam drops his eyes and pushes away his food. The effort of eating now beyond him. "I'm not much good with words." He feels defeated, worn out by trying to explain himself.

She sits still and silent for so long, he begins to plan a withdrawal that will leave his pride intact.

"Have you always been a risk-taker?" she says at last, smiling.

Sam wakes in his own bed in the middle of the night. He lies there for a while, listening to an owl hoot mournfully on a single note, the slurp of an incoming tide. He lets his mind drift. He is shocked by how much he wants Kate to like and understand him. He trawls back over their evening together. He might have rabbited on a bit too long but you've got to start somewhere, haven't you?

Out of the blue, he remembers what was bothering him about *Ciao Bella*. He sits bolt upright. It was the phone call, he thinks, struggling to recall the details. There was the roar of an engine, a shout, then the phone went dead. The Weasel must have had a visitor. Happier now, he settles down. He'll check with Artie in the morning. With a bit of luck, he'll find out that the Weasel has slunk off once and for all. Except why'd he want his mooring serviced if he was planning on disembarking for good?

He closes his eyes, trying to go back to sleep. He thinks of Kate again. He doesn't delude himself that their relationship will blossom in the same way as Ettie and the chef, who are old enough to desire contentment instead of hunting for thrills. He knows instinctively that with Kate, for every step forward, he'll have to take two back. He worries she is too young to settle for what to him is the nirvana of Cook's Basin. That the fire in her belly for more, much more, still smoulders. But there's only one way to find out and even if it ends up hurting him like hell, he's willing to take the risk that at some point she might vanish with a laptop and a backpack. Off without a twinge of regret and only a casual goodbye, on some new quest on the other side of the world. He sighs. Of all the coffee joints in all the world . . .

Unable to go back to sleep, Sam gets up at dawn. A light breeze off the land stirs the bush into life and ruffles the water. A single kookaburra makes a staccato start, before bursting into a full-throated declaration of his territorial rights. One by one, his family joins him until the air is filled with raucous joy. If only everyone, he thinks, set boundaries with laughter. He does a quick check of the barge and starts the engine. Cruises across pink water towards a pinker sky. He hopes the Misses Skettle are awake to see their favourite colour splashed about so extravagantly.

At the stern of Artie's yacht, he thumps the hull to announce his arrival. The old bloke's already up and about. Sam can smell burnt toast and coffee.

"You decent, Artie?" Sam asks, hoisting himself into the cockpit.

"Indecent, mate. And it's too late to change the habits of a lifetime," he replies.

"Glad to hear it."

Sam goes down the ladder into the cabin.

"Mate, wanted to ask you. Did your sleazy neighbour have any visitors late yesterday afternoon?"

"As a matter of fact he did. Four blokes wearin' suits pitched up in one of them speedboats that look like shiny black arrowheads. The Weasel gave them a big hello like they were best buddies, so I pulled me head in and had me dinner."

"Went off with them, did he?"

"Well, he got on their boat. That's the last I saw. Not me job to look out for the Weasel. By the way . . . that Kate."

"You know her?"

"Yeah. She's popped by a few times now. Brings me some goodies from the café on her way home."

"Did she ding your boat, Artie, or is she learning to come alongside decently?"

"Anyway," Bertie says, ignoring Sam. "Ya better watch out. That girl's showin' signs of bein' a stayer."

"I'm not going anywhere."

A collective cheer erupts when the locals hear of the Weasel's departure. For the next couple of days, people drop by Artie's yacht with words of congratulations for a job well done. Artie conveniently forgets to point out that he's done nothing but observe events and tells them firmly that one good turn deserves another. If they'll just step aboard for a while, he can find plenty of ways for them to show their gratitude.

As a result, the galley is scoured, the foam mattresses turned out to be aired. Old bed linen is ripped into useful rags, while new sheets, still crackly from their packets, are spread in luxurious splendour in the forward cabin. Artie's motley collection of shorts, T-shirts, trackie dacks and wind-cheaters are removed to the laundromat. They are boiled at 95 degrees, which has the double benefit of blasting out all stains and shrinking them to fit his dwindling body. The toilet shines like it's new and the bilge pumps are primed, oiled and any rusted wires replaced.

The only thing that isn't touched – on Artie's insistence – is his look-out post, a pile of bolsters arranged in a series of steps so he can haul himself to the top with comparative ease to keep watch through the forward hatch. He may not have to spy on the Weasel any more but it is a prime spot, he says, with a wink and a nudge, to keep abreast of Cook's Basin goings-on. Everyone understands that between Artie and the Misses Skettle, there will be even fewer secrets than normal.

"Betta watch yarselves," he says to all comers. "Or I'll be foldin' little good behaviour reminders and stuffin' 'em in bottles to send across the water. So ya know I'm on the job." He slaps his withered thighs, finding the thought hilarious. "Don't write me off yet, maties."

Another slap, then a beer appears in his fist and for the umpteenth time he recounts how a spiffy boat with four blokes in suits and dark glasses – like gangsters out of a movie

– arrived at the tail end of a cracker day to take the Weasel off into the sunset. Hopefully never to be seen again.

"No bugger was willing to dive over the side to give the old girl's bum a good scrape," Artie tells Sam when the barge-man arrives with a bottle of Bundaberg rum that smells so *medicinal* he's forced to take an immediate swig.

Sam ignores the hint to volunteer for the job and refuses a nip at the same time. "Too early for me, mate."

"Nectar of the gods," Artie says, wiping his lips with the back of his hand. "Can feel it doin' me good already."

For a second, Sam worries whether he's done the right thing, but the colour floods back into Artie's face, his eyes take on a low sheen, and he cracks a smile that's almost beatific.

"Go easy, mate," Sam says gently. "Quality should be savoured."

"Remember that the next time you see Kate."

"Don't want to appear rude, Artie, but it's none of your business."

Artie looks taken aback. "You're serious, then?"

"No bloody secrets, are there?"

"None worth knowing," he grins.

Cook's Basin News (CBN)

Newsletter for Offshore Residents of Cook's Basin, Australia

DECEMBER

Goodbye, Dear Bertie

The wedding may have turned into a wake but, in typical Islander fashion, guests rose to the call and instead of toasting the bride and groom, gathered to farewell Bertie who died on his wedding day. Bertie will be warmly remembered as a true member of the offshore community even though, technically, he lived onshore. He will be missed by one and all and we wish Julie all the best in the trying times ahead.

DOG RACE

Yes, it's on again this year on Christmas Eve, All entrants should be at the Spit by 5 p.m. with a long-neck bottle of beer and a can of dog food, any size. Last year, for the first time in the history of the race, one or two participants were over-ambitious and pushed their dogs beyond their capabilities. Please remember the race is meant to be fun for the dogs as well as the owners and we hope that this year there will be no need for the rescue boat. Jack the Bookie will be on site in his usual position in the Square. Memorabilia T-shirts can be ordered through CBN.

Car Vandal Nabbed

Good news! The person vandalising cars has been caught. It's a story that's unbelievable but true! The police finally began their investigations and started asking questions. One of them asked Fast Freddy if he'd seen anyone suspicious during his nightshift. Freddy remembered he'd seen a bloke prowling along the foreshore of the car park.

"Did you see what he looked like?" "Nope, too far away," Freddy told him. "Did you see which way he went?" "Nope, too far away." Freddy let the cop go about ten steps then called him back. "Might have somethin' that could help," he said, wearing that poker face of his. "Yeah?" "Couldn't tell you where he came from or what he looked like . . . but if you want his phone number, I've got that." The silly coot of a vandal rang the water taxi to get a ride to Cutter Island. Fast Freddy asked him where he was, and he waved from the car park! Freddy decided he looked suss, so he didn't pick him up. But his mobile registered the number, and best news of all . . . they've caught the bloke. He had a house full of stolen property and was on his way to the Island because he'd heard it was covered in weekenders and practically deserted. Hah! Well done, Freddy. The community owes you a great debt of thanks.

CHAPTER TWENTY-FOUR

Growing up on the water, Sam's developed a sixth sense for disaster, and right now, as he prepares to service the Weasel's mooring so Artie doesn't have to worry it might break loose in a storm, his instinct is working overtime. Nothing smells right about the whole situation. Not the derelict yacht, the Weasel's sudden disappearance, or even what he was doing living so damn squalidly anyway. Sam feels like he's missing some essential clue that will force all the pieces to slip into place. He hits the hydraulic switch and the chain begins a slow and steady rise to the surface. The huge concrete mooring block for *Ciao Bella* appears. Attached, but floating like it has a life of its own, is a dark green industrial-strength garbage bag tied at one end with a rope.

Sam stops the winch in a hurry. Goes over to the upturned milk crate and sits down. The bag is probably filled with empty bottles and takeaway food containers, dumped by some shyster too cheap to pay ten bucks at the council tip.

But it isn't. And he knows it.

After a short while, he stands and pulls his mobile phone out of his shirt pocket. He dials the water police. On the other side of the bay, a tinny flies past. The wake reaches the *Mary Kay* at the same time as a cop comes on the line. The bag is jolted by the surge. A foot appears through a tear.

"Dead body, mate," Sam says. "Stuffed in a bag. Look for the barge in Oyster Bay." He throws down his mobile and rushes to the edge of the barge. Heaves over the side.

It takes two boatloads of cops and forensic experts four hours to measure, tag, clip, assess, question Artie and finally leave. They tow *Ciao Bella* into custody as though the yacht is a credible witness.

Before the end of the day, word of the Weasel's murder quickly spreads from one end of Cook's Basin to the other. No one knows any details so speculation is rife. People gossip. Hearsay turns into truth. A guess becomes a fact. The camaraderie of friends and neighbours is thrown off-kilter because suspicion, once aroused, has a nasty way of taking hold.

A flock of sleek, fat crows, feathers gleaming like armour, swoops on the Square, scattering the seagulls and miner birds. Yellow-eyed, they loom like dark accusations, their dirge-like cries raising the hairs on the backs of necks.

"They're such doomsayers," Kate says, watching the birds from the doorway of the café. "First time I've ever seen them here. Do you think they're drawn to death? Like ghouls. Or do you think they know more than we do?"

"Stop it, Kate," Ettie says. "They're just scavengers. And today is garbage day." She grabs a saucepan and a wooden spoon and marches into the Square, banging like a drummer. The birds eye her menacingly, then slowly take flight. "No more witchery. Now there's work to be done. Let's get on with it." Ettie slips her arm through Kate's and guides her firmly back inside.

"You don't think Sam could have done it, do you?" Kate asks, unable to stop saying out loud what she dreads.

Ettie drops her arm and furiously rounds on her. "I'll pretend I never heard you say that!"

"It's just . . ."

"Sam is Sam. What you see is what you get. There's no dark side. Not even a grey side. He may do things his own way, get it wrong occasionally, even bend the law. But his motives are never in doubt. Sam tries to do good. End of story."

"None of us knows what we're capable of, Ettie, until we're pushed to the brink. He was so cut up about Boag and what that man was doing to the kids. I found him on the deck of the yacht, around the time the Weasel disappeared. I can't help wondering . . ."

"You really think a puny little drug dealer could tip Sam over the edge? I thought you knew him better than that."

Throughout her childhood Kate had felt like she was stuck on a runaway train heading for a smash. Now she feels she's on it again. "But I saw him there," she says, defensive. "I can't get that out of my head."

When Sam ties up to the deck of The Briny he hears footsteps and looks up, expecting – hoping – to see Kate. But it is Ettie who runs towards him with her arms out.

"Oh love," she says. "What a horror."

"Yeah. A shocker. He's no great loss, Ettie. But it's a terrible way to go. I've been up at the cop shop all afternoon."

"Police got any ideas?"

"Yeah. Those four goons Artie saw pull up in a stink boat. They're prime suspects."

"Ah," she says, thinking the sooner that bit of information makes it into the gossip mill the better.

"Coffee, love? Or something stronger?"

"Is Kate around?"

Something in the way Ettie hesitates makes him wary. He tries to think of how he might have upset her.

"Ah jeez, she thinks I did it, doesn't she?"

Ettie, who cannot lie although she's an expert at fudging the edges, shrugs. "The whole community's in a state of shock. It's only natural Kate is too." She sees the naked hurt on his face.

"Jeez," he says. "Tell Kate the bottom line of any decent friendship is trust. Without it, there's nowhere to go." Before Ettie can say a word, he jumps on board and reverses away from the dock.

Behind the wire screen door, Kate watches him leave, unable to move.

White-faced and silent, Sam lies on the red banquette out of sight of passing tinnies. He does not want to recount for one, and then inevitably all, the ghoulish details of the Weasel's murder, turning tragedy into pornography. The man is dead. That is enough to know.

After a while, the familiar rock of the water loosens his bunched neck muscles, the lock of his jaw. One by one, he slides the horror images into a far corner of his mind where he hopes they will, in time, dissolve into nothing.

He knows he should go home. Settle the kid who must have heard by now. But he isn't ready. Not even for Jimmy, whose capacity for trust is limitless and who would know, without any doubt in his pure heart, that Sam was incapable of hurting a living thing; who, unlike Kate, would follow him to the ends of the earth.

Christ, he wasn't a complicated man. No fancy frills. No slick dinner party repartee. No rubbing shoulders with power and money. No international travel. Just a man and a barge. Plain and simple. But not, he hoped, without his own brand of honour. If Kate couldn't see that, there was no point in trying. He feels his thoughts beginning to spiral in a million different directions again. He has responsibilities. To Jimmy, who is becoming a young man. To the community, that is like family. To the barge, that is not just his living but there for anyone in times of crisis. To the landscape, that's as much a part of him as breathing. He is a man of substance who sees a problem and wears it away.

He's about to sit up when he catches the whine of a boat close by. He ducks out of sight and the boat drones away. He waits until it is late and very dark before he slips over the side in his jocks and swims ashore. Tiptoes into his house. He chucks out the dinner Jimmy's left for him with a sharp pang – Boag would have loved it. Heads for the shower.

In bed, he tosses for an hour before he gives up on sleep. Instead he switches on the light, picks up a couple of books.

He chooses one recommended by Kate about a pig-headed Yorkshireman who took forty years to convince critics and cheats that he'd truly discovered the secret of measuring longitude. He reads the last ten pages of a heroic battle for recognition and justice then closes the book. Forty years. He sighs and switches off the bedside lamp. In the scheme of things, maybe it's too soon to give up on Kate. But three strikes and she's definitely out. Unless she has a bloody good reason for behaving like a twit. Love, as his father used to say, is an act of courage after all.

The next morning, the house is deathly quiet. Jimmy – the whirling dervish who has been Sam's shadow for weeks – is gone. His clothes are missing, his posters stripped from the walls, his two pairs of sneakers and his workboots nowhere to be seen. Believing Jimmy has done a runner after hearing the rumours, Sam is so hurt he doesn't bother to go looking for him.

He hauls out a bucket and a heap of cleaning fluids from the cupboard under the sink. He'll start on the house. Move to the barge. A clean slate.

Just then the door bursts open, whacking the wall with a bang.

"Where you been, Jimmy?" Sam demands without bothering to turn around to check it's the boy.

"Sam! Sam! Guess what?" Jimmy's face is excited. He hops from one foot to the other as if the floor is on fire.

"You know the rules, mate. You go out. You leave a note."

"But, Sam —"

"No buts, Jimmy. If you want to live with me, you follow the rules."

"Me mum's home, Sam! She's home for Christmas, just like she promised. I'm movin' home."

Sam gets up from the floor. He puts the bucket on the counter and holds out his hand, man to man. "Well, mate, that's good news. The best," he says.

"I'll still have me job, won't I? And a dog? We're still a team, aren't we, Sam?"

"Yeah, mate. A team. But I'm holding off on the mutt until we sort out a few logistics. You gotta understand, a mutt's a commitment. Like having a kid on four paws. Understand, Jimmy? Long as you're clear. Deal?"

"Deal, Sam. We're a team." Jimmy thrusts out his knuckly mitt, with its ripped fingernails and bloody scratches, to seal the contract. Then dashes off. "See ya, Sam," he calls from halfway down the jetty.

The official explanation of the Weasel's demise at the hands of a bunch of (apparently rival) goons lifts the pall that's been hanging over Cook's Basin. According to newspaper reports Leo Merrizzi, who'd been hiding out "on the isolated shores of a difficult to access island off the east coast of Australia" was the victim of a gang war that had been raging for more than a year.

It's the hottest topic of conversation – until everyone realises there's only two weeks to go until Christmas and rushes headlong into festive preparations. The Stony Point Tinny Yacht Club holds its annual Christmas party in a sandy little cove north of Wineglass Bay, far enough away from civilisation so the ruckus doesn't upset anyone. Mutts go into training for the annual Dog Race. Kids start jumping into the water in their school uniforms on the way home, knowing that by next term they'll have outgrown them anyway. The party season fires up with a vengeance and all the cooks trot out their best recipes to celebrate another glorious year.

Despite this, the Misses Skettle decide to take matters into their own gnarly hands to make extra sure lingering doubts about Sam are decisively quashed. They set themselves up in the Square with a few homemade sandwiches wrapped in greaseproof paper because, even though the tucker is certainly much improved at The Briny, fools and their pennies are easily separated. With a large Thermos of coffee doctored with brandy to perk their spirits, they hold court for a whole day at one of the scabby old picnic tables, like a couple of purple-crested galahs at a Sunday school gathering. Any possible doubters – and they know who they are – are plucked out of the passing crowds and forced to listen.

"Known him since he was no bigger than a jelly bean in his mother's belly," said one Miss Skettle through fuschia-pink lips. "His mother always had a sort of glow about her. I remember her old dinghy had more holes than a colander. She and little Sammy would head to the Spit, laughing louder than the penguins that quacked alongside. He would hold a jam tin bailer in his hand while she rowed. Sam's father was one of nature's gentlemen. Nothing was ever too much trouble. And what a body. Phew! Joanie, who lived in a house with a view of the boatshed, would hold her kettle out the window and hit it with a wooden spoon when he stripped to

his togs and went for a swim. There wasn't a woman in the
bays who didn't rush outside and go all goggle-eyed at the
sight of him. Joanie weaved baskets, you know. Very beautiful. Sold them to the big department stores, who could never
get enough of them."

While one pauses for breath the other Miss Skettle takes
over. At the first sign of antsy-ness from their audience, fingers are shaken. "Now, now, we haven't finished yet. Hold
your horses. The ferry's not going anywhere for a few more
minutes." And they take a firm grip of an arm, a hand – even
a thigh – and insist nobody move until they've had their say.

"Sam's mother and father raised him to love all living
things and once a boy's learned the sanctity of life, he doesn't
change. No matter how hard-pressed he is to put up with the
bad habits of blow-ins without any idea of common decency.
So if you're wondering about that shifty-looking fellow who
ended up in a garbage bag, well, if Sam says he had nothing
to do with it, then that's the truth. Now off you go. See you
at the next fireshed dinner."

"And don't forget to bring your torch."

When the old girls, hoarse by the end of the day, pack up
feeling they've done their bit, Ettie wanders over to ask if
they'd like a sandwich, a cake, a coffee, anything. "On the
house, ladies. You've done a magnificent job."

"Thank you, Ettie, dear. We put on our dinner before we
left this morning. It'll be perfectly cooked by the time we get
home."

"Slow cooking, always the best way," Ettie says, impressed.
"Eh?"

*

The Briny Café, caught in the middle of publicity surrounding the death of a man well-known to police as a "colourful underworld identity", does a roaring trade. Hordes of rubberneckers looking for vicarious thrills pound inside, desperate for coffee, cakes and the latest gossip. It doesn't take Kate long to develop a soft spot for some of Bertie's old rules, such as leaving the furniture in place. His insistence that people pay upfront also has its merits, as she discovers when a middle-aged couple complains about inedible food. Kate retrieves their empty plates and quietly insists they point out what exactly they couldn't eat. When they demand a refund she politely but very firmly says no.

The bloke, grey-haired with a middle-aged paunch, is red-faced. His wife, dyed black hair, too much jewellery, begins to look nervous and creeps towards the door. Fast Freddy materialises with a friendly smile. "Need any help, Kate?" he offers. The couple leaves, threatening action. Kate asks for their names. "You'll go on a list," she says. "You are never to be served in this café again."

"You can't do that!" shouts the man.

"Watch me," she replies with a smile.

The customer is not always right, she later tells Ettie, who would have refunded the money to keep the peace. "I spent most of my life being bullied by my mother. Those guys were amateurs."

That evening, when Ettie asks Marcus how he thinks the situation should have been handled, he tells her that Kate was absolutely correct. The couple were scammers.

"I hate confrontation," she confesses to him.

"One of many things I find utterly delightful about you," he replies happily.

He has arranged for them to enjoy a picnic in his glamorous timber runabout. The Christmas Choir, he announces taking her hand in his and tenderly kissing each of the oven burns, is rehearsing for its annual performance on the *Mary Kay*. The sound is exquisite and a boat in the middle of Oyster Bay would be the perfect spot to hear it, didn't she think?

They set off at dog-paddle speed under a turquoise sky, throwing down an anchor to the lilting strains of "The Three Drovers". The chef produces a basket of paper-thin pancakes wrapped around duck skin as crisp as toffee. They are laid alongside cucumber, green onion and a sauce he made himself using cinnamon and star anise. The skin, he tells Ettie because she asks for the secret, has been marinated in the same spices as well as ginger and garlic, then cooked at 60 degrees for three hours. At that point, he sews the skin to a rack to prevent it curling, ramps up the temperature of the oven and leaves it to roast for fifteen minutes. Finally, he ladles over smoking-hot vegetable oil until it turns the colour of beaten gold.

"All this for me," she murmurs on the end of a blissful sigh.

He fills her wineglass and reaches into the basket, this time to reveal bowls of prawn and rice noodle salad with a chilli lime dressing, roasted cashews. There are little vanilla cream pots with fresh blueberries to follow, he says, delighted to see her eyes are closed with what he hopes is ecstasy.

The choristers move on to "Silent Night", sung in German, and he joins in with a soft voice, knowing the words by heart. The carol is achingly beautiful with the rich tones of the basses folding into the mix like a layer of chocolate. A few minutes later, the descants rise to the challenge of "The First Noel".

"Ya gonna put a hole in me bleedin' boat if ya come much closer!"

Marcus and Ettie jump.

"My apologies, Artie, I did not realise the anchor was dragging. I was carried away by a beautiful woman, a beautiful night and beautiful music," Marcus says, throwing out his arm to fend off.

"Not bad are they?" Artie says.

"Magnificent!"

"Yeah. Well, you wouldn't have said that three weeks ago. They were singin' in the cracks, then."

"You know how to get to La Scala, Artie?"

"Eh?"

"Practise, Artie, practise."

"That joke's older than me, Chef, and that's sayin' somethin'."

"You okay? You need anything?" Ettie asks, straightening her hair, her dress.

"Nah. Good as gold."

"G'night, Artie."

"On the water, mate. Now and forever."

Ettie picks up on a plaintive note in his voice. "You sure you're okay?"

"Better than that bloody loser that went for a long sleep at the bottom of the sea! It's all relative, Ettie."

CHAPTER TWENTY-FIVE

A week before Christmas, summer is an explosion of red bougainvillea, blue, white and magenta hydrangeas and the sweet scent of star jasmine permeating the spongy summer air. Sam and Kate are still avoiding each other. He is hurt. She is ashamed. Neither of them will admit it.

The phone rings in the café. Kate and Ettie look at each other and Ettie shrugs helplessly. She is whipping egg whites for the lemon tarts. Egg whites, Kate now knows, do not wait for anyone. She slips the bowl of chocolate she is melting over hot water off the heat and wipes her hands. "We're going to have to put up a sign saying we don't do bookings, and put the same message on an answering machine," she says.

"Personal contact is the name of the game, Kate. No electronic speak in this café."

Kate smiles. "It's a good sign though. Business is building." She lifts the receiver.

"Is that Miss Jackson?"

"Yes."

"Kate Jackson?"

"Yep."

"I'm calling from the Coastal Shores Retirement Resort. I am sorry to have to tell you that your mother is very ill. You should come immediately."

Emily Jackson looks pale despite her green eyelids and pillar-box-red lipstick. She lies in a frilly pink nightie in the frilly pink bedroom of her frilly unit – she reminds Kate of a frill-necked scorpion.

With blue-veined hands Emily smooths the pink roses embroidered along the border of the top sheet. "They've told me I could die, you know. What would they know?"

Kate is shocked into speechlessness and a worm turns in her stomach. Her mother has always been invincible. The idea of her dying is absurd. She is the kind of woman who trails destruction in her wake but never lets it catch up to her. "Who told you?"

"Some baby-faced doctor who looks like she should still be in primary school."

"I thought your GP was a man."

"He's away. She's the locum. Not a brain in her head." Emily takes a long laboured breath before continuing. There's something missing from her voice. "I'll wait till George gets back before I do anything."

"What exactly did she say is wrong?"

Emily stares out the window over the mossy terracotta rooftops of the other "inmates", as she likes to call them. "Don't pretend to be interested, Kate."

Kate refuses to be baited. She picks up a little breathlessness in Emily's speech, sees blue tinges under her nails that are unpolished for the first time in Kate's memory. Her confidence in her mother's invincibility falters. "Maybe you should listen to her. What did she say?"

"She wants me to go to hospital for some tests. Something to do with my heart. Nothing that can't wait for George to sort out when he's back."

Kate loses patience. God, she might die and all because she'd rather consult a man than a woman. "Well, if you won't listen to the experts, there's not much I can do. It's your call." She stands then hesitates. Her mother suddenly looks indecisive. Sad. Maybe even fearful.

She is not yet old, Kate thinks, but she sees without a shadow of doubt that Emily is seriously ill. She sits back down.

"Are you hungry? I could make you a sandwich. I'm becoming quite good at cooking. Ettie says I'm a quick learner." A lifetime of anger and hurt begins leaking out of her. The waste makes her want to weep. Surely her mother, too, must be filled with regrets.

What was it that Emily chased with such manic intensity, plunging from one disaster to another? How many times had they packed their bags late at night and fled from debt collectors, lounge lizards and every kind of cataclysm?

Kate looks at her mother, lying so lightly on the bed she barely makes a mark. Her mind fills with a million questions, but one stands alone. She searches for the courage to ask it.

"What did I do to make you hate me?" she asks, her voice shaking.

"What are you talking about? You always talk such rubbish, Kate."

"I'm talking about the way you treat me." Kate takes a deep breath. "As though you hate me."

Her mother looks at her with eyes like black bullets.

"Do you really want to know?" she hisses, that old venom back in her voice now. "I'll tell you. You aren't your brother. And believe me, he's worth ten of you."

Kate is stunned. Feels like she's been punched in the stomach. "What do you mean a brother?" she almost whispers.

"What I said. Now stop your whining and leave me alone! I'm tired. You're making me feel ill."

Kate rises slowly from the faded pink armchair and walks out. She abandons her mother amongst her cheap knick-knacks and overstuffed wardrobes without looking back.

She has a brother.

No name. No address. Nothing to hint that he exists beyond Emily's words. Is it the truth, or the old girl's bid to control to the end? Whatever, the words are out there. Therefore he exists.

It is an end-shot of appalling virtuosity. From this moment on, every time she looks at a face in a crowd searching for a likeness, she will be forced to recall the angles of her mother's face, the colour of her eyes, the curl of her mouth, or a familiar expression.

Fighting anger and tears, she makes her way through a persistent drizzle and peak-hour traffic. The wheels of the car in front spray her windscreen with greasy slime. The wipers slap back and forth, leaving muck at both sides.

Suddenly the car in front slams on its brakes and goes into

a skid. It only takes a second to regain control, but her heart beats wildly. She slows. Recklessness will buy a plot alongside the old girl. No. Not alongside. Never that.

Calmer now, her old journo instincts kick in, as does the hard little kernel that has never cracked under a lifetime of Emily's hammering. She will return to her mother's bedside in the morning with a list of questions. If she has a brother, she must find him or spend the rest of her life wondering. She will not give Emily that satisfaction. She needs facts. At that moment, she almost turns the car around, but her anger still burns. In the morning, she decides.

It is dark by the time she swings into the car park at the Spit. If she cries, it will be self-pity, and as her mother always said, self-pity is for weaklings and weaklings get left behind.

She locks the car, skirting past the café, where she can see Ettie's lights blazing in the penthouse. If she is forced to speak to anyone, she knows she will scream. She runs down the ramp, jumps into her boat, and roars off without looking back.

Just before she falls asleep, she hears wailing and wonders if the sound is coming from her own throat. She blindly feels for wetness under her eyes but finds her skin bone-dry.

"Must be the wind in the casuarinas," she thinks.

At five she gets a call. It's the night nurse. Emily had a fatal heart attack in the witching hour between 3 and 4 a.m.

Kate throws the phone against the wall and lets out a howl of rage and regret. There is no going back. There never is.

When Kate arrives at the café the next morning, Ettie asks if she is okay. She is silenced by a look of red-hot ferocity.

She wants to tell Kate that unresolved bitterness turns on you, until you carry it like a scar. She wants to tell her that anger is pointless. She wants to tell her that if her mother is desperately ill, she must try to make peace. For her own sake, if not for Emily's. If she'd known Kate for years, Ettie wouldn't have hesitated to grab her by the scruff of her neck to march her back to her mother's bedside to do her duty. Their friendship is still too new, though, and every so often frailties surface. Perhaps if they weren't business partners she'd have been more inclined to take a risk. But the thought of seven days a week nursing a sullen offsider holds her back.

She watches Kate tie on her apron, and work in a frenzy that has nothing to do with the growing summer holiday crowds.

Kate attacks grease stains on the back deck with a steel wool, scouring so hard Ettie fears the timber is in danger of flaking away. The accounts are brought up to date and orders for new stock phoned through to suppliers. Island cooks are rallied to make a final effort to cash in on an anticipated last-minute rush for a great chutney to go with the ham or the perfect pickle to put under the tree as a gift. By late afternoon the café is polished to a glow and every dark corner is scraped hairpin clean. Kate nods at Ettie and goes home early without explanation or once mentioning that her mother is dead and she has to organise the funeral. Ettie, who has comforted and consoled so many over the years, hasn't the faintest idea what to do.

Just after closing, Sam calls in.

"I'm flat out with everyone wanting their deliveries before Christmas," he says. "Haven't got a minute to go to the supermarket. Thought one of your takeaway curries would hit the spot."

Ettie, looking worried, waves him upstairs to her penthouse. She makes him a cup of tea, even though he'd prefer a cold beer, and tells him to sit down.

"Kate's mother is ill," she explains. "She went to see her yesterday and something truly awful must have happened because she has barely said a word since and she didn't go to see her today."

Sam says nothing.

"Whether you like it or not, you're her friend. She didn't mean what she said about you and the Weasel. She's ashamed of herself for even thinking it. So get over to Oyster Bay tonight with a good bottle of wine – *not* a six-pack – and get her to talk to you." When he opens his mouth to speak, she cuts him off. "No ifs, no buts, that girl's in a mess and she needs help. I can't get through to her so you try. Okay?"

"I was going to ask if she might appreciate one of your curries, Ettie, that's all."

"I can assure you, she would hate one of my curries right now. But I'll get you one to take home to have later."

"You're the answer . . ."

"Oh shut up and get moving. Here, take this bottle of red with you."

It is just past dusk by the time Sam makes his way across the open water and swings towards Oyster Bay. Not at all sure of his welcome. Behind him on the banquette, the bottle of wine barely moves. He riffles through his memory of his mother's wise sayings, hoping he'll come up with a nice little homily that will help with what lies ahead. And for the first time in his life comes up blank. He's on his own.

He ties up at the pontoon as a strong sou'easterly peels loose sheets of bark from the trunks of spotted gums. They hurtle through the air and crash to the ground with a sound like bones snapping. He checks the ropes once more to make sure they're secure. Grabs the wine and goes up the steps to Kate's house at a rush to avoid being donged on the head by the debris.

He won't mention the distance that's been between them for the last few days. He'll open the batting by saying he needs some sound advice about buying Jimmy a Christmas present. Perfect, he thinks, knocking on the door. Terrible, he realises, the moment she flings it open with a look that makes his gonads shrivel.

"Bad time to drop by, is it?" he mumbles. And right there in front of him, she bursts into tears. He gathers her into his arms and whispers soothingly.

"My mother," she sobs, "is dead." She buries a face contorted by grief, and a large dose of anger, into the hollow of his shoulder until he picks her up and carries her to the sofa. "And . . . I have a brother," she adds, in little angry hiccups. "Or so she said."

He finds a blanket in the bedroom and covers her legs and bare feet. In the kitchen he puts on the kettle. He searches for a tea bag but finds an array of canisters with such bizarre names he soon gives up on the idea. He opens a drawer looking for a corkscrew instead. Outside, the wind starts to howl, the bush crackles and whines. He finds a couple of water glasses and pours the wine.

"It's from Ettie's private cellar," he says, with a wry grin. "She told me she'd kill me if I brought a six-pack."

Kate tries to smile. She takes a sip and then another. Two seconds later, she gulps half the wine in one go. "I have so many questions. I left her, you know, to die alone. But I never thought she would. Die, I mean." She finishes her wine and holds up the glass for a refill.

"She hated me. I mean *really* hated me. For as long as I can remember. Whatever I did wasn't good enough. I never measured up. From the moment I started breathing, I failed to live up to Emily's expectations."

Sam pours more wine and puts the bottle within reach on the floor. He's relieved, though, when Kate takes her customary small sip. Getting shit-faced, as he knows only too well, doesn't ease the pain, it only delays it.

"She used to make me wear silly frilled skirts when I was a little girl. I always ripped the hem, which drove her mad. Maybe that's where it all started. What do you think? I was plain, too. She loathes plain people. At least I've never been fat. I didn't fail her there." Another sip of wine. "I wish I could remember just one kind moment. Isn't that sad? God, all it takes is nine months in the womb and they own you forever. Whether it suits them or not."

Sam lets her ramble on and on without a word, indicating with a nod of his head when it seems she needs a reaction from him. Kate's memories ricochet from tennis clubs and pikelets to low-cut dresses and very high heels. From life in a country town to a string of business failures in the city. She and her father were clearly subjected to the whims of a woman who, he gathers, would disappear on and off throughout her marriage. Neither father nor daughter ever knew where.

"When I was twenty I fell in love," Kate says, holding his eyes with her own.

Sam sits up a bit straighter, listening intently now.

"He was a farmer. Every weekend, he drove three hundred kilometres to take me out to dinner. Red-checked tablecloths, candles in old wine bottles. You know?"

Sam nods.

"Afterwards, we'd lie on the sitting room floor at home, barely touching, listening to my parents' old records. I liked him, Sam. Thought I loved him. He made me feel . . . valued. 'This is the one,' I eventually confessed to Emily. A couple of weeks later, she told me that he'd gone into her bedroom and fondled her breasts. That he was a philanderer and I had to get rid of him. Anyone could reach into the gutter, she said."

Those words, Sam suspects, must have sent most of Kate's relationships careening off-course before they had a chance to take hold. How could she ever trust her judgement about men again? A single betrayal or a lifetime of them? The pieces begin to fall into place. So the house in Oyster Bay was a refuge, he thinks, making sense of it at last. Kate was not a misfit, certainly not a loner nor a drifter. She'd done a runner.

"And now," Kate almost shouts, "she tells – told – me I have a brother!"

He gets up from his chair then and slides in behind her on the sofa until her head rests against his chest. He puts his arms around her shoulders to stop her shaking. He smells lavender, rosemary in her hair. She fits in the hollow of his shoulder like it was carved for her.

"What am I supposed to do about *that*?" she says, beginning to cry again. "Does she mean a full brother? A half-brother? A step-brother? I have no idea. Was he born long before me? Did my dad even know? Who raised him? And now she's dead and I can't ask her."

"If it's true, what do you want to do about it?" Sam says, over the top of her head.

"Well, find him, of course," she says, twisting in his arms so she can see his face. "He's my brother, Sam. My family. We might even *like* each other."

"Or you might not."

"That too. But I have to give it a chance."

"I guess we'll just have to start looking then."

"You understand, don't you? I *have* to find him. I have to *know*."

"We'll find him. It's like any problem . . ."

"You wear it away." Her lopsided grin slithers off her face, but it was there, like a ray of hope. "We?"

He's about to say his mother always said that two heads were better than one but he swallows words he knows are banal in the current situation and strokes her arm. "Yeah, we," is all he says.

A few minutes later, she relaxes against him like a rag doll and is deeply asleep. A few *hours* later, she doesn't stir when Sam rests his lips on the soft white skin of her inner arm and then tucks the blanket under her chin. He lets himself out with barely a sound. It is three in the morning, the wind has dropped to a murmur and even the sea seems at rest.

Cook's Basin News (CBN)

Newsletter for Offshore Residents of Cook's Basin, Australia

DECEMBER

MERRY CHRISTMAS!

The Editor would like to take this opportunity to wish everyone a joyful and safe Christmas and New Year. See you all . . . on the water.

FUNNEL-WEB SPIDERS

Last week, while cleaning the bedroom, I came across a funnel-web spider about to take up residence in the laundry basket. Loath to kill any living thing, I managed to slip it into a jar. I then found that live funnel-webs are needed for regular milking of their venom for anti-venom serum for people who have been bitten. So next time you find a funnel-web, catch it safely and send it on to an authorised handler. Remember to put a hole in the jar for oxygen and moisten some cotton wool for fluids. You could save a life.

Christmas Day – Limited Service

The Community Vehicle is available for limited times. Please request or confirm your booking with the driver on duty on Christmas Eve. And have a great Christmas and New Year from the Community Vehicle Driver Team.

CAROLS AFLOAT – DEC. 21

Share the fun with family and friends. Load up your tinny with a picnic, a bottle of something festive, the kids and the dogs to sing along with the offshore choir. Either anchor in Log Frollow, starting around 7 p.m. Or catch the final performance at the Spit, at 8.30-ish. Look out for the lovely *Mary Kay* and follow the music! If you are boatless, call the ferry service to book a spot on the *Seagull*.

Wanted – House to Rent

For family with two young boys now returning to Sydney after seven years abroad. We would like to try offshore living before committing to buying a property. We've just given up managing a game reserve with lions, elephant and leopard, so the wilds of Cutter Island shouldn't pose too many horrors. Required from June for one year. We figure that's long enough to know whether it will suit us.

Bill and Tracey

Recycling over the Holidays

Recycling will be the same as usual. There are still a number of residents who are not separating bottles and paper. Please make an effort! If you receive gifts in large cardboard boxes, please break it down into small pieces for easier (and tidier) disposal. Merry Christmas one and all.

CHAPTER TWENTY-SIX

Three days before Christmas, Kate leaves Oyster Bay in the cool light of morning that turns the landscape satiny. She does not want to attend this last performance of Emily Jackson. But if there is an adored son, surely he will come to see his mother buried. Say goodbye.

If he exists.

And if he does, does he know of her existence?

She tries, but cannot visualise a sibling. And yet it's not impossible. Her childhood was riddled with secrets.

"Your mother's going out," her father would say.

"Where?"

"Just out."

And when Emily returned home, often a day or two later, glassy-eyed and dishevelled, Kate would ask: "Where did you go?"

"Out."

When she was old enough to understand, Kate suspected Emily was having affairs. Now she wonders if she dressed up and took flight not to meet a lover but to see a son she'd given up. If only she'd asked a single question, received a single answer. But Emily, she suspects, would have lied. Lying was a compulsion, as though the truth was too boring to waste time on.

Kate bans Ettie, Sam and Fast Freddy from attending the funeral. "The old girl wanted it to be private," she lies. They step back from her then, and let her go.

At the service Kate searches the small group of faces for a man who looks like her or her mother. There is no one. Just a line-up of stooped, white-haired "inmates" from the retirement village, hardly looking grieved. More likely *relieved* that it is not their turn yet.

At the graveside, she squeezes a clump of dirt. She knows she should toss it gently on the lid of the coffin in a gesture of regret and sorrow but hesitates for too long. Curious eyes turn towards her.

She hurls it then, like a fast bowler. The soil lands on the polished wood with a dull thud. Without waiting for the end of the service, she turns and tramps away. Rain begins to fall in big, round drops, as hard as pebbles.

She marches through silent lines of weather-beaten marble slabs with names and sentimental messages chiselled into the granite. How many lies are neatly etched forever on the tombstones? Beloved? Adored? Really, truly? Surely not everyone is a model husband, wife, mother, father, grandmother, grandfather. How many are sunk into the ground with a collective sigh of relief?

She'd cited cost when the undertaker had asked for an epitaph. "Name and date. Nothing else." No hypocrisy. Not now, not ever.

Ignoring the rain, Kate keeps on through the ordered, silent army of the dead. For a split second, she thinks she sees wraiths swooping through the air. There is a crack of thunder, then a deluge. She comes to her senses. The earth turns fragrant and water runs down her face, stings her eyes. Salty.

So many cemeteries located in the best real estate in town, she thinks, detaching herself, like a journalist, from emotion. As though the dead have eyes and feelings. She climbs into her car and drives aimlessly until the late afternoon. Emptying her mind. Knowing that if she doesn't, she will go mad. Then she turns around and heads home to Cook's Basin.

It is early evening when she reaches the Spit. The landscape gleams in the rain-washed summer twilight. She walks slowly towards the Square, her eyes on the ground, dodging the massive pothole that Ettie says will one day swallow a baby and a pram if the council doesn't pay attention.

A few people sit on the damp seawall holding fishing rods. The *Seagull* is tucked cosily on her mooring. The café is closed. Not even a lamp shines in Ettie's penthouse. A night out with the chef, Kate thinks, happy that her friend is happy.

It is almost dark now, with a white moon already high in a fading sky. She continues to Commuter Dock where she hears the steady diesel thrum of the *Mary Kay* and looks up. The barge glides into the drop-off and pick-up zone and waits there.

Sam jumps onto the pontoon and walks towards her. "Need a lift?" he calls out softly.

"I'm good," she says.

"Magic night."

"I'm tired, Sam."

"Well, love, I'm sorry to hear that because I am under strict orders and I've always been a bloke who does as he is told."

"Orders?"

"Yep." He grabs her hand. "Follow me."

"No, Sam. Thanks. It's really kind of you but . . ."

"Don't force me to throw you over my shoulder, mate."

"I am not your bloody *mate*!"

They chug smoothly over the water. Neither of them speaks.

He nudges into the rear deck of The Briny and waves at Ettie, who's watching from her penthouse. She gives a thumbs-up and disappears. In a few moments, Fast Freddy, Marcus and Ettie emerge carrying baskets, blankets and iceboxes.

"We all decided it was a top night for a picnic," Sam says. "Long as you don't mind a wet bum when you sit on the ground."

Way beyond Kingfish Bay, they anchor a few metres off a crescent-shaped sliver of beach that shines whitely in the night. Ettie and Fast Freddy row a dinghy ashore and set out blankets, cushions and an old washing machine drum that Sam had hoisted out of the hold where he stores the mooring chain. They twist it into the sand and then fill it with wood to make a campfire. Quickly, smoke curls upwards, a spectre against the night sky. The flames are warm, inviting, offering comfort.

In the wheelhouse, Sam fiddles with cables and switches. He shoos Marcus away when he offers to help. "Never touch the workings of another man's boat, mate. That way you can't be blamed for the explosion." He eventually hits a switch and it happens all at once. Music fills the air and a few lights strung around the gunnel flutter into red, green, yellow and blue life. The chef slides overboard into water up to his knees to join Ettie and Fast Freddy. On the beach, he swings both of them in a waltz. They plough into cool damp sand and fall in a laughing heap.

"Now," Sam says, reaching for Kate. "You can teach me to tango."

"As a matter of fact," Kate replies, almost smiling, "I happen to be very good at dancing."

"So. Who taught you?"

"My mother," she says softly, and a scant golden moment of her shadowy childhood eases the hurt.

"Anyone at the funeral who could be your brother?" he asks, spinning her round. Deliberately talking about it so it doesn't fester.

"Nope."

"Hell of an inheritance, if you don't mind my saying so."

"Well. She was always a bit of a drama queen. God, Sam, you've got the grace of an elephant."

"Easy on. It's early days. Give a bloke a decent chance."

"I think Ettie's waving to say our picnic is ready," she says.

"That woman . . ."

"Is the answer to every man's dreams. Move on, Sam, you have truly worn that line to a shred."

"Everyone's a critic," he grins, knowing he's trumped her. He jumps off the bow into the knee-deep shallows and reaches up to lift her off.

*

By nine o'clock on the morning of Christmas Eve, the sun already burns hot and the air is thick with moisture from a tropical northerly. Swarms of white moon jellyfish rise and fall hypnotically in a gelatinous sea. It's the last few hours before shops and offices close down for the silly season.

Sam drops in on Artie with enough supplies to get the old fella through the close-down period when over-partied locals can be found lumped on beaches, decks and sofas in a state of such lethargy it would take a cyclone to budge them.

"Got a message from Ettie and Kate," he announces, after turning down the offer of a pre-lunch rum. "Christmas dinner at The Briny. No excuses. It's sorted. Jimmy and I are going to strap you into a bosun's chair and use the crane on the *Mary Kay* to hoist you off your boat so we can transport you in regal splendour to Ettie's magnificent top deck. A comfortable chair already has your name on it and is waiting patiently for your arrival."

"Ya gonna lower me into an appropriately comfortable receptacle for the voyage over? Not leave me swingin' in the sunshine like a newborn hangin' from the beak of a stork?"

"Would I do a mongrel act like that?"

"Ya bloody would."

Inside the café, the rush is on to prepare for crowds that flock to the shore to watch the Dog Race. Ettie and Kate expect the usual chaos and mayhem, as well as a massive jump in orders for hot chips and cold beers.

In the remains of the afternoon, the Spit is a seething mass of wall-to-wall people. They line the shore, the ferry wharf.

Some are stacked four-deep on the roof of the cabin of the old *Seagull*, which has sunk so low in the water it is inches away from a death roll to the bottom of the sea.

Kate takes a quick break and rushes outside, pushing her way through the throng until she finds Jack the Bookie. She lays an astonishing fifty dollars on a rank outsider called Joy.

"Not in the know, are you?" asks Jack, who is more accustomed to one-dollar flutters.

"Nah. I just like the name."

Jack snatches her money, relieved. "Ah. A girl bet. All show and no form."

"Probably."

He gives her odds of twenty-to-one which adds up to a thousand bucks if it comes home. He leans around Kate to check his ancient tinny is still tied up in a handy spot. If Joy wins, he's fully aware he'll have to do a runner.

To hedge his financial exposure, Jack lowers the odds on the mutt to evens – a critical mistake. Suddenly everyone wants to plunge because they figure it must be a good thing. Nervous sweat trickles down Jack's face and a rush of queasiness swamps him as he tries to remember how much petrol he has in the tank. He sits down abruptly on a picnic bench, short of breath. So he misses seeing the start of the race when all the dogs swim with their owners across the two-kilometre stretch of sparkling blue sea. He realises he has no idea what Joy looks like. For all he knows, it could be a poodle or a Portuguese water dog. "Please," he prays out loud, "not a Portuguese water dog."

Jack looks up nervously from his battered sandshoes when the crowd begins to roar. He stands and eases his way to the front with an apologetic smile. "I'm the bookie," he explains. "Need to see the winner for myself."

The cry rises: "Joy! Joy!"

Out to sea, sodden canine heads jut out of the water and paddle into focus. Black dogs, white dogs, brown dogs, brindle dogs, long-haired, short-haired, curly-haired and just plain summer-shorn-down-to-zero dogs. Closer and closer. The chant is hysterical.

"Joy! Joy!"

Jack closes his eyes and crosses his fingers.

"Joy! The winner!" yells Sam, the race facilitator, from his official position in the western corner of the beach.

Jack opens his eyes just in time to witness a moment he later refers to as "divine deliverance from bankruptcy". He leaps from the seawall like a grasshopper, scrambles across the sand and grabs Sam's arm.

"Mate, mate," he shouts above the cheering, pointing at the red ribbon of the finishing line. "The mutt landed outside the barriers. She's gotta be disqualified."

Sam scratches his head and consults the scrawl on a torn-off envelope he's pulled from the back pocket of his blue shorts. He makes a quick phone call to a long-time Islander who invented the rules more than three decades ago. Jack waits, with his eyes squeezed shut. He hums fervently.

Sam grins. "You can keep your shirt on, Jack. Joy's out!"

With that, the bookie sinks to his knees in the soft yellow sand and shouts a mighty *Alleluia*, thrusting his clenched fist to the sky in triumph. Noticing, the crowd looks up towards the bright blue heavens, expecting to witness a Christmas epiphany. The sky is blue and empty. Whatever prompted

Jack's seraphic outburst must have been deeply personal. They return to the partying with renewed gusto.

CHAPTER TWENTY-SEVEN

In the pre-dawn heat haze of Christmas morning, Ettie wanders downstairs in her white cotton nightie. She checks the *Closed* sign is clearly visible, the locks still in place. No matter how piteous the plea for a container of milk or a loaf of bread, she is not opening for anyone today.

This year, she thinks as she prepares her early morning cuppa, she has so much to be thankful for. She takes the first hot sip with a sigh of pleasure before going outside to the deck. She picks a spot in the eastern corner, where the sun will hit in a while, and puts her feet on the rails. The peace, she sighs. The pleasure of not rushing.

Ten waifs and strays will gather at her table on the top deck for lunch: Marcus, Kate, Sam, Fast Freddy, Artie, the Misses Skettle, Big Julie, Jimmy. And his mum, Amelia, who has already told Ettie that she had so much time in minimum security she became an expert patchwork quilt maker. She hopes everyone is fond of the style.

Ettie drains her cup and checks her watch automatically,

finding it difficult to set aside the daily muffin-baking time-table. She gazes into water that's picking up thin strands of light now. The seabed begins to take shape. Tide-moulded sand, swaying seagrass. And fingerlings, barely bigger than tadpoles, flicking nonsensically back and forth. The air is already thickening with heat, the sun not even nudging the horizon. Why do we do it? she wonders as she does without fail every year. Hot turkey, hot potatoes, hot pudding in a hot climate.

She picks up the steady, high-pitched whine of Kate's boat and tells herself to get moving. A shower, clean clothes, an apron and on with the show. She has less to do than usual today. The pudding, heavily based on oranges, lemons, ginger and butter instead of suet, was wrapped in calico and steamed a month ago. Anyone passing through the café during the mixing process was invited to have a stir and make a wish.

Fast Freddy will do a quick run upriver to the Fisherman's Co-op for fresh prawns and oysters. To go with them, the chef will create a collection of perky little palate-pleasers using combinations of lime, chilli, shallots, rice wine vinegar and sesame oil. Marcus is also cooking the turkey with his famous pork, veal and chestnut stuffing.

Ettie elects Kate to make the sauces for the pudding – brandy, hard sauce, custard, and cream whipped with brandy and icing sugar. She aims to keep Kate busy all day. And anyway, it is part of her culinary education.

She waves at the young woman as she approaches the café, so utterly transformed from the reserved character who pitched up a little more than three months ago looking for a place to belong. She watches her dock her tinny precisely, hop out and tie on with two perfect bowlines. By the end of another year, Sam will teach her to read the sky for storms, the winds for danger, the sea for changing seasons. In turn, she will teach him to venture beyond the boundaries of tiny Cook's Basin, and hopefully only partially cure him of the boy bravado that he so often finds refuge in. And which is also, it has to be said, part of his charm.

Kate tramps up the jetty, steep with a low tide. "I'm ready to tackle the crème anglaise!" she announces.

"Custard."

"What?"

"It's custard, not crème anglaise. Close relation but a fraction sturdier from the addition of a little flour."

"And there I was, trying to impress you with my newfound knowledge. But I'll do my best, Ettie."

"You always do, Kate. And I love you for it."

Kate swallows. "Well. 'Tis the season to be jolly." And arm in arm they walk into The Briny Café as the sun breaks loose of the horizon.

On Ettie's top deck, the table is laid with a white cloth and red gingham napkins, courtesy of Marcus who seems to have cupboards full of tableware for any occasion. Jimmy's mum, Amelia, has made a Christmas tree centrepiece out of scraps of red fabric and five red candles. Jimmy made the bon-bons with some gentle instruction. She says she had to stop every now and then to stare at her boy who, in her three-month absence, had grown into a very decent young man.

The Christmas tree, which fills the penthouse with the

clean scent of pine, is covered in handmade decorations that Ettie's mother and grandmother cherished. A single silver star is attached to the tip. Every so often it catches the light off the water and shimmers.

Gifts are wrapped and tagged and piled under the tree in colourful abandon, ready to be opened over a glass of champagne.

At noon on the dot, the *Mary Kay* glides into sight like the dowager queen of the bays that she is. So much an everyday sight that she brings comfort and a sense that while she chugs across the water, all is well. Her deck and funnels froth with festive garlands that twinkle in the sun. Amelia, Jimmy, Fast Freddy and Marcus are dressed in a mix of red and green with reindeer antlers on their heads. The perennially pink Misses Skettle have abandoned their favourite colour and are swathed in strawberry from top to toe. At the front of the barge, like an admiral of the fleet, Artie sits on a white cane chair. Wet-haired, he is resplendent in his best long pants and a voluminous red-checked shirt, with a broad-brimmed cream straw hat tilted at a rakish angle.

Big Julie arrives at the café on foot pushing a wheelbarrow full of presents. She tells Ettie that hoarding money didn't do Bertie much good and she plans to live for the day and spend without remorse. "It's no good to you in the hereafter," she announces.

"You've taken care of the drainage pipes, though, haven't you?" Ettie says, concerned.

"Relocated them to a safety deposit box. I've also booked a world cruise," she adds with a wink.

When the barge docks, Jimmy flies off like a rocket and

roars upstairs to the penthouse, his eyes darting in all directions. He ignores the gifts under the tree and instead opens doors and cupboards, searching frantically.

When he fails to find even one of Boag's old hairs, he flops in a chair, holding back tears of disappointment.

"This what you're looking for, mate?" Sam says, grinning. He reaches under his shirt and holds out a wriggling little black-and-white mutt that will one day grow into a handsome border collie.

The kid leaps to his feet, his eyes ready to pop from their sockets. He tenderly takes the pup out of Sam's huge hands. "Hiya, Longfellow," he whispers, kissing the pup on the head.

Longfellow? The chef is the first to react. "A noble poet," he says, approvingly. "And therefore a noble name for a noble breed. It is a perfect choice."

Jimmy rushes downstairs, slams through the screen door leading to the deck and jumps on board the barge. He races to the bow where he sits cross-legged and explains to the pup, in a very serious voice, that when he is old enough this will be his look-out post and that he is to bark at the very first sight of a shark. "Isn't that right?" he calls to the adults who are watching from the deck. They raise their glasses in reply.

An hour later everyone sits on the pontoon, feet hanging over the edge in the cool water, champagne glasses topped up. The Misses Skettle are already giggly. Amelia bursts into tears whenever she looks at her son. Artie consoles her with a pat. Fast Freddy and the chef expertly shuck oysters with the tip of a sharp knife. A glorious array of dipping sauces is lined up on a red lacquer tray not far from a bucket filled with ice and glossily fresh king prawns. Cook's Basin meets three-star.

Ettie fluffs around making sure the Misses Skettle are comfortable, and that no one fills their glasses for a little while.

Upstairs, a golden turkey rests under a covering of foil. The ham is due to be taken out of the oven in ten minutes. In her only nod to the heat of summer, Ettie has prepared a bean and cherry tomato salad but – to everyone's relief – couldn't bring herself to give up crisp potatoes roasted with garlic, rosemary and sea salt. The chef has brought a pot of his cranberry sauce made with cinnamon and orange peel, as well as a light gravy created from scraping the pan drippings into a long reduction of a bottle of white wine.

"Kings . . ." Sam announces, when Kate emerges from the kitchen declaring her custard has thickened nicely.

"Never lived this good!" shouts the crowd.

They dine in the splendour of a perfect Cook's Basin afternoon, watching the light fade and gulls fly across the milky blue sky. As evening falls, they light the candles and sit around while the worn-out puppy sleeps soundly in one of Ettie's old baskets. Jimmy is fast asleep right alongside.

When it seems the Misses Skettle have had enough celebration for one day, Sam tucks them onto the banquette in the wheelhouse of the *Mary Kay* and takes them home. He kisses them goodnight and thanks them, as he always does, for their open hearts and endless generosity.

By the time he returns to the café, Fast Freddy is ready to help him restore a sleepy but impressively sober Artie to his floating palace. Kate offers to take Amelia and Jimmy home in her tinny.

The chef announces he and Big Julie will take charge of the cleaning up and that Ettie is to lie back on the sofa in ease and comfort. Ettie, who can't remember a more effortless Christmas, murmurs that yes, perhaps she is a little tired after all. And does exactly as she's told.

The moon is high in the sky by the time Sam climbs the steps to Kate's house. He tells himself he is simply dropping by to check she is okay. And that is true.

He tells himself that he can help her if she will let him. And that is also true.

He also tells himself that if he is met with resistance, he must accept that is how she feels. And that she needs time. True. But God, how he hopes for so much more.

"What took you so long?" says a soft voice from the verandah, and his stomach flip-flops. He laughs out loud and bounds up the steps three at a time.

Cook's Basin News (CBN)

Newsletter for Offshore Residents of Cook's Basin, Australia

JANUARY

The Editor wishes to report that her modem is sick and CBN will be unavailable for the short term. The modem doctor has been called. Do not be alarmed if you hear sirens. In the meantime, anything you wish to communicate to the wider Cook's Basin community should be pinned to the noticeboard in The Briny Café. It is up to each individual to check so that they can keep up to date with current affairs. (Yes, that means you, too, Seaweed!)

Recipes from
The Briny Café

ETTIE'S FIERY ROGAN JOSH

Prep time: 20 minutes + overnight marinating
Cooking time: about 1 hour 30 minutes
Serves 4–6

2 tsp ground cumin
2 tsp mild paprika
2 tsp ground coriander
6 ground cardamom
¼ tsp garam masala
1½ tsp ground fennel
1½ kg boneless shoulder of lamb,
cut into 3 cm pieces
¼ cup vegetable oil
2 brown onions, finely chopped
6 cm piece fresh ginger, grated
4 red chillies
8 garlic cloves
¼ tsp saffron threads (soaked in 1 tbsp warm water)
2 cassia leaves
2 cinnamon sticks
400 g can tomatoes
280 g plain yoghurt
Basmati rice, to serve

Combine ground spices in a medium bowl then add the lamb and toss until the meat is coated. A dedicated cook will leave it overnight in the fridge but it's fine to continue cooking.

Heat half the oil in a large heavy-based saucepan over low heat. Brown the lamb. Don't put too much meat in the pan at once or you will stew it and it will become dry when slow-cooked.

Heat the remaining oil in the same pan and cook the onion, ginger, chilli and garlic until the onion is soft and slightly browned.

Add saffron, cassia leaves and cinnamon sticks to the pan. Cook for a minute or two, until fragrant. Increase the heat to high, add the tomatoes and meat. Add the yoghurt spoonful by spoonful, stirring until it blends into the sauce. Bring to the boil then reduce heat and simmer, covered, for about 1½ hours or until the lamb is tender. If you like, sprinkle a pinch of garam masala on the finished dish just before serving. Serve with basmati rice.

ETTIE'S LAMB BURGERS

Prep time: 20 minutes
Cooking time: 8–14 minutes per batch
Serves 4–6

plain flour, for coating
vegetable oil, to fry
1 cup plain yoghurt
1 cucumber, chopped
1 garlic clove, crushed
handful of chopped mint

Turkish bread, split, toasted and buttered,
approximately three serves per loaf
Butter lettuce leaves, sliced tomato,
sliced red onion, to serve
Tamarind chutney, to serve

Patties
1 kg lamb mince
2 brown onions, grated
½ cup flat-leaf parsley, finely chopped
1 tsp ground cinnamon
1 tsp ground allspice
1 tsp ground cumin
1 tsp freshly ground black pepper
2 tsp sea salt
2 eggs
3 thick slices sourdough bread,
processed into fresh breadcrumbs

To make the patties, use your hands to mix all the ingredients together. Divide into four to six portions, depending on your appetite, and shape into patties about 2 cm thick. Coat in flour and shake off excess. Heat a little oil in a large heavy-based frying pan. Sear both sides on high heat then reduce heat to medium and cook according to taste. Rare takes about three to four minutes each side, well-done takes about seven minutes each side.

Combine the yoghurt, cucumber, garlic and mint. To assemble burgers, lay out toasted bread bases. Arrange lettuce, tomato and onion onto them. Place the burger on top, add dollops of the yoghurt mixture and tamarind chutney, and finish with the top pieces of toasted bread.

ETTIE'S CURE-ALL CHICKEN SOUP

Prep time: 15 minutes
Cooking time: 1 hour 5 minutes

Stock
1–2 cooked chicken carcasses (from
home-roasted, free-range chickens)
1 brown onion, quartered
1 carrot, quartered
2 stalks celery, roughly chopped
1 bunch parsley
2 garlic cloves
1 cm piece fresh ginger, finely sliced

Soup
2 tbs Chinese rice wine
2 tbs light soy sauce
1 tbs fish sauce
suggested vegetables: green beans, fresh
corn kernels, snowpeas, red capsicum
bean sprouts, to garnish

For the stock, crush the bones and place into a large saucepan. Add remaining ingredients, and enough water to cover.

Bring to a simmer over low heat and cook, covered, for 1 hour. Allow to cool, then strain and discard solids.

To make the soup, transfer the stock to a clean saucepan and bring to a simmer. Add the wine and sauces. Trim the vegetables into bite-sized pieces. Add the beans and corn to pan and cook for a few minutes, until just tender. Add snowpeas and capsicum just before taking off the heat. Serve topped with rinsed bean sprouts.

Optional extras: Add a serve of cooked ramen or udon noodles. Don't be tempted to cook the noodles in the broth, it makes it cloudy and slightly gluggy. Add chopped chilli to taste, which is great for colds and flu.

Note: Use 12 chicken drumsticks if you don't have cooked chicken carcasses. When the stock is done, remove cooked meat from bones, put in a separate bowl, and add to soup to heat through when you are ready to eat. Alternatively, use the meat to make sandwiches. The vegetables listed above are just suggestions, you can use whatever you have in the fridge.

ETTIE'S RASPBERRY MUFFINS

Prep time: 10 minutes
Cooking time: 20 minutes
Serves 12

    2½ cups self-raising flour
    90 g butter, very cold
    1 cup caster sugar

1¼ cups buttermilk
1 egg, lightly beaten
30 g desiccated coconut
200 g fresh raspberries (frozen raspberries
can be too wet and turn the muffins mushy)
4 tbs shredded coconut

Preheat oven to 200°C. Prepare 12-hole muffin tin by greasing or with paper cups.

In a food processor, briefly whizz together flour and butter.

Tip into a mixing bowl and add sugar, buttermilk, egg, desiccated coconut and raspberries. Mix lightly and until barely combined (over-mixing toughens the muffin).

Sprinkle with shredded coconut.

Bake for 20 minutes or until lightly browned on top. Leave in the muffin pans for about five minutes before turning out to cool on a wire rack.

LEMON DELICIOUS PUDDING

Prep time: 20 minutes
Cooking time: 45 minutes
Serves 6

125 g butter melted
2 tsp finely grated lemon rind (try to find strong-
tasting lemons such as Eureka or Lisbon)

1½ cups caster sugar
3 eggs, separated
½ cup self-raising flour
⅓ cup lemon juice
1⅓ cups milk
2 punnets blueberries
150 ml lemon butter – a good commercial brand
is fine or make your own cream if desired

Preheat oven to 180°C.

Grease six 1-cup ovenproof ceramic bowls.

Combine butter, rind, sugar and yolks in a mixing bowl. Stir in sifted flour and then add the juice. Stir in the milk in small amounts until the mixture is smooth but still runny.

Beat egg whites until soft peaks form and then fold into lemon mixture.

Divide mixture between the dishes and place in a large baking dish with enough boiling water to come halfway up the sides.

Bake for about 45 minutes and serve immediately with lemon butter and blueberries on the side.